In This
Sign
Conquer

LEGACIES OF FAITH SERIES

In This Sign Conquer

Irene Brand

kregel
PUBLICATIONS

Grand Rapids, MI 49501

In This Sign Conquer

Copyright © 1996 by Irene Brand

Published in 1996 by Kregel Publications, a division of Kregel, Inc., P.O. Box 2607, Grand Rapids, MI 49501. Kregel Publications provides trusted, biblical publications for Christian growth and service. Your comments and suggestions are valued.

Cover illustration: Ron Mazellan
Cover design: Alan G. Hartman
Book design: Nicholas G. Richardson

Library of Congress Cataloging-in-Publication Data
Brand, Irene.
   In this sign conquer / by Irene Brand.
      p.   cm.   (Legacies of faith series)
   1. Church History—Primitive and early church, ca. 30–600—Fiction. 2. Rome—History—Constantine I, the Great, 306–337—Fiction. I. Title. II. Series: Brand, Irene B., 1929– Legacies of faith series.
PS3552.R2917I5   1996   813'.54—dc20   96-10340
                                        CIP

ISBN 0-8254-2144-6

Printed in the United States of America
1 2 3 4 5 / 00 99 98 97 96

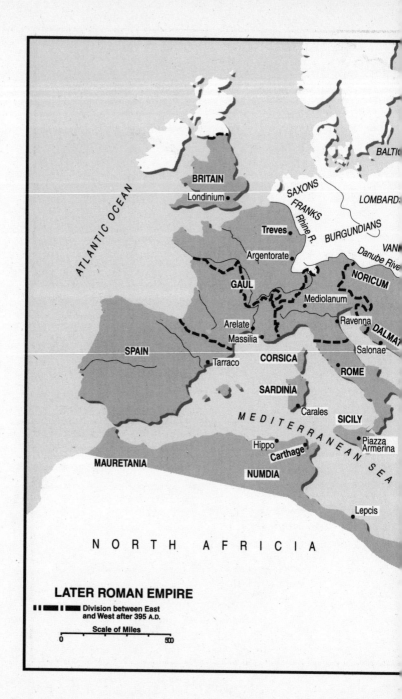

ATLANTIC OCEAN

BRITAIN
Londinium

BALTIC

SAXONS
FRANKS
Rhine R.
LOMBARDS

Treves

BURGUNDIANS

Argentorate

VAN

Danube River

GAUL

NORICUM

Mediolanum

Arelate
Massilia

Ravenna

DALMAT

SPAIN

CORSICA

Salonae

ROME

Tarraco

SARDINIA

Carales

SICILY

MEDITERRANEAN SEA

Hippo
Carthage

Piazza
Armerina

MAURETANIA

NUMDIA

Lepcis

NORTH AFRICIA

LATER ROMAN EMPIRE

▮▮▬▮▮ ▮▬ Division between East
and West after 395 A.D.

Scale of Miles

0   500

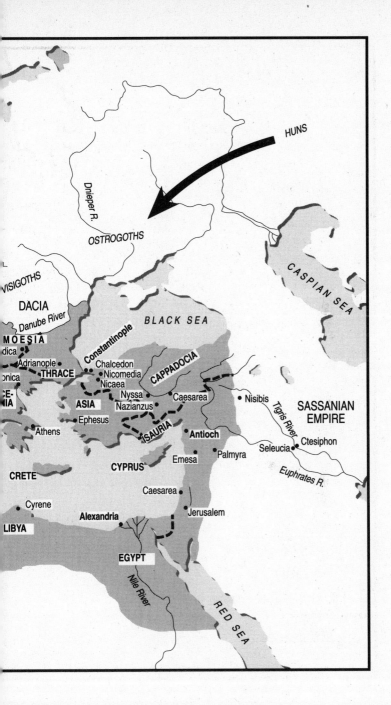

PART I

ROME—MISTRESS OF THE WORLD

ROME, NICOMEDIA, CARTHAGE, A.D. 300

O Rome, the world is yours and you its queen;
O Rome, bright star of stars in heav'n above,
Mother of gods and men, hear us, we stand
Within your temples and feel heaven near.

Claudius Rutilius Namatianus I
Fifth-century Roman poet

1

Rome, 300

The labored breathing of Ignatius Trento echoed throughout the room. His anxious family watched the rise and fall of the old man's chest, fearing each breath would be his last. Fifteen-year-old Lucius stood by the window watching as the imperial capital started its day. The usual clamor was somewhat subdued, as if passersby knew that the patriarch of the Trento family was dying. Plodding horses quietly pulled iron-wheeled carts along the stone-paved street. The butcher, who visited the house each morning, spoke in low tones as he conversed with the Trento staff over its needs for the day. As the cook opened the kitchen windows, the smell of bread fresh from the oven wafted into the room, mingling with the odor of medicinal herbs.

Lucius fidgeted from one foot to the other, until finally he crept to the foot of the couch and looked at his grandfather. Fear as sharp as a sword seized his heart when he saw the wizened form. The old man had been his friend, his guide, his mentor. His security would be gone when Ignatius died, for even without the diagnosis of pneumonia by the Greek doctor hovering over the old man, Lucius knew that his grandfather's days were numbered.

Suddenly Ignatius groaned loudly and struggled to a sitting position, aided by the arm of the physician. He pointed a trembling hand at Lucius. "Boy, bring the Alabaster. Quickly."

11

Lucius sped from the room and down the stairs into the peristyle where a servant was trimming the cypress hedges. "Angelo, come quickly," Lucius called. "Grandfather wants the Alabaster. Please open the chapel."

The servant dropped the knife he held and hurried toward Lucius. Chief of the other servants, Angelo carried keys to all the rooms and cupboards, and he soon found the heavy key that unlocked the chapel. Angelo swung open the door, but despite the need for haste, Lucius crept into the little sanctuary. It was a simple room with a few marble benches facing a wall decorated with a painting of Christ's resurrection. A single candle shed a soft-glowing light in the room, and Lucius's eyes fell immediately on the cedar chest that stood on the marble pedestal below the painting. His hands hovered briefly over the chest before he lifted it lovingly. Motioning to Angelo to relock the chapel, Lucius raced back to his grandfather's room.

He halted on the threshold and quickly looked to where his grandfather lay. His father, Bernini, had moved to the head of the couch. Father's arm supported the dying Roman, whose eyes were fixed on the door watching for his grandson. Lucius knelt beside the bed, carefully opened the chest, and removed the ornate alabaster vase with trembling fingers. He had never been allowed to touch it before. The slender, delicately carved alabaster, gleaming golden in the morning sunlight, began to warm to the touch of Lucius's hands. Streaks of black punctuated the golden background, and around its smooth sides, a carved Old Testament scene depicted Abraham at the moment he would have killed Isaac had God not provided a ram for the sacrifice. On the bottom of the vase, the numeral three had been carved.

The feverish dullness in Ignatius's eyes changed to rapture as he took the Alabaster and clasped it to his sunken chest. Looking up at Bernini, he said, "The tomb was empty, son. There was no need for the spikenard. The body was gone. Jesus is risen, and He waits for me at the right hand of the Father." Lifting his eyes, the old man gasped, "Lord, let Your servant depart now in peace, for my eyes have seen Your salvation. Thank God, the tomb was empty."

Ignatius slumped in the arms of his son, and Lucius knew that his grandfather had died. Trying manfully to stifle the tears pushing at his eyelids, he took the Alabaster from his grandfather's lifeless fingers and placed it back in the chest.

Lucius retreated toward the door and surveyed his grieving family. His father and the doctor laid Ignatius back on the bed and pulled a blanket over him. Domitilla, Lucius's slender, petite mother, crept to her husband's side, but he ignored her. Lucius wondered what his father was thinking. Like many other times in the past, the boy wished he knew his father better.

Bernini, a tall, barrel-chested man of immense physical strength, was one of the most successful merchants in Rome. His travels took him throughout the world as he searched for rare items to dispense from his warehouses in Rome and Ostia. He was gone more often than he was at home, and he rarely took time for the children when he was in residence. Ignatius had been the real father of the family, but that would change now. Bernini, as the oldest son, would inherit the authority of Ignatius.

Across the room, Lucius's twin brother, Marcus, caught his eye and lifted his hand in a slight salute. Beside him, their sister, Bernice, drooped on a bench and sobbed. The Nicomedia branch of the Trento family hovered near the bed. They had only arrived yesterday, spurred on by an urgent message from Bernini to his brother, Octavian, that the death of Ignatius was imminent. Octavian's wife, Atilia, and his son and daughter, Cassus and Octavia, had accompanied him. As Lucius walked out of the room to return the Alabaster to the chapel, his cousin Cassus fell into step beside him.

"Who will inherit the Alabaster now that Grandfather is gone?" Cassus asked.

Lucius shook his head. "I don't know. Grandfather was always somewhat secretive about his plans."

"My father hopes it will come into our family. He says that he's more devout in the faith than your father—no insult intended."

"How could I be insulted when you speak the truth? No one knows better than I that Father's primary interest is making money. He puts that first, even before his sons."

After the Alabaster was safely locked in the chapel, Cassus asked Lucius to show him around the brick, mortar-covered family domus built fifty years before. It had been several years since his last visit and much had changed. Copies of Greek paintings hung on the walls. Greek scenes were also incorporated into the mosaic floor. The two boys sauntered into the atrium, which served as the family reception room. Fresh air and light filtered through a vent hole in the roof. Their sandal-clad feet padded quietly on the decorative marble tiles as they sidestepped the pool placed in the middle of the floor to catch the rain.

"These brightly colored wall paintings must rival those found in the emperor's palace at Nicomedia," Cassus said, pushing aside the protective shutters from the atrium's decorative panels. "I had forgotten the beauty of this courtyard."

"Grandfather had it redecorated, so it has changed a lot since your last visit. I trust that this time you'll stay longer with us so we can show you the famous sites of Rome. And I'd like to learn from you about the emperor's household."

Cassus laughed. Then, perhaps remembering the reason for his presence in Rome, he sobered. "I have little firsthand knowledge of the palace. Father and the emperor are not friendly—Diocletian has no sympathy for Christians. My friend Constantine attends the court, and he brings me the news."

"That must be interesting. You'll have to tell me more about him," Lucius said.

When the rest of the family joined Lucius and Cassus in the atrium, several servant women entered bearing trays of fruit and cheese. Angelo followed with a cask of sweet wine. To their credit, Lucius noted that the death of Ignatius had left his family with little appetite; all of them had revered the elderly man. Lucius had often suspected that Bernini chafed at the restraint placed on him by his father. Still, Bernini and his father had agreed upon most things except religion. The older son had participated in the family's worship, but apparently he had done so to please his father rather than from any deep commitment.

Within a few hours, Ignatius's toga-clad body was placed in the atrium on a high marble catafalque. For two days, friends of the family would come by to pay their respects.

❀　❀　❀

After watching the young people fidget away the tedious hours of the first visiting day, Domitilla drew Lucius and Marcus aside. "It isn't necessary for you to stay here all of the time. Escort your sister and cousins out to the peristyle today. The weather is pleasant, and you should take some time for pleasure. After the funeral tomorrow, there will be nine days of mourning when you'll have to limit your activities."

Marcus cuffed his mother on the shoulder. "But tonight, we have a big feast. Make me completely happy by saying that Plotina will be here." Marcus had a particular interest in the daughter of his grandfather's lawyer.

Domitilla smiled fondly at her firstborn. "Cornelius Flavius is coming to read the will and Plotina will accompany him, but she will be under the supervision of a senior Vestal, so behave yourself accordingly."

Marcus lifted his arm in a sign of victory, but he stifled his joy when he observed his mother's warning frown reminding him that the family was in mourning. Watching the jollity between Marcus and Domitilla, Lucius wished—as he had done most of his life—that he could be more like his brother. They shared the same brown eyes and curly black hair, but whereas Marcus was a tall, broad-shouldered youth, Lucius possessed a well-knit, light figure. The bone structure of his face was finely modeled with a smooth complexion, making him as handsome as a woman. Marcus, on the other hand, had high cheekbones and an arching nose that gave his face a rugged appearance.

As Lucius followed his relatives out of the atrium, he reflected that the greatest difference in the two siblings was internal. Whereas he was quiet, reserved, reflective, and studious, Marcus was outgoing, adventurous, and willful. Marcus was the joy of Bernini's life, but even so, he and his father often clashed. Bernini had never found it necessary to discipline the more controlled Lucius.

When the young people entered the garden, Marcus said, "Bring in some of your menagerie, Lucius. That should entertain our guests."

Marcus was amusing Octavia, Cassus, and Bernice with an account of one of his misdeeds when Lucius returned. He was leading a chained red fox, and a sulfur-crested cockatoo sat on his shoulder. The bird turned his beady eyes on Cassus.

"Good day," he squawked. "I'm Caesar Augustus. Off with his head." Bernice clapped her hands and the bird screeched, "Cleopatra, Cleopatra. Mark Antony be cursed."

Lucius glanced toward his brother. "I see you've been teaching Bento some new phrases. I wish you would stay away from the animal building." Touching the cockatoo on the beak, Lucius said, "Some Scripture, Bento. You're a Christian bird."

"God is love! God is love!" Bento chortled as he left Lucius's shoulder, flew into the branches of a Persian walnut tree overhanging the garden wall, and closed his eyes.

Octavia knelt beside the fox. "Is he tame enough for me to pet?" When Lucius nodded, she passed her hand across the animal's soft fur. After playing with the animals for a while, Bernice and Octavia joined hands and went to sit on a marble bench near the garden wall.

"Do you have many pets?" Cassus asked Lucius.

"One fox, three dogs, and several cages of finches and thrushes. Father imports animals for the gladiator games, and occasionally he has the opportunity to buy some pets for me. Working with the animals gives me a break from my studies. Our tutor is a relentless taskmaster, but I do find a few hours to work with my pets each day."

"And don't forget your goat, brother," Marcus said as he dropped to the ground and leaned against a giant cedar of Lebanon. "Bento has given me a good idea. I'm going to sleep so I will be alert for the feasting tonight."

Cassus and Lucius wandered around the garden, with Lucius pointing out the trees that Ignatius had imported from China. "What a magnificent area to be found in the midst of Rome," Cassus said. "The city has built around this domus."

"Yes, since his home is close to the Forum Romanum, Grandfather has fought hard at times to keep away those who want to buy this area to build monuments. But now Father is apt to sell it."

The garden was a favorite spot for Lucius, and his fingers caressed the trunks of the locust tree and junipers that Ignatius had imported from Jerusalem. The myrtle shrubs had fragrant flowers and spicy-sweet scented leaves that periodically perfumed the area. Lilies and roses bloomed in profusion near the splashing cherub fountain. But the garden had been planned with utility as well as beauty in mind, for pomegranate, olive, and nut trees mingled with the ornamental plants. The crowning glory of the area was a tall date palm tree that towered above the garden walls.

At the eighth hour, a maidservant summoned them to the triclinium for the feast. The dining area was the largest room in the house, its length being twice its breadth. Three sloping couches were arranged around a square table with one side left free for service.

The tables were covered with damask cloths, and silver knives, spoons, and toothpicks were placed conveniently for the diners. When the young people arrived, the adults were already reclining crosswise on the couches, their left elbows resting on cushions.

Marcus immediately maneuvered Plotina, the frail daughter of Cornelius Flavius, toward a vacant place where he positioned her to his right as they reclined on the mattress-covered couch. Lucius took the place to the left of his twin, with Cassus beside him.

Cassus stared when servants hustled around the couches removing the diners' sandals and washing their feet. "I thought Grandfather didn't own any slaves."

"These aren't slaves—they're all paid servants," Lucius said. "Though Grandfather didn't believe in slavery, he did like his luxury and was willing to pay for it."

Horace Livius and his son, Cato, who had been Bernice's betrothed for several years, were ushered into the room and introduced to the Nicomedia relatives. In spite of the fact that Horace was pagan, Ignatius had agreed to the match because he and Horace had been friends since boyhood. The Livius household was nearby, and Cato had been a playmate of the Trento siblings.

Dinner began with shellfish, hardboiled eggs, and olives, served with decanters of wine sweetened with honey. The main course was a flamingo boiled with dates and dormice and stuffed with pine nuts. By the time the feast ended with pastries, fruits, and nuts, Lucius was stuffed to his limit.

"Too much food," Cassus said as he took another pastry, proving to Lucius why his cousin was a bit on the plump side, "but I keep remembering that during our mourning period, food will be scarce."

Throughout the meal, Marcus had given Plotina his undivided attention, feeding her fruit and nuts with his own hands. This action was not lost upon Plotina's father, a graying, gimlet-eyed little man whose visage grew angrier as the meal progressed; nor did it escape the notice of the white-clad Vestal standing against the wall.

Once Lucius nudged his twin. "Marcus, you are making the revered Cornelius quite angry. It might be better if you allowed Plotina to feed herself." Marcus shrugged an indifferent shoulder.

Lucius had never been able to understand his robust brother's attraction to this slender girl whose phantomlike movements reminded Lucius of a wraith. When she was a child of eight years, Plotina had been chosen to serve in the temple dedicated to Vesta, the goddess of the hearth. After three years, Plotina's health had failed, and she had returned to her father's home. Observing the dreamy look in the girl's eyes, Lucius wondered if her early training had spoiled her for life in the real world.

Perhaps echoing his thoughts, Cassus said in an undertone, "The lady Plotina is a beauty, but she seems a poor mate for the virile Marcus."

Lucius nodded in agreement, but didn't respond because Bernini had indicated that the feasting was over. "Let's assemble immediately in the atrium where Cornelius will read Father's last will and testament." Upon Bernini's signal, servants swarmed around the table with ewers of fresh perfumed water that they poured over the diners' hands, wiping them with towels they carried on their arms.

Lucius had laid aside his silk toga during the meal, but he slowly draped it over his short tunic as he followed the others from the dining hall. Since the reading of the will would have no consequence for him as the younger son, he wished he could be spared this further evidence that he had lost his grandfather, but he didn't want to call attention to himself by his absence.

The will carried few surprises. The import business and the other family property went to Bernini, who had managed both for several years. A generous portion of Ignatius's wealth was also bequeathed to Octavian, but when Cornelius Flavius reached the end of the scroll, he paused dramatically, and with a puzzled glance toward Lucius, he read:

> To my grandson, Lucius, I bequeath the Alabaster. Of all my descendants, I consider the boy to have the necessary qualities to provide a healthy climate for furthering the family's spiritual heritage symbolized by the Alabaster. And

my last request to all of you assembled to hear this reading
is that you will pattern your lives after the example of Jesus
of Nazareth, our crucified and living Lord.

Cornelius spat out the last words as if they left a bitter taste in
his mouth. "That is all," he said ponderously, obviously displeased with the will's conclusion, "although I should like to
add what my good friend Ignatius told me. He didn't intend to
favor one twin over the other, but whereas Marcus will someday inherit the family's business, he believed that Lucius was
the most studious of his generation, the one more likely to preserve and teach the tenets of the Christian faith. He wanted the
tradition carried on by his firstborn's descendants."

The gathered family sat in stunned silence for several moments. *Had any other holder of the Alabaster skipped over the
first generation to bequeath it to the second?* But since the relic
had belonged to the family for almost three hundred years and
its past was shrouded in mystery, no one could answer that question. Bernini broke the silence by thanking Cornelius for his
service and handing him a bag of coins. Marcus sidled over to
his brother to say jokingly, but still with a touch of malice, "Well,
schoolboy, your efforts have paid off."

Lucius wasn't concerned with Marcus's reaction, nor even
with that of his father, who probably resented having his lack of
spirituality questioned, but he did feel sorry for Octavian, who
drew Lucius to one side and said, "Let's go to the chapel and
pray. You've been handed an awesome responsibility."

As they entered the room, Lucius said, "Uncle, I'm sorry that
you didn't receive the Alabaster. I'm too young to have this duty
thrust upon me."

"I would have liked to be its guardian," Octavian said, "but
we must remember that no one really owns the Alabaster; it's to
be passed down from generation to generation by the one most
likely to appreciate its meaning and to perpetuate it. God has
chosen you to be the one in this generation to have that privilege

and responsibility. For some reason you've been selected over me, and God alone knows why." Lucius went to the stand that held the Alabaster, stunned by the solemnity on his uncle's face, as the older man continued.

"The message of the Alabaster is needed more than ever in our day. Perhaps you are not aware of it, but the church may be facing perilous days. Unworthy leaders have infiltrated our ranks. Bitter feuds are erupting between bishops and their congregations. Among the leadership there is hypocrisy and deception, wickedness, and many apostates who have denounced the faith of their fathers and are forming new sects."

"If Grandfather knew this, he had not told me."

Octavian nodded. "Perhaps he wanted to spare you that knowledge, but I want to pray with you that you will have the wisdom to handle the Alabaster wisely."

After the prayer, Octavian left Lucius alone in the chapel. He stared at the Alabaster in its cedar chest on the marble pedestal. So conscious was he of the responsibility placed upon him that he was not aware of Octavia's presence until she joined him on the bench.

"Why is it so important?" she whispered, looking in childish wonder at the small vase.

"I will tell you the story as I heard it from Grandfather," Lucius said. After a long pause, he cleared his throat and continued, "Three centuries ago when Jesus was crucified, our ancestor Suetonius, a merchant from Trento, was in Jerusalem. He witnessed the crucifixion, and he was still in the country when the news of the resurrection circulated. His specialty was Hebrew antiquities, and before he left Judaea, he went to a shop operated by Mary and Cleopas to buy some pottery."

"Mary of Magdala?" Octavia asked, wide-eyed.

"No, this Mary's identity is vague, but we do know that she was one of the women who went to the tomb to anoint the body of Jesus after His burial." Lucius pointed to the Alabaster. "She took that container of spikenard with her, but it was never opened because Jesus was gone from the grave. When our ancestor visited their shop and learned that she still had the vase of precious ointment, he bargained until he was able to buy it."

Octavia turned luminous eyes on Lucius, and then stared at the Alabaster. "Just to think—that container was carried to the tomb of Jesus! Is the spikenard still in it?"

Lucius nodded. "It has never been opened. Our ancestor brought it home with him as a symbol that the tomb was empty. He decreed that the vase should always remain in our family as a symbol of our Christian heritage—a reminder that we serve a risen Savior. That fact is what sets Christianity apart from all other religions."

"Didn't the family lose the Alabaster once?"

"During the persecution under Emperor Nero, our ancestor hid the Alabaster to keep the soldiers from destroying it. He was imprisoned and put to death before he could tell anyone of the hiding place. It was fifty years or more before it surfaced."

"Do you feel frightened to have such a trust given to you?" Octavia questioned.

"Yes," Lucius admitted. "The least Grandfather could have done was to tell me in advance. I've been thinking about so many things he should have told me. I wish he would have advised me how to plan my future so that I can be a fit guardian for the Alabaster."

"But he paid you a great compliment by not advising you! It seems to me that he knew you would make the right decisions. You only have to depend upon God to guide you in the right way."

Lucius looked at the girl wonderingly, almost as if he hadn't seen her before. Serenity and mystery shone in her long-lashed eyes, which radiated unusual wisdom for a girl of twelve years. *Grandfather, probably Octavia should have had the Alabaster,* he thought, but he only said, "I pray that you're right. I wish I could see into the future and know where the faith represented by the Alabaster will lead me."

"Perhaps it's just as well you do not know," she said.

2

ROME, 300

G ood day. Good day," Bento squawked when Lucius pushed open the door of the building attached to the outside wall of the domus. One-half of the enclosure was reserved for the family's horses, which the servants tended, but Lucius fed and cared for his menagerie, as the family was fond of calling it. Lucius took a deep breath as he entered the enclosure, for the odors of animal and fowl refuse were overwhelming until he became accustomed to the stench.

"Good day," he returned Bento's squawk. He opened the cages, and the cockatoo and other birds swooped over his head while he poured hot stodge into the stone feeding troughs for his Siberian huskies and the fox. Steam rose from the cold stone, for the temperature had cooled overnight. The goat's protest rose above the chatter of the birds as he impatiently waited his turn. After the feeding was completed, Lucius shooed the birds into their cages and opened the outside door to ventilate the odorous room.

He whistled, and the huskies and fox rushed to romp in the field between the barn and the small stream that marked the border between the Trento property and the wooded area surrounding the dwelling of Cornelius Flavius. With head down, Lucius paced back and forth in the field, lifting the hem of his

toga to protect it from the dew-studded grass. Before he left the
domus, Lucius had paid a last visit to his grandfather. Ignatius
would leave his home today, never to return, and Lucius's
thoughts were tormented.

The guardianship of the Alabaster sat heavily on his shoulders this morning. He was obligated to perpetuate the Trento
tradition of belief in the resurrection, yet he had no clear conviction of where his grandfather was at this time. He had been
instructed carefully in the Scriptures, but he apparently had much
to learn. Up until this time he had depended upon the faith of
his grandfather; now it would be necessary for him to make his
own commitment to faithfully follow the risen Lord. The sun
peeped over the trees and was chasing the dew away before
Lucius received some comfort by remembering the words of
Jesus, "I am the resurrection and the life, and anyone who believes in Me will never die." For the time being, he would have
to be content with that assurance. Ignatius had gone to be with
Jesus, and perhaps that's all he needed to know. The contented
cooing of doves from the nearby trees brought a subtle reminder
that also eased his spirit—God cared for all creatures, and surely
He would have His eye on Lucius Trento.

The household bell signaled that the morning meal was being served, and Lucius whistled for the huskies. They ran to his
side, the fox in their midst. Lucius ruffled the soft red fur—
strange how the fox had accepted its traditional enemies as
playmates.

By the time the Trentos had eaten a brief meal of bread and
cheese, a crowd had gathered in the atrium where Horace Livius
gave directions to the funeral participants. Six trumpeters headed
the procession, and directly behind them, the official female
mourners assembled.

Ignatius's body, still wrapped in a rich white toga fringed with
purple, was placed on a litter, and eight of his male servants
lifted the conveyance to their shoulders. Bernini's family came
next in line, and the Nicomedia relatives lined up behind them.

Many friends brought up the rear as the cortege wound its way on foot through the streets of Rome toward the first stop in the Forum Romanum.

The din of the trumpets resounded over the procession, and Bernice covered her ears to shut out the ear-piercing vibrations, but loud as they were, the instruments didn't muffle the howling, shrieking mourners.

"I'd forgotten how noisy funerals are," Marcus said to his twin. "I don't remember Grandmother's funeral being like this."

"It wasn't. Grandfather planned it, and he omitted many of these pagan practices. But Father is in charge of this procession, and he wanted all of the ancient customs included—he would like for Romans to forget that Grandfather was a Christian."

"No doubt it's to the Trentos' advantage if such knowledge isn't widespread," Marcus observed.

Lucius would have retorted, but his attention was drawn toward two paid actors cavorting on each side of the family impersonating Trento ancestors and wearing masks taken from wooden cabinets at the Trento domus. One actor wore a beeswax mask of a Trento who had lived two hundred years ago, while the other's face was covered with a marble mask bearing the image of Ignatius's own father.

The procession slowed when it neared the congestion of the Forum, which had been built over a filled-in swamp at the foot of Palatine Hill and for years had been the center of the city's business and government. Since it was also a place to shop, meet friends to exchange gossip, and watch public ceremonies, the area was always crowded.

Lucius felt a surge of pride in his country as he always did when he entered the Forum Romanum. The oldest of the city's public squares, it had grown through the years into a complex of open streets, government buildings, temples, and shops. Its main concourse was closed to wheeled traffic, but senators, priests, businessmen, shoppers, and hawkers thronged the area on foot. In deference to the funeral procession, the hawkers ceased their cries momentarily, but as soon as the cortege passed on, their voices followed the mourners. "Honey cakes. Dried figs. Salt fish."

When they passed the Golden Milestone, from which all roads fanned out of Rome to connect with major cities throughout the empire, Lucius motioned to be sure his cousin Cassus didn't miss this famous landmark. The Roman world was united with a network of straight, level roads, originally laid out as military highways to move men, pack trains, and siege equipment, but after the empire was established, the routes had been utilized by caravans hauling silk, spices, and provisions. Each mile along these thoroughfares was marked by a six-foot pillar measured from this Milestone.

"Roman roads are great," Cassus whispered edging his way to Lucius's side. "Otherwise, we could never have made it to Rome before Grandfather's death. And all along our route, I saw markers inscribed to the emperor who reigned at the time of that portion of road construction."

"I envy you, Cassus, for your travels. I haven't been farther from Rome than our country villa."

"Your time will come, Cousin. Father intends to invite you to visit us in Nicomedia. Since you're the guardian of the Alabaster, he wants to counsel with you."

"I shall look forward to that. I need some help to understand how to assume the responsibility thrust upon me."

The cortege halted in front of the Temple of Saturn, and Horace Livius mounted the steps to read the panegyric he had composed in honor of his friend. The business of the forum continued without interruption, so Lucius moved closer to hear what Livius had written.

"Ignatius Trento, leading Roman merchant, was born in this city during the reign of Severus Alexander. Until recently, good health attended his long and productive life. His achievements are many, chief of which was his export business that has been a mark of the Trentos for generations." For almost an hour, Livius enumerated and discussed in depth the political life and the numerous philanthropies of Ignatius, then he concluded, "He leaves behind him a host of friends and a grieving family, namely his sons, Bernini and Octavian, and their descendants."

Livius rolled the panegyric compactly and moved down the steps to rejoin the cortege. When it was obvious that the oration had ended, Octavian turned angrily to his brother. "Why was there no mention of father's Christian faith and his role in nurturing the church of Rome?"

Bernini presented a stony face to Octavian. "Because it was not to my interests to do so. There are times when it pays to be pragmatic. You don't live here—I do."

"But you know that Father would have wanted his Christian faith mentioned above all things," Octavian persisted.

"It's over and done with now," Bernini said, and he gave the signal for the procession to continue.

Lucius fell into step beside Octavian. "Don't grieve about it, Uncle. Grandfather's contributions to the Church will live on whether or not it's recognized in the official oration."

Octavian laid a heavy hand on his nephew's shoulder.

"You're right, of course, but it will be up to us to see that the torch is passed on. Your father will not do it."

Since no wheeled vehicles were allowed in the center of Rome during the daytime, the cortege wended its pedestrian way slowly to the family tomb, on the outskirts of the city, where Ignatius's wife had been interred a few years before.

"At least Bernini adhered to Father's wishes to have his body preserved rather than for the bones to be cremated. This is one evidence that Ignatius of Trento was a Christian," Octavian said.

The Trento tomb was located along one of the main roads entering the city. Built underground, the tomb was a series of rectangular grave plots enclosed by walls and separated from one another by narrow passages. The side walls were constructed of squared stones at the base, topped by bricks, and rounded out with a wide, plastered opening sculpted with projecting foliated stems and floral scrolls. The stair risers were richly carved in the same type of relief.

When they arrived at the tomb, a large group of people awaited them, whom Lucius recognized as members of the Christian church in Rome. Bernini ignored their presence, but when Lucius told Octavian who they were, the younger son went to the Christians.

"Thank you for coming today. After we are gone, will you commit my father's soul to the God who gave it, in the manner of the Church?" The placement of his father's body without even a prayer had concerned Octavian, an anxiety that Lucius shared. With their assurance given, Lucius's gloom lifted considerably as, without further ceremony, the servants conveyed his grandfather's body to its underground resting place.

Lucius chose a seat beside his mother when the family entered litters to be conducted back to the city. As they moved slowly along the Appian Way, he asked Domitilla, "What exactly can we do during the mourning period?"

"It's not so much what you can do as what you cannot do," she said, smiling. "Activities within the domus will not alter a great deal, but we will not take part in any of the city's entertainments."

"Will the wedding of Bernice and Cato go on as planned?" Lucius asked.

Domitilla nodded. "Yes. That isn't scheduled for twenty days. Your Nicomedia relatives are staying for the wedding, so after the days of mourning, I want you children to entertain them, but we will honor your grandfather's memory until then."

"One advantage of this mourning is that we'll be excused from study, I hope," Marcus said, his dark eyes glistening.

"That will be up to your father," Domitilla replied, "but I surmise that he'll intend for your lessons to continue."

"I hoped there might be one advantage for these days of enforced inactivity," he grumbled, but his mother quelled him with a stern look.

The nine days didn't prove to be as tiresome as Lucius had expected, for he spent most of his time with Cassus, and he formed a bond of friendship with his cousin that he hadn't had the opportunity to do before. Cassus had a clean-cut profile, full lips, and piercing, coal-black eyes. He was two years older than Lucius and they found much in common. Both were interested in the activities of the empire, which Cassus had observed first-hand by living in Nicomedia where the emperor resided most of the time.

On the third day of mourning, Cassus and Lucius went into the garden to lounge on the soft grass and nibble on ripe figs that had fallen during the night. As the sticky sweetness of the fruit dribbled over his chin like a fountain, Lucius said, "How did the citizens of Nicomedia react to the emperor's decision to share the power of the empire?"

"There are various opinions," Cassus replied, "but I believe that most people approve, for it's a well-known fact that the Roman Empire has become too large and unwieldy for a lone ruler. Besides, it's worked remarkably well."

"Grandfather was of the opinion that this move will eventually lead to civil wars, and he was usually right. He favored a central authority."

"This reorganization of the empire's administration will go down in history as the principal and most permanent achievement of Diocletian," Cassus said.

"That remains to be seen," Lucius argued. "Granted that the emperor wanted to insure the empire from the type of would-be usurpers we've had in the past few years, his plan is yet to be tested to the full."

"Many people think that Diocletian is on the verge of abdicating, and when he does, the purple will probably fall on Constantine's shoulders, and he could handle the empire alone, I'm sure."

"You've mentioned Constantine before, but I don't know who he is," Lucius said.

"Constantine is the son of Constantius, Diocletian's Caesar in the West, and his first wife, Helena. In 293 when Constantius was appointed Caesar, Diocletian compelled him to abandon Helena and to marry Theodora, the stepdaughter of Maximian."

"And since Maximian is Diocletian's co-Augustus, it was a political move."

"Yes, the emperor has a long-range plan whereby rule of the empire will move along smoothly to handpicked successors, and he's trying to keep the Augusti and the Caesars bound with family ties."

"So Diocletian rules in the East with his son-in-law Galerius as his Caesar, and Maximian is the Augustus of the West, and Caesar Constantius is his son-in-law." Lucius laughed. "That's the kind of political tangle that baffles Marcus when he's studying Roman history." Lucius paused in thought. "But where does your friend Constantine fit into this plan?"

"In order to keep control over Constantius, Diocletian brought Constantine and his mother to the court at Nicomedia. In one way, Constantine has been a hostage, but he's also a favorite of the emperor, and Diocletian has given him every advantage to learn political administration and military tactics."

"So it does appear that Diocletian has plans for him."

With a smile, Cassus said, "According to my father, God may be the one who has destined Constantine for great things, and Diocletian is only the instrument God has chosen to prepare the way. But whatever the reason, the emperor has taken his young protégé on many journeys throughout the East. His military training has been thorough, and he saw service not only in Persia and Egypt, but in Asia and on the Danube. He's had the best of education—he loves literature and he speaks Greek as well as Latin. He is known for his moderation and wisdom. Besides this, he even looks like an emperor—he possesses a noble carriage and an air of authority."

"You make a good case for him, but if I understand Diocletian's governmental system, Constantine won't figure in the succession. Let's see if we can reconstruct the order of the tetrarchy he set up in 293."

Cassus picked up a wax tablet and a stylus. "Let's outline what he's done. Diocletian surmised that as long as there was only one emperor that someone would always be trying to unseat him. So he chose a colleague to share the rule with him, both of them to be called Augustus, with each one to have a Caesar as an assistant and eventual successor."

"So he chose an old comrade in arms, Maximian, as his brother Augustus."

"Which is a good choice, for Maximian has proved his bravery and loyalty to Diocletian."

Writing on the wax tablet, Cassus said, "For his own Caesar, Diocletian appointed a soldier called Galerius, and Constantius became Maximian's Caesar. Father thinks he made a good choice in Constantius, who is a man of high merit, but he's not so sure about Galerius. So we have:

Augustus Diocletian, Caesar Galerius (married to Diocletian's daughter, Valeria)

Augustus Maximian, Caesar Constantius (married to Maximian's stepdaughter, Theodora)

"My tutor says that Galerius is a rough Illyrian soldier, uncultured and brutal, albeit, he's an experienced general. Diocletian considered an orderly succession possible only if upon the death or abdication of an Augustus, his Caesar, also his adopted son and heir, takes his place, and in turn selects a new Caesar. So it looks to me as if Galerius will be the next emperor, rather than Constantine."

"Time will tell," Cassus said, and he shook his head worriedly. "Father is distressed already at how events at court are heading, for some Christians have been forced to recant. Galerius is anti-Christian, and he seems to have unusual control over Diocletian, who in spite of his ideal of sharing the power is conducting himself as a sole monarch. He dresses like a king and lives surrounded by pomp and mystery. Only a privileged few are admitted to his presence, and they have to greet their emperor by kneeling and kissing the hem of his garment."

Settling the problems of the empire soon proved too much for the two boys, and they ambled back into the atrium where the rest of the family had assembled.

On the tenth day after Ignatius was buried, Domitilla called the youth together early in the morning. "Lucius and Marcus, I'm giving you the responsibility of entertaining your sister and cousins today by taking them to the Caracalla baths. I've also sent an invitation to Plotina Flavius and Cato Livius to join you there. Marcus, visit your father's steward to obtain money for the day's activities. Enjoy yourselves but return before darkness falls."

Marcus bade Cassus and Octavia walk beside him as they pushed their way through the crowded streets. "I want to explain to you about the use of the baths," he said.

"We have public baths in Nicomedia, too," Octavia said.

"But I doubt they compare to the immensity of these, which are considered one of the greatest engineering triumphs of the last century. They sprawl over more than thirty acres. Aqueducts bring mountain water into the system. The baths are so large they can accommodate more than a thousand bathers each day."

Marcus pointed out other points of interest in the city as they sauntered along, and Lucius was glad that his more verbose brother was in command of the tour. Not responsible for entertaining guests, he could settle in on his own thoughts. While he was at the baths, he would visit the library and see if he could borrow a copy of Cicero's *De oratore* to study as an aid to improve his oratory skills which, according to his tutor, he was notably lacking.

Although lost in his own contemplation, Lucius sensed that his sister was unusually quiet, and he shifted his attention to her.

"Why such a long face, Bernice?"

She flushed and lifted troubled eyes to him. "Ten days from now is my wedding. I will not like leaving the rest of the family."

Bernice was not as mature as many fourteen year olds, and Lucius knew this break would be difficult for her.

"You've known Cato all of your life. He will be kind to you. Besides, you've been betrothed for five years now; you should be used to the idea."

"But the Livius family has no Christian beliefs. Even though Father will not openly display his faith, he at least does not worship the pagan gods, but I will be compelled to do so when I live with Cato's family."

"Perhaps as Queen Esther you can be a witness of your faith to the Livius family. If you set an example of Christian principles, you may influence them."

Bernice's face brightened. "I hope so, but I don't know what I can do if they insist that I offer sacrifices to their household gods."

"You'll know what to do when the time comes."

Her mood lightened, and by the time they reached the baths, Bernice and Octavia were chatting companionably. Marcus took them on a tour of the spacious central building that provided access to many dressing, bath, and game rooms. "There are three progressions to the system," he explained. "We should take the cold bath first, then move to the warm bath, and finally to the steam room."

"How's the water heated here?" Cassus asked.

"By wood-burning furnaces beneath the floors that connect to a network of steam pipes."

Checking the schedule on the wall, Lucius said, "Bathing for women starts soon. While you bathe, we can go to the gymnasia and work out. It will be more than an hour before males can enter the baths."

"What will you girls do when you finish? We need to know where to find you," Marcus asked, but he paid scant heed to their answer, for Plotina entered the building followed by her senior chaperone. Marcus hurried toward her, and Plotina languidly extended her hand toward him.

"You're just in time," he said. His eyes grazed her richly clad frame, which in spite of her illness exhibited a more mature body than would be commonly expected in a girl of her age. Lucius noted a flame kindle in her eyes when she looked at Marcus but when she joined Bernice and Octavia, her face was calm and inexpressive.

The three boys spent the next hour in the gymnasia lifting weights, jumping rope, and doing calisthenics. Cato Livius waited for them when they returned to the central hallway.

"I bathed at home," Cato said to Marcus, "so I will take the young ladies to see a musical performance scheduled in the library. A flutist will be entertaining."

"That will be fine," Marcus said. "Mother doesn't want them unattended, but they have asked to visit the shops, too." He pressed some coins into Cato's hand. "Use this money if they wish to make a purchase."

Cato waved aside the money. "I'm sure they will be ready for a sausage or a cake now that they've finished with the baths, but I'll gladly stand the expense."

Marcus pounded him on the back. "You're a great fellow, Cato," and Lucius agreed. Bernice couldn't be in better hands, but he would be more optimistic about her future if their families shared the same religious beliefs.

Trusting the young women to Cato's care, the three Trentos entered a vestibule, stripped off their tunics and togas and left them with a servant. Lucius and Cassus donned leather shorts, but Marcus preferred to bathe nude. Arriving at the frigidarium, they found the pool already crowded with other bathers, many of whom Lucius and Marcus greeted. Seeing Lucius gingerly lowering his body into the cold water, Marcus grabbed him and ducked him under. Lucius howled and pulled his brother down beside him. They wrestled in the bracing water, as they'd done since boyhood, until the other bathers loudly denounced their antics.

Next Marcus led the way into the warm bath and then into the sweat rooms where hot moisture soon oozed from their bodies.

When they left the last pool, Lucius submitted to the hands of a masseur, who rubbed and oiled his body until he was completely relaxed. As the man pommeled his shoulders, his hips, his thighs, the numbness of mind and spirit he had experienced since the death of Ignatius eased away from him. In the past, he had depended upon the guidance of his grandfather; he acknowledged that, from now on, he must be his own man.

Lucius wrapped a clean loin cloth around his tingling body and leaned against one of the huge marble pillars that supported the arched ceiling. Closing his eyes, he listened dreamily to the hubbub around him. Gymnasts panted as they swung heavy dumbbells. Men argued over a game of knucklebones. Servants pattered over the marble floors bearing trays of wine for rich men who were being groomed and perfumed by their slaves. Hawkers paraded through the area with cakes, sausages, and pies, and over all this clamor echoed the loud tenor of a happy man singing in his bath.

Cato and the girls waited for them when they emerged from the building. As they started their return, Plotina motioned for Marcus to join her, and their steps lagged behind the others, with her companion following at a discreet distance.

"Father is very angry," she said. "He hesitated about permitting me to come today, but he didn't want to insult your mother. After today, however, he has forbidden me to see you. "

"What does he have against me? One day I'll be the head of the house of Trento. I can lay the treasures of the world at your feet. Why does he think I'm inferior?"

"He said that your actions at the feast we attended bordered on lust. You must remember that Father still considers me a Vestal Virgin though my poor health made it necessary for me to leave the temple. It isn't you more than any other man. Even if my health doesn't permit me to serve in the temple, I'm sure he intends for me to lead a celibate life."

Marcus's dark eyes snapped angrily and a determined look overspread his face. "Well, I don't intend for you to do so. I'll speak to my father—he'll make the proper arrangements."

Plotina shrugged gracefully as if the matter was of small interest to her. "You should know by now that Father will not be thwarted. You'll only make things worse for me."

"I won't give you up," he insisted.

"The consequences will be on your shoulders. I told Father I would talk to you about it. I can do no more. "

Running a few steps, she caught up with the others. Marcus started to rush toward her, then he cursed, savagely kicked a loose pebble on the street, and stomped in the opposite direction.

During the next few days, Lucius introduced Cassus to the best and worst of Rome. They visited the Tiber wharves and watched grain being unloaded into warehouses and observed the varied street activities. Peddlers hawked racks of used clothing. Merchants displayed fabrics imported from all parts of the empire. They investigated jewelry shops, booksellers' stalls, and vegetable markets. Fortune tellers tried to lure them to their tents. Prostitutes beckoned from their lairs.

"People have flocked to Rome since the early days of the empire, and there seems to be no ceasing," Lucius explained as they walked along the streets where impoverished Romans crowded into ramshackle multistoried tenements. "Most of them have been attracted by the free doles of grain that the government hands out. These flats have no plumbing. Water has to be carried up from the street, and residents dispose of their garbage by tossing it out the windows under cover of darkness. They heat with charcoal braziers or open flames that pose a constant fire hazard."

Since he was interested in engineering, Cassus examined the aqueducts bringing fresh water from the hills into the city. Some of the structures were triple-tiered, made of stone without any mortar to bind them together.

"They raise these huge slabs with block and tackle, I've heard,"

Cassus said. "I'm apprenticed to one of Diocletian's engineers, and he helped to build these aqueducts in Rome."

"They have made life easier for the city's residents because the Tiber is too muddy for use. Although few private homes can tap into the system, the water is piped to businesses and to the farms on the outskirts of the city."

"I've seen enough to believe that Rome will last forever, although it's obviously not self-sufficient. Grain is still imported to feed the populace, water is abundant, though brought from outside, and fresh vegetables pour into the city."

They spent one whole day on the Palatine.

"The Seven Hills of Rome!" Cassus exclaimed. "It was here that Rome was born about a thousand years ago. I've also visited the site of ancient Troy where the defeated prince Aeneas, a son of Venus, was ordered to lead his people to a new land in the west, and they came to the Latin peninsula."

"Our tutor says that after the Trojans reached Italy, they joined forces with the Latins, and their descendants Romulus and Remus, the legendary founders of Rome, established a settlement on this very hill. Although the tutor is Greek, he teaches us to take pride in our country. He's brought us here many times."

As they looked out over the city and at the busy Tiber many feet below, Cassus said, "It's easy to see why the city originated here—this would have been a natural refuge for the early inhabitants to defend their homes."

When they circled the Imperial Palace, Lucius said, "The palace was started by Caesar Augustus, but succeeding emperors have added to it."

"Too bad it isn't used much anymore, but Diocletian believes that Rome is too far removed from the center of the empire to be ruled exclusively from this city."

As they returned to the Trento residence, they surveyed the brick Senate building and the basilicas dedicated to Julia and Ameilia in the Forum Romanum. The Temple of Vesta stood slightly back from the square, flanked by the House of the Vestals.

"This is the order that Plotina entered when she was a child," Lucius explained. "It's considered the most important in the Forum, probably in the whole city, for the Vestal Virgins have custody of the Sacred Fire, symbol of the life of the city and therefore never allowed to go out."

Interested as he was in architecture, Cassus took delight in the round temple, with an opening in the domed ceiling to make it similar to the primitive hut dwellings used by the first inhabitants of Rome.

Without their parents' knowledge, one night Marcus and Cassus secretly left the house and mingled with nocturnal Romans. The din was even louder than during the daytime as delivery wagons clattered along the narrow streets. Taverns offered bread and wine to the poorer men who fled the drabness of their tenements for a night of revelry. A few rich Romans traversed the streets carried in litters by slaves, with a vanguard of servants to protect them from the cutthroats lying in wait at every corner.

After several hours of pushing their way through the crowded, noisy streets, Cassus breathed deeply when they entered the safety of the Trento domus. "Thanks for taking me to see the nightlife, Marcus, but it's a relief to have returned safely."

Two days before the wedding, Bernini planned an outing for the Trentos and the Livius family to see the chariot races at Circus Maximus. Though he had been to the Circus many times, Lucius never failed to marvel at the immensity of the place that seated nearly 250,000 spectators, and most of the seats were filled when they arrived.

As the large party moved into their wooden seats, acrobats were walking on wires high above the tracks, while clowns somersaulted their way back and forth on the sandy turf. It was not long before trumpets sounded; the crowd cheered noisily and looked toward entrances at each end of the arena. White-robed females tripped merrily into view, stepping in time to the drumbeats of the marchers and the melody of trumpeters dressed in short white tunics. The twenty charioteers who would be competing today followed the musicians, and behind them two yoked oxen pulled a wagon bearing the winner's palm wreath of victory. The cheering increased to a volcanic rumble demanding the commencement of the first race, on which people were still placing bets.

Another blast of the trumpet, and five chariots erupted onto the sandy course for the two-and-a-half-mile race, which necessitated seven laps around the track sparkling with bright mineral grain. Four horses pulled the small chariots, each manned by a daring charioteer with whip held high. The wild-eyed animals lunged forward when the official driver slammed a whip on their backs, following two horsemen who led the chariots around the track to set the pace. At intervals a sprinkler threw water on the chariots' smoking wheels to prevent an accident.

Rectangular basins containing ceremonial figures for marking laps were located in the center of the track supported by towering obelisks at each end. Seven bronze dolphins spewing water from their mouths were on the outer bar of each basin, and seven wooden eggs were placed on the inner bars. After each lap, an official reversed a dolphin and removed one egg.

Women screamed when a chariot overturned on the hairpin curve at the end of the stylized track, and the squealing of the injured horses added to the uproar. Bernini placed many bets on the red team, sponsored by one of the clubs that the gambling charioteers represented. Bernice and Octavia waved red banners to spur their team to victory.

It took most of the day for the opposing clubs to compete and to have a winner declared, and over an hour for the crowd to disperse and the Trento family to find transportation for the homeward journey.

On the morning of the wedding, Lucius found Bernice in the chapel sitting listlessly on the front bench. He watched his sister for a moment before he moved to sit beside her. She held two wooden dolls and some tunics on her lap.

She smiled wistfully at Lucius. "Cato's mother told me that I must dedicate my toys and childhood dress to the household gods. I suppose I should have told her that we didn't have any idols in this house, but I was too timid. I thought the Alabaster was the nearest we had to an idol."

"Oh, but it isn't an idol. The Trentos have never worshiped the Alabaster; it's nothing more than a symbol that the women found an empty tomb when they went to anoint Jesus's body. And as for your childhood toys, they don't have any place in the chapel. Why don't you leave them with Mother? She'll keep them until you have children of your own."

"I'm frightened about that, too."

"Surely Mother has talked with you about the physical part of marriage," Lucius said with embarrassment, knowing how incapable he was of advising his sister. When Bernice nodded, he continued, "No doubt all brides are scared at first, but you'll be all right. I'm sure Cato will be kind to you. And if you do have rough times, come here to the chapel and pray. In fact, let's pray now." Lucius held his sister's hand, and they sat quietly for several minutes.

"God, in the name of Your son, Jesus, we ask that you take away Bernice's fears. Give her the strength to become a good wife and mother and a vibrant faith that will transcend the pagan environment where she must dwell. May she be an example to her husband so that he will be drawn to You. Amen."

"That was beautiful, Lucius. I feel better about the whole situation. I think you should train to be a pastor."

Lucius laughed away her suggestion, and putting an arm around Bernice, he led her from the room. "A young woman should be happy on her wedding day. Let's anticipate an enjoyable time—no more tears."

Carrying the playthings of her childhood carelessly under her arm, Bernice smiled at her brother and hustled up the steps to her room. The smile remained on her face as she recalled the few times she had been alone with Cato. She had found pleasure in his caresses, and the flame in his eyes when he cast a gaze over her had caused her breathing to accelerate and a flush to warm her skin. Maybe marriage wouldn't be so bad after all. She skipped into the bedroom where her servants waited to dress her for the nuptials.

After her body was washed with perfumed water, the servants dropped a white silk tunic over her shoulders. Around her waist, she fastened a woolen girdle in a Hercules knot that could only be untied by Cato. She fidgeted impatiently while the front of her hair was curled with a heated iron. Then her shoulder-length tresses were braided and arranged in tiers on top of her head to fashion a coiffure resembling a halo. A crown of white roses was secured to the halo, adding an inch to Bernice's height.

"Just a touch of rouge and some eye shadow, and you will be ready for your lover. What jewelry are you wearing?"

"The gold bracelet in the form of a serpent and the gold earrings that belonged to my grandmother. When she died, Grandfather gave them to me, requesting that I wear them at my wedding."

Bernice put on orange shoes and threw a saffron-tinted cloak over her shoulders, while the maidservants topped her attire with a veil of flaming orange. She touched the ring Cato had given her when they were betrothed—a simple metal ring on the third finger of her left hand.

Musingly, she said to her attendant, "Do you think a nerve from this third finger leads directly to my heart?"

The woman laughed lightly. "So it is said, my dear one, and I believe that it's true."

Bernice waited almost an hour before Bernini came to escort her to the atrium where the ceremony would take place. Two priests conducted the ritual—one a pagan priest and the other the bishop at the Christian church, a concession to his father's faith that even Bernini would not ignore.

Bernice and Cato sat before the two priests with their fathers standing beside them. The pagan priest read the marriage contract, and Bernice was amazed at the size of the dowry her father had provided. Her spirits lightened considerably when she heard the stipulation, that "in case of divorce or a legal separation resulting in the return of the bride to her own home during a period of five years, ninety percent of the dowry is to be returned also."

She was feeling better about Cato, although ill at ease with his parents, but that provision would go a long way to insure her good treatment—Horace Livius was too tightfisted to want to relinquish that much money.

Bernini and Horace signed the parchment, and Flavius was present to affix his seal. To solemnize their vows, Bernice and Cato clasped hands and shared a piece of wheat cake. After the ceremony, Bernini invited the guests into the triclinium where tables of food had been laid out.

Centering the serving table was a roast boar, and when a servant severed the roast in two with one sweep of his knife, live thrushes flew out into the room. For appetizers, the guests had their choice of jellyfish and eggs or salted sea urchins. With the roast boar, vegetables cooked in heavy sauces seasoned with pepper, marjoram, honey, and oil, were served. A light wine, cooled with ice from the mountains, soothed their throats before they finished the meal with a dessert of stoned dates stuffed with nuts and fried in honey. A wedding cake made of meal and steeped in new wine was served before Bernice and Cato started toward the Livius domus.

Two trusted Trento servants hoisted Bernice to their shoulders and carried her along the uneven street. Other servants with flaming torches held aloft lighted the way for the wedding party. Flutists scampered among the guests, their eerie music lending a sense of magic to the scene, while three small boys swung tambourines in time to the music.

Bernice's hands moistened when they reached the Livius household—not that she was afraid of marriage now, but there were certain rituals she was supposed to perform upon entering the house. Although Domitilla had coached her well, she still feared she might do the wrong thing and displease her in-laws.

But as if she'd done it many times, Bernice anointed the door with the oil a servant held in a small vase, and then she hung woolen ribbons on the doorpost. Two Livius servants lifted her over the threshold. Cato brought her a lighted whitethorn torch and a filled vessel, the pagan symbols of fire and water. Bernice dipped her fingers in the water and used the torch to ignite a fire on the hearth before she returned to the door and threw the lighted torch toward Octavia. The surprised girl caught the torch and held it high. Why she should think of it at that moment, Bernice couldn't imagine, but as she saw her cousin holding the torch aloft, she thought of the Alabaster and the responsibility the Trentos had of passing on the faith symbolized by it. Could she do so in this pagan home?

With a wave toward her family and friends, Bernice closed the door and turned to her husband. She was no longer a Trento, but the faith fostered by her grandfather still burned in her heart.

3

NICOMEDIA, 300

Jupiter reigned in majesty on the carved wooden altar supported by a stooping Atlas, whose muscular body strained to support the major deity of the Roman pantheon. The ancient god was encompassed by an oval backdrop containing the signs of the zodiac. Below the altar, kneeling white-robed priests lifted oblations of fruit and meat to insure blessings upon the worshipers assembled in the spacious shrine. As the priests chanted, the pungent odor of Persian incense pervaded the temple.

Constantine prostrated his body before the altar, praying for a cessation of the anguish in his heart. When the bells chimed softly, indicating that the ritual was over, he left the Temple of Jupiter, his heart and mind still burdened. Next he stopped by the shrine dedicated to the Emperor Augustus, who was depicted in a marble relief leading Romans in sacrifices to their ancient gods. Constantine ducked his head to enter a small alcove and stopped before a cameo reproduction of Augustus, father of the imperial line. Augustus, flanked by two other Roman emperors, Tiberius and Caligula, was depicted wearing a tiara and holding a golden scepter. Constantine knelt before these emperors—who had been deified after their deaths by the Roman Senate—until his knees were numb from contact with the marble floor. Still, he received no ease for the pain smoldering in his heart. In other parts of the temple, supplicants voiced their petitions, some in shrieks for mercy, others in mumblings that only the gods could have understood. As Constantine heard their pleas and listened to the faltering footsteps of distressed persons entering and leaving the shrine, he wondered if they had found what they sought or if their souls were as desolate as his. With lagging feet, he left the shrine and came face-to-face with Cassus Trento. The two men joined hands in greeting.

"I've missed seeing you, Cassus. Have you been away?"

"To Rome for the funeral of my grandfather, where we tarried for a few weeks to visit with the family. And what about you, my friend? You appear troubled," Cassus said, noting the anguish in the dark eyes of his companion. Even his stern face with its beak of a nose and protruding jaw seemed less formidable today.

Constantine motioned to an inn. "Do you have time for a meal?"

Cassus nodded and followed the tall, angular centurion into the small boarding house. When their food was delivered, Constantine said, "My wife is with child, due to deliver any day. The doctors do not give much hope for a successful birth, and no man wants to lose his firstborn."

"The doctors do not always know the future."

Constantine shook his head worriedly. "My mother is not hopeful either. I have visited several temples today to pray for mercy, but my mind is still uneasy."

Cassus munched slowly on his meal. *Is this the time to introduce Constantine to Christianity and its balm for the troubled soul?* He had often longed to talk to his friend about the Trento faith, but the time had never seemed right. Up until recently, being the favorite of the emperor had given Constantine an assurance that all was well with him, but now that he had been brought low by the illness of his wife, Constantine might be more receptive. It could be the opportunity Cassus had been waiting for.

Praying for the courage to speak and for the right words to approach his friend, Cassus hesitated and lost his chance. Standing abruptly, Constantine said, "In all my worries, I'd forgotten that I've been summoned to see the emperor this morning. I'll have to leave you." Constantine rushed from the building, and Cassus hoped that his friend wouldn't be late for his appointment. It didn't pay to ignore a command from Diocletian.

As Constantine hastened toward the palace, he considered his friend, wondering at the radiant spirit Cassus always exhibited. *From what source does he find this inner peace?* In spite of his rush, when Constantine arrived at the palace, he spent more than an hour waiting in the peristyle. Worried about his wife and concerned over the reason behind the emperor's summons, Constantine paced the area. It was lined with columns in the Greek fashion, and a fountain bubbled in the center; flowering lilies grew at the edge of the water. Though citron and myrtle trees emitted their fragrances, Constantine was only semiconscious of the beauty around him.

He had been attached to Diocletian's court for nearly ten years since the elevation of his father, Constantius Chlorus, to Caesar of the West. Though Constantine had not wanted to stay at the emperor's court, he couldn't complain about the treatment he had received. Constantine and his mother, Helena, had been given an apartment in the palace. Tutors had been employed for him, and he had accompanied Diocletian on several military campaigns throughout the East. The political and administrative genius of the emperor had been freely imparted to Constantine. Still, Constantine sometimes felt like a prisoner, for Diocletian would hardly let him out of his sight. Apparently he was keeping Constantine as a pampered hostage in order to insure Constantius's loyalty to the state.

Last year during the emperor's extended illness, Constantine had escaped from Diocletian's heavy hand and had secretly married Minervina. Diocletian soon learned about it, and relations between them had been strained for the past year. Now the elaborate court ritual initiated by the emperor was one more thing to provoke Constantine. No one questioned the emperor's importance, for though of humble origin, Diocletian had enjoyed a brilliant military career and his genius as an organizer and administrator rivaled that of Caesar Augustus.

In spite of his colossal achievements, until recently Diocletian had remained accessible to anyone who had a problem, but with the change from monarchial rule to that of the tetrarchy, Diocletian had surrounded himself with pomp and ceremony. He had brought a sanctity to his position by assuming the title of Jovius, setting himself up as Jupiter's earthly representative destined to regenerate the Roman Empire. On Maximian, the other Augustus, he had bestowed the name of Herculius. Along with the titles, they had demanded the reverence and adoration due gods, and their palaces, courts, and bedchambers were considered sacred and holy. Although initially this was done to discourage the usurpation of their positions, Constantine feared that Diocletian was beginning to think that he indeed *was* a god.

When a servant finally summoned him, Constantine, though seething with impatience and indignation, calmly entered the room where Diocletian held court. The emperor wasn't on the high platform he usually occupied, but rather he stood gazing out the window. He was arrayed in a purple toga decorated with gold weavings and sparkling with numerous jewels. But he wasn't wearing his crown nor carrying his scepter, and he made no indication that Constantine was to do obeisance, so Constantine risked his anger by omitting the customary bow and kiss on the hem of his robe.

"What do you know about those people?" Diocletian demanded, and Constantine moved closer to see that the emperor's attention was focused on the Christian church, an unpretentious structure of stone, covered with masonry, across the street from the palace. The only thing that distinguished it from other buildings in the vicinity was a fresco over the front door depicting a dozen men gathered around a table. The central figure represented Jesus, the founder of the Christian church.

"Nothing," Constantine said. Until he knew the emperor's thoughts, it was not prudent to volunteer any information. Diocletian turned from the window and sat at a small table. Constantine remained standing.

Sipping moodily from a flagon of wine, the emperor said, "Then I'll tell you something about them. Christians are a subversive and hostile sect, and they become more numerous every year. In spite of imperial efforts to stamp out this religion, it continues to grow. Christians have infiltrated the army, the government, and the imperial court—even the emperor's own wife and daughter have come under their spell. They have to go."

"The emperor's policy of religious toleration has seemed to work well," Constantine dared to say, not really caring what happened to the Christians, but hoping to preserve peace in the empire.

"It's been almost forty years since Emperor Gallienus issued his edict of toleration, and the number of Christians has grown until it's now estimated that more than a tenth of the empire's inhabitants follow this religion. They are like a state within the state, and they would like nothing better than to overthrow the empire. I plan to stamp them out," Diocletian declared.

"May I inquire into the manner of their subversive movements?"

"A few months ago, during a public sacrifice when the augurs were inspecting the entrails of slaughtered animals to determine the will of the gods, a hostile presence kept them from reading their signs. It was later determined that some Christians stood on the outside of the temple that day chanting one of their psalms."

Constantine well remembered the outcome of that defective sacrifice. Fearing a plot to overthrow the old gods and usurp his leadership, Diocletian had reacted furiously. He had ordered that all residents of the imperial palace must offer sacrifice to the traditional gods or suffer the consequences. When everyone complied to his satisfaction, his fury had abated, and life had returned to normal. Surely no sane man would suspect any group on such unsubstantial evidence, but Constantine decided it was to his advantage to refrain from saying so.

"You've worked hard to promote peace and prosperity within the empire, sire, and if the Christians are disruptive to the state, then perhaps you should move against them." Even as he said it, Constantine wondered if the statement was wise. The only Christians he knew were the Trentos, and he couldn't think of any citizens who were more loyal to the state.

"Ah, but it's a great decision. I've been told that in the persecutions of this sect under Emperors Decius and Valerian, the Christians emerged stronger and more united than before. They seem to thrive on persecution, but Caesar Galerius has been pressing me to move against them."

So that's it! Constantine thought. He had wondered why a cool, clearheaded statesman like Diocletian would consider such an uncertain move. It appeared that Galerius, the emperor's Caesar and son-in-law, had been exerting more and more power in governmental policies.

Diocletian waited for Constantine to answer, and when he didn't, the emperor continued, "I am not ready to order a full-scale purge at this time, but I do intend to clear the army of these subversives. Several months ago I drafted orders demanding that all members of the military offer sacrifices to the Roman gods or risk dismissal from the service, but I didn't circulate the edict. However, I have decided to act, and I want you to deliver a copy of that order to Augustus Maximian so that he may deal with the army under his command. And you will personally see that copies of this order are taken to all the army barracks within my jurisdiction here in the East. I have ordered a century of Balkan cavalrymen to accompany you. You will leave at daybreak tomorrow."

This unexpected command deflated Constantine, and without an invitation, he sunk onto a bench. "But sire, my wife is ill and scheduled to deliver our child at any time. May I be excused from this mission?"

"Stand on your feet when you address your emperor!" Diocletian shouted, and reached for the rope to summon his palace guards. Before he could ring the bell, Constantine staggered to a standing position. "Do I have to remind you that you are under my authority and under obligation to this court? Yet for the past year, you have seen fit to make your own decisions. Perhaps you think that you're destined to wear the purple," Diocletian added with a sneer.

Anger boiled up in Constantine, but his rage was tempered by fear for his family—his father in Treves, his mother and his wife under the emperor's thumb. He had no recourse except to submit, but in that moment when he confronted the angry emperor, Constantine made up his mind that he would part company with Diocletian as soon as possible.

"Very well, sire. I'll be ready to ride at dawn." Diocletian curtly dismissed him, and as he left the palace and hurried toward the small quarters he had been occupying since his marriage, Constantine calculated the necessary time for him to carry out Diocletian's orders. It would take no less than twenty days of hard riding to reach Maximian's headquarters at Milan and return, and twice that many days to deliver the orders to the army stations in far-flung regions of the eastern empire. *Why has the emperor suddenly seen fit to entrust me with such leadership?* "He said I wasn't old enough to marry, yet he puts me in command of soldiers who are more hardened and experienced than I am," Constantine mumbled.

Has Diocletian planned this deliberately as punishment because I disregarded his wishes in marrying? Does the emperor think that I won't be able to handle the command and perhaps will lose my life as a result? Constantine was sure of it, but he stubbornly compressed his lips. If Diocletian thought this treatment would cause him to set aside his wife, he was doomed for disappointment. Regardless of the consequences, Constantine didn't regret his marriage to Minervina, the daughter of a farmer from the nearby countryside. Constantine had met the girl in the vegetable market in Nicomedia where she came to distribute her father's produce. His attraction to her had been immediate, and he paid many visits to the farm. Sensing that his mother, as well as the emperor, would react badly to his marrying a farmer's daughter, he had secretly wedded the girl, but when Minervina had conceived in the first month of marriage, he had brought her to the court.

His mother had accepted his wife, but Diocletian wouldn't allow Constantine and his bride to live within the walls of the palace. With the small pittance he received from his father, Constantine had rented a second-floor residence. They had been content until his happiness had been shattered by his wife's illness. Now with this command from Diocletian, Constantine was at his wit's end.

Constantine pushed his way through the crowded streets until he reached his building. His steps slowed as he ascended the stairway. Quietly, he opened the door into their quarters. Minervina reclined on the couch opposite the door, listlessly awaiting his return. His wife had not taken well to living in the city, and, especially now that she was ill, she dreaded the hours she had to spend alone. He knelt beside the couch and leaned over to kiss her. In her fever-flushed face and swollen body, Constantine could see little to remind him of the petite, vivacious girl he had married. "Are you feeling better?" he asked gently.

"I will be all right. Don't fret about me, husband." Minervina had never complained, though Constantine sensed the pain that tormented her. She laid her hand against his face and he lifted his hand to cover her limp fingers.

"I cannot help but worry, especially now. The emperor has commanded me to fulfill a mission for him that will take me away from Nicomedia for several weeks. If you deliver on schedule, I will not be with you."

A look of panic crossed Minervina's face, but she swallowed and spoke reassuringly, "Then I will have our child to show you upon your return. If you carry out this mission to his satisfaction, perhaps the emperor will look favorably upon you again. It distresses me that I've been the cause of his displeasure."

"You're worth it, my dear wife." He rose from his kneeling position. "But I must make plans. I've been ordered to leave in the morning, and there's much to do. I will arrange for a midwife to stay with you at all times, and I will also ask my mother to see to your welfare."

Constantine spent the rest of the day packing his gear and preparing his horse for travel. From the imperial stables, he commandeered a pack animal to carry his provisions. Meeting with the leader of the century, he told the man, "We'll be traveling fast, and that means light—take only as many provisions as you think we will need between cities. We can restock our supplies along the way."

Not trusting anyone to see to his mount, Constantine made the needed repairs to his saddle and bridle, combed and curried his horse, and checked the hooves of the animal. Being assured that the horse was ready for the journey, Constantine fed him a generous portion of grain and headed toward the palace again.

Entering through the garden area, he soon reached the apartment that had been the dwelling of his mother since their exile to Nicomedia. Voices indicated that Helena was not alone, and he entered the living room to find Atilia Trento with his mother.

Helena rose to meet him. "Son, what a pleasure!" Gray glistened in Helena's hair, but her skin was unwrinkled and rosy. She was a tall, willowy woman, not much shorter than her six-foot son.

Constantine revered his mother more than any other earthly person, and he cherished every hour spent in her company. He kissed her cheek and turned to greet Atilia. Then he sat beside his mother and said, "I'm in trouble, Mother, and I need your help." He hastily related his interview with the emperor and the condition of Minervina's health. "We have a part-time servant, and a midwife will stay with her until she delivers, but will you visit her daily? The time will be long for her."

"Yes, of course I will," Helena assured him.

"And I, too, will go to see her," Atilia said. "That way, if Helena is obligated to be at some court function, you will know that someone is seeing to Minervina's welfare."

"I'm most distressed over this action of the emperor," Helena said, and she and Atilia exchanged glances, causing Constantine to wonder as he had before how much connection his mother had with the Christians.

"I, too, would prefer that the emperor leave the army alone, but he believes this action is necessary," Constantine said. "I must leave now, but my thanks to both of you. Your promises have eased my mind, but be assured that I shall hasten my return."

"Will your journey take you to see your father?" Helena asked.

"No, only to Milan. It's my understanding that Augustus Maximian will relay the edict to my father."

When Constantine took his departure, his burden was lighter, for he knew he could depend upon the two women to see to Minervina, but the tone of Helena's voice when she spoke of his father saddened Constantine. Although he honored his father, Constantine didn't understand how he could abandon his wife for political expediency and marry Theodora, the stepdaughter of Maximian. Helena had accepted his action because she wanted what was best for Constantius, but she had never ceased to love him.

As the door closed behind Constantine, Helena looked with pity on her friend Atilia, who had cringed when Constantine had revealed the content of Diocletian's edict.

"So it's started again," Atilia said. "Just when our congregation has been growing, too."

"I had hoped that the emperor would be satisfied with his purge of the palace a few months ago." Helena shuddered and stood to pace the room. "Up until then Diocletian had been tolerant of our faith. He had ignored the Empress Prisca's leaning toward our Savior, and some of us had gone freely to worship with her and her daughter Valeria. But then he became suspicious, fearing that the ancient gods would be supplanted. That was a horrible time."

"Yes, even those of us outside the palace prayed daily until the storm of his wrath passed."

"I think he would have ignored the accusation of the augurs that some evil force was ruining their magical powers, but he became angry with his family and demanded that everyone under this roof offer sacrifice to the traditional gods."

Atilia remembered the time quite well. Diocletian's anger had been unleashed shortly before they left Nicomedia to go to Rome for Ignatius's funeral. All during their visit in Rome, she and Octavian had longed for news of what form the persecution had taken, and it was a relief to learn upon their return that no new outrages had been perpetrated against the church. Apparently their confidence had been premature.

"If I had it to do over again, I would not submit," Helena said. "I feared for Constantine more than myself if I had proclaimed publicly that I am a Christian, but until the day I die, I'll carry the burden that I recanted in the face of persecution. I've offered every penance I know, but still I do not believe I've been totally forgiven."

"We will pray that you'll receive a sign that God has forgiven you."

"But in the meantime, my lack of faith weighs heavily upon my mind." Helena sat down on the couch and leaned her head against the wall. "Now to the more immediate problem of Minervina. Whatever prompted my son to marry the girl is more than I know. He had risen steadily in Diocletian's favor, and I'm sure the emperor had great plans for him and intended Constantine to make a politically important marriage. Then he ruins everything by marrying the daughter of a farmer!"

"She is a lovely girl," Atilia observed.

"Granted, but hardly the woman for a young Roman with the future of my son—just as I wasn't the proper woman for Constantius. Though it nearly broke my heart, I knew he couldn't become a high official with the daughter of an innkeeper at his side."

"But they *are* married, so I hardly know what you can do about it."

With a sigh, Helena agreed. "There is nothing I can do but accept the girl, and I've done that, for there's no likelihood that Constantine will put her aside. He loves her dearly. If that baby dies, and doctors have warned Constantine of the possibility, it will be a blow to my son."

"It would be to anyone. I must go now," Atilia said, "but you can depend on me to help you with Minervina. I will send Octavia to sit with her also."

❋ ❋ ❋

Octavia Trento loitered along the street. She was not eager to visit Minervina. Surely if Atilia had any idea of the way Octavia felt about Constantine, she wouldn't have asked her daughter to visit the woman who would soon bear his child. Her mother would have been shocked to know that one as young as Octavia already possessed a mature, all-encompassing love for the young soldier.

She wended her way through the narrow streets where the shopkeepers sold their wares. She bypassed the rope maker, the blacksmith, and the butcher shop, but she dawdled momentarily at the stalls of the jeweler, the wool seller, the dye maker, and even longer with the woman who sold lingerie and bridal veils. Octavia allowed the woman to place one of the saffron veils over her head, while resigning herself to a loveless life. If she couldn't have Constantine, she would never wed.

When Octavia finally climbed the steps to the second-floor room and saw the suffering woman, all thoughts of jealousy fled. Helena sat beside her daughter-in-law wiping the glistening sweat from her face. Another woman, whom Octavia took for a midwife, stood on the other side of Minervina, ringing a bell softly to chase away the pain of childbirth. Helena pointed to a bowl on the table beside the bed and whispered, "Please fill it with fresh water."

Octavia moved into the small kitchen, and when she found the water jar empty, she rushed downstairs and filled it from the public fountain in front of the apartment dwelling. In her hurry, she spilled much of the water before she arrived back in the room, but she had enough left to fill the clay bowl, which she carried to the bed.

Helena motioned her aside because Minervina was writhing on the couch and the two women were hard put to keep her in bed. A thin blanket revealed the bulge of the woman's swollen body. A sour, offensive odor hovering around Minervina sickened Octavia, and she stifled the urge to retch. At the same time, she began having second thoughts about being any man's wife, if this was the result of marriage.

"We must get her on the birthing stool," the midwife said, and Helena helped her lift Minervina from the bed and place her on a padded, tilted stool.

"Octavia," Helena said, "this is no place for you. Please go home and send your mother to help us."

Octavia took one last look at Constantine's anguished wife before she rushed out of the apartment.

Atilia arrived within the hour, but when she entered the room, she grabbed the doorjamb for support. Though she was a mother herself, nothing in her sheltered life had prepared her for the scene she beheld. Helena and the midwife supported the wilting woman on the stool. Their clothes were stained, and the floor was splotched with blood. A putrid stench pervaded the area.

"Come, help me," Helena cried, "so the midwife can assist Minervina."

Reluctantly, Atilia moved to support the ailing woman in a sitting position. Minervina's face was as white as any cloth maker could have bleached it, and her face mirrored the pain she was enduring, but not a sound came from lips held between her teeth.

"Don't hold back your cries," the midwife said as she tried desperately to induce the birth of the child.

Long before dawn, Atilia had collapsed on the bench, and Helena didn't try to rouse her. By now, Minervina was so weak that Helena could hold her without assistance. At daybreak, Helena nudged Atilia. "Please bring our bishop. She must have the blessing of the church."

Even though Minervina was a pagan, Helena couldn't let her die without a Christian committal. And there was no doubt she would die. *But what of the child? Will Constantine return to find that he is bereft of both his wife and child?*

The bishop arrived, and as he prayed over Minervina, the midwife gasped, "The child is coming at last."

When the baby burst from her body, Minervina straightened on the stool and gave a scream that raised the hair on Helena's head. When she heard the child's weak cry, Minervina opened her eyes. "What is it?" she whispered.

"A fine boy," the midwife answered.

"Then I will have left Constantine something," Minervina gasped with her final breath. "Call him Crispus."

Helena had never cared much for her daughter-in-law, but during that grueling night she had learned in some small measure what her son had seen in the girl. Never had she known anyone to endure pain and suffering with such courage and fortitude, and she prayed that those qualities might be found in the newborn child.

✸   ✸   ✸

Two months had passed without news of his wife, and Constantine couldn't wait any longer. He bounded up the stairs of the apartment building after having left his horse to be cared for by servants. He pushed open the door to his quarters, and a slatternly woman greeted his entrance with a snarl. "Knock before you come in here."

For a moment Constantine was speechless, but he stammered, "I beg your pardon. I thought this was my apartment. Surely I don't have the wrong floor."

"I moved in here a month ago. The other tenant gave up the place—sickness or something."

Constantine turned on his heel. *Where are my wife and child? Surely with my mother.* He rushed toward the palace, speaking to no one. Not once on the recent journey through perilous areas had he felt the fear that engulfed him now. He paused briefly at the door of Helena's apartment, but he heard the cry of a baby within, and with a smile, he knocked.

Helena bade him enter on his first tap, and he opened the door. Octavia Trento sat on a stool holding a baby on her lap.

Constantine turned questioning eyes to his mother. "It's Crispus, your son," she said. "A fine healthy boy."

"Why the name Crispus?"

"That's what Minervina wanted to call him," Helena explained.

Constantine walked into his mother's bedchamber, thinking he'd find his wife there, but the room was empty. "What of Minervina? Where is she?"

Helena's hands clasped her throat, tears filled her eyes, and when she remained speechless, Constantine turned to Octavia. His body trembled and his lips refused to voice the fear that overwhelmed him.

"Minervina died giving birth to the child," Octavia said quietly. She held Crispus out to his father, but without looking at the boy, Constantine ran from the room.

4

ROME, CARTHAGE, 300

"Too bad, Lucius, that you can't make this trip to Carthage," Marcus said. "I'm the lucky one to avoid school for a month or more." Too excited over the proposed journey with his father to sleep, Marcus had entered Lucius's bedchamber before dawn. Lucius yawned, propped himself up on his couch, and lighted the wick in the oil lamp on the table.

"Has it occurred to you that it's a bit early to rise? Especially for those of us who aren't going anywhere. Father will not leave until midmorning."

Marcus ran his hands through his heavy black curls, laughing excitedly. "I can't sleep, but the main reason I'm up so early is that Plotina promised to meet me at dawn. She's coming to the copse of trees between their domus and ours."

"But Flavius has forbidden her to see you."

"I sent a note that preyed on her emotions. I told her I was going on a long journey and didn't know when I would return. That jolted her out of her lethargy," Marcus said with a smile.

"I don't consider a trip to Carthage a particularly long journey," Lucius said wryly. "The crossing will take a few days at most." He fanned away the fumes of the oil lamp, yawned, and shifted to a reclining position.

Marcus pushed the shutters away from the window, and the

59

early morning sounds of Rome infiltrated the room. It was that quiet time after the activities of the night had ceased and before the day's rush had started. Male pigeons cooed seductively on the rooftop of the domus as they spread colorful wings before their mates. Doors softly opened up and down the street as servants prepared for their masters' awakening. A slight breeze brought coolness to the room, and Lucius drew the blanket over his shoulders.

"It's the longest journey I've ever taken," Marcus said. "You're just jealous because Father didn't ask you to go along."

"You know my opinion of using animals for slaughter in the arena, Marcus. I would hardly want to go on a journey to capture them."

Marcus cuffed Lucius on the shoulder. "I'm going to miss you anyway." Leaning out the window, he saw a slight tinge of pink on the eastern horizon. Marcus waved good-bye to his twin and walked quietly down the stairs. He reached the garden, hurried through the field, crossed the creek, and found that Plotina had reached the meeting place before him. She wore a dark gray toga with a cape over her head, and in the darkness under the trees she was hardly visible. Obviously she had dressed to escape the disapproving eye of her father, should he be looking toward the woods.

Marcus hurried toward Plotina and took her hand. "Did you have trouble getting away?"

"No, a trustworthy slave helped me, but I cannot stay long. I don't dare risk Father's wrath should he learn that I've been seeing you against his wishes."

"I don't know why you fear him. He adores you, and your punishment would be slight, I'm sure."

"I hope you're right. But what of the journey, Marcus? Where are you going?"

"Father is taking me to Carthage on a trading expedition to obtain more animals for slaughtering in the arena."

Plotina shuddered. "I didn't know that the Trentos were

involved in that type of trading. I don't like having you mixed up in such a venture, Marcus. Although Father likes watching the gladiators and animals fighting, it has never appealed to me."

"But it's business—Father makes a great deal of money importing these animals. If we didn't do it, someone else would. While Grandfather lived, Father didn't say much about this part of the family industry, but it doesn't matter now." Marcus pulled her deeper into the woods. "But let's talk about us. Do you think your father will consent to our marriage?"

"He hasn't even mentioned to me that your father has made overtures, so I don't know what he's thinking."

"I intend to have you, Plotina," Marcus said, and lowered his face to hers. As their lips clung, Marcus exulted inwardly. Though Plotina often appeared to be distant, at times when he kissed her she responded with an intensity that set the blood pounding through his veins. Even when he would have released her, she clung to him until a muted whistle sounded and she pulled away.

"That's my servant—she was to signal when she heard Father rousing. I must go. May the gods hasten your return, Marcus," she said and ran with light feet across the dew-sparkling grass. Marcus watched her out of sight, then he raised his hand in an exultant signal of victory.

❀ ❀ ❀

All of the household staff gathered with the family in the atrium to bid farewell to Bernini and Marcus. Domitilla's gestures toward her husband were restrained because she didn't approve of his favoring Marcus over Lucius, but she couldn't resist Marcus's excitement, and she fondly embraced her firstborn.

"You're going to be plunged into a somewhat different culture, Marcus. Remember your upbringing," she warned. He nodded, but he paid little heed to her words. He wanted to get underway, and he fidgeted until Bernini came from his office with a chest of coins and his official papers.

The miles from Rome to Ostia were covered quickly in the family carriage driven by one of their servants, and by midafternoon Marcus and Bernini boarded the cargo ship *Dido*. After Marcus deposited his belongings in one of the small cabins, he explored the ship.

Sailors worked expertly and steadily to ready the *Dido* for departure. One of the vessel's masts towered from the center of the ship, and the other sloped forward over the bow, supporting a small, square sail that made steering easier. Marcus knew that the Romans had learned much of their seafaring knowledge from the Greeks, who used tight joints to fit the planks of the hull together and inserted a system of ribs to strengthen it. Set above the mainsail was a triangular sail; two huge oars were attached to the ship near the stern.

Bernini owned several similar vessels that carried grain from Alexandria to Rome in amounts of ten thousand pounds or more, but the hull of the *Dido* was fitted into stalls and cages to transport wild animals. Marcus inspected the empty hold, sniffing appreciatively the cedar wood of which the ship was constructed. He stopped a seaman and asked the size of the craft.

"Fifty-five paces long and fourteen paces wide," the man snapped and hustled on his way.

As the son of Bernini, Marcus expected to receive some respect, but as the commander bawled out orders and the sailors hurried to do his bidding, they ignored Marcus or pushed him aside. When he complained, his father said, "Even though I'm the owner of this ship, I'm not in command. Stay out of the way."

When he was younger, Marcus had fantasized about becoming a sailor, but after observing a day in the rigorous life of a seaman, he decided his destiny lay in some other direction. For diversion, he struck up a friendship with Matthew, the ship's only passenger other than the Trentos.

Matthew studied ancient writings and taught at a school in Alexandria. He had been in Rome for two months looking for rare manuscripts. "But I had a desire to see Carthage, and so I shall visit there before I return home," the man said.

"Will you be looking for manuscripts in Carthage, too?" Marcus asked.

The man spat derisively over the rail and replied angrily, "Yes, but nothing of true antiquity will be found. The Romans took care of that when they destroyed Carthage completely many years ago."

"Our tutor has told us that over four hundred years ago our soldiers leveled the city, plowed the site, and sowed the furrows with salt. The Carthaginians were sold into slavery. It was a wasteland for years."

"Nothing to be proud of, young Roman. But your tutor was wrong. Some ruins still existed when Julius Caesar saw the usefulness of the harbor and started a Roman colony there a hundred years later. The colonists were the ones who destroyed the past by taking the old stones to build their own structures. The sad part is that you can't reconstruct ancient artifacts and treasures. Once destroyed, they're gone forever. The Romans are great destroyers."

Marcus had been taught not to dispute his elders, but he did resent the man's criticism of Rome.

"But isn't the present Roman colony superior to the old Phoenician city?"

Matthew cast a pitying look toward Marcus. "Not in my opinion. The Romans have laid out roads in all directions and built up communities that they have linked with bridges, dams, and aqueducts, but they've taken advantage of the skills of local craftsmen and laborers to do this."

"What kinds of manuscripts do you hope to find in Carthage?" Marcus changed the subject.

"Some writings of the Christian leader Cyprian, who was martyred in 258."

"Oh, are you a Christian?"

"Of course, and I've assembled quite a collection of Christian manuscripts for our school."

"I didn't know the Christians were strong in Africa."

With a perplexed shake of his head, Matthew seemed to forgive Marcus for his ignorance. "Carthage is the site of one of the most important bishoprics in Christendom. It's where the diplomatic and forceful Cyprian served until his death in 258. North Africa is the homeland of many powerful leaders, and Christianity has made great headway there, much more than on the continent. In his writing of a century ago, Tertullian wrote that Christians were more numerous than pagans in Africa. That is probably still true today. You will see many Christian basilicas in Carthage." Matthew abruptly ended his discourse, and fixed a stern gaze on Marcus. "But what of your faith, young man?"

"I have no faith at this point. My grandfather was a Christian, but my father leans toward worship of the old gods. I've yet to make up my mind." With a snort, Matthew walked away.

Marcus's excitement grew when he could no longer see land, and he swayed back and forth as the *Dido* smoothly rose and lowered on the gentle swells of the Mediterranean. Gulls followed the ship and occasionally swooped down on the deck to snatch up some grain that a seaman had scattered near the bow. Before evening, Marcus's joy changed to agony when the rise and fall of the ship churned the contents of his stomach. Added to his physical discomfort was his embarrassment that he was the only person on the ship who had succumbed to seasickness. He would have expected the crew to be seaworthy, but it was degrading to be incapacitated when Matthew and Bernini walked the deck as if they had been born on a ship. Although he felt better by morning, Marcus nonetheless longed for the end of the journey.

❋   ❋   ❋

"Land, ho!" a sailor atop the main mast called out. Delighted to hear the words, Marcus ran on wobbly legs to the bow of the

Dido, careful to stay out of the way of the sailors who were unfurling ropes and clearing the deck of anything that would disrupt their duties as they prepared to land.

Bernini indicated points of interest to his son as they approached the city. "You will see two harbors, although there is a common entrance that can be closed with iron chains to ward off attacks. The first port is for merchant vessels like ours. The second is an island, with docks set at intervals around it for the use of smaller craft."

Aided by favorable winds, the *Dido* moved rapidly toward the circular harbor. As they veered toward the commercial port, Marcus glimpsed a walled island connected to the mainland by a wooden bridge. Ionic columns in front of each dock gave the appearance of a continuous portico in the harbor. *No wonder Carthage has been an important trading center for centuries!* Marcus thought. As the crew expertly maneuvered the *Dido* into place, Marcus observed merchant ships from Alexandria and other vessels from all ports along the Mediterranean.

Marcus bade good-bye to Matthew as the old man shuffled toward the city. After Bernini discussed a return sailing date with the ship's commander, he hailed a litter to bear them to the home of his friend Vergeil Brescello. Vergeil's family had been a long time on the African continent, for his ancestor had come to Africa during the reign of Gaius Gracchus, who had promoted colonization near the ancient site of Carthage. At that time, many people had settled on large farms, which they had later been forced to vacate when the Roman Senate refused to approve the colonization venture, but Vergeil's ancestor had stayed behind, continued to prosper, and had built a huge villa on the outskirts of the present city.

In spite of Matthew's disparaging comments about the colony, Marcus marveled as they rode through the streets of Carthage at how Roman the city was. He saw a colossal bath complex, an amphitheater, and an arena for chariot racing. Marble public fountains bubbled with sparkling water brought into the city by aqueducts. The areas where the lower-class people lived had twelve houses each, six on either side of a common border wall. The more elaborate villas of the wealthy were surrounded by stuccoed walls, and Marcus couldn't see what they were like.

When they arrived at the Brescello villa, Bernini dismissed the litter carriers, and a slave rushed from the monumental entry to collect their baggage. Remembering Matthew's comments on the many Christians in Africa, Marcus half expected that the Brescellos might be members of the church, but an altar at the entrance dedicated to the ancient household gods of Rome discounted his assumption. They entered the atrium, where a Neptune fountain spewed water into a rectangular basin set in the middle of a mosaic floor. The floor featured ceramic fish enclosed in glass cubes, making it appear that the fish were swimming when the water overflowed them.

Another servant appeared and led them up a mosaic ramp into an open-air garden. Beyond this peristyle were several small, squarish guest rooms, and the Trentos were shown to two of these. Their luggage was already in the rooms. "The master will greet you in the atrium as soon as you are refreshed." Bowing, the man left them. Marcus took advantage of the warm jug of water to remove the salt and grime from his body and donned a clean toga. In spite of Marcus's haste, Bernini was already waiting for him in the peristyle.

Marcus knew Vergeil Brescello since the man had visited them in Rome, but he had not met his son, Otho, who stood beside his father when they entered the family's living quarters. After Marcus bowed a greeting to Vergeil, the older man said, "And here is Otho. It will be his privilege to entertain you, Marcus, while your father and I transact business."

Otho's most striking features were dark, piercing eyes set in a noble head with a poise like that of an eagle. Until the family gathered for dinner, Otho conducted Marcus on a tour of the villa. The dwelling was quite similar to the ones around Rome, and Marcus felt at ease with his host, though Otho was four years older. They arrived at the triclinium while the slaves were still carrying in the food from an outside kitchen. The dining area opened out into a garden containing a huge fountain laid with mosaics. Here, also, mosaic fish offered the illusion that they were swimming through the cascading waters.

If possible, the Carthaginians enjoyed their feasting more than the Romans, Marcus decided as he sat through seven courses. He savored the strong taste of the turbot fish preserved in brine, but he found the roast stork to be a tough, stringy meat that left a scorched taste in his mouth. He passed that by for several servings of ground pork marinated in a spicy quince sauce that tantalized his palate and trickled warmly into his stomach. The plump yellow apples were not as tart as the ones imported to Rome, and the juice was as sweet as the light wine served at his mother's table. Before the evening was over, Marcus squirmed in the chair, wondering more than once why the Carthaginians didn't recline at their meals.

Before they parted for the evening, Otho said, "I can offer you a variety of entertainment. How long will you be here?"

"Father will not leave until he has enough wild animals to satisfy his demand, and I should like very much to go on a hunt. I mentioned it to Father and he didn't object. Do you think that can be arranged?"

"Certainly. I will see to it. We will also attend the public baths and the gladiator combats if you wish."

"I should like that. My grandfather disapproved of the gladiatorial contests, and I have never been allowed to attend one."

"Then we will have plenty to keep us occupied during the daytime. I've also arranged for your nightly entertainment," Otho said with a wink.

Marcus didn't realize the meaning of this conspiratorial gesture until he was almost ready to retire. Answering a discreet knock at his door, he opened it to a male servant who ushered a young woman into the room. Bowing, he said, "Compliments of Master Otho."

The man started to leave and Marcus grabbed his arm. "Wait! What's the meaning of this?"

"In this household it's customary to provide a night companion for our guests. You have been honored—Elissa has not lain with anyone before."

That makes two of us, Marcus thought, and before he could protest further, the servant exited and closed the door. Marcus looked wildly around the small room seeking a way of escape, but the woman stood between him and the door. *What can I do?* This situation was not to his liking, but pride would not permit Marcus to admit his inexperience to Otho. And the servant had indicated it was customary. *Does this mean that Father, too, has a sleeping companion for the night?* Marcus's mind reeled at that thought until he decided it was probably for unmarried men that this service was provided.

Marcus's surprise dwindled and he took note of his companion. She was veiled, and he lifted the filmy covering. The woman stood with bowed head, and when he tilted her chin, she stared at him with dark, luminous eyes gleaming with a mixture of fear and anger. A tangy scent of some exotic perfume surrounded her.

"Are you a slave, Elissa?" he asked.

She nodded.

"Why?"

Swallowing, she said in halting Latin, "I'm from the city of Tyre, ancient city of the Phoenicians. A shipload of us were fleeing from our homeland toward Egypt to escape the Roman legions, and we were captured. All of us were brought to Carthage and sold into slavery."

Momentarily, Marcus remembered his grandfather and his opposition to slavery, but Marcus knew he was on his own in dealing with this dilemma. Promiscuity was common in Rome, even among boys his age, but Ignatius had held a tight rein on his household, and Marcus had not been introduced to that side of empire living. "Were you forced to come here?" he asked.

She stared at him with contemptuous eyes and did not answer. Marcus hesitated, unsure of what to say or do. *Should I tell her that I am committed to another? What if she laughs at me?*

Elissa stared at him impassively, as if trying to read his thoughts. Marcus did not want her to sense his trepidation or inexperience. *I must keep my composure and take control.* His pride and desire overtook him. What followed made Marcus wish he had never come to Carthage. When it was over, he was filled with self-loathing and shame at having turned against his family's faith. He wanted to throw himself at her feet and beg forgiveness, but his pride forbade him to show remorse. *I must remain in control of my emotions.* He turned his anger outward onto Elissa.

"Dress and return to the slave quarters," he ordered.

Her sobbing grew quiet. "Do you mean I do not stay with you? In our culture sexual union is the same as marriage. You do not cast away the one you have taken."

His anger abated as he noted the pleading look in the eyes of the woman. She was no female of loose virtue, but a noble woman who had been taken prisoner. Now she had been abused, and Marcus was shamed by his lack of courage to admit that his senseless act repudiated all of his training.

"I am sorry that this happened to you, but if it hadn't been me, you would have been given to some other man."

"Do you think that excuses your actions?" she asked bitterly.

Marcus bowed his head. "No. No, it does not. I'm sure that I have caused you pain, but you see, I was inexperienced, too."

"Then will you take me with you? You do seem to have some degree of compassion. Don't leave me here as a plaything for these lewd Carthaginians. I'll even go as your slave."

He shook his head. "The Trentos own no slaves. Besides, I'm to be married to a Roman girl when I return home."

"Then you don't care what happens to me?"

"Yes, I do care, but—there's nothing I can do. You'll have to leave."

She rose from the bed and draped the garment around her shoulders. The spicy scent of the woman's perfume radiated from her body as she passed him. When she reached the door, she turned and stared at Marcus for a long minute. The shame, loathing, and dismay mirrored in the young woman's face haunted Marcus the rest of the night, and when he rose wearily to face the day, he wondered if he would ever forget this night's experience.

Otho knocked on his door before he had dressed. Entering the room breezily, he asked suggestively, "All alone?"

"Yes," Marcus said. To his dismay, his face reddened with embarrassment.

"Did you have an enjoyable night?"

"Yes," Marcus lied, "but I should have told you before. I am much in love with a young woman in Rome and we intend to wed soon. Please do not provide another slave to be my companion."

"Suit yourself," Otho said. "I'm to be married within the year also, but I fear I'm not as discriminating as you."

"What will happen to Elissa—the young woman who was here?"

"Depends on how she behaves herself. She's only been in the slave quarters two weeks. If she's a good worker, we may keep her here in the house, but she seems of aristocratic bearing and therefore probably won't be capable of heavy labor. We may use her to entertain our guests for a while and then sell her to a brothel."

Marcus hoped he didn't show it openly, but his host's callous evaluation of the slave caused him to cringe. Having grown up in a household without slavery, he had not been exposed to such brutish treatment of other human beings. For a moment he was tempted to ask to buy Elissa and take her back to Rome, but how could he explain her to his mother and to Plotina? He couldn't, so Marcus made up his mind to forget the incident. Elissa's enslavement had not been his fault, and if he hadn't taken her, another man would have. He forced himself to enter enthusiastically into the plans Otho was describing.

"Today we go to the circus, tomorrow we will visit the arena, and on the third day, we start on a hunting expedition into the interior of the continent," Otho explained.

❋ ❋ ❋

At first, Marcus considered the afternoon's performance to which Otho took him to be as good as anything he had witnessed in Rome. Trained panthers pulled chariots, lions licked the hands of their trainers, and several combats between wild animals were featured. Two male bears fought a water buffalo, and a rhinoceros and elephant engaged in a hard-fought battle, which the elephant won. The crowd roared with laughter when the rhinoceros bolted from the amphitheater with the elephant in hot pursuit. What Marcus liked best was the six elephants who walked across the arena on a rope suspended high above the stands.

As the afternoon wore on, the entertainment became more grisly, and though Marcus made an effort, he could not derive the satisfaction from the cruel sport that the other spectators did. A slave with only a knife for protection was chained to a post where he fought off an enraged panther. Before the man finally killed the animal, he was streaked with blood from the fearsome assault of the panther. The man was carried from the arena and Marcus wondered if he, too, would die.

After this example of cruelty at the circus, Marcus had little anticipation for a visit to the amphitheater the next day to watch the gladiators fight. When Bernini learned where he was going, he said, "This will be a new experience for you. Do you think you can witness these spectacles like a man and not make a fool of yourself?"

The doubt in his father's voice spurred Marcus to claim, "Of course I can. Don't think that I'll embarrass you."

The show started with competing gladiators performing the dance of death to the strident sound of trumpets and horns. Bets were placed on the crowd's favorites—those men who were trained, pampered, and adored by fans. These favorites, armed with swords and helmets, would fight the underdogs—the slaves, captives of war, criminals, or even vagabond sons of good families lured to the arena by promises of possible glory and wealth.

Each gladiator wore a broad-rimmed helmet, some of which had a covering over the face. Metal protectors enclosed their legs below the knees. They carried shields, and each gladiator chose the individual weapons most convenient for him. Some held swords and spears, others were armed only with daggers.

After two hours Marcus had seen enough, but to his frustration, the display went on and on. At the beginning of each bout, Otho would place wagers. Marcus joined in at first, but he soon wearied of the senseless bloodshed and stopped betting, trying to blot the scene out of his mind.

Several slaves were killed by the star gladiator, and their bodies were dragged callously from the arena. After each bout, fresh sand was sprinkled on the ground to soak up the blood, but as the afternoon passed, the fetid stench arising from the arena swirled around Marcus. His head ached and a bitter secretion tainted his mouth. Loud music accompanied each of the combats, and when the moment came to either save or kill the opponent, the music ceased suddenly in a moment of great suspense and silence. Once the man was given mercy or his life taken, the crowd resumed their shouting.

In every event, the underdog was defeated, but one fought so valiantly that when the gladiator should have taken his life, the crowd roared over and over, "Give him his life," and the gladiator lowered his raised sword.

The rescued slave walked proudly from the arena. "What will happen to him now?" Marcus asked.

"Oh, he's only been saved to fight again, or he'll be sold in the marketplace. He's still a slave."

The crowd's leniency to the slave encouraged Marcus enough that he leaned back, determined to endure the rest of the slaughter. His determination, however, would be tested with the next event.

A condemned criminal, dressed in a loincloth and armed only with a knife, was brought into the arena to be put to death. Four lions stalked the victim, and Marcus's tension mounted as the half-starved animals surrounded the criminal, coming closer and closer each time they circled him. The frightened man clutched the knife and turned constantly, trying to keep his eyes on the lion closest to him.

One animal lunged and clawed the man's shoulder, and the frenzied human struck at him with the knife until the lion roared and fell backward. The man pulled away from the lion and ran screaming for cover with all the animals in hot pursuit. He stepped behind one of the obstacles placed in the arena to prolong the exhibition, and the lions halted, only to start stalking him again.

Marcus half rose from his chair several times, his hands clenched until his knuckles whitened, but he endured the situation until the four lions closed in to kill the man who had exhausted every effort to save his life. The man screamed as the four animals leaped on him, and this sound of agony propelled Marcus from his seat.

"I'll wait for you at the gate," he said to Otho and rushed from the stands. He covered his ears to dull the bloodthirsty roar of the spectators and the bellow of a victorious lion. Gagging on the hot liquid that threatened to choke him, he gasped for enough air to make his escape.

He was angry at the crowd, angry at the system, even angrier at himself because he hadn't had the stomach for such murder. This whole trip to Carthage had been a disappointment. He had anticipated it as an exciting time, but everything had turned out wrong. He thought he would enjoy life once he was out from under Ignatius's restraint since it was obvious his father wouldn't deny him any experience, but his mother's last words kept ringing in his mind, "Remember your upbringing." *Have the years under the tutelage of my mother and grandfather made me unfit to take my place as head of the Trento family?* He wanted to be like his father, but something held him back. *And what will Father say? Will Father think I humiliated him?*

Most of the crowd had filed out of the arena before Otho joined Marcus. Otho was joyfully counting his earnings. "A thousand aureus. I haven't won so much for months. You should have bet more, Marcus."

Marcus didn't mention that he hadn't claimed his winnings. While they waited for the Brescello slaves to bring the litter, Otho, not one to ignore an issue, said, "I take it you didn't care for the slaughter."

And Marcus, tired of pretending, answered, "No, I didn't, but I should have stayed for my father's sake, who will question my manhood because I couldn't watch."

As they settled themselves on the litter, Otho said, "Oh, I don't know—sometimes manhood is more apparent in someone who won't go along with the crowd, but has a mind of his own. I won't tell your father how you reacted."

"Thank you, but I'll have to tell him. I know he will ask."

"Does this mean that you don't want to go on the hunt tomorrow?" Otho inquired.

"Not at all. Hunting in the wild, where the creatures have a chance of escape and a man pits his skill against them is good sport. There was too much cruelty displayed today for my liking."

"You're not alone in your opinion. Many efforts have been made—especially by the Christians—to stop the contests, and they are becoming less frequent. Not like in the early days of the empire."

"That's true. Even in Rome, they don't occur with the frequency of the past. For one thing, wild animals are harder to come by, and therefore they cost more. I've heard Father talk about this."

"One of the slaves in our household is a Christian, and he's continually preaching that all men should live as brothers. He says that their Jesus is going to set up a kingdom where even the wild animals will live together in peace and harmony." Otho turned piercing black eyes toward Marcus. "Do you believe that?"

"I don't know, but my grandfather believed it," Marcus added grudgingly.

Otho remained silent for the rest of the journey, but he said musingly when they reached his home, "At least it won't happen tomorrow, so we'll have our hunt together."

5

CARTHAGE, 300

The next morning after a light meal of bread, cheese, and soft, fuzzy peaches that tasted as sweet as honey, Otho took Marcus to the kennels, where lanky brindle greyhounds pawed their cages and barked vociferously.

"Ready for the hunt, are you?" Otho said as he stroked one after another of the noisy animals. Most of the dogs drew back from Marcus, although one stuck a pointed muzzle through the bars allowing him to rub its bony nose and the soft spot around its mouth. "These are the best hunting dogs available," Otho said. "Note the streamlined body, arched back, slender waist, and long, powerful legs."

"Do you breed your own animals?" Marcus asked.

"Yes, although occasionally Father imports some males from Egypt to improve the line. These dogs hunt by sight, not scent, and as fast as they are, they have no trouble keeping their prey in view."

Moving on to the stables, Marcus was introduced to the hardy horse that he would be riding. Encountering Vergeil and Bernini, Otho asked, "What time will we get underway?"

"We'll meet at the hunt club when the sun reaches its zenith, and we will start from there," Vergeil said.

"Then Marcus and I will ride this morning so that he can

become acquainted with his horse. Have you done much riding, friend?"

"Not for long distances, but we do have some good riding stock at our domus, and I learned to ride as a child."

Otho pointed out the horses they wanted to two slaves who hastily, but carefully, saddled the animals. Once astride his mount, Marcus realized he had not ridden such a brawny animal before, and he anticipated many sore muscles before the journey was long underway.

Otho led the way on a narrow trail that started behind the stables. He kept to a canter until they came to open countryside, then he slowed so that Marcus could ride beside him.

"Your hunting expedition seems to be highly organized," Marcus commented.

"Indeed it is. Father and I belong to a hunting club that was started a century ago when animals were in great demand for the amphitheater. In fact the animal population on this continent has been greatly depleted, and it takes a good bit of skill to supply the orders now. Unless one is well organized and has expert guides, the take is poor. Of course, the Brescellos hunt mostly for sport, but occasionally for a friend like Bernini, Father will hunt for profit."

Their return route brought them by the hunt club, which was also a private bath for members and their families. Otho pointed out the vast amount of equipment being readied. "Here are decoys that we use to lure the wild animals into our cages," he said indicating the stuffed goats and sheep tied to carts. Spears, shields, and firebrands also needed in the hunt were stacked neatly on wagons. A supply of wheeled cages held nets, lures, snares, and protective gear for the runners who would chase the wild animals toward the hunters.

"This venture is a major expedition, and we'll be gone for a few days," Otho explained, "but we also engage in smaller scale hunts lasting no more than a day. In those hunts, riders follow trained dogs that track game such as hares, ducks, plumed larks, and thrushes."

"I believe I would have preferred the smaller hunt," Marcus said. "After witnessing the slaughter of the animals at the amphitheater yesterday, I fear I won't enjoy capturing them. Since you didn't sneer at my squeamish behavior then, I feel free to say that to you. What's the matter with me, Otho? I want to be a Roman in every sense of the word. Why can't I enjoy these events as you do?"

"Probably because you have not been exposed to them before. This has been my life since I was a child. I know nothing else. No doubt in time you will learn to enjoy them."

Marcus shook his head. "I hope so. I remind myself of my twin brother, Lucius. He's the quiet one and would not even consider going to the amphitheater or on one of these hunts. I've always chided him for not having any courage, yet he would not hesitate to stand up and voice his disapproval of this needless slaughter of animals and human life. I believe he would say it to the emperor's face. So wouldn't you say he is more courageous than I?"

Otho placed a hand on his shoulder. "You worry too much about such things. You should be more like your father—when he comes to Carthage, he falls right in with our ways. It doesn't bother him, even though his behavior is apparently more reserved when he is at home."

"Definitely, but that may change. As long as my grandfather lived, his wishes dominated our way of life."

Otho nodded. "That is as it should be, but since your grandfather is no longer living, your household probably will change."

Marcus doubted that his mother would change her behavior, and she had a great deal of influence on Bernini. It had always amazed him that his huge, strong father should be swayed so often by his mother's quiet ways. Yet he couldn't help wonder if his own attitude toward the games and hunts had been influenced by what Plotina had said, the day before he left home, about her distaste for such things.

Before noon, about twenty-five hunters arrived at the club,

and Vergeil led the way into a small temple. A mosaic of the Roman goddess of the hunt, Diana, was depicted on one wall, garbed in a knee-length tunic, holding a spear, with a greyhound sitting at her feet.

Marcus stood to one side as the men prostrated themselves before the image of Diana while their leader prayed for her blessings on them, petitioning for good luck on the hunting expedition. Laughter bubbled up in his chest, but Marcus suppressed it, wondering why these men didn't realize the absurdity of praying to an image on the wall. He thought of the Alabaster that had graced their chapel as long as he could remember. He had not forgotten the warning of Ignatius. "It is not a god. It is not to be the object of your worship. There is one God and Father of us all—pray to Him. The Alabaster is only a symbol of what Jesus Christ did for us."

As Marcus looked at the men again, he wondered, *How could Father, who had also sat under the teaching of Grandfather, bow before this mosaic?* Although he was not sure he believed everything that his grandfather had taught, still it annoyed Marcus to see Bernini so easily disregarding the Christian faith. Soon the petitioning was over, however, and the hunters were off.

The caravan lengthened for more than a mile as they wound their way from the hunt club across the wide expanse of the Brescello estate. The gentlemen hunters took the lead, while behind them rattled the wagons filled with baggage, supplies, hunting equipment, and cages. Twenty slaves trotted in the rear, trying to control the excited greyhounds, who strained on their leashes each time a hare bounded away into the brush or a horned lark took wing.

Marcus and Otho were the youngest in the group, and they had been designated as outriders, which suited their pent-up energies. They frequently circled the whole caravan, scouting for possible danger. Otho explained, "We don't anticipate any problems, but it's always wise to be on the lookout for that occasional tribe of natives who might go on the offensive."

The farther south they traveled, the hotter the sun and the more oppressive the heat. The caravan halted by midafternoon. Slaves hurriedly erected canvases to shield the party from the blistering sun. When Marcus sprawled under one of the tents, it was gratifying to see that Otho was as exhausted as he.

Bernini cast an anxious glance toward his son and said, "Stretch out and take a nap, Marcus, and you'll feel like a new man." Marcus was glad to take his advice, and after swigging a long draught of cool water from a clay jar, he lay down beside his father. A slight breeze blew across the prairie, and with the thick canvas for protection from the sun, the heat was more bearable.

Several hours later, Marcus awakened to activity around him. Long shadows indicated the rapid disappearance of the sun, and he drew his cloak around him, surprised at how rapidly the sun's rays had given way to the coolness of evening.

"We will travel by night until we get through the desert. Eat well, for we will cover many miles before daybreak," Bernini advised.

Marcus stretched to relieve his aching muscles, gratified to know that he was more fit than he had imagined. The many hours on the exercise bars at the public baths had kept him in good shape.

The gentlemen ate leisurely, seemingly in no hurry to resume the journey. One older man started reminiscing. "I'll never forget the time I participated in an elephant drive organized by the state. An overpopulation of elephants was causing a problem to the villagers in Numidia, destroying their crops and homes, and a whole army was sent in to capture the animals. So many of them had already been killed that the natives used their tusks for fence posts."

"I hear they drove the elephants into pits to capture them," another man said.

"They tried all kinds of things. Even sawed through the trees where the elephants habitually leaned, hoping the elephants couldn't get up once they fell." He laughed. "That wasn't true. Once they toppled to the ground, it wasn't long before they bellowed and started off again."

"Will we be capturing any elephants?" Marcus whispered to Otho.

"Not this trip. Usually when they take elephants they don't capture the wilder animals. Besides, the elephants are found farther south than where we're going."

❀　❀　❀

Marcus lost count of the days they traveled before the earth started looking green and heavy vegetation appeared. Each day's journey was marked by an oblation poured out to placate the goddess of the hunt.

"One more day, and we'll be in hunting territory," Otho said.

Excitement spread through the party as they neared their destination, and the weary slaves were hard put to control the aggressive dogs that had been as docile as puppies in the desert.

Much to his disappointment, Marcus was not allowed to participate in the actual hunt. He was delegated to be an observer only, but after watching the hunt for two days, Marcus realized the wisdom of that decision.

First, the stuffed sheep and goat decoys were placed in strategic positions to lure the wild animals into one area, which was closed off with huge nets. Then the mounted Roman provincials rode down their prey with the aid of the greyhounds. They carried javelins, stones, and spears to use only if a life was endangered. Once the animals were cornered, the beaters, protected by shields and carrying long firebrands, closed in on the frenzied beasts and drove them into cages.

On the first day, one of the beaters was attacked by a crazed leopard, and the man was dead before a hunter slew the beast with a carefully aimed spear. A large number of ostriches, lions, and panthers were captured alive, though several animals were killed in the fighting. One lioness, with two cubs at her side, was distracted by the hunters, and Marcus ran in to capture the cubs. With only a few scratches for his efforts, Marcus grabbed the cubs and shoved them into a cage.

After suffering a tirade from Bernini for his carelessness, Marcus said, "Let's take them home to Lucius. You know how he dotes on animals. These will make wonderful pets." Half-heartedly, Bernini agreed and galloped away to head off an ostrich bent on escaping. Marcus reached out a hand to stroke the soft fur of the cubs, but he jumped backward as they stood on their hind feet and spat at him. "Lucius will tame you," he cried.

The longer he was away from Rome, the more Marcus thought about Lucius. They had never been separated for more than a day, and although Marcus picked on his brother a lot, he found that he missed his twin's companionship.

❀   ❀   ❀

Within four days, the cages were full and the caravan turned homeward. None of them had much rest on the return journey because the captured beasts pawed at the cages, jumped at their captors, and screamed displeasure of their captivity. The slaves had to be wary each time they pushed food and water into the cages, but every care was taken to preserve the beasts until they could be sold for use in the arena, where they would be mistreated, goaded, and starved to make them more ferocious and more entertaining for the thrill-seeking crowds.

Because of the commotion all around him, Marcus slept little, and as he lay wakeful, the image of Elissa's face haunted him. *Will I see her again?* Thoughts of their intimate encounter pervaded his mind, and, in spite of himself, he compared her hot, dusky beauty with the languorous Plotina. He groaned in misery as he wondered if the gentle Roman girl would provide him the excitement he had known with Elissa.

Marcus was glad to see the buildings of Carthage and to smell the salty breeze from the Mediterranean. He was ready to go home, but he knew he wasn't the same person who had left Rome. He'd been a boy then, but he had plunged into many adult situations in a short time.

The night of their return to Carthage, Bernini told him, "We'll not be leaving for two days. Tomorrow I'm going to the slave market."

"But, Father . . ."

"I don't need any advice, son. To take my place as head of the Trento family, I'll do it my way. As much as I revere your grandfather, his ways are not mine. I have to make my own destiny. I'm going to buy a few slaves tomorrow, but I will not introduce any into the household until I see how your mother reacts. There will be one exception—I want you to buy a slave for your own personal servant. You're to follow in my footsteps, and you need to learn how to order and control men. In a few months, I'll introduce you to the business side of our family, but owning a slave will be a good way for you to start exercising authority. I will expect you to choose the one you want."

So Marcus spent another sleepless night wondering how he would know what kind of a slave to buy and what he would do with one once he had him. He thought of Lucius and his certain disapproval if Marcus brought home a slave. And he thought of Elissa, the slave girl. *Was she tonight sharing the bed of some other Brescello guest?* Maybe he should buy *her*—but he knew that Bernini hadn't had a female slave in mind.

The next morning, Vergeil was busy so Otho ordered the family carriage and accompanied Bernini and Marcus to the slave market located near the harbor. The slaves were separated by sexes and ages—men and women, boys and girls—in groups around the large room. Prospective buyers jostled one another, and if one showed an interest in a certain slave, a hawker would push that one forward and give a rundown on the slave's capabilities.

Marcus wondered how and why so many nationalities had been enslaved. There were Greeks of proud and noble bearing who covered their inner feelings with haughty disdain when a buyer punched at their muscles, looked at their teeth, or pulled down their eyelids for inspection. Black men and women obviously from the inner continent rolled white terrorized eyes at their inspectors. Prisoners of war from the eastern countries were being offered for sale.

As he looked over the prospects, Marcus grabbed Otho's arm. "Look, isn't that the slave we saw fighting in the arena—the one who fought so bravely that his life was spared? Those scars on his chest look as if they have been inflicted recently."

Otho looked at the muscular, dusky-skinned man whose arms were manacled behind his back, but the proud bearing of his shoulders indicated that his spirit had not been captured. "I believe you're right. Would you consider him?"

"Perhaps. If I could win his loyalty, he would make a good bodyguard. Let's find out what we can about him."

When they expressed interest in the man, his owner shoved him forward. "His name is Sulla. Speaks no Latin as yet, though I've tried to get him to learn. He is from the eastern coast of the Mediterranean, from one of those tribal groups who have inhabited that area for centuries. He's a prisoner of war."

"But didn't we see him fighting in the arena a few days ago?" Marcus asked.

The hawker showed discomfiture that they knew something of the slave's background, but he soon recovered. "Then if you saw him fight, you know he's a brave, strong man. Since he was spared because of his bravery, his life was not put in jeopardy to fight again in the arena."

"Better dead than a slave, perhaps," Marcus said, and the quick glance the slave gave him caused Marcus to wonder if he didn't already know the Latin language.

Otho tugged at Marcus's toga. "Come along," he whispered. "You don't want to show too much interest."

Though they looked until the auction started, Marcus couldn't see anyone else who pleased him, and he asked Bernini to examine the slave.

After a close inspection, Bernini said, "I don't know, son. He seems to be a few years older than you, which is well. And he is strong, but I don't like the look in his eye. I'm not sure that he would be trustworthy—too much hatred mirrored on his face."

"But isn't that to be expected in someone who was enslaved by force? These who look defeated probably wouldn't make worthy servants."

"You may be right, Marcus. The decision is yours."

Apparently many others agreed with Marcus about Sulla's worth, for the bidding was active. With Bernini's blessing, Marcus raised the price until he bought the man. *I have a slave now, but what am I to do with him?*

"You may put your slaves in our quarters until it is time for your departure," Otho said, solving the immediate problem for them. He took charge of the money exchange and sent Sulla and the three slaves Bernini had bought to the Brescello's slave house.

"I want to buy some gifts to take home," Marcus said to Otho on his last day in Carthage. "If you're busy, I can wander around the stalls by myself."

"Very well," Otho agreed. "I do need to exercise the greyhounds. The nearer you get to the harbor, the more reasonable the prices. I'll order a litter to take you to the center of town, and you can be on your own."

Marcus wandered among the shops most of the morning before he made any purchases. The lion cubs would be all the gift he needed for Lucius. For Domitilla, he bought a brooch made in the image of a bronze dove to keep her cloak in place. For Bernice, he found a jar of jasmine perfume. He hesitated over that purchase, for the pungent odor reminded him of his experience with Elissa, but he was sure his sister would like it. Plotina's gift was the hardest to choose, but he finally settled for a length of sea-blue silk to set off her fragile loveliness. As the merchant wrapped the material in a thin strip of parchment, Marcus dreamed of the day he could see her wear the toga made from his gift.

Armed with his purchases, Marcus looked for a litter to carry him back to the Brescello home.

"Greetings, young man," he heard a familiar voice say. It was Matthew, the scholar whom he'd met on the *Dido*. "How have you enjoyed your stay in Carthage?" the scholarly man continued.

"Very well," Marcus started, but he hesitated. "I guess that isn't a true statement. I've encountered many things that have disturbed me."

"I knew that you would be initiated into the cruel culture displayed in Carthage. What displeased you?"

"The callous disregard of human life, especially at the gladiator games and the slave market." He didn't think it wise to confide to this learned man about his experience with Elissa.

Matthew nodded sagely. "This province is like Rome used to be under the first Caesars. Christianity is slow to have an impact on the barbarian practices, for although our faith has grown here in Africa, Carthage hasn't changed much. Come with me, young man, and I'll show you some other things that might stun you."

Matthew led the way to a high point overlooking the harbor. "Before the Romans destroyed Carthage, this was the site of Tophet, where children up to four years of age were sacrificed. You must remember that this area was settled by the Phoenicians from the eastern coast of the Mediterranean. That was the place where the worship of Baal was practiced, as you probably remember from the Scriptures, and the Phoenicians brought their religion to this region."

"Child sacrifice was common in all those countries, I believe."

"Yes, even Abraham, our revered ancestor, did not find it an unusual command when God told him to sacrifice his son, Isaac."

Marcus's mind wandered for a moment when he thought of

the Alabaster and the scene it depicted concerning Abraham. He started to tell Matthew about the vase, but some intuition of danger caused him to curb his tongue.

"In one of the scrolls that I've uncovered here written by Tertullian more than a hundred years ago," Matthew continued, "he states that the rite of child sacrifice persisted in spite of Roman efforts to stamp it out. And I wouldn't be surprised if it is still carried out in secret. So you see a culture that tolerates child sacrifice will not be averse to killing in the amphitheater."

"One thing that has caused me to question the religion of my grandfather is the slow pace of the Christian movement. If the God of the Christians is so powerful, why after three hundred years has there been so little change?" Marcus questioned.

"There has been more change than you imagine. God works through humankind, but transformation first has to take place in the human heart. These changes aren't always apparent, but I believe that we are on the eve of a great awakening." Matthew looked northward across the sea, and he waved his arm in a wide arc. "Somewhere out there God has planted a seed in some man's heart, and when that seed is nourished, Christianity will become a powerful force in this world. I pray to God that I will live to witness it."

Marcus stared at Matthew's enraptured face, and the visionary certainty in the man's eyes almost convinced Marcus that his words were true. While the possibility excited Marcus, it also scared him. If Christianity became a dominating force, then his Roman lifestyle would be threatened, and Marcus didn't think he would like that. *In a struggle between pagan Rome and Christianity, which will be the victor?*

6

Rome, 300

Will this journey never end? Marcus thought as he looked anxiously toward the continent although he could see nothing except haze on the horizon. To pass the time, he counted the seabirds accompanying the *Dido*. He lolled on the deck and watched fast-moving clouds streak across the azure sky to disappear in the distance. Deriding himself for becoming a philosopher like Lucius, he wondered if the pattern of a man's life was like the clouds—to spend a few days on this planet and then to fade forever into nothingness.

Marcus shook his head to rid his mind of thoughts too deep for him and contemplated the clouds' imagery. It was not difficult to find Plotina in the graceful spirals highlighted with pink hues that glided temptingly across his vision. His musings were pleasant when he thought of her, but his spirits plummeted when one cloud bore the stern face of Ignatius, who beheld his grandson with a disapproving stare. When the accusing eyes of Elissa glittered at him from a dark cloud filled with showers, Marcus left his lounging position and prowled the deck, shaking a fist at the gulls protesting his presence.

Except when he took them their food, Marcus avoided the end of the deck where the slaves were chained. When he approached Sulla, whose aloof gaze refused to lower in his presence, Marcus had the uneasy sensation that he was the slave, not Sulla. Marcus tried to convince himself that his strange attitude stemmed from a concern over his family's reaction to these slaves, but he feared it was more than that. *Had the empire risen to its present greatness on the backs of slaves?* He knew that was so, and his pride in his country lessened considerably when he considered how he would feel in Sulla's position.

As soon as a seaman on the platform atop the ship's mast cried, "Land, ho," Marcus quickly gathered his belongings and rushed to the bow of the ship. He fidgeted as the *Dido* eased into the busy harbor at Ostia, then he hurried to hire a carriage to transport them to Rome. With Sulla's help, he loaded the caged lion cubs that had adjusted well to captivity, and then climbed into the carriage to wait. At his signal, Sulla sat in the rear of the vehicle in the company of the slaves Bernini had bought. Though the other slaves chattered a lot, Marcus had yet to hear Sulla speak in any language, and he wondered if the man was mute.

Clutching the gifts he had purchased for his family, Marcus pulled a fold of his toga over his head as protection against the bright sun that had intensified during the hour before his father had finished his business with the captain of the *Dido*.

When Bernini entered the carriage and gave the command for departure, he said, "Do you think I have money to throw away, Marcus? It will be necessary to pay this man for a carriage that stood idle for over an hour. You should have waited until I had finished before hiring a carriage."

"But I'm so eager to get home. I miss Mother and Lucius."

"Unless you want to walk, you still have a delay. I need to stop by the warehouse here in Ostia before we continue our journey."

Marcus groaned his displeasure. He had no choice except to wait, but they arrived home at last, and the Trento domus had never looked so good to him. He bounded from the carriage and rushed into the atrium.

"Mother! Lucius! We're home!" he shouted. His call brought

the family on the run. He thrust his gift toward Domitilla and grabbed Lucius by the arm. "Come see what we brought you." Marcus propelled his brother toward the street, but Lucius stopped at the doorway when he saw the slaves unloading the baggage.

"Who are these people?" Lucius demanded.

"Oh, Father bought some slaves," Marcus answered offhandedly.

"You surely don't intend one of those for me?"

"No, no. Come over here." Marcus pulled his brother toward the caged lion cubs. "We brought you some more pets. I captured these for you myself."

Lucius smiled at the energetic animals rolling on their backs and playing together. "I'll be happier if I don't know how you captured them. I'll give them good care. Help me take the cage to the barn." But Marcus had already learned how to use a slave, and he motioned for Sulla to carry the cage. The twins walked behind him.

"You don't mean this man is a slave?" Lucius said as he side-stepped to avoid the playful paw that a cub extended from the cage.

"Yes, his name is Sulla. Father insisted that I buy a slave. He's my own. I think I made a good choice, but he doesn't speak our language, and I find communication difficult. I want you to teach him."

Lucius noted the disdainful look in the man's eyes, and wondered if his brother had bought trouble for himself. Sulla didn't appear the kind of man to be easily enslaved. "I know nothing about teaching someone to speak our tongue and even less about training lions," Lucius said after the slave placed the cage in the entry of the barn and stood to one side awaiting further orders. "I'll have to keep them caged until I gain their confidence. How old do you think they are?"

"The experienced hunters with us judged the cubs are about three months old because they're already eating meat. There's one male and one female, but they won't be old enough to breed for three or four years."

"That's a small consideration," Lucius said in amusement. "I have no interest in breeding lions." Lucius experimentally rubbed his hands across the brownish yellow hides. Only a bit of black at the end of the tail and on the back of the ears varied the color of the cubs. When the male cub grazed his tongue across Lucius's finger, he smiled. "I'll name them Dan and Beersheba—those are good biblical names."

"I'll leave you to your pets," Marcus said. "I have better things to do. It's been six weeks since I've seen Plotina, and I must try to smuggle a message into her house."

He turned to leave the barn, but Lucius said, "Marcus . . ."

Marcus paused impatiently.

"Marcus," Lucius continued with an effort, "there's something you need to know."

"Surely it can wait. I told you I want to see Plotina."

He moved forward again but stopped when Lucius said, "It's about Plotina that I must tell you." Lucius's face paled and he swallowed convulsively, hesitant to voice the words that would destroy his brother's future. "She's gone, Marcus. Her father has sent her back to the Temple of Vesta."

"What?!"

"Cornelius Flavius saw you and Plotina meeting on the morning you left Rome in spite of the fact that he had forbidden her to see you, and she had promised that she would not." Seeing that Marcus was stunned into silence, he explained further, "Her health has improved a great deal and Flavius considered that she was still under the vows she'd taken before."

"I won't allow it! Why didn't she protest? He did this to spite me!" Marcus exploded.

Lucius didn't consider it wise to remind Marcus that he had brought this problem upon himself, but he said, "She only has to remain a Vestal for thirty years. If you're a faithful lover, you can wait for her."

Remembering his experience with Elissa, Marcus protested, "We would both be old by then. I won't wait."

"You'll have to, Marcus. You have no choice."

❋ ❋ ❋

For days Marcus haunted the Forum Romanum with his eyes on the Temple of Vesta and the House of the Vestals. At least once a day the Vestals were brought out for exercise under the guardianship of a temple eunuch. Marcus mingled with the crowd that always followed the Vestals, but though he once caught Plotina's eyes, she looked away as if she hadn't seen him.

That night Marcus sought out his brother. "Lucius, tell me what you know about the Vestals. I want to know what I'm fighting."

"The worship of Vesta is one of the oldest religions in Rome," Lucius explained. "You can't fight it. To be a Vestal Virgin is an honor reserved in ancient times for the daughters of royalty only, but now the virgins are chosen from leading families. A Vestal is sworn to chastity for thirty years. They spend the first ten years learning their duties, the second decade practicing them, and their final years teaching the duties to novices. The sacred fire that they tend is a symbol of the well-being of the state, and it's a heavy responsibility to be sure that flame doesn't go out."

"But Plotina's father is the one who took the vow for her— she was only a child of six years old."

"That's true, but don't fool yourself, Marcus. I believe that Plotina is perfectly willing to be a Vestal. You'll cause trouble for her if you continue this course. You know that the populace honors them so much that they can even pardon condemned criminals. Leave her alone, Marcus."

When Marcus realized that he could expect no sympathy nor help from his brother, he sought out Bernice. Marcus hadn't seen his sister since her marriage, and he carried the perfume he had bought for her. In spite of his own troubles, he took her hand and smiled warmly. "And how are you, Bernice? Do you like being a matron?"

"It is not as I feared it might be. Cato is good to me and so are his parents. Anytime I become lonely for my family, I'm free to return home for a visit. They have asked me not to go to the Christian church, but they do not object that I worship as I please here in this home. But what about you, Marcus? How did you like your journey to Carthage?"

"Some of it was terrible, Bernice, but I've practically forgotten about it because of my disappointment over Plotina. Will you take her a note from me?" he pleaded.

"Why, Marcus! How can I?"

"She's out walking around the Forum each day. Surely you could brush by her and give her a note."

Bernice hesitated, then said, "Write your note. I'll do it, though it's against my better judgment, and I won't take any blame for the consequences."

He grabbed her hand and kissed it. "I'll bring it to you in the morning."

Marcus agonized over what to put in the note, and he was far from pleased with the final version.

Dear Plotina,
    You are mine. Don't you feel that in your heart? How can you remain a Vestal Virgin? If it were only a few years, I could be patient and wait. Please slip out of the temple and meet me tonight. I'll wait until you come.

                                     Marcus

Marcus accompanied his sister to the Forum, and he kept guard while she mingled with the crowd, but he stayed hidden when the Vestals came out for their daily exercise. When Bernice rejoined him, she said, "She has the message. I greeted her briefly and slipped the note into her hand. I watched, and she didn't discard it, so I'm assuming that she'll read it."

When dusk was falling, Marcus took up his vigil outside the school for the Vestals. Torches on high pedestals lighted the Forum Romanum, and he stood in the shadows of the Temple of Vesta. It was a beautiful circular building, and, according to tradition, it was built by Numa, who placed there the image of Minerva and other sacred objects brought to Italy by Aeneas. The safety of the city depended on the preservation of this building and its relics, and as Marcus thought of that, a chill crept up his spine. Although he was not as superstitious as most Romans, still he could not help but question if his convincing Plotina to leave the temple might have national repercussions.

As he stood in the shadows, Marcus kept looking around him, wondering if he had been detected. Although not as busy as it was in the daytime, the Forum bustled with people, and in the murky light they looked like ghosts floating in heavy fog.

Within an hour, Plotina came to his side. "I have taken a great risk to come here, for we are always under surveillance," she said at once. "I must not stay, but I thought I owed you an answer."

He tried to take her into his arms, but she eluded him.

"Marcus, this won't do. You must give me up. I have taken a vow and I mean to keep it."

"But you love me!"

"Yes, I do, but I also revere my father and the gods of Rome. I will not do anything to discredit either of them. Don't you understand that if I should do as you wish some great calamity might come upon the empire, and I would be at fault. Find another girl and marry her. You can be happy."

A vision of Elissa flashed into his mind, but Marcus asked huskily, "Don't you even care?"

Plotina didn't answer, but she didn't resist this time when he drew her into his arms. Though all the ardor of his youth surged into the caress he gave her, he drew no spark of response as he had always done before. She remained cold and unresponsive to his touch. Finally, he admitted that he had lost her and pushed her away.

"Go then. Go back to your sacred fire—your Vesta. Keep your vows." In his haste to leave her, Marcus stumbled over a man hidden in the shadows and fell to the ground. Cursing, he righted himself and reached for the person who had caused his fall, but the man eluded his grasp.

❂   ❂   ❂

Swathed in a white robe, Plotina knelt in front of the altar with the senior Vestal who was training her, and the soles of her bare feet shone in the muted light. On the pedestal above her head, the sacred flame burned steadily in the copper pot. Plotina periodically ladled a few droplets of oil on the blaze to keep it alight. Automatically, she cleared away the ashes that accumulated around the sacred flame, and with tongs added coals to the fire.

Plotina longed for her daily service to be completed. Today she could find none of the peace that she normally experienced when she tended the altar of Vesta. Always before, the eight hours passed quickly without any sign of fatigue, but today, the oil fumes caused aching eyes, her arm was numb, her lower back ached, and her thoughts rioted as she recalled the meeting with Marcus last night. *Why couldn't I make him see that I have dedicated my life to the goddess?* This service had nothing to do with her love for him, and it disturbed her to know that she desired him physically, an unworthy emotion for a Vestal Virgin.

Plotina's eyes closed and her head nodded forward, but her sister Vestal shook her gently. "Plotina, do not go to sleep. I am going for a short break."

Plotina roused and walked around the circular room flexing her arms and stretching her back. The flame flickered and she rushed to the pedestal. With shaking hand, she lifted a ladle of oil and brought the flame to life again. Assured that the light was safe, Plotina knelt in worship before the goddess and closed her eyes. Marcus's face rose before her.

"Plotina, awake! The flame is out!"

Plotina thought it was a dream until she was pulled rudely to her feet by the other virgin. She stared at the pedestal, where only a small spiral of smoke moved upward from where the flame had been. She leaped to the platform and pushed coals to the center of the pot.

"Maybe no one will ever know. It couldn't have been out for more than a minute."

"The goddess will know," the woman said, "and if some great calamity befalls this city, everyone will know. You have been remiss, Plotina, and all of us may suffer for it."

Plotina stirred the coals and found a small spark that still burned. She poured a full ladle of oil on it and the flame burst forth again. Not until then did she realize how her heart was pounding in her breast. On shaking knees she knelt again before the altar.

When her service ended for the day, a chill of terror engulfed Plotina when she was summoned into the presence of the chief priest of Vesta. Two eunuchs accompanied her to the inner sanctum of the temple, where she had never been before. All of the virgins feared this man, who had the power of life and death over them, and when Plotina entered his presence, she dropped to her knees and closed her eyes. She could not look upon his face.

The silence was deadly. *What does he know?* She had been warned when she had first come to the order that there were peepholes throughout the buildings where spies kept watch over the Vestals.

"Look at me!" the priest demanded.

Plotina could not see his face because of the white hood he wore, but she stared at the tall figure. "You have committed a crime against this temple and the state. Dire results may come because you let the sacred flame go out."

Plotina dropped her head. She wanted to beg for mercy, but the words came slowly. "It was not out—a spark still burned. I only dozed for a minute."

"Perhaps you would not have been sleepy if you had not been out of the temple last night. Who was your companion? Who took your virginity?"

Plotina jumped to her feet. "No! No, I am still chaste. If someone spied on me, they can tell you that. I did nothing wrong."

"You have lost your chastity, otherwise the flame would not have gone out. The future of the empire is at stake. You will be sacrificed to save the state."

Across Plotina's mind flashed a vision of a small underground chamber with access only by a ladder from above. It had been shown to her when she first came here—the place where unfaithful virgins were imprisoned and left to slowly starve and suffocate. She was not guilty; surely this would not be her fate.

"Who was your companion?" the priest shouted, but Plotina shook her head. She would not betray Marcus, for she was as much to blame as he. She need not have seen him last night; she could have sent a letter, but she had longed to see him one last time.

"You have betrayed our trust. You have broken your chastity vow. You will die for your sins," the priest said.

She again opened her mouth to assert her innocence, but one of the eunuchs jerked the white toga from her body and covered her with a black robe, trussing her arms and legs within it. A gag was thrust between her lips, but with her eyes she pleaded for mercy. The priest turned his back on her, the eunuch threw her over his shoulder, and they headed toward the lower reaches of the temple. The gag loosened and Plotina screamed, but her voice faded into the distance. The echoes of her terrified shrieks swirled around the virgins now tending the sacred flame, and they shuddered.

❀　❀　❀

The news of Plotina's death reached the Trento household in a message delivered by a servant from Cornelius Flavius. When the Trentos had assembled in the atrium, the servant read the message aloud.

"In spite of the fact that the Trentos and the Flavius family have been friends for years, this is to notify you that the friendship is severed. The stream between our properties will serve as a barrier that I do not expect any person or animal from your household to cross. There will be no discussion of the matter."

After reading Cornelius's message, the servant handed the scroll to Bernini, who sat with his mouth wide open, astonishment evident on his face. "But why? Why?" Bernini finally stuttered.

"The master's daughter is dead. She was buried alive in an underground chamber at the Temple of Vesta, condemned to death because she had broken her chastity vow and had allowed the sacred flame to snuff out. Though she refused to name her guilty partner, Master Cornelius lays the blame to a member of your household." The servant looked directly at Marcus before he exited.

The eyes of his family turned toward Marcus, and Bernini shouted, "What have you done?"

Marcus's eyes glazed and his whole body quivered like a branch during a north wind. His lips trembled when he answered his father. "Nothing! Nothing, I tell you. She had not broken her chastity vow, at least not with me. She was chaste!"

"But they must have some reason to suspect her."

"After I returned home and learned that her father had sent her back to the Temple of Vesta, I sent Plotina a note by Bernice and asked her to meet me. She came out one night, but she made it clear that she wanted to stay where she was. I kissed her, but nothing else."

"It's hard to believe that she would be put to death for that," his father said slowly.

"But it's true. Don't you believe me?" Marcus turned to his twin. "Lucius, surely you believe me."

Lucius placed an arm over his brother's shaking shoulders. "Of course, I believe you."

"But I'm to blame. If I'd left her alone as you told me to, she would be alive today. Now I don't have any reason for living," Marcus wailed.

"But we have another pressing problem," Bernini said. "Traditionally, a partner in the guilt of a Vestal is flogged to death."

"I don't care! I deserve to die!" Marcus shouted.

"Well, I care," his father said determinedly. "Especially since you are not guilty. I will make discreet inquiries, and if your life is endangered, you will have to leave this city."

"I'll leave the city, all right," Marcus shouted, bolting from the atrium with Lucius pursuing in his wake, and Sulla following them. Though Lucius could normally outrun Marcus, he didn't catch up with his twin until he reached the banks of the Tiber. Marcus had already thrown off his toga and was clad only in his tunic. He was unbuckling his sandals when Lucius arrived. "Wait, wait, I beg you. Give time a chance to heal," Lucius pleaded.

"But I sent her to a horrible death," Marcus sobbed.

"You are not all to blame. Plotina came out to see you of her own free will. You invited, that's true, but she didn't have to come. You couldn't have compelled her to. Besides, it's too late to do anything about it. Come back with me to the domus," Lucius said gently.

Marcus finally succumbed to Lucius's pleading, and with Sulla helping him, Lucius half-dragged his distraught brother back to the domus. Lucius knew Marcus would need a lot of watching in the next few months. Although he did not trust the slave, Lucius would have to enlist Sulla's help. Upon entering the domus, Lucius led Marcus to the chapel. Marcus sat passive, staring at the Alabaster, while Lucius prayed.

After he finished praying, Lucius said, "Go to the Christian services with me tomorrow. You would be able to bear your loss easier if you trust your problems to Jesus. He's the Way, the Truth, the Life. It's time you act upon the truth you've been taught."

Much to Lucius's surprise, Marcus did go with him the next day, but he sat through the Scripture reading, the prayers, and the message with a stoic attitude. Lucius could not persuade him to go again.

"I need to be forgiven, Lucius. I have blood on my hands. I must make atonement for my sins," Marcus said over and over when Lucius tried to reason with him. "And I committed another grievous sin when I was in Carthage. I lay with a slave girl who was a virgin, but cast her aside because I was coming home to Plotina."

Lucius hid his horror at this additional transgression of his brother. "Your sins were atoned for when Jesus died on the cross. If you did sin in beguiling Plotina, that sin has already been forgiven. That's God's grace—it's a free gift. The atonement has been made."

Marcus shook his head. "That answer does not suffice for me. I must work out my own salvation, and there's no provision in your belief for that."

"I believe you would be happier if you had been accused and flogged," Lucius said.

"That's true. I would have ended it all in the Tiber, but I thought that the priests of Vesta would take me prisoner and end my life the same way Plotina was killed. That would have been just retribution. I'm guilty, Lucius, I must atone."

❀ ❀ ❀

Although the family anticipated a move against Marcus, no attempt was made to arrest him. After Bernini's investigation produced no threat against him, all of the Trentos except Marcus settled back to normal living. Marcus, however, refused to go to the classroom again, and since Bernini decided that Lucius had learned all the tutor could teach him, the man was dismissed.

Lucius continued his studies, but he was freed to work at his own pace, giving him more time to train the lions, which turned into lovable pets. Teaching Sulla to speak Latin was not as easy, although Lucius considered the slave to have an excellent mind. Sulla openly resented his bondage, though he was careful not to step over the line of disobedience. Lucius always guarded his back when he was in a room with Sulla.

Marcus, too, was uneasy with the slave. Each time he caught the angry, rebellious look in Sulla's eyes, he was reminded of the slave Elissa and the disdain she had displayed when he'd rejected her. Marcus began to seek Sulla's company more often when he discovered that the slave practiced a secret religion. Marcus had come upon Sulla in the courtyard one day holding a small statue of an oriental god dressed in the flowing robes of the East. All that he learned from the slave was that the statue was of Mithra, an ancient god. This led Marcus to do some reading to learn what he could about the religion. Marcus liked what he learned.

Mithra was a legendary Persian god born out of a rock. Only the bravest men could become his followers. First they had to go through many painful ordeals, such as spending the night in a cramped box, which was placed in water to make things worse. At last, Marcus had found a religion that might allow him to work out the guilt in his life, for as the weeks passed, his burdens only intensified. Not only did he mourn for Plotina, but his rejection of the slave Elissa preyed on his mind.

Marcus often wandered in the Forum, looking long at the round temple of the Vestals, and one day when his condition was desperate, he enlisted in the army, to become a part of the *comitatenes*, a mobile field force consisting largely of cavalry, stationed at strategic points well behind the frontiers and capable of moving at a moment's notice to any point of danger. This seemed the answer for Marcus; if anything could take his mind from his guilt, the army should do it. Only after the commitment was made did Marcus realize what a blow his choice would be to his parents, and it was two days after his enlistment before he found the nerve to mention it.

"You've done what!" Bernini exploded.

"I've enlisted in the Roman army," Marcus repeated.

Lucius bowed his head in his hands, doubtful, but accepting this move that Marcus had made as a possible answer to his twin's dilemma.

"But don't you feel any family responsibility? You're the heir to the family business. Does that mean nothing to you?" Bernini raged.

"It's only for twenty years, and you're still in your prime. You can carry on until I've served my enlistment."

Bernini tried for days to reverse Marcus's decision, but Marcus remained adamant. Since his brother's burden seemed to have lifted somewhat, Lucius approved of the enlistment, although he knew that the closeness they had enjoyed as twins would never come again. Lucius went with Marcus to the Forum where he met the other volunteers, thankful that Sulla would be accompanying his brother. When the legion of would-be soldiers marched away, Lucius returned to the barn where his animals were housed. Unashamed of the tears that flowed over his cheeks, he put his arms around the playful cubs and buried his face in their soft manes. The lions seemed to understand his grief, for they left off their frolicking and softly licked his face.

❁   ❁   ❁

Sulla had not been too secretive in leaving the tent, and Marcus had no trouble following him. Sulla hurriedly moved through the quiet countryside, his way lighted by a full moon. Marcus stayed several paces behind him. Inside the city, the trail took Marcus down a set of steps, and he entered a small antechapel that led into a shrine—a long, narrow, dark room that resembled a cave. At the far end stood an altar and behind it a mosaic god wreathed in a radiant and fiery crown. Time was represented by a sexless creation with a lion's head and a human body. Around this body was entwined a serpent to represent the passage of the sun. Time held a scepter, thunderbolts, and the keys of heaven, and its body bore the signs of the zodiac.

Marcus stayed in the background as Sulla knelt before the altar with about a dozen other worshipers. The priest, robed in the disguise of a wolf, led the devotees through a long liturgy in a language Marcus didn't understand. Incense burned in small vials on an altar and the fumes burned his eyes.

When Sulla left the shrine, Marcus fell into step beside him. "Tell me something about your worship."

Sulla seemed surprised to see Marcus but answered in a worshipful tone, using much better Latin than he had evidenced before. "Mithra is a deity of my religion. He is the genius of divine light, associated with fire and the sun. Our religion emphasizes self-reliance and is identified with destiny, as well as light and fire. We emphasize the power of the stars."

Marcus's sandals crunched noisily on the hard turf, in step with the soft patter of Sulla's bare feet. *Self-reliance. Destiny.* He liked those words.

"We believe that darkness is populated by devils who once carried on a vain assault of heaven and were condemned to wander on the face of the earth spreading misery and plague."

"How do these devils work? Do they prey on the mind?" *This is beginning to make sense!* "How does your religion bring ease of mind to the troubled?"

"The devils work in many ways, but Mithra has fought the powers of evil. His life's journey symbolizes the duration of human suffering, for we believe that life is a battle and that victory can come only when the faithful observe divine laws."

Marcus understood why this religion would appeal to a slave, and he conceded that he was also enslaved to actions of his past. He listened eagerly as Sulla continued.

"Redemption does not come at once, but the faithful should strive for perfect purity, symbolized by continence, repeated washings, and abstinence from certain foods. Even if we do not have peace in this world, we know that after death there is a promise of immortality. The soul travels through a series of zones, ridding itself one by one of the passions it has acquired during its stay on earth."

As Marcus listened to Sulla's explanation of his religion, he compared it to the teaching he had heard from Ignatius. His grandfather had always said that salvation came through faith only and that people could not be saved by their works. That belief had never appealed to Marcus because he was geared toward action. In the depressed state of mind he was in, Marcus longed for anything that would diminish his anguish, and Mithraism seemed to be the answer. It was a man's religion, rigorous and virile, providing orders of membership with its sense of fraternity and its emphasis on combat in the cause of good. He decided he must look deeper into this faith. The religion of the Alabaster might be good enough for the other Trentos, but Marcus wanted something different.

PART II

THE RISE OF CONSTANTINE

NICOMEDIA, ROME, GAUL, TREVES, A.D. 303–312

As far as sunlight spreads its gift of life,
Where Ocean's lapping waves enfold the world,
You rule. Through southern sands,
  through northern snows
The march of Rome went unimpeded on.

Claudius Rutilius Namatianus I

7

NICOMEDIA, 303

The burning candelabras radiated a warm light on the gray walls of the little sanctuary. Octavian carefully rerolled the manuscript from which he had been reading and started singing a favorite hymn. When Atilia's soft voice joined his, he reached for her hand and lovingly beheld his fellow worshipers lifting their voices in praise.

> The day draws on with golden light,
>   Glad songs go echoing through the height,
> The broad earth lifts an answering cheer,
>   The deep makes moan with wailing fear.
> For lo, he comes, the mighty King,
>   To take from death his power and sting,
> To trample down his gloomy reign
>   And break the weary prisoner's chain.

The outer door burst open and Dorotheus, one of their number, rushed into the room. The singing stopped abruptly. Dorotheus was a servant at the imperial palace, and Octavian trembled when he saw the grave look on the face of this loyal Christian. Octavian tightened his hold on Atilia's hand, and she clung to him, as if she too sensed the terror that gripped his heart.

"The news is not good, brothers and sisters," Dorotheus said. "The emperor has issued an edict calling for the destruction of churches and the confiscation of all church properties, as well as the immediate stoppage of assemblies and any sort of worship."

"But why?" someone stammered. "We have not harmed the state nor anyone else. Why should he start the persecution again after forty years?"

"You surely know that Caesar Galerius has been visiting the Augustus for several weeks," Dorotheus said with a grimace. "He has been quite persuasive that Christians are a subversive sect and damaging to the state. We do know that in some parts of the empire our brethren have been rebellious."

"But we're so few in comparison to the population as a whole," Octavian said. "How could we do much harm?"

"Diocletian suspects Christians because we will not sacrifice to the Roman gods. But why should you be surprised? We've seen this coming for years. The emperor's edict to cleanse the army had the desired effect to weed out those who were determined to follow their Christian leanings. He believes these edicts will do the same thing in the empire as a whole. Diocletian no doubt feels the empire would benefit from our eradicaiton. It's estimated that more than ten percent of the inhabitants of the empire are Christians."

"How much time do we have?" Octavian asked.

"I don't know. As soon as I learned of the edict, I rushed to warn you, but I suggest that you disband worship immediately and take steps to preserve the sacred writings and the relics we have here. According to two other edicts, the clergy will be imprisoned and forced to sacrifice to the gods under threat of torture. Those who sacrifice will be released, those who refuse will be persecuted."

"Before we abandon our worship, I think we should pray," Octavian said, "that we might not falter under persecution."

After the prayer, Dorotheus hurried back to the palace to learn more news. Some Christians hurried out of the building, intent on protecting themselves. The few who remained quickly gathered the scrolls and relics, and Cassus was chosen to transport the items to a safe place. "And I don't know where that will be, son, but take our sacred writings away from here. And stay with them," Octavian added with a meaningful glance. "I don't want you coming back into the city."

"Where would you suggest? Rome, perhaps?"

Octavian shook his head. "This persecution is apt to spread across the whole empire, and the cities will be targeted. Better try to find refuge in a rural area. When the trouble passes, you can return."

"How can I flee and leave you to face persecution? Let me stay and you go," Cassus suggested.

"Yours will not be a safe task either. If you're discovered with these scrolls and relics, you will be in immediate danger. We will try to send Octavia to safety also."

Cassus embraced his father, kissed Atilia, and took the bundle entrusted to him. The streets of Nicomedia were quiet as he furtively left the basilica. He had almost reached his home before Cassus heard the din of a crowd before him. His rapidly beating heart seemed as clamorous as the noise in the street when he darted into an alley and cautiously made his way forward. Peering from behind a building, Cassus breathed more evenly when he saw that soldiers weren't behind the uproar, but rather a group of street urchins who had surrounded a man and were advancing on him. "Jew. Dirty Jew," they called as they pelted their prey with stones.

Forgetting the precious items entrusted to him, Cassus dropped the bundle and rushed toward the boys. "Stop it!" he shouted, as he grabbed two of the urchins and banged their heads together. His action distracted the boys momentarily, and when their prey darted into a nearby house, the attackers fled.

Seeing that they were gone, the man opened the door and beckoned Cassus to come inside. He retrieved his bundle of scrolls and joined the stranger, who was trying to stop the blood flowing over his face from a wound on his forehead.

"Why were you attacked?" Cassus asked.

"Jews are unpopular everywhere, young man. The children have taunted me before, but they had not attacked until today. Thank you for coming to my aid. I'm Matthew of Alexandria, a collector of rare manuscripts."

"Would you be the same Matthew who journeyed a few years ago with my cousin, Marcus Trento, on his trip to Carthage?"

Matthew smiled. "Oh, yes, that pompous young Roman who had much to learn."

"Well, he's learning it now in the imperial army," Cassus said with a laugh. "But we have our own problems. Have you heard that the government is destroying Christian scrolls and manuscripts? I'm fleeing this city now with these from our basilica." He looked around the room that had several cases of ancient-looking scrolls. "Perhaps you should join me," he added significantly.

"Gladly. My work here is almost finished, anyway. Give me a few minutes to collect my belongings. Do you have any destination in mind?"

Cassus shook his head. "This happened suddenly and I've made no plans."

"Then may I suggest the small seaport town of Alexandria Troas. I have friends there who will shelter us."

Open to any suggestion, Cassus agreed. He fidgeted while Matthew wrapped his clothing around the scrolls he had collected, then led the older man down a back street to the Trento home. Within an hour, the two men mounted swift horses and departed from Nicomedia.

❀   ❀   ❀

Constantine crossed the peristyle and entered the personal quarters of Diocletian. Since the death of Minervina three years ago, he had been restored to the good graces of the emperor, resulting in almost constant attendance upon Diocletian. Early each morning, he was expected to arrive in the royal chambers during the time the emperor was being dressed by his servants. From then on, he was in Diocletian's company until nightfall. *At least he doesn't require me to sleep in the room with him,* Constantine thought. *Not yet!*

Though Constantine chafed at his near-imprisonment, he was thankful for the opportunity to be near his son and to watch him grow. Crispus's intelligence had even caught the attention of Diocletian, who had hired Lactantius to be his tutor, a man whom Constantine revered as a friend.

Surely I'm not late! Constantine thought when he saw that Diocletian was already dressed and had been joined by Caesar Galerius on the jewel-studded dais. Diocletian nodded curtly and demanded, "Where is the commander of the palace police? He should have been here long ago."

"Shall I go look for him, sire?" Constantine asked.

"No, then I wouldn't know where you are. Ah, here he comes," Diocletian added as a huge, helmeted man entered the room.

"Within the hour," Diocletian ordered, "take your men and raid the Christian basilica across the street. Destroy all of their religious writings and relics and completely level the building. Caesar Galerius, you secure copies of my edicts from the scribes, post them around this city, and see that they are distributed throughout the empire."

"Shall the edicts be posted first, sire?" the guard asked.

"No, destroy the basilica today. Tomorrow will be soon enough to post the edicts. The Christians don't need any advance notice. If their God is so powerful, perhaps He will already have given them warning," the emperor said with a gleeful laugh.

The soldier raised his javelin in salute and departed, and Galerius said, "Let's go to the rooftop and watch the destruction." He smiled contentedly.

Constantine followed the two officials to the roof of the palace in time to see the soldiers enter the building and drive a small group of clergy and laymen out into the street. A clergyman cried out in protest when soldiers tore the door from the basilica, but he was held back by one of the armed men.

In a short time, the soldiers returned from the basilica empty-handed. Striding across the street to the palace, the commander of the guard called, "Sire, there are no relics nor writings. The place is empty."

Remembering Diocletian's caustic words, a thought made Constantine's flesh crawl. *Did the Christian God warn them of this persecution?*

Diocletian turned with an angry visage to Constantine. "See, what have I told you? These people always evade state orders."

He shouted down at the soldier. "Destroy that building."

"Shouldn't it be burned?" Galerius said.

"No, there are too many other edifices nearby that could catch fire, including the palace."

Constantine watched wrathfully as the soldiers moved against the building with rams normally used to attack a walled town. In a short time the walls crumbled. A small group of Christians huddled in the square with heads bowed and shoulders slumped, witnessing the destruction of their basilica. Constantine recognized Octavian and Atilia Trento, as well as Octavia, their daughter, who had been a big help to his mother in caring for Crispus. Anger boiled in his heart at Diocletian and Galerius. He couldn't speak for the Christians across the empire, but certainly the emperor had nothing to fear from the Trentos.

As Constantine thoughtfully left the roof, he felt a moment of fear for his mother. She no longer made any secret of her Christian sentiments. Indeed, she had even tried to persuade him to join the sect, though Constantine had remained impervious to his mother's veiled remarks.

The next morning, Galerius commanded Constantine to accompany his group of soldiers as they moved through the city to post the edicts in conspicuous public places. Octavian Trento and Euethius, a man of great distinction in Nicomedia, stood in the square viewing the remains of their church building when the soldiers nailed the edict on the only pillar of the basilica that hadn't been destroyed. With a roar of rage, Euethius grabbed the piece of parchment, tore it to shreds, and trampled it underfoot.

"Arrest him," Galerius ordered. Constantine jumped from his horse, and with the help of another man, soon had the enraged Euethius tied securely. Diocletian must have been watching from the palace, for he rushed into the square and confronted Euethius. "You dare to destroy an edict of the emperor?"

The angry red of Euethius's face quickly faded to a gray pallor, as if he suddenly sensed the enormity of what he had done.

Diocletian turned from Euethius and commanded Galerius, "Execute him immediately. Burn him."

Even Galerius seemed daunted at the order, for his voice faltered, "Burn him?"

"Yes. Right there in the middle of that basilica."

Galerius's soldiers tied the condemned man to the pillar where the poster had been, gathered the rubbish from the destroyed church interior, piled it around Euethius's feet, and ignited it. Constantine watched in horror as the fire smoldered and then blazed upward. Euethius screamed when the flames engulfed his clothing, and the smell of burning flesh and singed hair drifted throughout the square. Constantine's mouth felt as dry as sand and his hands clenched as he held on to his horse for support. A wave of heat engulfed his body, nausea surged into his stomach, and Constantine reeled in his saddle, his eyes seared by the hot flames.

Euethius's screams soon ceased, but his voice was still strong as he spoke aloud, and Constantine wondered if he prayed to his God. A small group of Christians hovered close to the dying martyr, and their voices raised with his. To take his mind off the tragedy being enacted before his eyes, Constantine concentrated on their words.

"Be merciful to me, Lord, in this time of distress. My eyes are feeble with sorrow. My soul and my body are overcome with grief. My life is full of affliction and my lips will soon be stilled. My strength is failing, and my bones are almost consumed. My enemies have made me the scorn of my friends. But I trust in You, God. You are my Lord. My life is in Your hands. Deliver me from my enemies."

Noting the bravery of this man, Constantine longed to rush into the square and douse the flames, but should he sacrifice himself for a man he hardly knew? Now that he was in the good graces of Diocletian, he had better stay that way—at least, until he could leave Nicomedia and join his father in Gaul. Constantine turned slowly and mounted his horse.

As if the heavens themselves were angry at the martyrdom of Euethius, a strong wind erupted and lightning and thunder filled the square. Constantine could hardly hold his horse in check as streaks of lightning danced along the soldiers' metal helmets and a driving wind brought an onslaught of rain that doused the fire around Euethius's charred body.

Galerius ordered the troops to the safety of the castle, but Constantine gave the reins of his horse to one of his comrades and dismounted to help Octavian and a few other men remove the remains of their friend from the post. He stamped out a few sparks and found it difficult to meet Octavian's eyes.

"Thank you, Constantine, for showing some mercy," Octavian said. "I trust this will not bring you disfavor at court."

"I trust so, too, but he died as a brave soldier. I couldn't seem to do otherwise."

"All Christians will soon be called upon to take a stand," Octavian said. "I may meet a similar end myself."

Constantine marveled at the lack of fear on Octavian's face. "What of Cassus?" Constantine asked, hoping his friend wasn't slated for such a fate. Octavian only shook his head, and Constantine haltingly questioned, "What words was he speaking before his death?"

"He repeated one of the psalms written by the Hebrew David many years ago."

As Octavian and his friends carried the remains of Euethius away, Constantine stared after them. *When these Christians preserve their sacred writings in their hearts and minds, how can Diocletian hope to destroy them?*

❊ ❊ ❊

An uneasy calm settled over Nicomedia for a week. Christians discontinued public worship, and even the soldiers must have been repulsed by the death of Euethius, for they raided no more churches despite Diocletian's orders. As if nature was still protesting, wave after wave of thunderstorms drenched the city. During one of them, Constantine was awakened by a servant pounding on his door, shouting, "Fire! Fire! The palace is ablaze."

"The lightning has caused it," Constantine deduced as he rushed out into the atrium, where flames and smoke poured from a room not far from Diocletian's chambers.

With the help of the huge palace staff, the fire was soon extinguished, but Diocletian's rage was not so easily quenched. "Who tried to burn the palace over the emperor's head? The villains will be punished," Diocletian cried as he stalked into the atrium. He was clad only in a short tunic and Galerius strode at his side.

"No doubt the lightning started the fire," Constantine suggested. "The storms have been fierce all night."

"Or perhaps it was the Christians," Galerius said persuasively. "They have not taken kindly the extermination of one of their own."

Diocletian looked quickly at Galerius, and it was obvious that the suggestion found root in his mind. "All of the major leaders of this sect and their families must be imprisoned. If they do not recant of this spurious religion, kill them."

As Constantine left the presence of the angry emperor, Lactantius, his son's tutor, fell into step with him. "The story around the palace is that Galerius himself set the fires, but he'll make Christians the scapegoats."

"Why? What have they done that's so horrible?" Constantine asked.

"Caesar Galerius is ambitious, and he wants to learn the identity of all those who owe allegiance to another."

"I wish I could leave here," Constantine said. "I don't want to witness another scene like that execution last week. I haven't been able to put it out of my mind. It haunts me."

"You can't leave now, so make the best of it, but I would suggest that if you know anyone within this palace who is a Christian that you remove them at once."

Lactantius held Constantine with a piercing look then moved away from him. *Is he referring to Mother?* Constantine had always thought that his mother was safe in the palace since some of Diocletian's own family favored the sect, but that was apparently not the case.

In a roundabout way, he approached his mother's apartments. The storm still raged outside, but inside, he could hear the laughter of his three-year-old son. Constantine knocked quietly and entered. Octavia Trento sat on the floor playing with Crispus, who came running to be swooped into his father's arms. Upon Constantine's entry, Helena came from the inner room.

Constantine spoke at once. "The emperor has just given the order that all Christians are to be imprisoned, and if they won't recant their faith, they'll be put to death."

Helena gasped, and Octavia half-rose from the floor. Before they recovered their composure, he continued, "Don't you still have a brother who operates the inn at Drepanum? This would be a good time for you to pay him a visit and to take Octavia and Crispus with you."

"I won't leave my parents," Octavia protested at once.

"I'll send them word where you are," Constantine said. "Believe me, they won't want you to stay here. I'm going to hire a driver and carriage for you to leave tonight. There's no time to delay."

"But how can I explain my absence?" Helena asked.

"Write to Empress Prisca and tell her you were called away temporarily because of sickness in your family—don't say where. State that you didn't want to bother the emperor during such troublesome times and ask her to relay to him the reason for your absence. I feel sure that she'll 'forget' to tell him for a few days."

"It seems cowardly to run away."

"Someone has to take Crispus out of harm's way, and I certainly can't go." He started out the door. "Be ready to leave by nightfall."

The next day, in an effort to cleanse his household, Diocletian ordered that all persons in the imperial palace offer sacrifice to the traditional gods, and anyone failing to do so would be beaten. Constantine dropped a pinch of incense on the altar without any compunction for he held to the sun god anyway, but he felt sorry for Diocletian's wife and daughter who, with tear-stained faces, walked by the altar and did obeisance. Dorotheus and a few of the other servants refused and were taken into the square and flogged repeatedly until they fainted.

In the following months, soldiers surged throughout Nicomedia searching for leaders of the Christian church. Many who had gone into hiding were betrayed by others and dragged into prison. Knowing that it was just a matter of time before he was taken, Octavian wrote a letter to Lucius.

Dear Nephew,

In reality, this letter should be written to your father, but since he has little patience with my beliefs, I will write a final message to you, for I believe that the time has come for me to join our Savior in heaven. I do not long to stay on this earth any longer, but I do wish that I could have persuaded Atilia to leave the city so that she would not have to suffer imprisonment and death, but she would not. So we will die together, and I trust God that we will die bravely.

Thus far, Cassus and Octavia are safely out of

Nicomedia, and I believe that it's God will for them to survive this round of persecution. I have pondered why this travesty has come upon the church, and I do not lay the sole cause to the enmity of the emperors, for I believe that they are the agents of God, who in His wrath, has unleashed His long-deserved judgment upon the church. Even though Diocletian is a pagan, God has anointed him as a modern-day Cyrus to do His will. The church has become wicked and self-seeking, and God has withdrawn His hand. This awful punishment will continue until the time of penitence is fulfilled.

I urge you to look carefully to the guardianship of the Alabaster, for the persecution will soon move to Rome. Here, all religious relics were ordered destroyed, and that will also be the case in Rome. Guard the Alabaster well, but when and if you are caught up in the persecution, hold dear the memory of what the Alabaster stands for, as Atilia and I shall do. Jesus is the Resurrection and the Life—whoever believes in Him will never die. Because the grave was empty, I do not fear what death may hold.

Your loving uncle and brother in the Lord,

Octavian

Nicomedia, 303

After a few months of this persecution, Constantine was overwhelmed with the blood lust of the officials, and he was hardly able to countenance the stories reaching Nicomedia of the wholesale butchery of Christians in some parts the empire. Some were executed by fire, while others, bound by the public executioners, were dumped in small boats and thrown into the sea. And the thing that seemed most strange to Constantine was the mystical fervor of these men and women who went to their deaths rejoicing.

In one of his sudden mood changes, the emperor relaxed his hold on Constantine and it was with some relief that he obeyed the orders of Diocletian to take a century of soldiers to put down a rebellion in the seacoast town of Alexandria Troas, where the citizens were attacking government officials. Within a few days of his arrival in the town, Constantine had uncovered the problem and was in complete sympathy with the citizens rather than the officials. Two years before, Diocletian had issued an edict setting a ceiling on prices to curb inflation. The edict had set ceilings on over a thousand different items, but soon speculators and profiteers—most of them soldiers and government workers—had removed many of those items from the economy and were selling them on the black market. The rebellion on the part of the people had resulted from hunger. Profiting from the administrative lessons he had learned at Diocletian's side, Constantine had imprisoned the speculators, thrown open the warehouses to the people, and within a few weeks was searching for honest administrators to take over the work of the government.

One day he looked up from his work when a man walked into the room. He reached for his sword when the stranger closed the door.

"Would you take your sword to an old friend, Constantine?"

Constantine stared in amazement at the bearded man before him. The voice sounded familiar, and when he looked in the smiling eyes, he said hesitantly, "Cassus?"

"Yes, but I hope you won't make it known. I'm trusting my life to you, depending on our past friendship to keep you from betraying me."

"What have you done that could possibly make me betray you?"

"I'm a Christian, remember? I left Nicomedia before the persecution began, and as yet it has not extended to this remote area. At first, we feared you had come for that purpose, or I would have contacted you before."

"Sit down, Cassus. I'm sick of this bloodshed, and I have no notion of betraying any Christian." While Cassus sat, Constantine hesitated, then said, "Have you heard that your parents were martyred?"

Cassus nodded, his face grave. "It was their choice. They could have escaped, too, but they would not. I was entrusted with a task for the church or I would not have run away. Do you know the fate of my sister?"

"On the eve of persecution she left Nicomedia with my mother and Crispus. I believe all three are safe in Drepanum."

"God be praised for sparing them."

"What have you been doing here?" Constantine asked with a curious glance at Cassus's shabby clothing.

"Making myself inconspicuous by working at the wharves. But I'm secretly abiding in the home of one of the richer men in the city, and he has done me the honor to betroth me to his daughter, Lanitra. I heard you were looking for honest administrators, and I would recommend that family. They are Christians and will treat everyone fairly."

Constantine rose quickly. "You have solved my problem. I knew no one in this city whom I could trust. You have my thanks, Cassus."

"In exchange, I will ask a small favor of you. Will you send word to my uncle in Rome, Bernini Trento, that Octavia and I have thus far come safely through the persecution?"

"I will send the message by military post, but in the event it does not reach your relative, I will deliver it in person, for Diocletian has commanded me to travel to Rome with him in a few weeks."

❀ ❀ ❀

Since the return to Nicomedia from Alexandria Troas lay in the direction of Drepanum, Constantine planned his return route along the Sea of Marmara. It was nearing dusk when they entered the ancient town. Careful to keep a secret from his men as to where they were going since he feared a report would be given to the emperor, Constantine hesitated to ask any directions to the inn operated by his uncle. He remembered that his mother had referred to it as the Gladiator, so he rode through the streets of Drepanum hoping that he would find the inn by chance.

His problem was solved when a tribune riding beside him said, "I understand the Gladiator is a good inn, sir. It's not large enough to provide housing for all of us, but there's an army barracks close by."

"Let the soldiers find shelter in the barracks; the officers can try the Gladiator. I look forward to a comfortable night after this hard day of travel."

This is going to be easier than I'd hoped, Constantine thought as he waited for the soldier to carry out his orders and to guide him to the Gladiator.

The smell of roasting meat tantalized his nostrils as he entered the semidark hostelry. *Will I recognize my uncle? Will there be some family resemblance?* A maiden working at the fireplace looked up at their entrance.

"Is the owner here?" Constantine said. She nodded, disappeared behind a curtain, and returned with a man who must surely be his own relative. The middle-aged man stood six feet tall in his sandals, and his broad shoulders were held straight, his head set solidly upon them. Constantine had the sensation that he was beholding himself in a mirror.

Looking straight into the man's gray eyes on a level with his own, Constantine said, "I'm Centurion Constantine serving the Roman Empire. I would like lodging for ten of our company tonight. We do not have any official business in Drepanum, we're simply in need of overnight lodging before we return to Nicomedia." He placed a slight emphasis on the word "official," hoping that his uncle would understand that he wanted nothing mentioned of their kinship.

"We have a public room that could take care of most of your men, and your servant would consider it an honor if the centurion would share the quarters of his family for the night."

This is too easy, Constantine thought, but he said, "Your hospitality is accepted. We'll bring in our gear."

Within the hour, Constantine was sitting with his mother and holding Crispus on his knee in an apartment far removed from the merrymaking soldiers in the public room of the inn. The one window, now heavily shuttered, looked out upon the Sea of Marmara.

"Have you fared well here?" Constantine asked his mother.

"Yes, but we've stayed in hiding, awaiting news from Nicomedia before we make any plans. My brother has heard rumors that all is not well."

"Members of the Christian church have been practically eliminated in Nicomedia. If they haven't been killed, they've run away or recanted. Many reasonable people have dared to publicly express their indignation at this outrage perpetrated against blameless people whose only crime has been to worship their God and live reverent lives. The persecution has about run its course in Nicomedia, but it will soon spread to other cities."

"What about my parents?" Octavia asked anxiously.

Constantine hesitated before answering. "I'm sorry to bring you the sad news that they were condemned to death by strangulation, but they went to their deaths rejoicing. Cassus is safe in Alexandria Troas."

Helena put her arms around Octavia's trembling body. "I'm so sorry, my dear. I hope you know you'll always have a home with me." Turning to Constantine, she asked, "What are we to do?"

"You must remain here indefinitely, and I would suggest that you take on a new identity for the time being. Perhaps Octavia could pass Crispus off as her child, and you could work as a serving maid in the inn. I hate for you to have to do that, but for your own safety, you must."

"I am no stranger to hard work—indeed, I worked in this very inn before I married your father. I daresay I'll be happier here than in the imperial palace."

"But you are destined for better things, and I look forward to the time when I can make your life easier. In the meantime, I prefer for you to be in seclusion. Diocletian is going to Rome soon to celebrate the twentieth anniversary of his reign, and that's all he has on his mind now, so it's possible the persecution will die down, but I want my loved ones safe. My own position is precarious at best, and if the opportunity comes, I'm going to join my father. If I should do that, then the emperor might bring his judgment down upon you. Someday, I will heap upon you the honor you deserve, but now isn't the time."

After darkness fell, Constantine wandered outside and sat on a bench behind the inn. A slight fog hovered over the water, and he breathed deeply of the damp air. A loon cried shrilly as it rose from its place of concealment, and the soft breeze from its wings brushed Constantine's face as it lifted into the air. Hoping that he could spend a few peaceful moments, he was dismayed when his thoughts turned to the Christian persecution. *Will I ever forget the martyrdom of Euethius? What makes the Christians choose death rather than recant their faith*? He was startled from his musings by Octavia, who appeared at his side.

"I'm glad you came out, Octavia. I want to thank you for the way you've taken care of my son. Mother says that you've relieved her of much of his care."

"I love Crispus. It isn't difficult to watch over him. But I would hear more about my parents . . . did they leave a message for me?"

"I don't know. When I saw Cassus recently he had no message from them, but he is grateful that their deaths were instantaneous rather than by execution in the arenas. I'm sure your parents would want you to go on with your life and not grieve over them."

"That's just it—I don't have a life. Most of my belongings were left behind when I fled with your mother, and I'm simply existing here at the kindness of your uncle. What is my future?"

"As soon as the persecution ceases, I'm sure that Cassus will arrange a marriage for you."

Silence stretched between them, and Octavia said nervously, "You mentioned that you didn't want your loved ones to be persecuted. Am I included in that?"

Constantine had only meant Helena and Crispus, and it startled him to realize that Octavia was in love with him. *Is this the reason she has taken over the care of my son so willingly?* Not since Minervina's death had he had any yearning toward another woman, and he must not give this girl any false hopes.

"Actually I was thinking of Mother and Crispus, but I certainly count you as a friend and do not want you persecuted. Nor would your parents. They would want you to be safe. You need not fear you are a burden here. If Mother goes to work in the inn, we will pay you to look after Crispus."

More silence greeted his remark, and he continued, "I'm glad I'm learning to love my son. When my wife died, I blamed him for her death and I didn't want to be around the child, but now he's filling that empty place in my heart that Minervina left. Of course, most of my heart will always belong to her, but I'm happy that I have Crispus as a reminder of my beloved wife."

Octavia sighed and returned to the inn without further comment.

8

ROME, 303–305

Lucius lounged in the atrium, thinking about the letter he had received from his uncle. Absentmindedly, he fondled the thick mane of Dan, who was sprawled beside his chair. Trying to blot from his mind the hideous persecution his aunt and uncle might have suffered, he concentrated on the two lions. Beersheba coyly switched her tail while Dan tried to catch it. As they had matured, their spotted hair had given way to brownish yellow coats the color of dead grass.

How old are they now? Almost three years, Lucius calculated, since Marcus had brought them to Rome. For the first year he had wrestled with the cubs, but they soon grew beyond that. In a wrestling match, he now came off second best with the four-hundred-pound animals, yet they had made the most docile of pets. They followed him around the domus as if they were kittens, and he'd taught them many tricks. One trick that often entertained the family was when he said, "Play dead," and the lions flopped on their backs.

Occasionally, when Lucius least expected it, one of the animals might leap on his back and force him to the ground, and he always experienced a moment of terror when the huge, ruffed head with sharp teeth bared snarled above him. But after a moment's tussle, the lion would dash away, and if it were possible for lions to laugh, he figured the animal laughed at him. The two lions had taken it upon themselves to be Lucius's guardians, and once Dan had attacked Marcus, who had been playfully cuffing his twin. Marcus still had Dan's tooth marks on his arm. After that incident, Bernini had demanded that Lucius get rid of the lions, but he hadn't enforced the order, so the lions still had the run of the property.

Lucius's peaceful musings were interrupted when Bernini stamped into the atrium holding a letter from Constantine saying that Octavian and Atilia had been martyred. Copies of the two edicts that the Christians had disobeyed were enclosed. "The fools! Why did they have to be so obstinate? Why couldn't they drop a pinch of incense to the emperor, and then go on praying to the Christian God?"

"But what of Cassus and Octavia?" Domitilla asked, following closely behind Bernini. "Does the letter contain any news of them?"

Bernini handed the letter to his wife. "He sends a message from Cassus that both he and his sister are safe."

He stalked out of the atrium into his office and slammed the door. Domitilla looked fearfully at Lucius. "Do you think the persecution will spread this far?"

"Without a doubt," Lucius said gravely. "Persecution feeds itself, although I feel we are safer here than many places since the Roman populace is more sympathetic to Christians than people in some cities. However, that could change very quickly."

"I wonder if I would have the courage that Octavian and Atilia had," Domitilla mused fearfully.

"You won't have to find out. You know that at the first sign of persecution, Father will sacrifice to the emperors and force you to do so as well. He believes in being pragmatic."

"But you, Lucius—what will you do?"

He paused many seconds before he answered. "I don't know. I hope I'm courageous enough to remain faithful, but I don't suppose I'll know until the testing comes."

"You must remember Octavian's warning about the Alabaster. Think of a hiding place for it, should it be necessary."

Lucius studied the two edicts. "One edict orders the arrest of the clergy, and the other stipulates that the prisoners will be released if they offer sacrifices, otherwise they will be forced to do so by any means. So far, it seems that across the whole empire, only the clergy are affected. What happened in Nicomedia may have been an isolated incident, and with any luck, it will not extend further."

"But the edict says that churches are to be razed and relics and writings confiscated. Anyone who resists such measures, clergy or laity, will be violating the law of the land," Domitilla said with a concerned look at her son. "It worries me Lucius. I know what you'll do."

✸   ✸   ✸

The deaths of Atilia and Octavian had occurred in the spring of 303, but it was late summer before the news had reached Rome. Throughout the rest of the summer and fall, news filtered in about persecutions in the realms of Galerius, but the believers in Rome were undisturbed, and they carried on their worship as usual.

Marcus came home in November, after almost a year's absence, saying that he had been transferred to duty in Rome and would be staying in the city for several months. Sulla followed him when he bounded into the peristyle where Domitilla and Lucius were enjoying the late afternoon sun.

"Why, you hardly seem like twins anymore!" Domitilla exclaimed as her burly son wrapped his mother in a hug that left her breathless. Marcus grabbed Lucius's hand and shouted, "Brother!" But Lucius folded his twin in a tight embrace and buried his head on the muscular shoulder encased in armor.

As she watched the reunion between her two sons, Domitilla absorbed the noteworthy changes in Marcus. The rigorous life of the army had caused him to develop muscular legs and arms, and he appeared to weigh at least fifty pounds more than Lucius. But the greatest difference was in the eyes. Lucius's eyes were peaceful and compassionate, but as for Marcus, that desperate look brought about by Plotina's death had given way to a hardness not only in his eyes, but in his whole character that dismayed his mother. *And what of his faith? Has he abandoned all of the teachings he learned from Ignatius?*

Dan and Beersheba were draped around the pool watching the goldfish. Dan looked up quickly at Marcus's entrance, and when Marcus broke the embrace and wrestled Lucius to the floor, Dan stood to his feet and growled menacingly.

Paling somewhat, Marcus said with a laugh, "I guess I can't wrestle with you anymore, brother, as long as you have a protector. I may yet regret the day I brought those animals home to you."

Marcus stretched out a hand for Lucius to help him rise, and when Dan padded to his side, Lucius laid a hand on the broad back. "It's all right, Dan. He's a bully, but I love him."

"I thought Father told you to get rid of those animals."

"As you can see they're still here, and from the size of you, I may need their protection. You're looking great, Marcus."

"Besides being a bit puny, you look good, too. What have you been doing with yourself?"

"I have continued my studies even though our tutor has gone to another household. Besides that, I've been working in the nearby basilica, that is, with what time I have left after I do the work you should be doing as heir to this estate. Someone has to take over when Father is away on business."

"You would be the next to inherit if something should happen to me, so the practice may be good for you."

"What concerns me is whether there will even be an heir after the two of you, since neither of you seems to have any plans to marry," Domitilla complained. "Most of your friends are married by now and have their families started."

"Mother, we're only thinking of you. You look much too young to be a grandmother," Lucius said.

She was pleased at the compliment, but she was not to be diverted. "You do have a responsibility to your family—someone has to carry on the story of the Alabaster. Besides, if you aren't married by the time you reach twenty-five, you'll have to pay a fine."

"Not I," Marcus said. "Although soldiers are permitted to marry now, we're exempt from the fee. But I have no intention of taking a wife, so it's up to Lucius. Being a Roman soldier is a great experience, but life is somewhat uncertain, and I don't want to be responsible for a family."

Noting Domitilla's expression, Marcus switched the subject, "But I don't like having you associated with the Christians, Lucius. Don't you know what's happening throughout the empire? I had expected the persecutions to have spread here."

"Yes, we've heard," Domitilla said, and told him what had happened to Octavian and Atilia. "I hope, son, that you haven't been involved in any of these persecutions."

"No, I've been too busy fighting the barbarians. And I suppose I should tell you that I'm now a devotee of Mithra."

Domitilla gasped, and Lucius said without inflection, "That's your choice. But why are you in Rome now?"

"Diocletian is coming to Rome next month to celebrate the vicennial of his reign. Maximian will be here, too, so it's necessary to have many troops in the city. And my century will be supervising the games that the emperor is sponsoring as part of the celebration."

❀　❀　❀

The next morning, Marcus came to Lucius in the chapel, where Lucius knelt for his morning devotions. He sat on a bench in the rear of the room until Lucius rose.

"You could have joined me, Marcus," Lucius said.

"My new religion meets all of my needs, and it's one that has escaped persecution. You would do well to become a follower."

"A man can't change his religion to suit the political situation of the day, Marcus. Besides, Mithraism is a religion of the lower class. What can it possibly offer you?"

"The opportunity to work for my salvation. I've gone through several of the castigations. I've fasted for fifty days, touched fire, suffered scourging for two days. Little by little, I'm making recompense for the death of Plotina and my responsibility for it." *But I still haven't received pardon for the way I treated the slave Elissa!* his conscience prodded, and inwardly Marcus cursed the part of his memory that would not forget the incident.

"But what purpose do these rituals serve? What do you gain from them?" Lucius asked.

"Let's face it, Lucius. Life on earth is merely a transition to a higher plane. Earthly existence is nothing but hardship and bitterness. Mithra guides souls from the earthly situation into which we've fallen up to the light from which we originally came. During my last sacrament, the lion degree, I washed my hands in honey and vowed to keep them pure of all misdeeds. Then a garland was tossed from a sword, which I pressed down upon my shoulder. Mithra is now my garland and crown."

Lucius could see why this religion had appealed to his brother, for there was much in it that paralleled the Christian belief that he had learned as a child. When he was reaching out for a religion of redemption, the war god of the army, Mithra, had obviously been presented as a redeemer of the soul. But Lucius was troubled and momentarily his faith faltered. *How can Christianity survive the onslaught from these pagan religions and the persecution the church is now enduring? And what can I do for the church as a whole when my own father and brother deny the faith?*

"Has your childhood training completely deserted you?" Lucius questioned. "Remember Grandfather Ignatius taught us that a man can't work for his salvation—it's a free gift from

God and comes only by faith in the death, burial, and resurrection of Jesus."

Marcus shook his head stubbornly. "I'll admit those teachings enter my mind occasionally, but I've made my choice. I'll stick by it. Which brings me to the purpose of my visit." He paused to clear his throat before he continued, "It concerns me to hear that you have embraced so wholeheartedly the faith of the Christians. It is not safe. In Grandfather's day, even though it was against the law to follow the Christian religion, the emperors paid no attention to the law. It's different now. This last edict against the clergy has filled the prisons with bishops and deacons, even readers and exorcists. The prisons are so full of Christians there's no room for criminals. Besides that, many have been killed. Lucius, be reasonable. I don't want you to pay the same price our relatives paid in Nicomedia."

"I can only answer you with your own words. I've made my choice—I'll stick by it." Lucius looked toward the pedestal holding the Alabaster. "Or perhaps it was made for me when Grandfather made me the guardian of the Alabaster."

Marcus strode angrily around the room. "But it's all so simple. All the emperor is demanding is a show of loyalty. Why can't you drop a pinch of incense upon the burner in front of the emperor's statue and still practice your religion?"

"The Roman Empire has deified its emperors, thus to pay homage to Diocletian is acknowledging him as a god, especially now that he's taken upon himself the title of Lord. Christians have but one Lord, and dropping a pinch of incense to the emperor is in reality denying our faith in the one Lord, Jesus Christ."

"You may change your mind when the persecution reaches Rome," Marcus said darkly.

"I pray not. I trust that I can face the executioners as bravely as Octavian and Atilia did."

"And I've always been accused of being the stubborn one," Marcus said as he stormed from the room. Lucius followed his brother into the atrium, where Marcus slumped on a bench.

Marcus looked up at his brother. "I must confess that I'm troubled about Sulla," he said. "Although I had no trouble disregarding Grandfather's religious teachings, I can't forget his dislike of slavery. It disturbs me to own a slave, especially one as intelligent as Sulla. He's the one who introduced me to Mithra."

And enslaved you more than himself, Lucius thought, but he didn't speak his opinion, hesitating to add to his brother's despondence. "Set him free then," he suggested instead.

"And make Father angry?"

"You've made him angry before, and he's always forgiven you."

The fountain splashed softly in the tile basin, and Lucius heard his mother's voice in the distance giving orders to the kitchen staff. Marcus seemed to be thoughtfully considering Lucius's suggestion.

"I've come to depend on Sulla," he said, "not so much to meet my needs, but I like the man. There are times when we've worshiped before Mithra that I think he looks upon me as a friend, but then I'll see a resentful, hateful look in his eyes when he turns toward me, and I'm almost frightened of what he might do."

"You can hardly expect him to feel kindly toward a man who keeps him in bondage."

Marcus remained thoughtful and soon rose to wander out of the atrium without making any response.

❀   ❀   ❀

Diocletian arrived in Rome two weeks later, to be met by Maximian, the other Augustus. He sponsored a festival to celebrate Roman victories and his twenty-year reign. Compared to other emperors, Dicoletian's festival was frugal, and the people were unhappy. The complaining populace seemed to forget the colossal bath Diocletian had built for them and his large gift of money. The people made no effort to hide their disappointment that the games had not been more elaborate.

Diocletian had never liked Rome anyway, and when he experienced the ingratitude of its citizens, he made no secret of the fact that he would not stay long in the city. Constantine knew that if he were to see the Trentos he must do so right away, before the emperor took a sudden notion to leave.

One morning when Diocletian seemed in an amiable mood, he approached him. "Sire, with your permission, I request a few hours leave this afternoon to visit a family here in Rome. They are friends of my mother."

He knew he didn't dare tell the emperor the truth, that he wanted to take greetings from Cassus Trento, for Diocletian might remember the martyred Trentos in Nicomedia. Expecting to have to persuade the emperor to grant his request, Constantine was surprised when Diocletian said, "Be back in the palace before nightfall. I don't trust these Romans."

Constantine hurried to his quarters to write a short note.

Constantine of Nicomedia would like permission to call upon your family this afternoon. Please reply if that will be convenient.

He found a man who was familiar with the maze of Roman streets to deliver the message. In about an hour, a knock sounded on his door, and he opened upon a young man of medium height, whose smile radiated from a pair of the most intelligent brown eyes Constantine had ever seen.

With a slight bow, the youth said, "Lucius Trento at your service, Centurion."

Constantine laughed. "I didn't expect you to come in person to answer my note."

"I've come to conduct you to our home, sire. The streets of Rome are a maze to a stranger. My father and mother await your arrival with pleasure. I've a litter waiting outside the palace to take you to our home."

As they rode through the streets, Lucius indicated points of interest, and Constantine was happy to find a friendly Roman after the reception the imperial court had received.

Bernini stood on the street in front of the domus when they arrived. "Welcome to our home, Centurion Constantine! We are honored. My brother has spoken well of you."

Domitilla waited for them in the atrium, and she motioned for the servants to bring in wine and honey cakes. "Please be seated, sire."

After they'd discussed trivialities, Constantine said, "I must come to the purpose for this visit. I bring you greetings from your relatives, Cassus and Octavia."

"Oh," Domitilla said with feeling. "Thank you; we've been quite concerned about them since we learned of the death of their parents."

"And we thank you for your communication about Octavian and his wife," Bernini said. "Are Octavia and Cassus safe?"

"For the present, although they are both in hiding. I will not tell you where they are, for your protection as well as theirs, but they wanted you to know that they had escaped the persecution that claimed their parents."

"I've wished especially that Octavia could have come to us," Domitilla said. "Poor child—she will miss her mother."

Constantine smiled. "Octavia couldn't be in better hands, I assure you."

"Then we will be content with that," Domitilla said resolutely.

After a light repast, Lucius escorted Constantine back to the palace. When they were parting, Constantine said, "And what are your plans for the future, Lucius?"

"My future is a bit uncertain at this time, sire," Lucius said simply. "Presently, I'm helping my father with the family's affairs. I do not know what lies ahead for me."

"It's been my pleasure to meet other members of the Trento family, and I trust our paths will cross again." The dark pall of the future seemed to drift away at that moment, and Constantine had a momentary revelation of things to come. He saw his own life burst into prominence as bright as a meteor hurtling from the heavens, with Lucius Trento boosting the tail of that star.

❋ ❋ ❋

Since emperors customarily granted amnesty to many public offenders on special occasions relating to their reign, there was widespread hope that Diocletian would release the imprisoned clergy during the celebration of his vicennial, but no such announcement came. During Diocletian's stay, Lucius and members of the church in Rome awaited the persecution they expected to be unleashed against the general church membership, but the Emperor left the city without taking any notice of the church. Thinking that it was wise to retain some hold upon the emperor's court, one Christian clergyman was persuaded by his fellows to pretend to recant and join Diocletian's march in order to feed information to the Roman Christians. It was from him that they learned of Diocletian's movements over the next few months.

The emperor celebrated the New Year at Ravenna, and then became ill on his return to Nicomedia. In spite of his ill health, he spent the spring and early summer of 304 inspecting the Danube frontier, traveling for the most part in a litter. In the fall, Diocletian appeared in public to dedicate the circus adjoining the palace at Nicomedia, and for several weeks thereafter he was hardly seen by the public. Reports circulated that he had died, and although this proved to be false, Caesar Galerius decided to issue a fourth edict during the emperor's incapacitation. The edict stated that without exception, every man, woman, and child in the empire was to sacrifice and pour a libation to the gods of Rome. The Christians knew that perilous days were descending upon them.

Outside the city of Rome, guards were stationed, and a statue of the sun god was set up near the gates. All who passed were asked to offer a libation of holy oil on the altar. Those who refused were imprisoned. To forestall persecution, the church stopped its corporate meetings, but Lucius knew it was only a matter of time before he would be imprisoned, for soldiers constantly patrolled the streets and went from house to house to find offenders. Each person was asked, "Are you a Christian?" And those who steadfastly acknowledged their faith were arrested.

What to do with the Alabaster was Lucius's greatest concern. Finally, he wrapped the chest in a piece of leather, took it to the stable, and placed it beneath the trough where he fed the two lions. It wasn't likely that even the bravest of soldiers would trespass in the cage where Dan and Beersheba lived. On the pedestal in the chapel, he substituted a jar of perfume that his mother had recently imported from Arabia.

The family wondered how much Marcus was involved in the arrest of Christians, for they had not seen him for weeks. One night he arrived after dark and came into the atrium. The light from the oil lamp flickered on his armor as he looked gravely from one to the other of his family. In a guarded tone, he addressed his parents and Lucius. "The time has come for you to leave Rome. I may lose my head for warning you, but there's a limit to how far I can go."

"Then we're marked for arrest?" Bernini said.

"Tomorrow. Lucius is the main target, but it's well known that there is a chapel in the house and that Grandfather was a leader in the church. If you'll sacrifice to the traditional gods, you won't be bothered."

Bernini looked toward his wife. "Well, will you?" he asked gruffly.

Domitilla's face paled, but she said, "Not if I'm brave enough."

It seemed strange that Bernini didn't try to persuade his wife into the sacrifice, for he had bent her to his will more than once, but without argument, he said, "Then we'll leave Rome tonight. Perhaps we will be spared if we go to the country. Lucius, you are going with us?"

"No, Father. I want you to take Mother, but I will stay. I've been praying for days about my decision. The only answer I've gotten has been to see Jesus hanging on the cross. He died for me. I can do no less than that for Him."

Marcus struck his sword against the wall of the atrium. "I've done all I can do. I only hope the gods will grant me one favor and not have me assigned to arrest my own brother."

Domitilla and Bernini departed within the hour, and as Lucius stood in front of the house and watched them leave, he marveled at his father's departure. He could have sent Domitilla with trusted servants, and if he had sacrificed, he would have had no trouble. *Is the example of Ignatius so deeply ingrained in my father that when the test has come, he can not bring himself to deny the lordship of Jesus Christ?*

Lucius spent the night in the chapel praying for courage to endure persecution. He didn't have long to wait the next morning. He had just returned from feeding his animals when a knock sounded, and Angelo admitted ten soldiers to the chapel where Lucius awaited. With relief, Lucius noted that Marcus was not in command. His heart pounded, but he stood to face the intruders, thankful that the trembling inside didn't show outwardly.

"Are you Lucius Trento?" the tribune in charge demanded, and Lucius nodded.

"Are you a Christian?"

"Yes, I am," Lucius said in a voice that reminded him of his grandfather's. Ignatius would have been proud of him today.

"You have an opportunity to recant—to say that all religions except the worship of Roman's traditional gods are wrong."

"I believe that Jesus Christ is my Savior, that He died on a cross, but rose again to live in heaven where He has a home prepared for me."

"Then we will see that you soon occupy your new home." Upon the tribune's gesture, two soldiers seized Lucius's arms. "Destroy this place," the command was given, and Lucius watched with a sad heart and a sober countenance as the room's furnishings were demolished. The pedestal with the substitute Alabaster was the first to fall.

The prison where Lucius was taken was as crowded as Marcus had said, and he wondered where he would even find a place to sit down. One of his fellow Christians greeted Lucius when he was pushed into the dungeon. "It won't be this crowded tomorrow," the older man said. "I hear the prison will be emptied to provide fuel for the games."

Lucius suppressed a moan. *Anything but that!* He was prepared to endure months of imprisonment and hardship, even to have his head cut off, but to be torn into bits by wild beasts was too horrible to contemplate.

"We will spend the night in prayer and song," the Christian leader said. "We must not forget what happened to Paul and Silas in the Philippian jail. Perhaps God will work a similar victory for us."

Lucius was ashamed to admit that he was afraid, but he was. Now that he was at the point when it seemed he must die, he wanted most to live. *Why can't I be like Octavian and Atilia and face death with a song on my lips?* Lucius was thankful that he'd had the strength to refuse to recant, but wondered why he couldn't face death with courage.

Confused and ashamed, he sought a solitary corner rather than joining in the prayers of his fellow believers. Dampness from the continual dripping of water along the walls seeped into his body, and he pulled a woolen cloak around him. The stench of body odor from people who had been deprived too long of their baths stung his nostrils. Nearby a man coughed and sneezed. When food was thrown to the prisoners, Lucius chewed on the heavy brown bread that tasted like sand in his mouth.

Over and over, throughout the long night, Lucius mumbled what words he could remember from David's prayer when he was facing death.

"Have mercy upon me, God, show mercy toward me. I trust You to protect me under Your wings and become my refuge until this evil has passed. I beg of You, God, who does all things for me. Send Your Spirit from heaven and save me from my enemies. Thank You, God, for showing Your mercy and truth toward me. My soul is among lions, and I'm in the company of evil men with spears and arrows. But I would praise You, O God, who live higher than the heavens. Let Your glory be above all the earth. They have prepared a net to catch me, to bring my soul low. They've dug a pit in front of me, but, God, let them fall into it themselves. You have great mercy, O God, and regardless of tomorrow's outcome, I pray Your glory will fill all the earth."

In spite of Lucius's prayers and the songs and praise of the other prisoners, no miraculous happening had occurred by morning. Lucius and twenty-four other Christians were separated from among the prisoners and marched toward the arena. Lucius tried to join the others in rejoicing that they were counted worthy to suffer for Christ, but even as his lips voiced the words of the songs, inwardly over and over he prayed, "If it's possible let this cup pass from me. Not my will, but Yours be done."

With head down, he approached the gates of the arena and thought of the times he had been here with his family. His grandfather would never permit them to witness the executions, but they had good times watching the chariot races and acrobatic stunts. Now it was his turn to provide entertainment for the masses. The prisoners were surrounded by soldiers, and Lucius looked up quickly when a Roman soldier nudged him roughly.

Marcus!

"There's a horse ready for you on the street behind the arena beyond the stables," his brother muttered. "He's saddled, and I've provided enough provisions for several days. When you get free, leave this city at once."

Marcus moved on, and Lucius looked down with some mirth at his bound hands and shackled feet. *When I get free!* There didn't seem to be any danger of that.

Lucius's body shook, sweat glistened on his face, and his

throat was parched as one after another of the prisoners were led to their deaths. He heard the bellows of the tortured, starved animals as they pounced on their victims, and the clamor of the bloodthirsty crowds. The waiting was the worst of all; he wished he'd been taken first! What courage Lucius had disintegrated, but he held tenaciously to his faith. *Don't let me deny You, God, not even in my mind. Even if You don't deliver me, I know You have the power to do it.* He tried to remember every instance he could of Christians who had gone to their deaths bravely, their lips still praising the Lord. *Thank You, God, for Stephen and his example. Thank You for Octavian and Atilia. Blessed be the name of the Lord. The Lord giveth and taketh away.*

At last the soldiers came for him, and as they cut the thongs that secured his arms and removed the shackles from his feet, a sense of peace came over Lucius, and he had no desire to run. He had met the test, and his faith had remained. His captors gave him one more chance to put a drop of incense on the altar, but smiling he shook his head, and when they pushed him forward, Lucius didn't go with the faltering steps he had feared he would.

With a courage that he didn't know he possessed, Lucius strode into the arena inviting the attack of the animals. *Will it be lions or panthers that will attack me? Or perhaps a brown bear from India?*

He didn't try to elude the attackers by hiding behind the posts, but stood unprotected in the middle of the area already stained with the blood of his fellow Christians. The clanging of a gate alerted him and he wheeled. A lion and lioness bolted across the empty space toward him. When they almost reached him, the lion stopped, bared his teeth, emitted a throaty roar, and switched his tail.

Dan!

Lucius quickly turned his gaze to the lioness watching him with a friendly gaze. Somehow Marcus had exchanged these two pets for the ferocious beasts; now the rest was up to him. *Is it God's will that my life is to be spared?* He jumped at Dan as he had when the lion was a cub. Dan took his cue and wrestled Lucius to the ground. After a short tussle, Lucius pushed him aside and started to run. Beersheba leaped on his back and rolled him to the ground. Then with a thrust, she hurled Lucius through the air toward Dan. Lucius was on his feet when he faced the lion. The wrestling went on until exhaustion swept over Lucius. He whispered into the animals's ears, "Play dead." And they both flopped over on their sides and appeared to be lifeless.

The entertaining threesome had kept the audience in an up-roar, and when Lucius leaped to his feet without a scratch upon him—although he hoped that wasn't too obvious—he bowed before the officials asking for mercy.

"Release him! Give him his life," the crowd chanted, and the director of the games lifted his arm.

Not knowing how long his reprieve would last, Lucius lost no time heading for the gate. He did take one look to see what had happened to Dan and Beersheba. The attendants were drag-ging the still-immobile lions from the arena. He wished he could stay and see that they, too, were out of danger, but he owed his life to Marcus, and he knew he had to leave the city before this hoax was discovered.

Lucius hurried around the stable and found a saddled horse loaded for travel. A note was attached to the roll of provisions. "If this scheme works, put on the clothes in the bag, hide in the woods until night, and leave Rome. Don't go back home. I'll explain to our parents."

Lucius headed toward the nearest woods, the forest belong-ing to Plotina's father, not sure he was safe even there, for Flavius had never spoken to any Trento since her death. When he was safe from scrutiny, he searched in the pack Marcus had pro-vided. He found a bag of gold coins and, instead of the rich toga of a Roman, a dark gray garment, wax tablets, and a stylus. No doubt Marcus is expecting me to pass as a scribe. *It isn't a bad idea,* Lucius thought with a grin.

The hours of waiting seemed interminable as he pondered the miracle of his delivery. *God has saved me for some purpose, but what is it?* When it was sufficiently dark that Lucius thought he could safely mingle with the mounted throng that always crowded Rome's streets at night, he headed his horse northward. He felt uneasy about leaving because he didn't know when he could ever return. He swung back into the forest and tied his horse to a tree. Then he warily crossed the stream and crawled toward the stable at the rear of the Trento house. He knew he might be in grave danger, especially if it were now known why he hadn't been devoured by the lions, but there was something he had to do.

He made it to the stable without incident, but once inside, Bento squawked at him. He quieted the bird and then lit a candle to guide his way to the lion's cage. A throaty growl greeted him, but when he spoke softly, the growling ceased. Only one lion was in the cage.

"Dan," he whispered, "how did you get back here, and where's Beersheba?" Not expecting an answer, Lucius unlocked the cage. He knelt beside the feeding trough, reached his hand underneath, and with a sigh of relief, pulled out the wrapped box he had placed there several days ago. He considered going into the house to find some weapons, but he supposed he must be content with the dagger he had found in his pack. Tucking the box under his arm, he started to relock the lion's cage, but upon impulse, he left the door ajar and whistled for Dan to accompany him.

They made a strange procession as they wended their way out of Rome—a gray-clad scribe holding a cedar box on the saddle in front of him, followed by a huge lion, whose padded paws made little sound—nor did they incite much interest. It was as if the eyes of the Romans had been blinded to the exit of Lucius and his pet.

9

NICOMEDIA, 305

The rainy season had caused the winter to seem long in Nicomedia, but today a brilliant sun had made the peristyle a place of warmth and beauty, and Constantine had sought his favorite chair near the fountain. Normally he never tired of reading Greek literature, but Constantine caught himself time and again squirming in the chair and staring into space. He finally laid aside his reading and paced the mosaic paths of the garden.

Glancing with a speculative eye toward the imperial bedchamber, he made a quick decision, draped his toga around his shoulders, and headed outside. Diocletian usually slept all afternoon, so surely he wouldn't be needed during the time it took for a brisk walk around the outer periphery of the palace.

Doves intent on nesting squatted on the stone walls and when a shadow passed over him, Constantine peered toward the sky and watched a falcon, graceful wings spread wide, swoop downward toward its prey on the ground.

Constantine breathed deeply as he strode along the street. Having been promoted to the emperor's bodyguard meant staying close to him, and Diocletian had rarely left the city for more than a year. *How much more of this inactivity can I stand?*

Jostled suddenly out of his reverie by a man who nudged his

left side, Constantine broke stride and moved his hand quickly to his sword.

"Pardon me, sir," the man said. "Excuse my clumsiness."

Constantine took in the drab tunic of the servant before he encountered his eyes. Instantly recognizing the man before him, he stifled his comment when a warning hand was laid on his arm.

"Allow me to introduce myself," Cassus said, once Constantine recognized the need for secrecy. "I'm a servant of Lanitra, a wealthy widow who is residing at the former Trento property in this town. Perhaps you would like to call upon her at your convenience."

"I'm not master of my own decisions, but I will come at the first opportunity, " Constantine said. Cassus bowed and passed on down the street, leaving Constantine with dozens of questions.

Two days passed before Constantine found another occasion to leave the palace, taking advantage of a time when Diocletian's physician stated that the emperor needed rest and should not be disturbed. In a roundabout way, he approached the Trento home, finding it still in a state of disrepair due to the attacks that had been made on the property of Christians.

Upon Constantine's knock, Cassus, still dressed as a servant, opened the door and ushered him inside.

"We've been waiting for you," Cassus said, and directed Constantine's attention to a fair-haired woman entering the vestibule from another room. "Friend, I want you to meet my wife of six weeks. Lanitra, this is my longtime friend, Constantine."

Once the greetings were exchanged, the three entered the atrium and Lanitra brought glasses of sweet wine.

"And when did you arrive in Nicomedia?" Constantine inquired.

"Ten days ago, and I've hovered around the palace often to catch a glimpse of you."

Constantine grimaced as he set his cup aside and waved away Lanitra's attempt to refill it.

"I'm seldom outside the walls. I now have the elevated position of being one of the emperor's bodyguards, and he wants his body guarded most of the time. I've chafed at being a near-prisoner for years, and this last year it's been worse."

"Diocletian is very ill, I've heard," Cassus stated.

Constantine nodded. "But why have you returned to Nicomedia? The ban on Christians is still in effect."

"Call it homesickness, call it stubbornness, or whatever, but I couldn't stay in exile any longer. I'm probably as safe here as in Alexandria Troas anyway, especially if I can effect this disguise."

"We went by Drepanum on our way here to see Octavia," Lanitra said, "and we bring you news of your mother and son. Crispus is a splendid boy, much taller than you would expect of a child of five, and your mother is lovely."

"Yes, I saw them about six months ago, and I felt that she thrives on the hard work in the inn. But I still want to take her away from that life. She's had enough hardship—I'd like for her to live at ease during her remaining years."

"Your mother doesn't impress me as being the type of person to be happy with folded hands," Lanitra said, "but your intent is honorable."

"Rumor has it that Diocletian is on the verge of abdication," Cassus said. "Do you think that is true?"

"I know no more than any other citizen, for since the emperor's extended illness, Caesar Galerius spends most of his time in Nicomedia, making imperial decisions. While it's understand-able that Valeria would want to be near her father and of help to her mother, still it rankles many of us that Galerius has assumed so much authority."

"By now I would have thought the persecution of Christians would have waned, but Galerius is apparently the one who keeps the fires of conflict fanned into a blaze," Cassus said.

"That's true, for Diocletian no longer cares what happens to the empire. He's only a shell of the man he was."

"How do you stand with Galerius?"

"Not well, and I fear for my life if he assumes the purple. I've been on several military campaigns with Galerius, and it seems that I'm always given the most dangerous assignments. I've often suspected that he has designs on my life, and I want to go away. My father would like for me to join him, but I dare not leave without an official dismissal."

❀　❀　❀

As he walked along the crowded streets after leaving the Trentos, Constantine contemplated the reasons he had come to distrust Galerius. He had thought all day about the narrow escapes he'd had over the past few years. Perhaps the near-accident yesterday when he had gone boar hunting with Galerius and some of his soldiers had brought the other incidents to mind. Galerius had apologized profusely when his horse nudged Constantine's as they were closing in for the kill on the angry boars, but when Constantine's horse had thrown him, he was left at the mercy of the two charging animals. *Did Galerius and his men react slowly in rescuing me? Would they have helped me at all if I hadn't jumped quickly behind a soldier's mount?* And Constantine could recall several battles the past few years when he had narrowly escaped losing his life, and always Galerius had been nearby. *Do I pose such a threat to Galerius? If so, I would do well to guard my back at all times.* Constantine had many friends here in the palace, but if Diocletian should die, Galerius would take command, and he would be quick to eliminate any opposition. Constantine decided he would have to be especially wary of strangers.

He recalled his need of self-protection the next morning when a man entered the peristyle from the east, stood hesitantly until he located Constantine, and came directly toward him. The man looked familiar, but remembering his thought about strangers, Constantine waited watchfully with a hand on the hilt of his sword.

"Ho, Constantine," the man said upon nearing. "It's been a long time since our last meeting."

Constantine studied the man's face, but recognition eluded him.

"Maxentius," the man said with a smile, "and I'm not happy that you don't remember your old comrade. We had many a good hunt when you used to visit our palace at Aquileia."

The men clasped hands and Constantine said heartily, "Maxentius! I haven't seen you since I joined Diocletian's court. That's sufficient reason not to recognize you. And how is your father, Maximian?"

"Worried! That's the reason he dispatched me to appraise the situation here in Nicomedia."

Constantine had last visited the court of Maximian, the Augustus of the West, the year Constantius had become a Caesar and had been forced to set Helena aside for a more advantageous political marriage to Maximian's stepdaughter, Theodora. Constantine had stayed at the palace for the wedding, then he had been ordered to Nicomedia to attend Diocletian.

Constantine resumed his seat on the bench and motioned for Maxentius to join him. "When did you arrive in Nicomedia?"

"Just this morning. I've paid my respects to the emperor and delivered my father's greetings, but I doubt that he even recognized me."

Constantine nodded. "He has days like that."

Maxentius lowered his voice. "We've heard many tales about the ill health of Augustus Diocletian, and my father thought it was in his best interest, and mine, to have a member of our family present at the court. Do you know what Diocletian plans to do?"

"No. I've never been invited to sit in on the conferences between Diocletian and Galerius, nor have I been taken into the latter's confidence. How goes the empire in the West?"

"All is well with both your father and mine. I hear that Constantius has built his capital at Treves into a place of beauty, and except for an occasional attack by the northern tribes, he lives in peace."

"What about the Christian persecution?"

Looking around him before he spoke, Maxentius said, "No one paid much attention to the edicts. Many Christians have fled to the West to escape persecution. Maximian and Constantius both made a few arrests and pulled down a ramshackle building or two, but the oppression hardly exists in the West."

"It makes no sense to wipe out an industrious group of people who make up a tenth or more of the population. I'm glad our fathers had the prudence to desist," Constantine noted.

"Which they probably couldn't have done if the emperor had not been beset by ill health."

"True. I look forward to your company, Maxentius. I've spent a year of boredom."

"If I judge correctly, there will be a change soon."

"But whether it will be worse or better for us, who knows?"

"No one, but the gods and Diocletian."

❋　❋　❋

Diocletian rallied from his illness, and after several days of consultation with Galerius, messengers were sent throughout the empire summoning important personages to appear at Nicomedia on the first day of May. When Maxentius received his notice, he sought Constantine out.

"What's going on, do you know?"

"The rumor is that the emperor is retiring."

"Then that will leave Galerius in charge. And what of my father?"

"Again the rumor is that Maximian will be ordered to resign also."

"That will not make him happy," Maxentius said with a laugh. "There's nothing wrong with *his* health!"

"But he owes his office to Diocletian, so I suppose he will step down."

"And then what?" Maxentius wondered.

Constantine shook his head. He didn't trust Maxentius enough to share his own anxiety and conclusions. If Maximian and Diocletian were both gone, then it seemed likely that Galerius and Constantius would be elevated to the position of Augusti, and didn't it follow that Constantine, as the son of Constantius, and Maxentius, as the son of Maximian, would become the Caesars? Since Galerius had no children, this seemed the only solution to Constantine.

❋   ❋   ❋

Whenever he could slip away from the court, Constantine continued his visits to the home of Cassus, and one day in late April when he arrived, the Trentos had company—a brawny, heavily muscled Roman soldier. Beside him, Cassus, who was not a small man, seemed dwarf-sized.

"This is my cousin, Marcus Trento," Cassus introduced. "He has come to Nicomedia as an escort to the governor of Rome, who was commanded by Diocletian to be here on May 1."

Marcus saluted Constantine. "You did my family the honor of visiting them in Rome two years ago. I'm sorry I missed you then."

"They received me well," Constantine said. "How did they fare during the recent persecutions?"

"Father is not a Christian, so he was in no danger. My parents did leave Rome for a few months, but they've returned now that the oppression is less severe."

"I've wondered often about Lucius, the young man of the family. A brilliant scholar, I perceived."

"My twin," Marcus said proudly. "He's always been the studious one, while I was the rebellious son. As the firstborn, I should be in Rome helping my father in the family business, but that life was too tame for me." With an amused smile, he added, "Lucius is not in Rome at this time, however."

"Is this your first time in Nicomedia?"

"Yes." Marcus said, his eyes glittering excitedly, "and I can hardly wait to find out what the emperor has in mind."

❋   ❋   ❋

Constantine was one of the soldiers who formed a mounted honor guard around the ailing emperor's litter as he was borne to a site three miles outside of Nicomedia. The gathering was to occur at the very spot where Diocletian had been proclaimed ruler of the empire in 284. Two chamberlains assisted the emperor from the litter and practically carried him up the steps of a small dais beneath a column topped with a statue of Jupiter, the patron deity of Diocletian.

"My friends, I've come here today to advise you of a decision that will make vast changes in the empire." His voice faded and the emperor's shoulders shook convulsively as he wept.

Constantine closed his eyes. He could not look upon this pitiful creature who had once been the most powerful man in the world. *What has brought about Diocletian's downfall? Was Lactantius right in saying that all enemies of Christianity will be brought to their knees in this fashion?*

Diocletian gained control of his emotions and continued, although his voice still faltered. "Here under the emblem of my patron god, where in my vigor I took upon myself the purple vestment of the Roman Empire, I lay aside that mantle in favor of others who are strong enough to carry on the work."

Constantine sensed that the eyes of many had turned toward him, but he kept his eyes focused on the dais, his heart pounding in his chest.

Diocletian turned toward his son-in-law. "In my place as Augustus, I pass the work to Galerius, who has been my right hand in the East for many years." No surprise there, for Galerius had obviously been groomed for the job.

"In Milan today, I have commanded my old comrade-in-arms, Maximian, to abdicate in favor of Constantius Chlorus, who will have precedence over Galerius."

Cheers from the crowd interrupted Diocletian, for many of these soldiers had served under Constantius in Gaul, and they had a high respect for him.

"I have also instructed Maximian to raise Septimus Severus to the office of Caesar of the West."

At Constantine's side, Maxentius gasped audibly, and all around him surprise was evident by the stirring of feet. Constantine still hadn't given up hope that he would be named until Galerius led his nephew, Maximinus Daia, forward. Diocletian removed his purple toga and placed it over the shoulders of Maximinus, making him the Caesar of the East.

Determined not to be a poor loser, Constantine stared straight ahead, hoping that his disappointment did not show on his face, but inside anger boiled up in him like a volcano. For sixteen years he'd danced attendance upon Diocletian only to be passed over without even an honorable mention. Although he acknowledged that Galerius was the instigator of these appointments, Constantine was disappointed that Diocletian had so misused him, but he kept his frustration to himself.

Maxentius was not so subtle. After their return to the palace, he stormed into Constantine's room without even knocking. "Are we going to accept this decision without a fight?"

"What else can we do? You should have been aware that this might happen—you know that Diocletian has never planned for the positions of Caesar to become hereditary."

"I could understand that if no heir was suitable for the job, but we've both proven ourselves as leaders. Besides serving admirably in the army, you're one of the best-read men in Nicomedia, and I've worked beside Maximian for years. I know everything that he knows. Galerius is the cause of this. Of course, I've never made any secret that I dislike him."

"Nor have I."

"But to think we were passed over for Severus and Maximinus."

"They're both excellent soldiers," Constantine reminded him. "In spite of his age, Maximinus has been a foot soldier, a bodyguard of the emperor, and a tribune."

"He has some good qualities, but he's a creature of Galerius and will do exactly as he says. And Severus is nothing but a violent, hard-drinking soldier."

"I repeat, Maxentius, there's nothing we can do about it."

Maxentius's face took on a secretive look, and he said, "I'm not so sure about that. I'm leaving Nicomedia today. I'm going to Milan to see my father before I make any decisions." He lifted his hand in farewell and exited quickly.

Constantine stifled his disappointment and stayed at the palace until the ailing Diocletian removed himself, his closest friends, and a few of his guards to the new palace he had built for his retirement years in his native Illyria. Constantine counted himself fortunate not to be chosen to accompany Diocletian.

While Constantine was wondering what he could do, an urgent message came to Galerius from Constantius Chlorus, pleading ill health and asking Galerius to send his son, Constantine, to him. A similar note was sent to Constantine, and upon receipt of it, he requested an audience with Galerius, but the new Augustus kept him waiting for a week.

Constantine noted that thus far Galerius hadn't assumed the trappings of an exalted monarch as Diocletian had done, and it was a relief, for he doubted that he could have brought himself to kiss the hem of Galerius's robe.

"I've had a communication from your father, Centurion," Galerius said, taking the initiative. "He cites ill health as a reason for wanting you at his side."

"That is right, Augustus, and I beg your indulgence in granting his request. You have your own protectors, so it's hardly necessary for you to keep the guard of the former emperor. At this point it seems that I can be of more benefit to the empire if I'm in the company of my father."

"What of your son and your mother? Where are they?"

Constantine hesitated. *No doubt Valeria knows their whereabouts, but would she betray a fellow Christian to her husband? Should I lie or dissimulate?* But even now, Galerius probably knew where they were and was trying to test him.

"My mother and son are at Drepanum, where her brother operates an inn. She left here several months ago when her brother was ill and has not returned."

"They would be welcome at the court of Galerius."

Constantine bowed. "The emperor is kind. I will send that information when I communicate with them again. But in the meantime, do I have your permission to visit my father?"

"Is this a visit or a permanent move?"

"I understand that Constantius is preparing to embark on an invasion of Britain. I should like to arrive in time to accompany him on that mission. Since he is now the Augustus in the West, I would await his further orders." It wouldn't hurt to remind Galerius that Constantius was the senior Augustus and therefore could have ordered the Augustus of the East to send Constantine to his father.

"I will think on the matter and give you my decision tomorrow."

It was late the next day before Constantine was called into Galerius's presence. "I've decided," Galerius said, "that you may journey to your father. Leave tomorrow. I've ordered a half-century of soldiers to accompany you at high noon."

Constantine bowed. "Thank you. I'll be ready."

When Constantine raised his head quickly, he noted a look of hatred in Galerius's eyes. As he left the room, he puzzled over the Augustus's attitude. He obviously didn't want him to go to Constantius, yet it was plain that Galerius disliked him. *Why would Galerius want me to stay in Nicomedia?*

Constantine went to the stable and saw to the grooming of his three horses. He would take the extra mounts because the journey across the Alps at any season could be hazardous, and he needed some extra animals. With this done, he checked the army barracks adjacent to the palace to see who would command the detail of men who would go with him tomorrow. He came away from that interview with additional disquiet. The centurion in charge of the group was Galerius's chief executioner. *Why would the*

Augustus want to part with the executioner for several months while he escorts me to the coast and then return? Or does Galerius not expect him to be gone long? Am I being overly suspicious? Constantine couldn't forget the narrow escapes he'd had in the past for which he had blamed Galerius.

Deep in thought as he left the barracks, Constantine would have passed by Marcus Trento without a word if Marcus hadn't called, "Ho, Constantine! You look as if you have the burden of the world on your shoulders."

"Greetings, Marcus. The emperor has given me permission to leave Nicomedia tomorrow to join my father, so I should be content since that's what I've wanted to do for many years."

"But you're not happy about it?"

"Happy to be leaving, but dare I confess that I don't always trust the emperor?"

Marcus laughed. "Then you join a host of other people who feel the same, including me. Augustus Galerius has not always dealt kindly with the Trentos, as you well know."

"When do you return to Rome?"

"I'm ready for further assignment, and I will tarry here until I receive my orders."

When they parted at the main entrance to the palace, Constantine said, "Convey my greetings to the senior servant in the Trento home."

Marcus laughed and went on his way. Constantine supped lightly, then sought his couch. He was not sleepy, but the events of the day had jaded him. *How can I protect myself from Galerius's picked men?* He closed his eyes, and as weariness overtook him, he seemingly slept, but ever afterward he would wonder if he had been dreaming or if he had experienced a vision.

"Constantine. Constantine." His name was repeated over and over, and roused at last, Constantine sat up and reached for the sword by his side. "Who is it?" he said, and his eyes scanned the dim light to find the speaker.

He sensed a presence in the room, but he could see nothing.

Frightened, he swung his legs over the side of the couch. "Who is it?" he repeated.

His question wasn't answered, but the voice spoke again. "Galerius is planning to take your life. He has arranged for an ambush the second day of your journey. The soldiers will join your attackers."

"But what can I do? I would be one against many," Constantine said, feeling foolish talking to nothing, but at his wit's end to know how to deal with this situation.

"Do not wait until tomorrow. You have the emperor's permission to depart Nicomedia. Do not delay. Leave tonight."

Suddenly, Constantine felt that the room was empty. Judging by the length of the burned candle, he must have been in the room four hours. It didn't occur to Constantine to disobey the command. He quickly gathered the items he had laid aside to take tomorrow and rolled them into a pack. He slung his heavy sandals over his arm and drew his warmest toga around his shoulders.

With bare feet, he crept out into the peristyle, waited until the guard at Diocletian's door turned his back for a moment, and then slithered along the mosaic path that opened on the street. At the stables, the guards were all in a deep sleep, and they didn't stir as he led out his three horses, tied his pack on the back of one of them, and walked the animals quietly away from the palace. Constantine had a strange sensation that someone was directing his steps, as if an unseen hand had put its protection around him.

No one intercepted him as he made his way quietly to the Trento home, and his persistent knocking finally brought an answer. Cassus held an oil lamp when he opened the door. "Constantine!"

"May I come in for a moment?" When the door closed behind him, Constantine said quietly, "I'm leaving Nicomedia tonight, and I wanted someone to know. If I shouldn't arrive at my father's, you can notify my mother."

"Why the secret departure?"

Constantine hesitated to talk about his dream. "I fear for my life if I wait until tomorrow. It seems prudent to leave tonight."

In spite of their low voices, they had disturbed Marcus, and he entered the room. "You're not planning to travel alone?" he said.

"I have no choice. I can't take the chance of asking anyone to go with me. I don't know who's loyal to the emperor and who isn't."

"But it's dangerous to go so far alone. If you'll give me a moment to prepare, my slave and I will accompany you. I received my orders this afternoon to proceed to the army led by Constantius. I was to travel with a legion of soldiers next week, but I will send word that an emergency dictated that I leave sooner."

"Won't that cause you trouble?"

"No, my centurion is quite favorable toward me."

"Then if you insist, I'll appreciate your company."

In a short time, the three men rode quietly out of Nicomedia. Once they were free of the city, they put their horses to an accelerated pace, wanting as much distance as possible between them and the city before daylight. A full moon lighted their way, and they made no stops until they came to the strait connecting the Pontus Euxinus with the Sea of Marmara. At the guardhouse there, Constantine slipped quietly into the stable, and in a short time, he had accomplished his purpose.

Mounting again, they swam their horses across the strait and headed eastward. At the next guardhouse, Constantine halted and entered the stable. When he returned, and they continued their journey, Marcus said, "I'm curious. What are you doing?"

"Killing the horses. That will cut off pursuit. If Galerius sends his legions, they won't have any fresh horses."

"I heard no cries of pain from the animals."

"Horses don't make much disturbance when they've had a spear thrust through their hearts."

"That's pretty hard on the horses," Marcus said, not quite approving.

"But on the other hand, my life is pretty important to me."

"You do have a point there. Lead on."

They traveled at night for over a week, avoiding army barracks and large cities and staying off the main Roman roads. Within a month, they reached the summit of the Alps, where they considered themselves safely out of Galerius's hands. They slowed their pace, knowing that the journey would go more quickly as they descended the mountains. Carefully wending their way downward, the roar of a lion wafted toward them, and Constantine said, "Surely there are no lions in these mountains!"

"There's one, at least, " Marcus said as they rounded a bend on the narrow mountain trail. Standing in the road before them was a lion, his golden mane raised, and his teeth bared in a snarl. He stood over the lifeless form of a man beneath his feet.

"Looks like we spoiled his feast," Constantine said. "Poor devil!" He lifted his spear and pointed it toward the lion, but Marcus caught his arm.

"Wait!"

10

Gaul, 306

The horses reared in fright, and Marcus had his hands full controlling his mount while at the same time trying to stay Constantine's arm.

"What do you mean, 'Wait'? As soon as the beast finishes that man, he'll turn on us."

"But the man may be my brother, and if so, that's his pet lion. If you'll hold my horse, I'll go closer and try to see if it is Lucius."

"If it isn't a pet lion, you're in trouble."

Dismounting, Marcus handed the lines to Sulla. Constantine looked at Marcus as if he'd taken leave of his senses, and he held his spear in readiness. "Pet or not—if he attacks you, I'm hurling the spear."

Marcus laughed warily. "And he may do so."

He inched his way forward. "Dan," he called. "Dan."

The lion is standing his ground, but is there a spark of recognition? The giant beast moved his head slightly, perhaps not so tense as he had been. Marcus dared to move closer, but the lion tossed his head, growled menacingly, and took a step forward. Marcus shifted his attention to the man. *It is Lucius, I'm sure of it, but is he dead or alive?*

"Lucius!" he shouted. "Lucius!"

The figure on the ground moved slightly and groaned.

"Thank God, he's alive," Marcus said, and even in that moment of stress, marveled that he had called on the God of his fathers rather than Mithra, the new god he'd now enthroned in his life.

"Lucius, it's Marcus. We'll help you, but you'll have to call off Dan. You know he has never liked me."

Lucius stirred and weakly lifted a hand to touch the lion. Dan deliberately scanned the three men before him, and he growled another warning before he slowly reclined beside Lucius, his face on his paws, heeding the command of his master but obviously not pleased about it.

Marcus eased forward, still not completely satisfied that the lion wouldn't attack him. Glancing over his shoulder, he saw that Constantine had not relaxed his vigil. Marcus knelt by his twin's side, placed an arm under his shoulders, and lifted him slightly. There didn't seem to be any sign of injury, so he apparently hadn't been set upon by robbers.

In spite of the cool air around them, Lucius's skin felt hot to the touch. "What's the matter, Lucius? Can you hear me? What happened to you?"

Without opening his eyes, Lucius smiled and said softly, "Marcus to the rescue again! Seems as if I owe you two favors now. I don't know what's wrong. I've been sick for days, and I can't find any habitation in these mountains or anyone to help me."

Marcus turned to Constantine. "Can we take him with us, sir? If not, I'll have to stay behind and care for him."

"Who's with you?" Lucius whispered.

"Sulla and Constantine. You remember Constantine, don't you? He's from Nicomedia, a friend of Cassus."

Keeping his distance from Dan, Constantine moved forward. "I can't delay long, or I might miss making contact with my father." Looking eastward, he said, "And I'm still not easy in my mind about pursuit from Galerius."

"Do you think you can ride, Lucius? Where's your horse?"

Lucius shook his head. "He may have wandered away. Must find him. The Alabaster is in the saddlebags."

"And what is the Alabaster?" Constantine asked.

"Oh, just a keepsake in our family," Marcus said offhandedly. "Sulla, see if you can find his horse."

Constantine knelt beside the two brothers. "I traveled this way when I went to Nicomedia years ago, and I believe we'll reach a village in a day or two. It seems to me that he has typhus. I have some herbs in my gear. We can treat him with those and take him with us. He can be tied on his horse, but what are we going to do with that big cat? Our horses are still skittish. If he's along, I daresay we'll all have a difficult journey, and these mountain trails are not designed for frightened horses."

"Dan is my brother's pet and not dangerous unless someone threatens Lucius."

"Marcus, any lion is dangerous," Constantine insisted.

Marcus stood to his feet and, with a stubborn set to his jaw, said, "I won't be a party to destroying the lion. If we take Lucius, Dan will come, too. I'll stay behind and take care of him if you want to journey on."

"Does it occur to you that you're disagreeing with a centurion of the first rank, soldier?"

"Yes, sir, but I might remind you that I haven't been placed under your command."

Constantine laughed. "Have it your way, but I'm keeping my spear ready. We'll try it, but if either your brother or his pet cause us any delay, I'll travel on."

"Fair enough," Marcus said. He heard shod hooves on the rocky ground. "I see Sulla has found the horse."

The rest of that day's travel was slow, not only because Marcus had to ride beside Lucius's mount and support him on the animal, but also because the trail was treacherous as they started their descent of the Alps. Marcus rode in front and set the pace, for the horses acted normally when they could see Dan, plodding along beside Lucius's mount. But if the lion was behind them, the horses broke into a run, which could mean disaster on the steep terrain.

Lucius had lost consciousness by the time they made camp for the night, but Sulla bathed his face in cold water until he roused.

"Do you want something to eat?" Marcus asked. "Our supplies are low, and about all we can offer is bread and cheese."

"I'll try the cheese and some sweet wine if you have any."

"No wine, but there is a stream with cold clear water nearby."

"That will be fine. I'm very thirsty."

Marcus leaned his brother against the trunk of a large fir tree because he didn't have the strength to sit erect without some support.

"What are you doing here? You were the last person I'd have expected to meet. I thought I was dreaming when you called my name," Lucius said.

"I was commanded to go to Nicomedia with Rome's governor as an honor guard to be present when Diocletian abdicated. Or did you know that had happened?"

"No, since I left Rome, I've stayed away from the major centers, going into villages only when I've needed supplies. I've slept outside most of the time, but one rainy night I took refuge in a vermin-infested inn, and that's where I picked up this fever."

"There have been many major changes. Diocletian abdicated and forced Maximian to do the same. Constantius and Galerius are the Augusti now, and Septimus Severus and Maximinus Daia are the Caesars."

"Those appointments will not benefit the Christians," Lucius predicted.

"No, except for Constantius, who has been tolerant of that faith. But you should rest, Lucius. We're hopeful that tomorrow we will reach a village where you can find refuge."

"But what of you? Where are you going?"

"Constantine feared for his life if he had stayed in Nicomedia now that Galerius is in control, and he's rushing to make contact with his father, Constantius, before he invades Britain. I've been assigned to take part in that expedition."

❀   ❀   ❀

Travel was not any easier the next day, but in late evening, they arrived at a small village, which offered little in the way of help, but the residents directed them to a farm outside of the town, and they moved on. After a few miles, they looked down on the most pleasant site Lucius had seen for many days.

Farm buildings were nestled in a narrow valley, and up the slopes of the steep hills, row after row of grapevines marched like soldiers on parade. Olive trees spread along the river valley, and grain fields shimmered and waved as softly as the ocean.

"I assume that's the Rhone River," Marcus said, and Constantine nodded.

Lucius had stayed erect most of the day, but he'd had little to say. "I'll have to put Dan on a leash," he said. "There's one in my gear, and if you'll help me off the horse, I'll try to walk and lead him."

"That's a good idea. No one would welcome us with an unchained lion," Constantine said.

As they drew nearer, farm animals scattered, instinctively fearing the big animal. Several men confronted the strangers as they rounded the corner of a large barn. The spacious house attached to the barn was surrounded by hedges of myrtle and roses blooming in well-kept plots.

Constantine held up his hand. "We come in peace," he said. "I'm Constantine, eldest son of Constantius Chlorus, Augustus of the West. I'm seeking shelter for the night and help for one of our company who is ill."

One of the farmers—a stalwart, bearded man—stepped forward. "We had the privilege of entertaining Constantius Chlorus a year ago. You are welcome here." To a boy who had appeared beside him, he said, "Tell my wife we have guests." As the boy sped toward the house, he said, "Conrad of Corneille at your service, sire."

Conrad personally conducted the travelers to a small room between the barn and the house. "You may stack your gear here, but I offer you the hospitality of my home."

Lucius tied Dan to a post, and at his command, the animal dropped to the ground. Conrad ushered them into his square, stone house, which consisted of a huge room that was kitchen, bedroom, and living room all in one. On the hearth of a stone fireplace that dominated the room, meat turned on a spit tended by two women. The room was dark because daylight entered only through thin slits in the walls. Flickering candles cast shadows around the room. The aroma of warm food permeated the place. The older woman, introduced as Hannah, came forward, bowed to her guests, and took charge of Lucius.

"You will lie on this pallet near the fireplace where I can watch you." With a grateful smile, he allowed her to lead him to the bed.

As Lucius passed the fireplace, the other woman looked up, and he saw her beautiful face, framed in blonde hair, with eyes as blue as the sky. She smiled at him, and Lucius lifted a hand to his heart. He felt as if he'd been stabbed.

"Felice," the older woman said, "Bring some warm water so I can bathe him."

Felice brought the bowl of water and returned to her duties at the fireplace without speaking. "Felice is my daughter," the older woman said as she bathed his face and hands. He had clean clothing in his pack, but he was too weary to search for it now.

In a short time, Constantine and Marcus were seated at the long wooden table with their host while the women set a platter of roast mutton covered with boiled leeks, and a pot of lentils before them. Barley bread fresh from the oven was served with a pot of warm honey.

"You should not have the meat," Hannah said as she brought Lucius a slice of bread covered with honey. "And here is a bowl of warm goat's milk. You have had a bad fever, but you're better now," she said running a hand over Lucius's forehead. He leaned against the wall to eat and listened to the conversation, but he was too weary to talk. After Lucius ate, Hannah gave him a potion of hot herb water. When Lucius began to nod, he motioned for Marcus to join him.

"What are your plans?" Lucius asked in Greek so that their hosts would not understand.

"We will leave here early in the morning, so this is our last opportunity to talk," Marcus answered in Greek.

"I need to know some things. What of our parents? Are they safe?"

"The persecutions have slowed down now, and they've returned to Rome. Father will not permit Mother to go to any worship service of the church, so they should be safe for the time being. They are concerned about you, missing you very much, but wanting you to stay away until all danger is past."

"Can you send them word that I'm safe?"

"Yes. Soldiers have access to the official government post, and I will send them a message."

"What happened after I left Rome? Was the hoax discovered?"

"Apparently not. No one seemed to suspect that I'd substituted your pets for the ferocious animals."

"But what about Beersheba? Why wasn't she in the stable when I returned there?"

"When you returned there against my instructions, I might add," Marcus said.

"I couldn't leave the Alabaster behind."

"I knew you wouldn't want to, but when I looked for it, there was no sign of it in the wrecked chapel."

"No, because I'd hidden it in the lion cage. And when I got there, it seemed a good idea to bring Dan with me, but what about Beersheba. Was she killed?"

"Not as far as I know, but I wasn't able to separate her from the other animals, and she's being used in the games. Once she got the taste of human blood, her wildness returned, and there was no way to rescue her then."

"Where is Dan now?"

"He's in the room where we stored our gear. Conrad wasn't keen about having him inside, but he didn't want him prowling around the farm either."

"Please help me out to that room. He might attack these kind strangers if I'm not with him."

Although Conrad protested that a guest should not stay in the shed, he obviously was afraid of the lion, so he provided sheep-skins to make a soft bed for Lucius.

"I've made arrangements for you to stay here until you're well," Marcus assured his brother, "but then what?"

"I don't know. I hope to find some kind of employment, for my funds are almost gone. There are several large cities here in Gaul, and I should find something to do. But how will I make contact with you? Where will you be?"

"Following Constantine, I suppose. Some of us thought he would be chosen as a Caesar, but since he wasn't, perhaps the gods have something better in store for him."

❀ ❀ ❀

Within a few days of the departure of Constantine and Marcus, Lucius was able to leave his pallet and sit in a chair, thanks to the nourishing foods and herb treatments of Felice and Hannah. All of the family took an interest in his recovery, and they counted it worthy of a celebration when Lucius joined them at the table for a meal.

The family used a local vernacular that Lucius couldn't understand, but Conrad spoke Latin fluently and the others could converse slightly in Lucius's native tongue.

"Now that you have regained some strength," Conrad said, "you must visit the hot springs. In the morning, I will take you in the cart to the waters where Julius Caesar is purported to have bathed. They will make a new man of you."

Lucius wasn't sure that his wobbling legs would hold him when he started outside the next morning, but he made it to the cart and Conrad lifted him to the seat. He whistled for Dan to follow, for the lion hadn't had much exercise since Lucius's illness. As the ox pulled the cart along a grassy cliff-rimmed plateau, Lucius glimpsed the river running through steep gorges widening into quiet runs and wide valleys.

"The most beautiful country I've ever seen," Lucius said, sorry that he must soon leave this pastoral area. "It's so peaceful here."

"But not always," Conrad said. "We often have to defend our homes from the Alemanni and other heathen hordes that swoop down upon us." He smiled. "But most of the time it is peaceful."

After daily visits to the hot springs for several weeks, Lucius was as healthy as ever. He knew he needed to find employment, but it would be difficult to leave. Not only did he like the area, but Felice had wrapped herself around his heart. The girl was quiet and had rarely spoken directly to him, but when she turned her dark-lashed blue eyes in his direction, he was hard put not to grab her in his arms.

By this time, Lucius had determined that the family were Christians, for they bowed their heads for a blessing over each meal and knelt by the fireplace for prayer each evening. So one night after the meal had been eaten and when the women had tidied up the serving dishes, Lucius said, "I'm sure I haven't thanked you properly for giving me refuge and restoring my health. I can't impose on your hospitality forever, so I must leave in a few days."

Felice gave him a sharp glance. "You are not able to travel yet," she said.

He smiled in her direction. "Not yet, but soon, I hope. But I want to tell you of the circumstances that brought me among you, if you would like to listen."

Hannah lighted a candle to ward off the approaching darkness, and she and Felice joined the men at the table.

"I'm a resident of Rome, where my family has lived for several centuries. My father, Bernini, is one of Rome's leading merchants. Since my grandfather Ignatius died six years ago, Father has made an effort to stay in the good graces of the imperial government. Although he appreciated the vast estate my grandfather passed on to him, there was one legacy that has been an embarrassment to him. Grandfather Ignatius was a Christian, and in Rome at this time it isn't prudent to be a follower of Jesus."

"And you, young man," Conrad said, "what of your faith? Do you follow the paths of your father or your grandfather?"

"I, too, am a Christian, for Ignatius taught me well. I have noticed your worship, and so I felt bold to speak. Have you had any persecution here in Gaul?"

"We, of course, have heard of the latest edicts by the emperor, but Constantius has not seen fit to enforce these orders. Nor did Maximian, so it is bad for us that he has abdicated. Neither Constantius nor Maximian are Christians, but their women are, and apparently they've had some influence on the men. But go on with your story, young man."

"After Diocletian became incapacitated and Galerius began to issue and enforce edicts, first the clergy and then the laity were persecuted. All that was necessary to escape this persecution was to drop a pinch of incense before the statue of the imperial gods. It shames me to admit that I feared I would deny my Lord because the ordeals inflicted upon the faithful have been terrible, but every time I passed before the statues, I seemed to receive a renewal of my faith, and I moved on without making an offering. Ultimately, I was arrested and condemned to death in the arena by wild beasts."

Felice gasped. "How did you escape?"

"I spent the night in prison with many other condemned Christians, and though we sang and prayed throughout the night like Paul and Silas, no miracle happened for us. We were led out to the arena the next morning, where deliverance occurred for me but not for the others. Although it was done through human hands, I still consider it a miracle."

Felice's face paled, and she looked at Lucius as if she could sense the pain he would have suffered if deliverance hadn't come.

"I don't mean to keep you in suspense, but I must give you some background to lead up to my escape. As I told you, my father is a merchant, and much of his business is with imports. Six years ago, my twin brother, Marcus, went with Father to Africa. When they returned, they brought two lion cubs that I adopted as pets. About this same time, a tragic death came to the woman Marcus loved, and he disavowed his role as Father's heir and entered the army. It so happened, or by God's intervention, whichever you want to believe, Marcus was on duty at the arena the day I was led to my execution.

"I still don't know how he did it, but he substituted my pet lions for the ferocious beasts. The two lions and I wrestled as we often had done, and when I said, 'Play dead,' they flopped down as if I'd killed them. The spectators were awed at my escape and clamored for my release."

"Then it's understandable why you travel with the lion," Conrad said with a laugh.

"Yes, he's more protection than a dog. Marcus provided a horse and gear for me and ordered me out of the city before the hoax was discovered, but I delayed long enough to go back home for something vitally important to me. While I was there, it seemed a good idea for me to bring Dan along for company. I've been on the road for six months, and it was fortunate for me that Marcus and Constantine found me when they did."

"That's an amazing story, Lucius. When so many Christians have been sacrificed in the past few years and you have escaped death two times, it must be that God has some important role for you to perform in the future," Conrad said.

"That's true, and I know what it is, so I should never have been fearful of my life. You see, Conrad, I'm the guardian of the Alabaster."

The three adults stared at Lucius without comprehension.

Lucius laughed apologetically. "It's also a long story. Perhaps you should hear it at another time."

"Not unless you're tired, Lucius," Hannah said. "You tell a fascinating tale."

Lucius went to his quarters and returned with the box containing the Alabaster. He removed the vase and placed it on the table, where the candlelight brought out the dark streaks in the gray substance. "That container of spikenard was carried to the tomb of Jesus to anoint His body for final burial by Mary. Since Jesus had risen, there was no need for the ointment. My ancestor, Suetonius of Trento, brought that container back from Jerusalem three centuries ago. It has been in the Trento family since that time."

His audience listened in fascination as Lucius told how the Alabaster had been handed down from generation to generation to remind his family of the certainty of the death, burial, and resurrection of Christ.

"May I touch it?" Conrad said and reached out a timorous hand to stroke the surface. "You have an awesome responsibility, young man. No wonder God has spared your life."

"I'm glad you see it as a responsibility instead of an honor. And while it is an honor, I feel strongly the duty of preserving the truth of the resurrection and passing it on to the next generation. I don't mind saying, sir, that it seems to me that the church is growing farther away from the real truth that Jesus died to atone for our sins, and that we're saved through faith in Him."

"Here in the West our worship is quite simple, but I've heard that in the large cities of the empire the form of worship and the role of the clergy goes far beyond the simple lifestyle of the first Christians."

"You're right, and the more thoughtful Christians see this present persecution as God's way of cleansing the church."

❀   ❀   ❀

For the next several nights, after the day's work was done, Conrad and Lucius discussed their mutual faith. One evening, Lucius said, "I'll admit I was relieved to find that you were Christians. If I were in the hands of a pagan family, I might not have fared so well."

"My family has been Christian for many generations. Christianity came to us along the commercial routes from Asia Minor by Greek immigrants. We now have several bishoprics in western Gaul and in cities along the Rhine. We haven't had any serious persecution since the reign of Marcus Aurelius, who disliked Christians because he thought they were undermining the civilization he was trying to maintain. Under his son, Commodus, the persecution abated, and the church grew rapidly. And as I said, these latest edicts have done us little harm."

Even after his complete recovery, Lucius delayed his departure. For a man who had spent most of his life within the walls of Rome, a whole new way of life opened to him. Conrad was a good farmer, and the neat fields of barley and rye with full heads waving in the breeze appealed to Lucius.

"The farmers in the Rhone Valley provide bread to the rest of Gaul. It's a good market if we get the rain we need, as we have this year," Conrad stated on one of their evening walks around the farm.

On the hillsides the grapes were turning slightly. "In one month, we will be picking grapes and preparing for winemaking. Conrad grapes are prized by the major winemakers. We tread out the juice, but make only sweet wine for our own use. The rest is sold to local wineries. You must not leave us before the grape harvest."

"You're making it harder and harder for me to contemplate leaving at all."

With a sly look, Conrad said, "Felice would like for you to stay."

Lucius felt his face flush under Conrad's pointed gaze. It was true that Felice had shown much interest in him, and if he could read their attitude, Conrad and Hannah looked with favor upon him as a son-in-law. *But what of my feelings? Gentle Felice would be a good wife for any man.* Having spent his life among brunette, dark-eyed people, Lucius was attracted to her contrasting blonde, blue-eyed beauty. She was a diligent worker, and her father boasted of the fighting skill of his daughter, who had fought more than once to ward off invasions by Frankish tribesmen from the north.

Lucius was twenty-two years old now, beyond the age when most Romans took a wife. If he were at home, his father would have arranged a marriage, but since that was impossible, Lucius took matters into his own hands. Late that evening, he asked Felice to walk with him to the top of the plateau. They sat silently for many minutes watching night settle over the valley, and when Lucius reached for her, Felice came willingly into his arms. He soon learned that this girl who worked vigorously and fought with boldness possessed an appetite for passion that at first Lucius wasn't sure he could match. But with amazement, he realized that the quiet twin could be aroused to a blazing pitch when it came to love—all he needed now to make his life complete was this woman in his arms.

Felice's parents welcomed their match, and Conrad threw his arms around Lucius in a hard embrace. "My boy! You will marry during the winemaking festival. And you will stay with us always. I have need of a scribe as well as a son."

Lucius asked to have their house built on the high hill overlooking the Rhone, and the one-room dwelling was completed by the time of their wedding. The weeks passed quickly for Felice and Lucius as they worked and played away the days.

Occasionally, word would come of Constantius's invasion of Britain and of the oppression still being unleashed in the East. Lucius would moodily wonder if he was fulfilling his goal in life by being sequestered in this peaceful place. He often thought of Marcus and his parents, but he lacked the motivation to interrupt this placid way of life where he and the neighbors worshiped

God simply and enjoyed the lifestyle they considered typical of the early church.

❀　❀　❀

Almost a year had passed when, one morning as he pruned vines on the hillside, Lucius saw a small group of soldiers entering the yard of the farm. He recognized Marcus as the leader of the group, and he had a premonition that the peaceful days had ended. With a mixture of sadness and eagerness, Lucius rushed to his brother.

Not even taking time to greet his twin, Marcus blurted out his news. "Constantine has been declared an Augustus," he said joyously. "I knew I made the right decision to throw in my lot with his."

He waved a hand to stop the stammering questions of Conrad and Lucius. "After we left here, we traveled quickly to Gessoriacum, where we found Constantius Chlorus ready to invade Britain. We crossed the English Channel, marched northward as far as Hadrian's Wall, and defeated the Picts. By the end of the campaign season, the Romans claimed a victory."

"We have had some news of the invasion, but it has been sketchy," Lucius said.

"Constantius set up court at York and gathered his family around him, but on July 25, Constantius died, and Constantine is now the Augustus. Constantius chose his eldest son above the other males in his family by his second wife. So this goes to prove the legitimacy of Constantine's birth, something that has concerned him. After setting key persons in control of Britain, Constantine is back on the continent, and he intends to make his home at Treves in the commodious palace Constantius built there."

"But why are you here, Marcus? Can I believe that you came simply to inquire of my health?"

"No, much more important than that. Constantine is trying to surround himself with advisors—learned men, those he can trust. You came to mind, brother Lucius, and I suggested you. The Augustus has summoned you to his court to be his chief scribe. Say you'll go with me, my brother. I've missed you."

11

TREVES, 307

Lucius laid aside the parchment he was copying and rubbed the back of his neck. His work as chief scribe for Constantine increased each month as he copied the ruler's messages and saw that they were dispatched throughout Gaul, Britain, and Spain.

Felice, heavy with their first child, entered the room and laid her soft hands on his neck in a gentle massage. "May I help you in any way?" she asked. "I have everything ready for the guests."

Lucius rose from the table and pulled her into his arms.

"That feels good," he said, "and definitely takes my mind off my work, but no more massaging, or we will not be here to welcome our guests."

"Your eyes, neck, and fingers have had enough for one day anyway," she said. "Since Constantine has returned from his victory over the Alemanni, you've hardly had a free moment."

"He's been sending reports of his exploits throughout his kingdom, but I'm almost finished."

Felice settled down by the window and picked up a garment she was stitching for their child.

"How do you feel today?" he asked.

"Clumsy," she said, smiling, "but I'm all right."

"I hope we can go to your mother for the delivery of this

child. I had never thought to keep you away from your parents so long."

Although her eyes saddened, Felice said, "My place is with you. I miss the farm, and I do not care for all the trappings of a royal court, but I haven't been sorry I came here with you."

As Lucius slowly paced the room, he marveled that it had been almost a year since they had left the Rhone Valley. He had anticipated that they would stay with Constantine for a few months and then return to the serenity of the farm, but the empire was in such chaos and Constantine's position was so often insecure that he had stayed out of a sense of duty.

"Do you ever think about our home on the plateau? I can close my eyes now and see the sun rise across the valley, the morning dew on the grapevines. I can almost smell the olive oil as it comes from the press."

Felice's eyes filled with tears and she nodded. "But as long as he needs you, we must stay, for I can't forget that Christianity owes Constantine a debt. When he gave Christians in his domains full restitution of what they had lost during the persecution, he tied us to his political star for as long as he wants you."

"We're wise to recognize it as a political move rather than tolerance for Christianity. By this gesture, Constantine asserted his right to legislate for his subjects, but it also made him popular as a potential liberator for Christians throughout the empire. Which outcome provided the most motivation, I don't know, but I won't desert him now. I'd be happier if Constantine would actually embrace Christianity."

Although Galerius had rejected the idea of having Constantine as an Augustus, he had recognized him as a Caesar, and for the time being, that had suited Constantine, for by so doing Galerius had approved his legitimacy for the office. Instead of Constantine, Galerius had appointed Severus to replace the dead Constantius.

Wisely, Constantine had accepted the appointment of Caesar and settled down at Treves, content to rule in Britain, Gaul, and

Spain for the present. His father had used Treves as his head-quarters for ten years, so it was a well-established center with a mint, imperial factories for the production of uniforms, court dress, shields, and spears, as well as the treasury for Gaul. And with the advent of Constantine and his legions, two immense stone warehouses had been constructed on the bank of the Moselle to store provisions for the town's residents.

Having lived in Rome most of his life, Lucius adapted well to life in the city, which was laid out in a rough circle enclosing more than a hundred blocks. During the first months of his reign, Constantine had constructed mammoth baths to serve the court. When Constantine was not fighting the savage hordes to the north, he enjoyed adding to the magnificent structures started by his father and hunting with his friends. Marcus continued to be a favorite with Constantine and had risen in the imperial army to the rank of tribune.

As soon as he had settled in Treves, Constantine had sent for his mother and son. Octavia, who was now an inseparable companion of Helena, had accompanied them. Octavia had cared for Crispus since his birth, and although her hope of ever becoming the wife of Constantine had been blighted when the Caesar had agreed to a political marriage, Octavia was so attached to Crispus and Helena that she had willingly come to Treves with them.

Marcus accompanied Octavia and Helena when they arrived at the small domus assigned to Lucius and Felice. Marcus had grown stouter over the past year, and although he laughed often and heartily, Lucius didn't think he had ever been happy. When Dan heard Marcus's voice, he padded in from the courtyard to stand protectively by Lucius's side. When he growled softly, Lucius put a restraining hand on his back.

Laughing, Marcus said, "Why can't that animal remember when I've saved your life, rather than the times I used to cuff you around when we were boys?" Ignoring Dan, he continued, "I come on official business. Caesar Constantine has issued an invitation for the Trentos to attend the royal wedding at Arles next month."

With a quick glance at Felice, Lucius said, "But will you be able to travel?"

"I should be. Tell the Caesar we will be there."

"But it's several week's travel to Arles and back. You may deliver before we return."

With a smile, Felice said, "I'll risk it. You're obligated to go, and I'd rather deliver along the route with you than to stay here alone. I would have neither friend nor family with me if everyone is away at the wedding. Besides, we'll be so close to my parents' home that Constantine may permit us to pay them a visit on the return. We'll go."

After Marcus left, Felice turned to Helena. "Are you reconciled to Constantine's marriage yet?"

"No, I'm not. The girl is only nine years old, which is at least three years too soon for a marriage to be consummated. She's more suited to a union with Crispus, who's only two years younger than she."

"Apparently Constantine believes it's to his advantage to marry the girl," Lucius said.

"I suppose it is, but I would have preferred he marry someone of a childbearing age if he must marry at all."

"Constantine will never love anyone except Minervina," Octavia said. "He's made that quite plain to me. Therefore, marriage is only a political expediency to him."

Leaving the women to discuss travel plans and details of the wedding, Lucius returned to his desk to finish copying the dispatch. Before he picked up the stylus, he contemplated the stormy political situation in the empire.

While Constantine had enjoyed victory on the battlefield and had settled down to a luxurious life at Treves, he had kept his court abreast of the worsening condition of the empire. A few months after Constantius's death, Augustus Galerius had angered the citizens of Rome by extending the imperial tax to their city and disbanding the elite Praetorian Guard. This had prepared a climate for Maxentius, Maximian's son, to plot an insurrection. Maxentius had been proclaimed Augustus on October 28, and all of Italy soon fell under the power of the usurper.

Galerius immediately dispatched his co-Augustus, Severus, to put down the rebellion, and Maxentius had appealed to his retired father to lead an army to stop the invasion of Rome. The majority of Severus's troops were Maximian's veterans, and they would not fight against their old general, so Severus surrendered, only to be put to death by Maxentius. When Galerius marched to avenge Severus's death, he was no more successful in dislodging Maxentius then Severus had been, but as he retreated, he left behind a scorched earth and an embittered population.

Maximian hurried to ask Constantine to cut off Galerius's retreat and annihilate him, but Constantine refused. In an attempt to win Constantine's support, Maximian urged the youthful Caesar to marry his daughter, Fausta, and thereby receive the title of Augustus. In return for these favors, Maximian hoped to persuade Constantine to fight against Galerius, but Lucius thought it unlikely that Constantine would involve himself directly with the senior Augustus, though he was willing to marry Fausta for the political advantage it might give him. And this marriage became even more desirable to Maximian when he and his own son began to disagree.

❈　　❈　　❈

Marcus's command was assigned to the rear guard for the Caesar's procession to Arles, and he held his horse at attention as Constantine's retinue moved out of Treves. An honor guard of British auxiliary cavalrymen passed first through the gates of the walled city before six official trumpeters announced the coming of the Caesar.

Dressed in new armor, a crested helmet, and wearing a gold-handled spear at his side, Constantine came next, arrayed in a purple toga. By his side was the former Augustus, Maximian, who had come to Treves to accompany his future son-in-law to his palace on the Rhone River at Arles. Behind them, the boy Crispus rode proudly on a small mare, dressed in garments identical to his father's, indicating that, in spite of this new marriage, Constantine did not intend to set Crispus aside in favor of any future children he might father with Fausta. But considering the youth of his future bride, it would be several years before Fausta could produce children. Because of the danger attached to the life of a Caesar, Constantine could easily succumb before he had more children. The grooming of Crispus for leadership was important to his father.

Helena's closed carriage followed, but she had the curtains pulled aside, waving to the palace servants who were staying behind. Octavia and Helena's personal servant rode with her. Marcus smiled when he remembered the change in Helena's status from a year ago. When Constantine had become established at Treves, he immediately sent for his mother. Marcus had headed up the soldier escort. When they found Helena in Drepanum, she had been working over a fire in her brother's inn. Her clothing was spattered with grease from a boar roasting on a spit, her hair was untidy, and weariness marked her carriage. But the woman had come alive when Marcus had delivered Constantine's message, and within a day, she was ready to leave the drudgery of the past behind her. Dressed today in silk with golden decorations and a jeweled tiara on her head, she bore no resemblance to the woman he had escorted to Treves.

Lucius and Felice were far behind the royal family in the procession, and they waved at Marcus fondly as their small carriage passed, although as a member of the guard, he could not respond. Not to be left behind, Dan padded along in the rear of their carriage, to which he was attached by a chain. The people of Treves had gotten used to the animal and no longer feared him. Still Lucius kept him on a leash when they were away from the house.

On and on the procession passed, and Marcus judged that the whole imperial retinue must extend for at least five miles. The important personages had one or more carriages piled with their baggage, some of which probably contained as many as six tunics, six shirts, lightweight coats, a heavy one, and several togas. By the time bedding, food, spices, and wines were added, a sizable amount of baggage had accumulated, and in Marcus's opinion, made the royal train an attraction for robbers.

Marcus judged there were at least five hundred people in the entourage, including the important government officials, their families, personal servants, and their baggage. How they could ever reach Arles by the date set for the wedding, he couldn't imagine.

Marcus allowed the long procession to travel at least a half-mile in advance before he motioned for his company to fall into line. At the best, they would be inundated by choking dust stirred up by the multitude of animals, so Marcus didn't look forward to the journey.

❀   ❀   ❀

Felice's squirmings on the hard pallet awakened Lucius, and he tightened his arms around her. No hint of daylight seeped into the tent, and he closed his eyes, hoping to sleep again, but his mind was too active. He buried his face in Felice's soft hair and rubbed his hand along her abdomen, feeling the faint stirrings of his child within her. *I shouldn't have allowed her to make this trek; each day finds her more weary, but how can I leave her behind?* Though it had been a smooth expedition, there were still many miles to cover, and Lucius dreaded it for Felice. *And if her time comes out on the march, will the cortege stop for her?* He groaned aloud and mumbled, "She shouldn't have tried this journey."

A muffled sound reached his ears, and Lucius sat up suddenly, causing Felice to voice a sleepy protest. Lucius crawled to the tent flap and peered out into darkness. A few fires burned around the camp, and a thin sliver of light along the eastern horizon signaled that the dawn was near. Lucius strained his ears. *Is that the muffled sound of horse's hooves approaching our camp?* He stepped outside and became aware too late that the ground was crawling with men. He shouted and dropped to his knees as an unseen assailant smashed a club over his head.

Lucius's shout had alarmed the camp, and as he lost consciousness, he heard the sound of the trumpet summoning the troops. By the time he roused, daylight revealed mounted guards racing around the camp. Felice was trying to pull him into the tent, but he picked up a javelin lying beside a fallen plunderer and rushed in the wake of the guards led by Marcus. The ragged band of robbers was no match for the Roman soldiers, and the fight was soon over.

Constantine, dressed only in his tunic, paced in front of his tent. "Where were the guards?" he shouted. "Cannot a Caesar of the Roman Empire depend upon his own men for protection? Find the guilty persons so they can be punished!"

Marcus stepped forward. "Those on guard duty are all dead, sire. The plunderers slit their throats before they could give warning. We've accounted for most of the attackers, although a few fled toward the hills on horseback. Do you want us to pursue them?"

His eyes still flashing with anger, Constantine turned back to his tent. "Let them go, but be on your guard. Now that we're all awake, we may as well continue our journey."

Lucius suddenly burst into the circle around the Caesar's tent. He grabbed Marcus's arm. "Marcus, the robbers pilfered some of the tents, and they took my pack containing the Alabaster."

Wheeling to his men grouped behind him, Marcus said, "After them. The robbers must be apprehended." He left the camp at a gallop with his troops falling into formation behind him.

A riderless horse stood nearby, and Lucius jumped on its back, kicking the animal into action.

"Halt!" Constantine shouted. "How dare you leave camp without my permission? Come back, I say." But all that came back was the rapid tat-a-tat of the horses' hooves as they raced across the rocky soil.

Lucius caught up with Marcus within a few miles, and Marcus called, "Is Felice all right?"

"Yes, otherwise I wouldn't be here. I dare say that she's more important to me than the Alabaster at this point."

The soldiers' horses had been resting all night, so in a short time they overtook the fleeing bandits, who kept peering back at their pursuers. When they came within twenty feet of their prey, Marcus lifted his javelin. "Take them," he cried, and a dozen weapons simultaneously hurtled forward into the backs of the robbers. Most of them fell out of their saddles, and it was only a short time before the horses were rounded up.

"Oh, ho," Marcus said as they examined the plunder recovered from the thieves. "Looks as if the looters were busy at work while their comrades kept us occupied." He lifted a small sword. "The Caesar would not be happy to have Crispus's specially made sword taken."

Lucius had opened his pack and quickly determined that the Alabaster had not been damaged. Then he said wryly, "Let's hope that will ease the Caesar's anger somewhat. Perhaps you didn't hear him, but he gave the command for you to turn back."

Marcus frowned. "No, I didn't hear him, but I doubt that will be sufficient excuse."

The cortege was organized and ready to move when they returned, but Constantine confronted Marcus and Lucius as they stopped by the carriage where Felice waited. "Perhaps the Trento brothers will be kind enough to explain to their Caesar why they deliberately disobeyed his command."

"Sire, I didn't hear your command to return," Marcus said, and he motioned toward the stack of plunder that people were joyfully searching for their belongings. "And as you can see, the looters had taken much of our goods."

"Perhaps you didn't hear the second command, but may I remind you that I'd already given an order to let the robbers go?"

Lucius stepped forward, hoping to take some of the heat from Marcus. "May I take the blame for this, sire? I hadn't heard your first order, and I was concerned about a possession I'd lost."

"Oh, yes, the Alabaster, I believe you said. I remember once before this Alabaster was mentioned, and when I asked what it was, you didn't tell me. Well, this time I mean to find out. We will continue our march, but tonight, I command both of you to attend me in my tent. After I hear about this Alabaster for which you would disobey your superior's orders, I will decide upon punishment for the Trento brothers."

Constantine turned on his heel and stalked back to the front of the procession. Marcus shrugged his shoulders and motioned his men to their position in the rear. As Lucius settled into the carriage beside Felice, she whispered, "Are we in trouble?"

He squeezed her arm. "Probably, but don't be concerned about it. There's always our home on the Rhone, and it seems to beckon me more often. Besides, the pressures of the office sometimes weigh heavily on the emperor's shoulders, and he makes statements that he really doesn't mean. No doubt, he'll be more forgiving tomorrow."

❊   ❊   ❊

Constantine was alone in his tent when Lucius and Marcus entered. His jaw was thrust forward in a menacing manner, and his eyes were stormy—as if anger had simmered inside him all day. The twins stood until the Caesar curtly commanded them to be seated.

Knowing that Felice was praying in their tent gave Lucius courage, and with a quick prayer of his own, *Father, help me*, he unrolled the leather protecting the box. He hadn't closely examined the ornate vase for several weeks, and he looked at it a moment before he lifted it from the box.

"The Alabaster, sire."

Constantine took the vase and turned it slowly, but suddenly a strange look covered his face, and he thrust it back to Lucius. "You hold it! But I want you to tell me why it's so important to you."

"This alabaster vase has been in the Trento family for over three hundred years, and when my grandfather died it was passed to me."

"I can see why you wouldn't want to part with it," Constantine said slowly, "but is there more to the story than that?"

The twins exchanged glances. And almost as if he had stood in Jesus' presence and heard His voice, the words came to Lucius, *When you are brought before rulers, don't worry about how to defend yourself, or how to speak, for the Holy Spirit will teach you what you should say.*

"For centuries this vase and its contents have served to remind the Trentos of the death, burial, and resurrection of Jesus of Nazareth, whom the Christians believe to be the Son of God."

"Are you a Christian, Lucius?" Constantine said, but the tension in his face had lessened, giving Lucius courage to continue.

"Yes, sire, and I'm emboldened to share with you the story of my family's faith because the Caesar has been so generous with Christians since he assumed the purple."

"As you would know, my mother is a Christian, so I wouldn't want the sect persecuted as they are under Augustus Galerius. Thus, you may be as bold as you wish. Tell me the rest of the story."

During the next hour, Marcus and Lucius fielded Constantine's questions as he pulled from them the story of Suetonius and the journey of the Alabaster to the present time. He looked often at the Alabaster, but he didn't reach for it again.

"Lucius has said that he's a believer, but what of you, Marcus?" Constantine asked. "We've been comrades on many a march, but I've not heard about your Christian beliefs."

"No, sire, I'm a follower of Mithra. The Christian religion could not meet my need. I had to make atonement for my own sins, and I've done that through the many rituals of Mithraism."

Constantine looked to Lucius for a rebuttal statement, and Lucius smiled sadly at his brother. "Although the organized church has sometimes strayed from the true doctrine, the early Christians taught that Jesus made the only atonement necessary for the sin of the world, and I believe that. Salvation is a free gift from God through faith in what Jesus has done. The Alabaster reminds me of that daily. It's a sorrow to me that my brother has not followed our faith."

Constantine reached for a piece of bread on the table beside him, and as he nibbled thoughtfully on the dry crust, Lucius, empowered by the Spirit, spoke again. "And may I encourage you, Caesar Constantine, to put your trust in the Son of God. Surely your mother has talked with you about her faith."

"Yes, and while I revere my mother highly, I have not been persuaded to assume her religious beliefs. As you know, I have taken the sun god for my patron."

"But your sun god could easily be the Son of God whom we worship," Lucius said haltingly.

Constantine was in a thoughtful mood when they left him at a late hour. As they eased out of the tent, Marcus lifted his hand in a gesture of victory—Constantine hadn't mentioned any punishment for their disobedience.

❁   ❁   ❁

The palace at Arles overlooked the Rhone Valley, and Felice thought longingly of her home when she saw the broad fields. Throughout the length and difficulty of the journey, she had often questioned her wisdom in coming here rather going on a shorter trip to stay with her parents. While she would have liked her mother with her during the birth of the child, she wanted Lucius, too, and since she had to choose, she had stayed with her husband. Now that they had been installed in a small room in the palace and she'd rested for a day, she was glad she was here. Their second-floor room was pleasant, and from the balcony she could see the river. Hearing shouts and laughter, Felice moved to a window that overlooked an inner courtyard.

Crispus, Constantine's son, and a young girl played tag below her. She watched as they chased one another across the tiled pavement, weaving in and out of the myrtle hedge that rimmed the spraying fountain. She surmised that Crispus's playmate was Fausta, the bride-to-be. If so, she could well understand Helena's aversion to this wedding. The girl was smaller than Crispus, and her long brown hair flowed gracefully behind her as she leaped from one spot to another. Once when Crispus caught her, he dragged her to the fountain, dipped up a handful of water, and sprayed it in her face.

Feeling a presence behind her, Felice turned into Lucius's arms. "Fausta," he said.

"I assumed as much. She seems a much better mate for Crispus than his father. He's thirty-two to her nine years!"

"Political marriages are often like that."

"How glad I am that we didn't have to wed for political reasons!"

"I might have been compelled to do so if I'd been in my father's household."

"Do they know about us yet?"

"I have sent two letters by the government's post, so I'm sure they've received them. Civilian mail can't move rapidly, so it may be months before we hear from them. Someday I hope we can visit my home, but even without your delicate condition, it isn't wise for us to go to Rome while Maxentius rules there."

"This wedding will make Constantine Maxentius's brother-in-law. How will he choose now in an argument between Maximian and Maxentius, which is bound to come?"

"I don't believe he will choose. He'll wait until father and son work out their differences, and he'll side with the victor. I have difficulty figuring Constantine. He's done a lot for the Christians, but I wonder if his actions have been motivated by religious conviction or if he's just a calculating politician trying to keep friends in both camps. I don't always trust his motives."

"I pray that you won't publicly say so, at least while we're still attached to his court."

"I don't intend to, but I'm not a slave, and if Constantine goes contrary to our Christian beliefs, I'll leave his court. We can always go back to your father's farm."

"I believe you want to return there as much as I do," Felice said, laughing.

A knock on the door interrupted them, and Helena entered at Lucius's bidding. Noting her distress, Felice led her to a couch and offered her some fruit and a cup of wine. "I had hoped," Helena said, "that there would be some semblance of Christian influence in this wedding, but that doesn't seem to be the case. Constantine is right now offering incense at the Shrine of Apollo. I'd prayed that your talk with him, Lucius, would divert him toward our faith. When I protested his visit to this shrine, he said it was a political expediency."

Lucius glanced quickly at Felice as if to say, *I told you so,* but to Helena he said, "Maximian's court is directing the wedding, and of course, he's a pagan."

"But Constantine could have disagreed with their arrangements, for Maximian is the one pushing this match," Helena said. "I wouldn't have come at all if I'd known I would have to witness a pagan wedding."

Felice rested her hand on Helena's bowed shoulder. "You should be here to share in the marriage of your only son."

"And have you seen Fausta? A mere child. She seems younger than Crispus. I shouldn't have bothered you since you can't do anything about it, but I had to talk to someone who would understand my uneasiness, and I can't talk to Octavia. She's really grieving over this marriage, even though Constantine made it clear to her years ago that he wasn't interested in her. Octavia is as near to me as any daughter could be, and I hate to have her hurt."

❁ ❁ ❁

Lucius was present when Maximian and Constantine final-
ized the marriage agreement. Maximian promised to transfer
his title of Augustus to Constantine, although Lucius personally
thought it was not his to convey. *Why can't the old man be content to go into retirement as Diocletian had done? Why did he
have to stir up discontent in the empire?*

Constantine was to inherit any claim that Maximian had held
in the empire, and in return Constantine transferred a sum of
gold to Maximian. They agreed that Fausta would become a
member of Constantine's household, but that the marriage would
not be consummated until after the girl had reached her twelfth
birthday. But when Maximian pressed Constantine to pledge
his support in a war against Galerius to drive him away from
Rome, Constantine absolutely refused.

This accounted for Maximian's stony look at the wedding the
next day, Lucius deducted.

When Fausta appeared, she no longer had the long hair Felice
had admired the day before. Her hair had been parted into six
locks fastened together by ivory combs into a cone-shaped coiffure at the top of her head. White ribbons adorned her restrained
tresses. The bride's veil of brilliant orange material, which left
her face exposed, topped a wreath of marjoram on her head. A
tunic of loosely woven muslin was fastened about her waist with
a woolen knotted girdle. The tunic was high enough off the floor
to expose her shoes, the same brilliant orange as her veil.

Dressed in a purple toga, Constantine waited for his bride
beside the chairs they would occupy for the ceremony. Lucius
wondered if this ritual seemed as ridiculous to others as it did to
him, for the Caesar towered more than three feet over his child
bride, but since this was the accepted practice throughout the
empire, no one else seemed to regard it as unusual. But Lucius
judged all marriages by his own, and he wondered how
Constantine could ever hope to find happiness in such a union.

The ceremony opened with the sacrifice of a pig and the diviners read the contents. Holding up the liver, one of the pagan

priests shouted, "The signs are favorable—a large liver without blemish." The marriage contract was signed by ten witnesses, of which Lucius was one. Fausta's attendant, a woman who had been married only once, joined the right hands of the couple, and the vows were exchanged quietly, including mutual promises of their desire to live together.

One of Constantine's closest advisors celebrated the union by reading a panegyric asserting the legitimacy of his claim to the rank of Augustus. If Lucius remembered Marcus's account correctly, Constantine was actually hailed as Augustus only by the troops of his father. But his right to hold the office was assured now with this marriage, and the orator asserted that Constantine was entitled to the succession not by reason of heredity alone, but by virtue of his abilities and by the appointment of his father-in-law. The panegyrist ended with the words, "And being taken into the family of Maximian, he is hereby inducted into the clan of Hercules, which divine ancestor he has emulated by his mighty deeds."

Helena sat with bowed head throughout the ceremony, no doubt distressed that her son was being drawn farther into dependence upon pagan gods.

Shouts of joy rose from the guests as they followed the couple into the dining hall for the banquet.

Felice had attended a few feasts in Constantine's palace at Treves, but none to equal this. The first course consisted of egg dishes, cheese, and brown bread. The main course was peacock and venison, with cabbages, leeks, asparagus, and artichokes. When the first pain came, Felice thought that something she had eaten during the long feast had disagreed with her, but when the agony became more insistent, she nudged Lucius. His eyes were fearful when he glanced her way, but when another pang caused her to writhe on the couch, he knew their child was on its way.

12

The peacocks announced Lucius's arrival as he crossed the courtyard and approached the palace entrance. The peahens squawked their displeasure, while the male spread his train of greenish feathers and strutted reluctantly out of Lucius's path.

Fausta sat in the shade of a Valonia oak trying to effect a regal appearance, but looking more like a child playing in her mother's clothes than the wife of a Roman Caesar. Now that the marriage of Fausta and Constantine had become a fact, Fausta spent hours each morning having her hair dressed in an elaborate creation of curls and waves. She further tried to disguise her youth with heavy makeup around her eyes and on her face, and with lavish applications of exotic perfumes that left the scent of a Persian harem in her wake. Lucius was of the opinion that Fausta went to all of this trouble to entice Constantine to her bed more often, though he had yet to see any affection between the Caesar and his bride.

Felice, on the other hand, thought that Fausta tried to make herself beautiful to catch the eye of her stepson Crispus, who at this moment lolled on the ground near Fausta, arguing with his tutor Lactantius over some point of rhetoric.

"Lucius," Crispus called, "come join us."

Since Octavia had often brought Crispus to the Trento house

during his childhood, Lucius and Felice were quite fond of the boy, but he had no time to visit with him today. "I have an appointment with your father." Lucius looked upward and saw Constantine observing the courtyard from a second-floor window. "See, he's waiting for me already."

As Lucius ascended the marble stairway, he wondered what Constantine thought about the friendship between Fausta and Crispus. *When he keeps them both in the same house, what can he expect?*

Constantine motioned for Lucius to enter his apartment, and after a servant brought them chilled wine, he said, "Your message indicated that you had received a letter from your father."

"Yes, sire, this letter is in response to my query about the political situation in Rome, which you wanted to know. Shall I read it, or do you prefer to study it yourself?"

"Please read it to me."

Lucius nodded and unrolled the parchment. With an apologetic look at the Augustus, Lucius said, "The first part is of a personal nature, sire."

"Read any of it you like. I'm most interested in the political situation."

Lucius glanced through the first paragraph and decided to read it all.

Rome, 312
Dear Son Lucius,

In spite of the turmoil in this city, your mother and I remain in good health. We rejoice to hear about the growth of our grandson and to know that Felice has also borne you a daughter. We look forward to having you bring your family to Rome when we again have peace in the land. Thank you for the news of Marcus, who never bothers to write.

At first, Maxentius was hailed as a savior by the populace of Rome, and they lauded his military victories. But with the estrangement between Maxentius and his father, it became obvious that it was Maximian's popularity with the army that had helped defeat the military power of Severus and Galerius.

There have been several riots in the city. The first occurred in 307, when the grain fleet from Carthage was held back by the rebellious Africans, and famine swept the city. Another riot grew from of the burning of the Temple of Venus and Roma, but the self-appointed Augustus provided an expansive reconstruction program that included a new temple to Venus and Roma, an arena for chariot races, and a basilica on the Forum Romanum. This effort to please everyone has scarcely pleased those who had to pay for it. Maxentius has been hard on the Roman senators, many of whom he has killed to confiscate their wealth. In a dispute with his soldiers, six thousand persons were slain. Our business has suffered some losses, but we are surviving. You will be interested to know that Maxentius has not been hard on the Christian community. He suspended the decrees of persecution, intervened in a papacy dispute, and restored churches and cemeteries seized by Diocletian. Still, I believe that the Christians do not like him.

Constantine held up his hand, and Lucius paused to give the Augustus time to ponder this information. When Constantine nodded, he continued reading.

In answer to your unspoken query, it is my opinion that few citizens of Rome would be willing to fight in Maxentius's favor should anyone be disposed to unseat him. I would assume by now that you have heard of the death of Galerius, and the Edict of Sardica, issued in 311 before his death. In the event that you have not, I will copy a portion of it.

"When we issued an order to the effect that they (Christians) were to go back to the practices established by the ancients, many of them found themselves in great danger, and many were attacked and punished with death in many forms. Most of them indeed persisted in the same folly, and we saw that they were neither giving to the gods in heaven the worship that is their due nor giving any honor to the God of the Christians. So in view of our benevolence and the established custom by which we invariably grant pardon to all men, we have thought proper in this matter also to extend our clemency most gladly, so that Christians may again exist and rebuild the houses in which they used to meet, on condition that they do nothing contrary to public order."

I trust that this information will be of help to you and those you serve.

Your devoted father,
Bernini Trento

After Lucius finished reading, Constantine sat for several minutes in silence. As he watched the face of his Augustus, Lucius wondered if he had aged as much as this man had in the five years they had been together. Constantine had gained some weight and was often referred to as "Bullneck," not in derision, but in affection from those who liked him—and most of his subjects did like the Augustus of the West. But being ruler of the western empire had not been an easy task for Constantine, and perhaps the hardest part had been the defection of his father-in-law, Maximian, two years ago.

After Constantine had married Fausta, Maximian had returned to Rome to try to effect a joint administration with his son, but they had disagreed violently. When it seemed that the whole government administration that he had planned was on the verge of collapsing, Diocletian had come out of retirement for a meeting at Carnuntum at the request of Maximian and Galerius. Diocletian had insisted that Maximian abdicate again, and he had named the Illyrian Licinius as Augustus to replace Severus, whom Maxentius had murdered.

Maximian had returned to Treves an embittered and defeated old man, and Constantine had received him well as his father-in-law and advisor. But while Constantine was on a campaign against the Franks, Maximian assumed the purple for the third time, took possession of the treasury and the arsenal, and returned to the palace at Arles. When Maximian had been apprehended, he was granted life and liberty again, but Fausta had informed Constantine of further intrigue by her father, and Maximian was killed by strangulation. Constantine was not happy that Maxentius had taken control of the Italian peninsula, and rumors had circulated around Treves for months that Constantine was planning to unseat his brother-in-law. Yes, the life of a Roman ruler was difficult, and it was little wonder that Constantine had aged.

So deep was Lucius in reverie that he jumped when Constantine spoke. "Please express my thanks to your father when you write, and tell him that I hope to call upon him again in the near future."

That should make Marcus happy, Lucius thought, for this statement indicated that Constantine did indeed plan to march on Rome and challenge Maxentius's right to rule.

❋ ❋ ❋

Lessons were over for the day, and Crispus and Fausta sat together on a marble bench while Lactantius waited for Lucius beside the gate. Constantine and Lactantius had been friends in Diocletian's court, and Constantine had brought the man to Treves to tutor Crispus.

"Have you heard about the death of Galerius?" Lactantius said.

Lucius held up the missive from his father. "Just now in a letter."

"It was an agonizing death," Lactantius said with some satisfaction. "May all enemies of the Christians die in that manner.

God has brought His vengeance on the great persecutors of the church. Diocletian is a disillusioned old man, stripped of all his greatness, and Galerius has succumbed after much suffering to a terrible disease—his maggot-infested body writhing to the end."

Lucius respected Lactantius as a learned man, but as he went on his way, he could not share in the man's rejoicing. Enemy of the church or not, Lucius could not pray for evil to come upon any person.

Reaching home, Lucius hoisted his son to his back, kissed Felice, and hastily answered her query about the outcome of the interview with the Augustus. "I don't know if Father's letter will have any weight in his decision. I personally think Constantine has made up his mind to wage war against his brother-in-law in spite of all the advice to the contrary he has received from his counselors and military men."

"Yet Marcus thinks Constantine should march on Rome."

"But my brother has less care for his life than most soldiers. He seems to court death."

"Why, husband? I've often wondered at the difference in the two of you. I can understand mere brothers being so different, but when you're twins, I would expect you to be more alike. You're such a sensitive, caring man, while Marcus goes through life caring for no one except you and our little Titus. What makes him different?"

"It grieves me that Marcus is the way he is. For one thing, he's thrown away the faith of my grandfather for a religion that does not include love and compassion. And since he's Father's heir, he should be in Rome now taking over the family business. I think his conscience hurts him that he has no interest in carrying on the family's tradition. Also, Marcus had a bad experience in his youth—he was in love with a pagan girl who was chosen to be a Vestal Virgin."

"What are Vestal Virgins?"

"The worship of Vesta, the household goddess, is as old as

Rome itself. It's a great honor when young girls are chosen as novitiates to keep the fire burning before Vesta's altar. Plotina was chosen, but ill health forced her to return to her father's house, and Marcus fell in love with her. His attentions did not please Plotina's father, and he refused to consider their marriage."

Felice listened with bated breath as she suckled Lucia at her breast. Lucius finished the story, saying, "She was condemned to death and buried alive."

Felice stared at him, wide-eyed. "How terrible!"

"Yes, it was a terrible death for Plotina, and for Marcus, who also died in a way. He would have taken his own life, but Sulla and I guarded him from that. Then secretly he enlisted in the army to court death on the battlefield, though he seems to bear a charmed life. He was influenced to follow a pagan religion by his slave, Sulla."

"There's a strange bond between those two, I've always thought. Not the usual slave and master relationship."

"Marcus has never been the same since he bought Sulla. Although the death of Plotina could certainly have caused Marcus's anguish, I've always thought something else is haunting my brother—something that happened to him in Africa."

"And when he hears this news from your father, he'll be more inclined to persuade Constantine to move against Maxentius."

"I fear so, for Marcus has this exalted belief that Constantine is destined to rule the whole empire."

"I sometimes wonder if Constantine doesn't hold the same opinion, since he's already the uncontested ruler of all the western provinces, and a legitimate Augustus. Now he's aligned his family with Licinius, Augustus in the East, by arranging an engagement between his half-sister, Constantia, and Licinius. That more or less pits Constantine and Licinius against Maxentius and Maximinus Daia."

"It's hard to believe how the political situation has changed since we came to Constantine's court," Lucius said. "Galerius, Severus, and Maximian are all dead. Maximinus Daia has taken over Galerius's domain from the Bosporus eastward. Licinius was chosen to succeed Severus from Italy as far as the Bosporus. Maxentius is ruling in Italy and Africa, and Constantine is supreme to the west and north. None of these four rulers likes or trusts the other. I fear we're in for a war." Lucius watched Felice place Lucia in her cradle. "Let's resign and go back to the Rhone," he said.

Felice put her arms around Lucius. How often they had talked of the peaceful farm life! How much they would prefer to rear their children in that atmosphere rather than among the trappings of an imperial court. Felice longed to be near her parents, but Lucius felt that his life was bound to Constantine, and she doubted he would ever leave him.

"Someday, husband, we will return to the farm."

"In the meantime, if Constantine marches, will we go or stay? I don't want to subject you to a march with the army, but if Constantine makes it to Rome, it would be an opportunity to see my parents and have them see us."

❊   ❊   ❊

Within three weeks of the receipt of Bernini's letter, Constantine started his eastward march, with forty thousand men drawn from Britain, Gaul, and the barbarian provinces. This was a small contingent to challenge the large army assembled under Maxentius, but Constantine couldn't risk taking any more men from Gaul without inviting invasion by the barbarian hordes from the north. Marcus was overjoyed to be chosen to go on the march, but Lucius received his command with mixed emotions. It would be a rough trip for Felice and the children, but he didn't want to leave them behind. On the other hand, he feared for his parents and sister if Constantine took Rome by assault, and he wanted to be there to intercede for them. When he learned that Constantine was taking Crispus, Lucius decided to risk his family also.

Lucius arranged for an extra cart to enable Dan to ride most of the way on the long trip, for the lion tired easily on long trips now. It pained Lucius to see his beloved pet content to spend most of his time sleeping in the sun.

After one day with the army, Lucius felt a pride in his country he hadn't known before, and he became well aware of why the Roman legions had been able to conquer the world. The soldiers marched quickly along the straight, stone-paved roads, carrying most of their gear on their backs. They wore their armor, but carried a helmet, shield, two javelins, and rations strapped on a forked pole slung over their shoulders. Mules were provided to haul tents, heavy camping equipment, and extra rations.

The situation for the Trentos was not much above that of the fighting men, for while Constantine had allowed Lucius and Felice to travel by cart, he insisted on everyone sharing the same food—grain for making bread, lentils, onions, occasional dried fish, and a daily ration of sour wine.

Each day the march proceeded in a special order—cavalry protected the flanks, the fighting units marched in front and the rear, surrounding the commanders, baggage, and heavy equipment in the middle. The centurions spurred their men to cover twenty miles each day, and the soldiers' work didn't even finish when they stopped for the night. As they approached hostile territory, each camp was entrenched to prevent the encampment from being overrun.

Before the main column arrived, advance surveyors chose a campsite—one that was situated on level ground near water and without nearby tree cover to invite ambush. While half of the troops stood guard, the other men dug ditches and piled the dirt into four-foot ramparts. Inside the camp, each group of tents was arranged in the same location every night to make pitching the camp easier and quicker, and to enable the soldiers to readily find their way around if they should be attacked during the night.

Constantine approached the Italian peninsula through the Mount Genevre pass, arriving first at Susa, where he quickly overcame that city's resistance when his legions burned and burst the city gates. At Turin, the enemy's heavy cavalry, some in suits of mail on armored horses, confronted the invaders outside the city in a gigantic wedge formation, but Constantine's army struck them down with iron clubs and entered the city with little bloodshed.

The enemy fought bravely, none of them capitulating to Constantine, so that the invaders had to fight every step of the way along the peninsula. One by one, however, Verona, Modena, Ravenna, and Aquileia succumbed to the lightning campaign of the soldiers. By October, Constantine was in sole control of northern Italy, and he began a more leisurely advance toward Rome, where he expected that Maxentius would barricade himself, making it necessary to storm the city.

As an advance measure, when they were within a week's march of Rome, Constantine asked for volunteers to enter the city as civilians to study the enemy's defenses. Marcus was the first to volunteer. He was also the first to return, and he made his report to Constantine.

"Maxentius has a large army with him, for he has enrolled deserters from the armies of Severus and Galerius, as well as recruits from Italy. He's also recalled regiments from Africa and reactivated the Praetorian Guard. He has us vastly outnumbered. Rome has enough supplies to sustain a long siege, and the city has been newly fortified with trenches. It seems Maxentius means to wait us out."

"Can we expect any help from the citizens of Rome?" Constantine asked.

"Probably not. They obviously want to be rid of their emperor, but he also has some strong supporters, especially since he's been worshiping the ancient gods and consulting the sibylline oracles regularly."

"You've done well, Tribune Marcus. I will await reports from the other scouts before I make a decision."

Within a few days, the other scouts returned, and their reports paralleled Marcus's—that it would not only be difficult, but nearly impossible to take the city of Rome. After a day's deliberation, Constantine ordered the troops to move forward, expecting to lay siege to the Imperial City, but with the approach of Constantine's army, the Roman population rioted, believing that Constantine was invincible. Faced with this tense situation, Maxentius moved out of the city to engage his enemies.

Hearing of Maxentius's action, Constantine was overjoyed to escape the boredom of a long siege, and his troops prepared for battle, but the emperor's strange behavior that afternoon puzzled those who rode with him.

❀　❀　❀

In order to keep the children from the campfire where Felice was baking brown bread and boiling lentils for the evening meal, Lucius held Lucia on one arm and rolled dice with Titus, but his mind was not on his children. *What had happened to Constantine this afternoon?* With the invasion of Rome pending, this was no time for the Augustus to lose his mind.

Lucius wasn't aware that Marcus had approached until Titus stopped playing and ran toward him. Marcus swooped him up in his arms for the rough greeting that the boy loved. Felice marveled that she and Lucius had produced this child, who was more like Marcus than like his own father. Marcus soon sat the boy aside and hunkered down beside his brother.

"I'm worried, Lucius. What happened to Constantine? Did you see anything? You were right beside him, weren't you?"

"Yes, but I didn't see anything. It seems to me that Constantine has been overly quiet since we left Modena. I thought the number of casualties might be weighing on his mind."

"But one of his bodyguards told me that he acted as if he'd been struck blind, shielded his eyes and said, 'Is this the answer?'"

"That's true. I was reminded of the incident where the apostle Paul was struck blind on the road to Damascus. I personally think that Constantine had a vision of some kind, but he didn't reveal anything to us. He kept turning to those around him asking, 'Did you see it? Did you see it?' When all of us answered in the negative, he seemed disappointed."

"Did you see anything at all?" Marcus persisted.

"A most beautiful sunset! It was at the hour when the sun is several feet above the horizon. Clouds hid the sun itself, but rays extended in all directions, highlighting and underlining the clouds. There were hues of orange, yellow, purple, and red superimposed over the bluish tints of the sky. I had been watching the changes in the display as we'd ridden along, and occasionally I saw cloud formations that reminded me of flowers, animals, or fish, but at the time Constantine became so agitated, I saw nothing."

Felice called the brothers to dine, and before they had finished their meal, a member of Constantine's bodyguard approached and handed Lucius a sealed message. "I'll wait for an answer," the man said.

Felice placed her hand on Lucius's shoulder, and Marcus cast a startled glance toward his twin. Lucius quickly broke the seal and read the message. Without hesitation, he answered, "Tell the Augustus I'll be in his presence immediately."

The soldier raised his hand in salute to Marcus, and as soon as his back was turned, Lucius handed the short missive to Marcus, who read it aloud, "Come to talk with me and bring your Alabaster with you."

"But what does this mean?" Felice asked.

"I think it's the opportunity Helena and I've prayed for. Constantine has been aware of the Christian message, but he has never been responsive to what his mother has said, and I must admit that I haven't dared to broach the subject."

"He brought Christian bishops along on this campaign!" Marcus said.

"But pagan priests also, so he isn't favoring one religion over another."

"Why the Alabaster?" Marcus questioned.

"You remember that time when we were on our way to Arles and the Alabaster was stolen, and when we recovered it, Constantine demanded to know its importance? Since I told him, he hasn't mentioned it, but apparently he hasn't forgotten about our family possession."

Lucius went into the tent, retrieved the chest from his gear, and kissed Felice good-bye. "I don't know what time I'll be dismissed. This may be a long session, so take the children to bed when you want to."

Constantine was alone in the tent when Lucius arrived. A tray of food on the table beside him looked practically untouched, and he held a goblet of wine that was almost full. He motioned for Lucius to take the bench opposite him. "I'm troubled in my mind, Lucius."

"I've been noticing that for several days, sire."

"Do you believe in divine intervention in the affairs of men?"

"With all my heart."

"I've experienced that intervention for several years—almost as if some force outside myself motivated me. But if it is a god, which one?"

Lucius opened his mouth to say, *There is only one God*, but Constantine continued, "Is it Apollo at whose shrine I've worshiped? Is it Mithra, the god of the army? Is it the sun god symbolized by the worship of our former emperors? Or is it the God of the Christians whom my mother and you worship?"

Recognizing that Constantine was in a reflective mood and that he wasn't expecting an answer, Lucius remained silent. He prayed for God to give him the right words when he did have the opportunity to speak.

"I've been hoping for a sign, and I may have received one today, but I'm not yet satisfied in my mind. I want you to tell me again about the Alabaster that was a sign to your ancestor."

Lucius tenderly lifted the Alabaster vase from the wooden box. He extended it toward Constantine, but the Augustus shook his head.

"As I told you several years ago, this is not an object of worship, but rather it's a reminder that the founder of our church, Jesus Christ, is not a dead leader, but the Son of God who lived on earth as a man, died on a cross, and rose from the dead. When I hold this small vase, I remember the death and burial of Christ, but more importantly, I'm aware of the hope of eternal life."

"And this Jesus was put to death on a cross?"

"Yes, sire. Roman soldiers did the deed, but the Jews were the instigators of His accusation and trial."

"And why did they want Him dead? I thought Jesus was a Jew."

"He was born to a Jewish mother, but the religious leaders feared Him because He preached a new approach to righteous living—namely that the motivation for a good life comes from the Spirit living within, and that salvation is of God, not what persons can do for themselves."

"Has the cross become a symbol of the Christian faith?"

"The early Christians didn't need any reminder of what Christ had done, but it seems to me that the church is introducing more imagery into its worship, for I have seen ornate crosses in several churches."

"I saw His cross this afternoon, Lucius, hovering above the sunset. It was studded with jewels, shining like gold, and the brilliance of it blinded me. The words, 'In this sign conquer,' were shouted to me from the heavens. It was so vivid that I was sure this was the sign I wanted, but since no one else saw it, I am doubting again. Before I can cast my lot with the Christian God, I need added assurance. I thought if I saw the Alabaster, that might be the sign, but while it may be for the Trentos, it doesn't suffice for me. What's your opinion of the cross I saw? Was it a vision or my imagination?"

"I have never had a vision of that nature, sire, but I do know that God has spoken in that manner to many people in the past. There is no reason that He couldn't communicate with you in the same way."

"My spies have told me that Maxentius has sacrificed to the gods, and upon their answer, he has decided to cross the Tiber and engage us in battle tomorrow. That's unsettling to me, Lucius, when I had expected a long siege. Now that I know I must fight another battle, I need a banner—a labarum to lead my troops to victory."

"May I inquire what message Maxentius received, sire?"

"The oracles told him, 'On this day the enemy of the Romans will fall.'"

Lucius smiled. "That's a rather vague answer depending on whom the real enemy of Rome is. I wouldn't be concerned with a message from a pagan god."

"But is there any sacrifice you can make—any rites you can perform to secure an answer for me? I'm desperate, Lucius. It's as if my whole future hinges on this moment."

"I can pray to God for an answer, sire. That is all that I can do. I will stay with you throughout the night, beseeching for guidance."

Lucius prayed for several hours, and each time he looked up, Constantine sat erect, staring at him. Rising at last from his knees to sit on the bench, Lucius said, "May I suggest that the Augustus lie down? If you are to direct a battle tomorrow, you will need some strength."

"I need a sign, Lucius, not strength. Under which god do I pursue this campaign?"

"I've had assurance that the answer will come. If the Augustus will rest, I will keep a vigil beside you."

Constantine leaned back on his couch, and before long, Lucius believed that he slept. Lucius spread a blanket over the Augustus, and drew his own cloak closer around his shoulders, for the night hours had brought added coolness.

Near dawn, the atmosphere in the tent changed, as if a presence had entered, and Lucius looked around quickly to see if one of the bodyguards had appeared, but he saw no one. Constantine must have sensed something unusual, too, for he raised up on his elbow with his eyes open, but Lucius did not believe that he was awake.

The room was light and Lucius thought the sun must be rising, but peering through the tent flap, he noted that it was still dark outside. Feeling almost as Moses must have felt when God told him he was standing on holy ground, Lucius slid to his knees beside the bench. He couldn't watch while Constantine received his answer.

Daylight had filtered into the room when Lucius arose. Constantine was wide awake now, and he sat on the edge of the cot, his eyes alight with purpose. "I have been cleansed, Lucius. Though I have not walked in the ways of righteousness in the past, I have been visited by a God who does not suffer a man to remain in the shadows, one who reveals the way of salvation to convert all people to righteousness. I have been redeemed. Until this moment I thought I was sufficient in myself, but now I know that I must yield to a Higher Power. How grateful I am that the almighty God has granted me that which I do not deserve, and that He has singled me out to be His servant."

"The sacred writings of the Christians teach us that our salvation is a free gift from God—it is only by God's grace through the death and resurrection of His Son, Jesus, that we are saved to a righteous life here on earth and an eternal home in heaven."

"At a later time I will dwell upon the wonder of it all, but, for now, I have the answer I desired. For months I have wondered if the power of the sword is sufficient without divine aid, and as I lay awake for most of this night, I've recalled the experiences of former emperors. Of all of them, only my father—who cast his lot with the Christians—was successful. I tended in that direction myself, and now I have the sign."

Constantine rose from the cot, walked to the door, and spoke to one of the guards who entered. "I've been instructed by God to place a heavenly sign on the shields of our soldiers before we start the battle. We are to place an X with the upper arm bent over—the sign of Christ—on all the shields."

"But, Augustus, will we have time?" the guard asked. "Our spies have just returned with the report that Maxentius is on the move. He believes that today, October 28, is an auspicious day for a battle since it marks the sixth year of his reign. He has built a pontoon bridge about twelve miles from Milvian Bridge, and his troops will cross there."

"Pass the order to march, but be sure that at least the advance guard has the symbol on their shields. Also, prepare a labarum of a cross. From this day forward, I declare that I will follow the way of the Christians. I fight under the cross of Christ."

As Constantine left the tent to prepare for the day's battle, Lucius dropped to his knees again. "God of our fathers, praise Your name for a speedy answer. May You continue to lead this great man. May he do mighty works in Your name. Amen." As he rose from his knees, Lucius wondered if Constantine's purpose would remain the same should he lose this battle. The idea didn't bear thinking about, and Lucius hastily dismissed the thought from his mind.

Lucius wrapped the Alabaster and its box carefully and hurried to tell Felice the good news. She joined him in rejoicing for a few moments, and then they quickly made preparations to strike the tent.

"I will need to go forward with Constantine to deliver his messages from place to place. But you and the children stay well to the rear. I do not want to be worried about you."

"May the God of our fathers and of Constantine watch over you today, husband!"

Once his decision was made, Constantine moved quickly and fixed his headquarters on a sandy-colored cliff at the Saxa Rubra, where he could maximize the best possible use of terrain and the possibility of surprise that it gave him. From this position about four miles north of Milvian Bridge, he stationed his army on the plateau below. The escarpment ran along the swift-flowing Tiber, out of sight of Maxentius, whose approach led along a straight highway, across a flat plain for two whole miles beneath the eyes of Constantine's pickets.

Constantine allowed Maxentius's army to cross the river and

to weary itself by scaling the height beneath the autumn sun. Then, like a thunderbolt, his own troops, fresh and ardent, burst from their cover to hurl the enemy back down the fatal slope. The army retreated, but the Praetorian Guard stood its ground, the river at its back, and Maxentius's standard floated in the air behind the guards, so it was evident that the self-proclaimed Augustus was with these troops.

Although the Praetorian Guard held firm, Maxentius's troops broke before the first charge. Apparently stunned by the ferocity of the invaders, the troops stampeded back to the river, and in their hurry to cross, jammed the passage. Constantine's men rushed in and slaughtered the troops while they vied with one another to cross. The onslaught of so many men at once sank the bridge, and thousands fell into the river and drowned.

The armored Maxentius clambered onto the last boat, and the invaders fought one another for the privilege of taking his life. But the boat tipped, and Maxentius, hampered by his armor, fell into the river. Several of Constantine's men swam into the river to retrieve the body of their enemy, which soon floated in an eddy. Maxentius was already dead when they dragged him ashore, but one of the soldiers drew his sword, cut off the head of Maxentius, and raised it on a pikestaff.

Constantine rode quickly amidst his troops and raised the labarum high. "The cross of Christ will from henceforth be the banner under which we fight. The victory goes to the God of the Christians."

Marcus worked his way over to Lucius in the midst of the shouts of victory and said, "Constantine might well have claimed this action as a great feat of arms. I've never seen him direct a battle with more expertise. What happened in that tent last night?"

"I'm not really sure, but the Augustus had a vision of some sort to make him believe that our God appeared to him. Now that his actions have resulted in this victory, I believe he'll continue to fight under the Christian banner."

"But I wonder about the fate of those of us who are not Christians?"

"He's been tolerant of most religions during the past six years, and I wouldn't think his attitude will change."

Constantine joined the brothers, his eyes alight with a destiny that only he could see. "I risked everything on this battle in spite of the fact my counselors advised against it, but we won. I can only explain that success by realizing the victory didn't come from mere human valor, but through a mysterious force that had its origin in God. I challenged the Christian God, and He kept the pledge."

The way was now open for Constantine's victorious march into Rome, and he gave orders for regrouping and the march forward. "Carry the head of that usurper at the front of our procession. Let it prove to the Romans that they have a new master."

Trumpets heralded the approach of Constantine and his victorious army, but no resistance was encountered as the hordes wound through the streets lined with crowds of Romans vying for a position to glimpse the victor. Constantine traveled through the Porta Triumphalis, along the Via Sacra, into the Forum Romanum, and to the palace that had been quickly vacated by Maxentius's followers.

The next day, Constantine met with the Senate and spoke to the enthusiastic people. The senators received him warmly and confirmed him in the rank of senior Augustus, granted him the nomination of government officials, and pledged to build a statue and an arch in his honor. Constantine, in his turn, rewarded the city with gifts and a weeklong holiday of extensive circus performances.

Once Constantine's authority was established in Rome, Lucius requested permission from the Augustus to visit his parents. As he hurried through the streets with Felice and his two children with Dan rambling along behind them, Lucius pointed out landmarks to her. "Just to think it's been seven years since I walked these streets, and I didn't even know about you then."

"I'm scared to meet your parents, but I suppose that's natural," Felice said nervously.

When they approached the door of the imposing Trento house, Felice held back. "I didn't know your family was so rich. Now I *am* scared."

"Remember that Marcus is the heir to all of this. I'm the son who's supposed to carry on the spiritual heritage of the Trentos. We won't be living here."

Angelo opened the door, and if Lucius needed any sign of the passage of time, it was Angelo's bent form, and the gray hair and wrinkles he noticed on the face of Domitilla when she rushed to greet them.

"Your father is away at the warehouse in Ostia. He won't be home until evening. Can you stay for a while?" Domitilla asked eagerly.

"We will be in Rome until after the first of the year while Constantine strengthens his political advantages. Felice and the children will stay with you, and I will come home each night. Does that make you happy?"

"Very much so," his mother said as she lifted little Lucia into her arms. "Welcome to the family, Felice. I've wanted so much to meet my son's wife," she smiled warmly and turned back to Lucius. "I suppose that Marcus has not married?"

"No, he hasn't, but he's with Constantine and will no doubt be here to visit you in a few days. Mother, it's so good to be home again."

Domitilla smiled, but she couldn't answer, for tears flowed over her face and splashed on Lucia's clothing. She hadn't expected to ever have all of her children with her again.

PART III

THE FIRST CHRISTIAN EMPEROR

ROME, CARTHAGE, ITALY, GAUL, NICOMEDIA, SARDICA,
THESSALONICA, NICAEA, CONSTANTINOPLE,
A.D. 312–330

Far distant tribes became one fatherland
Beneath your pow'r, which brought to conquered men
The rule of law; and through this common right
You made a city out of all the world.

Claudius Rutilius Namatianus I

13

ROME, CARTHAGE, 313

Lucius wrapped his woolen toga around him as a protection from the cold Roman weather and hurried toward the Trento domus. His father stood in the atrium as if he had been waiting. "The women and children are resting," he said in answer to Lucius's query. "I asked them to leave us alone. I have something to show you." Bernini laid his hand on Lucius's shoulder and gently propelled him toward the chapel room. Although he had been home for a week, Lucius hadn't had the courage to look into the room that had been destroyed the day he'd been arrested. Nor had he asked his mother about it.

Bernini pushed open the door into the room that had once served as a family worship center.

"Father!" Lucius exclaimed in surprise. Except for the absence of the Alabaster on its pedestal, the room had been restored to the way it had been in Ignatius's time.

"Father!" Lucius said again and dropped down on the bench nearest him. "The way this room looked when I last saw it has haunted me for years. Grandfather would be so pleased if he only knew."

Bernini sat beside Lucius. "Somehow I think he knows, son."

Lucius stared at his father with wondering eyes and Bernini smiled. "Yes, I at last have embraced the faith of the Trentos. I have become active in the church of Rome, which grew under the reign of Maxentius."

"But what caused you to change?"

"I suppose the teachings of Ignatius were too ingrained in my mind for me to escape them permanently, but I was also impressed by your faith, son, and that you gave yourself up for persecution because of what you believed. The deaths of Octavian and Atilia have also burdened me. If so many of my family believe Christianity is worth dying for, the least I can do is to follow its precepts."

"May I bring the Alabaster?"

Bernini pointed to the empty pedestal. "The chapel is waiting for its presence."

Lucius sped toward his room on winged feet, but he crept quietly inside so as not to disturb his sleeping family. The years had been hard on the cedar box that housed the vase, but when he removed the Alabaster and placed it on the pedestal, it gleamed as brightly as it must have done when it was new. "This will be its home as long as we're in Rome, but when we travel again, I will carry it with me."

As Bernini and Lucius regarded the vase in the illumination of the candle's glow, Lucius related the theft and recovery of the Alabaster, and how he had taken the family heirloom into the presence of Constantine. "I would like to think that our story of the Alabaster had some influence on the Augustus's leanings toward Christianity."

"It's good to see the Alabaster back in its place, so leave it here as long as you are in Rome. I suppose it's too much to hope that you will be staying with us."

"I will remain with Constantine until he releases me from his service. I hope that he will take Rome for his official residence because I long to be with my family, but he doesn't seem to be enthusiastic about living here."

"Surely he will not return to Treves now that he's taken the Italian peninsula?" Bernini questioned.

"He will probably follow Diocletian's example and establish

several places of residence, but Constantine doesn't always con-fide in his counselors nor does he necessarily take their advice."

Father and son sat quietly for several minutes until Bernini broke the silence. "I would also tell you of another change brought about by your grandfather's teachings—I have freed my slaves. I didn't have many, and though the church doesn't condemn the practice, I didn't feel at ease owning another hu-man." Bernini laid a hand on his son's shoulder in a manner that Lucius had coveted from him, a touch that always before had been reserved for Marcus. Lucius had to fight back his tears at this unexpected gesture. "I wanted you to know, for I realized the slaves had disturbed you, as well as your mother."

"Father, I'm proud of you," Lucius stammered, hardly know-ing how to cope with his transformed parent. "But what of Sulla? Will you have him freed also?"

"Marcus must make that decision."

Lucius and his father moved companionably from the chapel as Lucius pondered the difference in Bernini's attitude toward him. Now they were not only father and son, but also brothers in the Lord.

Bernice, Cato, and their two sons came for the evening meal, and as the adults lounged around the table after the children had been sent to bed, Lucius could feel the pride of his parents. When Marcus tramped into the triclinium in time for the final dessert course, Domitilla exclaimed, "At last all of you children together under our roof again! This is the first time we've all been to-gether since Bernice's wedding."

"Are you proud of us, Mother?" Marcus asked, as he gulped a large draught of wine to finish his dessert.

"Very much so," she said, her eyes bright. "Although you two men did not take the route we had envisioned for you as chil-dren, you've given us no cause for shame."

"At least none that you know about," Marcus said jokingly, but Lucius thought he detected a hint of anguish in his brother's eyes before he laughed again. Surely he had forgotten Plotina by this time.

When they moved to the atrium, Marcus spotted Dan lounging beside the pool. "So it is like old times—there's that cantankerous creature, but I believe he's begun to accept me at last. He hasn't growled at me for weeks."

"Dan is getting old and more docile," Lucius said as he sat beside the lion and rubbed a hand over the muscled back.

"I suppose he's safe enough," Domitilla said hesitantly, "but I don't like to see him unleashed around the children."

"We never leave him alone with them," Felice said, "and Dan is content to rest in the sun now. He's not very aggressive."

"What news do you have from the court?" Cato asked. "Now that Constantine has declared himself the champion of Christianity, can we pagans expect the same persecution that other emperors have handed out to Christians?" Bernice gave her husband a sharp glance and waited for one of her brothers to reply.

"You must understand first of all," Marcus answered, "that Constantine's foremost aim is to solidify his hold on the empire, and if he thinks he can do that by embracing Christianity, he will do so. But he's too practical a politician to disregard the religious beliefs of about 80 percent of his subjects and thereby antagonize the Senate, the imperial bureaucracy, and the army."

"But Marcus," Lucius protested, "there's more to it than that. I've told you about the vision that Constantine had. There's no doubt in my mind that he believes God is leading him."

"That may be so, but I'll wager if Constantine had not defeated Maxentius he wouldn't be so supportive of Christianity. However, since he believes that the God of the Christians gave him this victory—and I'll admit with our inferior forces, it does indicate divine intervention of some sort—he's going to do all he can for the church, but at this point, he doesn't have the type of spiritual faith you have."

Lucius didn't argue with his brother because he, too, remembered his question of how a defeat would have affected Constantine.

"Do you actually consider Constantine a Christian?" Marcus

hurled at his brother, not content to let the subject rest, but Lucius shook his head. "I don't honestly know."

"What's your opinion, sir?" Cato turned to Bernini.

"Probably Marcus and Lucius are both right in their assessment of the Augustus, but it seems to me that the world is ready for somebody like Constantine. Even most of the pagans disapprove of further persecution of Christians. You've told me that yourself, Cato."

Cato nodded. "Yes, as much as we hated Maxentius, we tolerated him because he put an end to violence by bloodthirsty mobs. We heard about the peaceful situation in Gaul where Constantine had given concessions to the Christians, so none of us mind if they're given freedom of worship." He tugged gently on Bernice's hair. "Besides, I'm living with one, and she isn't too troublesome."

Bernini thoughtfully rubbed his chin, and reminding Lucius of Ignatius, he said, "The times are favorable for the growth of the church. As I've watched Constantine's star rise, I've contemplated over and over the passage in the Scriptures about Jesus coming to the world at the right time."

Marcus exchanged a puzzled look with his twin, and Lucius lifted his arm in a sign of victory.

"One of the writers said that 'when the right time came, God sent forth His Son to be born of a woman,'" Bernini continued. "I believe God is intervening in human affairs again, and in His providence has chosen Constantine to execute His work here on earth."

Marcus was obviously stunned for a moment by his father's change of opinion, but he soon rallied. "You'll agree he's interfering in human affairs when I tell you my orders."

Domitilla moved to stand beside Marcus. "Will these orders take you away from us?"

Marcus placed his calloused, scarred hand over her delicate white fingers as they lay softly on his shoulder. "Just for a short journey, Mother."

"Tell us," Lucius said impatiently. "I've wondered why he was in conference with his chief advisors today."

"He gave us a long speech at first, obviously summing up what he's been thinking about for several days. To summarize what he said, he considers that the empire is in great danger because the citizens have neglected to worship God. He says that the state's near peril at the hand of men like Diocletian, Severus, and Galerius is directly connected with the lack of Christian worship, and only with the restoration of freedom of worship will the empire survive."

"There's nothing new about that," Cato said. "The welfare of the state being bound to religion has always been a part of Roman thinking, but from what you say, it appears that Constantine believes that devotion to Christianity instead of the ancestral religion like the Vestal Virgins is what will prevent the Roman Empire from extinction."

His comments about the Vestals brought a grimace of pain to Marcus's face, but he nodded. "And that's the reason I've been ordered to command an entourage to Africa, bearing several Roman bishops, and His Esteemed Excellency, Senator Anulinus, to oversee the secular administration of Constantine's orders. I'll be carrying letters to Constantine's proconsul in Carthage with orders to restore all confiscated property to the churches, and to exempt the clergy from all municipal tax burdens and public services. We'll be taking funds to Caecilianus, the newly elected bishop of Carthage, for distribution among the orthodox bishops and clergy in Africa."

"When do you leave?" Lucius asked.

"High noon tomorrow."

"Then that means I'll have a busy morning copying the dispatches," Lucius said as he sized up his brother's rigid jaw and the nervous tick in his right cheek.

Marcus absentmindedly caressed Domitilla's hand.

"You don't seem to be happy about your commission," Cato observed.

"I'm not," he answered, but with a finality in his voice that dissuaded further comments.

Bernini had been frowning since he had learned Marcus's destination, and he said slowly, "I hope you aren't going into trouble, son. We've been hearing about a possible schism in the church of Carthage."

"You mean that Christians are fighting among themselves? Haven't we had enough trouble from government persecutions?" Lucius said.

"Apparently not," Bernini said. "It may be rumors, but the church here has had reports that Carthage has two bishops. Since Constantine inserted that word 'orthodox' into his orders, he must be aware of it. A man by the name of Donatus is the leader of a radical group of dissident clergymen who have protested vehemently the election of Caecilianus as bishop."

"I've heard that, too," Cato said. "Doesn't it have something to do with the persecutions under Diocletian?"

"Yes," Bernini continued, "the state-approved bishop supposedly capitulated to pressure and has pardoned those who surrendered the Scriptures to be burned. Donatus, on the other hand, endured six years of imprisonment in a dungeon and survived several stretchings on the rack without recanting. His followers have elected him bishop, so it does look as if you'll have some trouble."

"I'll leave that up to the priests who are responsible for distributing the money," Marcus said. "My troops are only responsible for guarding the church leaders and the money."

"I trust you will have time to visit my good friend, Vergeil Brescello while you are in Carthage," Bernini said, but Marcus didn't answer him. He released his mother's fingers, which Lucius noted were reddened from the force of Marcus's clasp, and bid them all good-bye with a wave of the hand.

Although Marcus was obviously impatient to go on his way, Lucius called to his brother and followed him out to the street. "Another change in our father that might interest you is that he's freed his slaves," Lucius stated.

"What! After making me buy one that I didn't want?" Marcus said indignantly.

"He's had a change of heart—the impact of Grandfather's teachings were stronger than his practical nature. Besides, Father is growing older and is not so much interested in status and riches as he used to be."

"Why are you telling me this? Are you suggesting that I free Sulla?"

"You've never felt easy in your mind about him, have you?"

Marcus leaned against the wall of the domus. "No, and I'll tell you why—every time I've looked into his eyes, I've been reminded of an incident that happened to me in Carthage that I've tried to forget and can't. I told you about that night I spent with the slave girl."

"Perhaps your conscience has prompted you to make restitution to Sulla since you couldn't retract that incident."

Flinging his arms in a decisive gesture, Marcus said, "I'll do it! I've put Sulla in the servants' quarters now because I didn't want to take him back to Carthage, but if you'll take care of the necessary paperwork while I'm gone, I'll go tell him he's going to be freed."

Purposefully, Marcus strode toward the rear of the domus as Lucius followed him. Sulla sat on the floor of the kitchen polishing Marcus's javelin blade. He stood when they entered. Master and slave stared into each other's eyes while Lucius stood as a silent observer. Sulla no longer exhibited the haughty look of hatred he had worn for years. Although Lucius had never witnessed any softening of his attitude, at this moment he felt that Sulla had come to respect Marcus.

"Sulla," Marcus said, "I have just learned that my father has freed the slaves he bought in Carthage the same day that I purchased you. I didn't want a slave then, and I don't want one now. You'll be free as soon as Lucius can draw up the necessary papers."

Sulla turned his back to hide the surge of emotion that spread across his face. Marcus laid a hand on his shoulders. "I have appreciated the service you've given me. The Trentos will give you enough money so that you can make a new start in life."

When Sulla faced Marcus again, he still didn't show humility, a quality apparently lacking in his makeup. "I thank you," he said. "You have not been a hard master."

Marcus extended his hand and Sulla hesitantly took it. "Under different circumstances, Sulla, I believe we could have been friends. Since I must leave Rome tomorrow on business for the Augustus, I will consign you to Lucius." Even though he was relieved to be rid of this encumbrance, Marcus turned from Sulla, agony still searing his soul. The softened expression in the slave's eyes only heightened his memory of Elissa.

❀ ❀ ❀

As the ship approached the African shore, Marcus stood at its bow and remembered his first trip to Carthage. With one foot propped on a bale of rope, his body adjusted easily to the gentle sway of the boat as it slipped lightly over the rolling waves. He compared this stance to the seasick, cowering boy of a decade ago. That former trip to this Roman colony had changed his life completely—it had turned him aside from the easy life of a Roman patrician to the dangerous, exciting role of a soldier. He had gone to Carthage as a pampered boy but had returned as an experienced adult who was still not hardened enough to bear the brunt of Plotina's death.

If I had an opportunity to live my life over, would I change it any? In his memory Marcus had enshrined Plotina as a spiritual angel, but in retrospect he doubted that even with Plotina as his wife could he have been content to spend his life as a Roman gentleman. He liked the rough and tumble days of a soldier, he exulted in the danger and challenge of a battle, and he even reveled in the intrigue and jealousy of the Augustus's court.

He had become reconciled to Plotina's rejection and her death, but he'd never forgotten the slave, Elissa. *What has happened to her? Why hadn't I been man enough to turn her away that night?* Whereas thoughts of Plotina brought a calm and easy spirit, the memory of Elissa burned on his mind as a curse, as an evil demon that seared his conscience, and that curse had kept him celibate until this day. Whenever he had looked upon some woman lustfully as he'd celebrated with his army companions, the thought of that night with Elissa had dulled his passions.

When Constantine had issued his orders, Marcus had almost asked to be excused from this mission to Carthage, but he was too dutiful a soldier to disregard a command, so he had made preparations to leave. Even then, he hadn't intended to visit the Brescellos, but now with Bernini's specific request to do so, he didn't know what course to take. For his own satisfaction, he'd like to know what had happened to Elissa, but with Otho's utter disregard for slaves, he probably wouldn't have any idea. Besides, if she had ended up in some brothel as he feared, the fact would shatter him as much as Plotina's death had done.

He wouldn't have to deal with the matter of Elissa until he had carried out Constantine's orders, a duty that almost immediately developed into a trying situation for all of the Augustus's envoys. When through Constantine's edict the Donatists, as the followers of Donatus were being called, discovered that they were not included in the benefactions granted to the other congregations of Africa, they refused to accept the situation. After they had harassed the orthodox bishops to give them part of the funds, without results, they turned on Constantine's representatives with threats. Finally, they persuaded the Roman priests to carry back with them a petition requesting Constantine to select three Gallic bishops to serve as an impartial jury to arbitrate the dispute.

When it was necessary for them to wait several days before the petition was drafted, Marcus felt he had little excuse not to visit the Brescello villa as Bernini had requested. Marcus sent a message to the elder Brescello to acquaint him of his presence, and a servant returned speedily with an invitation.

Although it was several miles from the barracks to the Brescello home, Marcus set out on foot, wanting to delay the encounter as much as possible. *What a brave legionnaire, I am*, he thought disgustedly as he meandered along the crowded streets of the Roman colony, bemoaning what he considered a soft streak that he'd inherited in the Trento makeup.

Otho rushed to meet Marcus when a servant announced his arrival—an Otho who little resembled the slender youth Marcus had known. Paunchy and florid, Otho had the look of a man who had succumbed to a dissipated life.

"By the gods, Marcus!" he exclaimed, "if you aren't a sight for my weak eyes. Your father had apprised us of the fact that you had joined the emperor's army." He punched Marcus's sinewy arms and thighs that proved as hard as a stone. "What a specimen of manhood you are! But come in, come in!"

Panting slightly, Otho led the way into the courtyard. "Have you heard that my father died? I'm now the owner of the villa."

"No, I haven't heard—nor has my father, for he asked me to pay the esteemed Vergeil a visit. Accept my sympathy for your loss."

Otho nodded. "He died a month ago. It was a sudden death without suffering, and for that we are thankful."

"But what of you," Marcus said. "I haven't been in Rome for several years, so I know nothing about your life."

"I'm a married man now with two sons, one a babe in arms, the other a strapping boy of ten. You'll meet my wife at the evening meal. I've followed in the footsteps of my father, managing the family's affairs—I can't say that it's an exciting life as yours must be. Tell me, what brings you to Carthage?"

"I'm here on business for Augustus Constantine. I assume that you've heard about Maxentius's death and Constantine's rule of Italy."

"Yes, we receive news quite often from the continent, but life goes on much the same here regardless of who reigns in Rome."

Marcus's thoughts reverted often to the first night he had spent in this residence, but bedtime came and he still hadn't mentioned the slave girl. He feared that Otho would put him in the same room that he'd occupied before, or worse still, that he would offer to provide him a female companion for the night. Even when that didn't happen, Marcus slept fitfully and awakened with a determination that he would leave the villa without asking any questions. He had learned to live with that segment of the past, and he wouldn't revive it.

Marcus would have departed immediately after the morning meal, but Otho detained him by saying, "Oh, you can't leave without seeing my son, Vergeil. Come with me."

With his arm across Marcus's shoulders, Otho led him toward the rear of the villa. "Before he starts his day's studies, he goes riding. We will wait for him in the garden."

As they entered the garden where doves mourned plaintively and larks sang a greeting to the morn, Marcus sniffed the balmy air appreciatively. "Ah, what a change after the cold weather we've had in Rome. Sometimes I wish that I could be assigned to a warmer . . ." He stopped abruptly and clutched his companion's arm in a grip that caused Otho to gasp.

"Who is that boy?"

"Please, comrade, you're breaking my arm," and when Marcus relaxed his grip, Otho looked toward the stable where a boy stood with his ramrod-straight back to them. "Oh, that's Tonio, my son's slave." He winked at Marcus. "Some Roman guest left him as a present for us."

Marcus stalked toward the boy, who whirled and turned startled eyes on the burly Roman soldier approaching him, but then he dropped his eyes as any well-trained slave would do. Marcus tenderly lifted the boy's head. *Can this be a coincidence—the same graceful carriage, sensitive eyes, beautiful bone structure, brown curly hair, and skin as smooth as a girl's?* This was Lucius as a child—Lucius, at ten years old, reincarnated in this slave boy before him.

A lump rose in Marcus's throat, and he turned away so that

Otho might not see the tears in his eyes. His distress was so evident that even Otho was speechless, and Tonio dared to cast an upward glance at this stranger.

Just then, young Vergeil ran into their midst, and after he was introduced to Marcus, he turned to his slave and said importantly, "Come, Tonio, it's time for our lessons."

Marcus gritted his teeth at the masterful tone of the child's voice, and when the boys turned away, Marcus muttered, "Who is this boy's mother? What do you know about his birth?"

Otho looked sharply at Marcus and then directed a speculative gaze toward the departing boys. "Suddenly, I remember the first night you spent in this house, Marcus. I displeased you by sending one of our new slaves to be your companion for the night."

"And don't think I've forgotten, either! Her name was Elissa."

"Ah!—the name of Tonio's mother is Elissa also."

Marcus grabbed Otho by the shoulders and shook him. "Stop dallying with me, man. Why didn't you notify me about this boy? Didn't it ever occur to you that he might be mine?"

With as much dignity as he could muster, Otho extracted himself from Marcus's grasp. "Even if it had occurred to me, do you think I would have bothered you with it? Most Roman gentlemen would have had me on the rack if I'd gone through our slave quarters trying to match them with some of the children there. I have no idea how many of them I've fathered myself."

Marcus turned away in disgust, making an effort to stifle his emotions. Otho was simply a product of a brutal environment, and what Marcus looked upon as callousness was just a way of life for this Carthaginian. "I'm sorry, Otho—I shouldn't have vented my feelings upon you, but the memory of that woman has haunted me for years. To come upon this boy today—who is the image of my twin brother—made me forget my manners. Now let me ask you in a more reasonable tone—do you know where the boy's mother is? And what can you tell me about him? There's no doubt that he's mine, the resemblance is too strong."

"The boy does not look like you. I suppose if he had I might have suspected his parentage, but we have many visitors here from Rome."

"My brother and I do not look alike, nor do we have similar personalities, yet he has a son who resembles me more than he does his own father. It's a quirk of nature, I suppose."

"Tonio began to show outstanding qualities when he was a mere child, at least enough to catch my father's attention. When my son was born, father gave Tonio to him. They've grown up together, and Tonio has been educated along with Vergeil. I don't think you'll find fault in the way the boy has been treated."

"But what of his mother? I've feared all of these years that she ended up as a prostitute."

With a smile, Otho beckoned Marcus to accompany him. They climbed the rear steps to the second floor, walked along the gallery overlooking the courtyard, and Otho knocked on a door.

"Enter," a feminine voice said.

Otho opened the door, but he stepped aside to allow Marcus to enter first into a small office room. A tall woman dressed in a pale yellow tunic stood behind a desk. Despite the changes the years had made in Marcus, recognition lit the woman's flashing eyes.

"Marcus, I'd like for you to meet the housekeeper of Brescello villa. My mother took Elissa from the slave quarters several years ago for her own personal servant. After my mother died, Elissa took over management of the household. Along with a few other servants, Elissa was granted freedom by my father's last will and testament. Elissa, I believe you and Tribune Trento have met before." In the first thoughtful act Marcus had ever known his friend to exhibit, Otho exited and closed the door, leaving the couple alone.

"I've never forgotten you, Elissa," Marcus said quietly.

Elissa sat down and motioned Marcus to a seat opposite her desk. "Nor I you, sir."

"This is only my second trip to Carthage. I hope you can

imagine my surprise when I discovered a child this morning who is the image of my twin brother when he was that age."

Elissa's dark eyes flashed with fear and her hands trembled. She clinched her fingers tightly and dropped them to her lap.

"Elissa, you have nothing to fear from me. Tell me what happened to you after that night we spent together."

Elissa hesitated, then began her story. "Soon after that, Madam Brescello came into the slave quarters looking for house servants. She chose me to be her personal attendant, and I lived here in the villa." She lifted her eyes. "Because of her protection, no other man has touched me. The child is yours, sir, but I beg of you, don't take him away from me. Now that I'm free, I'm saving my funds to buy his freedom."

A light knock sounded at the door, and upon Elissa's summons, Tonio hastened into the room. He circled Marcus's chair to stand beside his mother, and she pulled him into a protective embrace. Tonio handed Marcus a parchment. "Master Otho asked me to bring this to you," the boy said in Lucius's soft tones.

Marcus unrolled the parchment, read it quickly, and laid it in front of Elissa. "It's freedom papers for Tonio, dated today. It seems my friend Otho has a generous streak under that hardhearted facade of his."

New fear blanched Elissa's face, but she turned to her son. "Tonio, you know I've always told you that your father was a Roman gentleman. This is Marcus Trento, your father. He didn't know he had a son until he saw you today."

Tonio turned wondering brown eyes toward him, and a tight pain gripped Marcus's heart. Speaking with difficulty over the lump in his throat, he said, "Would you like to go with me when I leave for Rome in a few days?"

Elissa gasped and interest flared in Tonio's eyes, but he shrank closer into his mother's embrace. Elissa's gaze caught and held Marcus's, and he said, "That is, if your mother will go, too, as my wife."

"Will you leave your father and me alone for a few minutes,

Tonio?" The boy looked searchingly from one adult to the other before he left the room and closed the door.

"How you can have the effrontery to make such a suggestion, I don't know. I said I've thought of you often, sir, but never with any kindness. I loathe you and the very thought of your disregard of my person. Now that I am free, don't ever think that I will submit to you willingly."

Marcus was struck dumb, and he stared at her for several minutes. He eased down on a bench before he answered her.

"If I hadn't taken you some other man would have."

"You don't know that, nor do I. The only pleasure you've given me is my son, and I want him to have the advantages you can provide as his father. So if there is a room in your home where I can live and see my son daily, we will come to Rome with you. Perhaps I can serve as housekeeper as I have done here."

"I really want to marry you," Marcus insisted because her beauty and queenly bearing were even more captivating than he had remembered. It would be easy for him to love this woman.

She shook her head. "Only on my terms."

With poor grace, Marcus stood and said, "It seems I have no choice."

"There is also another barrier between us," she said. "I could not go into any household where my brother is held as a slave."

"I don't understand," Marcus stammered.

"The slave Sulla that you bought is my brother. Didn't you know that?"

Weak-kneed, Marcus sank to the bench again. *How many more surprises would this day hold?*

"So that's why I always thought of you when I looked at Sulla. I deduced it was because you were both slaves, but now I see how many features you have in common. Sulla would never discuss his past with me." Still dazed by this surprising news, he added, "But that problem need concern you no longer. I freed Sulla before I left Rome."

"Then we will travel with you."

"Probably we will set forth within a week."

Marcus left her presence, feeling more cowed than he'd ever felt in his life. Here, at last, was a woman to make him a worthy mate, and she hated him. And on the heels of that disturbing knowledge, came the thought, *How am I going to explain Elissa and Tonio to my family? Lucius will have to help me.*

14

ITALY, GAUL, 313–320

By the first of February, Constantine was on the move again to Milan. Before he left the once-great imperial capital, Constantine abolished the Praetorian Guard, which for years had been the maker and protector of emperors.

At first, when Marcus was assigned to oversee the destruction of the Guards' barracks, he lamented inwardly the passing of this great institution. He was much annoyed at his concern, for he was supposed to be the hard-hearted twin, not the sibling who mourned for things of the past. *I must be getting old,* he thought as he watched the dismantling of the old barracks. Life was full of changes, some good and some bad. Without the passage of time, he wouldn't have a son now, so one had to give up some things to have the advantage of others.

He smiled when he remembered the tumult Elissa and Tonio had caused in the Trento domus, but his parents were so happy that their firstborn had at last produced an heir that they chose to overlook the nature of his conception.

As for Elissa, Domitilla was glad to transfer the oversight of their home to another woman, and she capably settled into her new role. Marcus saw Elissa often and discussed his plans for Tonio.

Did he sense less resentment in her attitude toward him, or was that only wishful thinking on his part?

When they arrived at Milan, Constantine took up residence in the palace that Maximian had built. Lucius had a room in the palace, while Marcus moved to the barracks with his men, but they saw one another often for the officers dined at the palace each evening, and whenever possible the two brothers shared the same couch.

One evening, during an entertainment that interested neither of them, Marcus said, "I had thought this would be a brief sojourn and then we would return to our families, but it seems unlikely."

"We knew, of course, that Constantine had come here to meet with Augustus Licinius, but now he's sent for his sister, Constantia, and Fausta."

"Rumor has it that a wedding will take place between Licinius and Constantia, and I suspect the emperor thinks he should spend a little more time with his own wife if he ever expects her to produce an heir."

"He has an heir in Crispus, and the way he dotes on the boy, perhaps he thinks he needs no other."

"Crispus has the making of a soldier, so it's little wonder the Augustus favors him, but life is uncertain in the Roman Empire, and it's not well for a ruler to base all his hopes on one son."

"Speaking of sons, I had a letter from our father. He says my Titus and your Tonio are acting just the way we did as boys."

"That bad! Then I suppose my son is getting the worst of all the tussles, even though he's the eldest."

"Serves you right for the way you used to treat me. Of course, Titus was born with your temperament, so he's hard on Tonio. However, just as in the past, Dan has elected himself to be Tonio's champion. In fact, Father said that they keep the lion caged all the time, for without me in the house to control Dan, they fear he might become violent. I should have brought him with me, but Dan is getting old. I don't know how many more journeys he can take."

"I had a letter from Father, too—an official paper. He wrote that since neither of us are interested in the family enterprise, he's made Cato the manager of the import business. The family dwelling will be mine, now that I have a son to inherit it, but he's divided the rest of the estate into three equal portions between us and Bernice. He thought this was the only fair way since we aren't involved in the business and Cato is willing to take over. I wrote him immediately that I agree with his disposition. Does Father think he won't live long?"

"If the shock of actually receiving a letter from you doesn't hasten his demise, then his chances are good for a long life."

❀ ❀ ❀

Lucius felt as if he were witnessing the presentation of a great drama as he participated in the events of the next few days. Licinius, Augustus of the East, arrived in Milan with trumpets heralding his approach and an honor guard of soldiers flanking him. In order to keep a large number of troops in Gaul, Constantine had arranged for his mother, Fausta, and Constantia to travel together under the protection of one century, and they arrived the next day after Licinius.

Because Licinius distrusted his Caesar, Maximinus Daia, he didn't want to be absent from his domain for long, and he insisted upon a speedy marriage. Constantine, however, wasn't to be hurried until he had accomplished what he wished. Before the marriage, an alliance between the two men was sealed and future empire policy drafted, and a concordat formulated that set the rules for treatment of Christians throughout the empire.

Lucius wept for joy when he copied the first draft of the edict that was to be circulated among Roman subjects everywhere. *What a day for Christianity! Surely there must be rejoicing in heaven by my Aunt Atilia and Uncle Octavian and the many others who have been martyred for their faith.*

Our purpose is to grant both to the Christians and to all others full authority to follow whatever worship each person has desired, whereby whatsoever divinity dwells in heaven may be benevolent and propitious to us, and to all who are placed under our authority. Therefore we thought it salutary and most proper to establish our purpose that no person whatever should be refused complete toleration, who has given up his mind either to the cult of the Christians or to the religion that he personally feels best suited to himself. It is our pleasure to abolish all conditions whatever which were embodied in former orders directed to your office about the Christians, that every one of those who have a common wish to follow the religion of the Christians may from this moment freely and unconditionally proceed to observe the same without any annoyance or disquiet.

Lucius laid down his stylus and thoughtfully studied the remainder of the concordat. The rejoicing he had felt at first turned to bitter gall in his mouth. His first thought had been that this agreement between the two emperors spelled freedom for the church, but as he read the words over and over, a warning bell rang in his heart. Not even the fear he'd experienced as he marched to his probable death in the arena could compare with what he felt now.

He wasn't dismayed because the emperors were recognizing other religions, too, for he believed in freedom of religion. He didn't want others to perish because of their beliefs. Even when Marcus had embraced Mithraism, he had not derided his brother, even though he knew he was wrong. No, it was more than that. Instead of the emperor's action being a forerunner in granting religious freedom to all, he had a vision of the future and realized that this first move of the Roman Empire to pass laws governing the religious conduct of its citizens was actually the death knell of the faith as it had been promulgated by Christ. Probably he wouldn't live to see it, but what of his descendants? *Will the day come when an established state church puts to death all those who cherish freedom and tolerance of religion?*

It didn't bear thinking about, and as Lucius picked up the stylus and finished copying the concordat, he decided that he would give Constantine the benefit of a doubt. Surely the man meant only good for Christians by this decree, which concluded,

> This agreement will ensure that the divine favor toward us, which we have already expressed in so many affairs, shall continue for all time to give us prosperity and success, together with happiness for the state.

Licinius stayed only two days at Milan before he departed with his youthful bride, affirming his fear to leave his provinces too long to the mercies of Caesar Maximinus Daia. As the residents of the royal palace gathered on the grounds waiting to bid good-bye to the newlyweds, Marcus joined Lucius, who stood near a stone pillar basking in the warm sun. Even his woolen cloak could not ward off the cold wind sweeping down from the Alps.

"I expected more celebration over these nuptials," Lucius said to his brother, "but I hear expediency dictated this quick departure of Licinius."

"That's part of it, but Constantine and Licinius neither like nor trust one another. They became allies until Maxentius was out of the way, and now each is wary of the other. It won't be long until the two of them are fighting. Will we ever have peace?"

"Strange words from a soldier. I thought you liked to fight."

"Once that was my only interest in life," Marcus said wryly. "Now I look forward to the end of my twenty-year stint, when I can leave all of this behind and settle down with my family in the Trento domus. If I were home more, I think I could persuade Elissa to marry me. I'm counting the days and the hours, but right now seven years seems like a long time."

"But it will pass rapidly, Marcus. It's been a bit longer than that since I had to flee Rome for my life. The days have passed quickly."

"When you decide you've had enough of court life, will you return to Rome, too?"

Lucius shook his head. "The peaceful life of the Rhone Valley beckons me. We will return there."

"Then we will be separated. I would not like that, brother. I've never said it before, but I thrive on your presence."

Lucius was surprised at his brother's melancholy mood—much out of character for him—but he had changed a great deal since his discovery of his son and the challenge of winning Elissa for his wife.

"It's my understanding that Constantine means to remain at Milan for several months. If so, I plan to ask leave to go back to Rome and see if Elissa will bring Tonio here. Do you want me to bring Felice and the children when I go for Tonio and Elissa?"

"By all means. But can you bring Dan, too? I miss the old pet. We've been through much together."

"There have been times when I've regretted my impulse to import that beast from Africa, but I'll bring him along—in a cage."

After the departure of Licinius and his bride, Marcus left for Rome and Constantine took a hunting trip, which gave Lucius the added time he needed to finish copying the concordats and dispatch them to all parts of the empire.

Crispus, too, had declined taking the trip with his father, although he liked to hunt. One afternoon, he stopped by Lucius's room. "My grandmother and Octavia have sent me to bring you to their apartment. They seem to think that you've neglected them."

Lucius laid down his stylus, closed his portable writing desk, and reached for his cloak. "I could take no leisure until the last of these dispatches was ready for the post. However, I have finished and will go to visit them at once. Where are they housed?"

"Come, I will show you. I'm going that way," Crispus said.

Lucius laid his arm over Crispus's shoulders as they walked along. "You're as tall as I am, Crispus. You're maturing rapidly."

"My father grew quickly, he tells me. I'm like him," Crispus said with a touch of pride. When they reached the west wing of the palace, Crispus pointed to a door. "That is where you will find Grandmother Helena," and he moved on down the corridor.

"Aren't you going in with me?"

"No, I spent several hours with them this morning. I'm going riding with Fausta now."

An hour passed rapidly as Helena and Octavia asked about Felice and the children, and they discussed the things that had happened in Treves since Constantine had departed.

"The Franks are getting bold again and have made several hits against our forces along the border," Helena reported. "I fear Constantine may have to teach them a lesson. If so, he'll move out of here quickly."

"I hope not before Marcus returns with my family," Lucius said.

Rapid hoofbeats sounded at the front of the palace, and Helena rose to look outside. A frown creased her face. "I don't like it. There go Fausta and Crispus again. They have ridden every day since Constantine left. I know that Fausta instigates these encounters. Crispus is on the verge of manhood, and I don't like the way Fausta leads him on."

Octavia's worried eyes rested on Helena. "Perhaps if you would talk with Constantine, he could put a stop to it."

"It may be that I'm being too sensitive about their relationship. What do you think, Lucius?"

"I can't see any problem, but Felice does, so it may be that men and women view these situations from different perspectives."

"I won't say anything to Constantine yet, but it may be time for me to have a talk with Fausta."

"Have you heard anything from Cassus?" Lucius asked Octavia.

"He's been married for many years, but I haven't seen him since we left the East to come to Constantine's court. He's working as an architect with Licinius in building up Nicomedia. He will be happy to hear about this agreement the two emperors have reached."

"Give him my greetings when you write again. We became good friends that time you were in Rome, and I've wanted to visit him in Nicomedia, but the time has never presented itself."

"The time will come," Helena said. "It seems to me that my son is looking eastward, and when he goes that way, he'll take us with him. And I hope so—Octavia and I have talked often about making a pilgrimage to the land of Jesus' birth, and it will break the length of the journey if we can depart from Asia. There are things God wants me to do, but we must have peace before I attempt them."

As he listened to Helena, Lucius recognized the same ambition that characterized her son. No wonder that Constantine had lofty aspirations when he had inherited a double portion of eagerness and drive from his two parents.

❀　❀　❀

One more day, Lucius thought, *and we'll be home*. It had been quite an undertaking to make this journey from Asia Minor to the Rhone Valley, but Felice was eager to see her parents, and both of them coveted a few months away from the rapidly ascending star of Constantine. They had traveled by ship from Thessalonica to Arles and overland from there.

Lucius's household had grown considerably in the years since he'd left the Rhone when he had only Felice and the two horses they'd ridden. Now he was the father of three children and employed a bevy of servants to look after them. But this was the first trip Lucius had taken without Dan, and he missed the lion's gentle padding steps by his side. Dan had died a few weeks ago at Thessalonica, where Constantine had settled into winter quarters. The absence of the lion was another thing to remind him of the passage of time.

Across the campfire from where he sat, Felice lifted her eyes and caught his gaze as she tested the contents of the baking oven. "It's been a long time," she said.

"Fourteen years since we were married, and no visit at all for three years. It's a great experience to be part of history in the making, but we may have missed the best of life."

She laughed at him. "Don't sound so gloomy. You know you wouldn't have missed being a scribe for Constantine."

Titus strode into camp, and as always Lucius marveled at this son who looked so much like Marcus. By some quirk of nature, Marcus had fathered a son in the image of Lucius, while even in temperament, Titus was a copy of Marcus. This often led to heated disagreements between Lucius and his son.

"What time will we arrive at my grandfather's tomorrow?" Titus asked.

"Around noon, I think, if we don't take too long to break camp in the morning."

"I'll sound the gong early," Titus said, "so there will be no reason for anyone to oversleep. I'm eager to see my grandfather." He looked pointedly at Lucius. "I've considered riding on by myself tonight. I could be there in a few hours."

Lucius shook his head, and without argument, Titus accepted his father's decision. After he left them, Felice dropped down on the rug beside Lucius. He pulled her close and nuzzled his face in her soft blonde hair. She returned his kiss, then looked over his shoulder at her stalwart son. "He's not as brave as he would have us believe," she said with a smile.

"No, but he has proven that he's on the verge of manhood during this trip. I'm proud of him."

"Yes, I know," Felice said, a bantering quality in her voice. "It shows."

"I wish our children could visit more often with your parents, but that seems an impossibility now that Constantine has turned his back on the West to spend more and more time in the eastern provinces."

"And I wonder why? Granted, the weather is wonderful in Thessalonica in the winter, but summer is beautiful in Gaul."

"It's more than the weather. Constantine is keeping his eye on Licinius, and now that he's established Crispus and his trusted advisors in Gaul, he doesn't have to worry about the West."

"With Crispus in Gaul and Constantine's household in the East, Crispus and Fausta are kept separated."

"Women!" Lucius exclaimed with a smile. "Will you never tire of scandalmongering?"

"Will you never believe the obvious?" Felice countered.

Bearing Constantine some sons hadn't lessened Fausta's interest in Crispus. Although Lucius and Felice rarely disagreed, the suspected mutual attraction between Crispus and his stepmother was a point on which they had vastly different opinions, but Felice wisely let the matter drop. The situation continued to concern Octavia and Helena, and although the two women missed the boy, they were relieved when Constantine had made him a Caesar and assigned him to Gaul.

Titus sounded the gong before daylight, and their company broke camp soon afterward. The sun had not yet reached its zenith when they saw the family farm in the distance.

Conrad and Hannah noticed their approach and ran to the courtyard to greet them. Lucius noted that three years had not made much difference in this couple, for they didn't look much older than they ever had. *That's what comes from living in this serene rural setting*, Lucius thought, not without a pang of regret that his own life had followed a different course.

Hannah had eyes only for the baby girl, Panetta, whom she had not seen, while Conrad grabbed Titus and Lucia in a tight embrace.

"We may as well leave," Lucius said to Felice. "You can see who the honored guests are."

Laughing joyously, Conrad boomed, "You can stay, too, since you brought our grandchildren. Why didn't you send word you were coming?"

"Emperor Constantine has settled at Thessalonica for the time being, and since events in the empire are peaceful now, we asked for a two-month leave, and here we are."

"Two months!" shouted Conrad. "Praise the Lord. If you stay that long, perhaps you won't leave at all."

"Don't tempt us," Lucius said.

In honor of their arrival, Conrad declared a holiday so he could visit with his family while his workers mingled with Lucius's servants. In the evening, Lucius and Conrad walked around the farm and eventually came to the house Lucius and Felice had built when they were first married. Lucius peered into the dark interior, which Hannah had kept clean and orderly.

"Felice and I would like to live here during our visit." When Conrad started to protest, Lucius laughingly said, "You can house the children. Felice and I would like a little time to ourselves."

Descending from the plateau, they settled on a wooden bench in the olive grove to watch the sunset, and Conrad said, "How goes the state of the empire? What's in the future for us as Roman citizens? What's in the future for us as Christians?"

"I'll answer the latter question first. The church is growing in numbers and strength. In fact, this rapid growth disturbs me. I'm not sure that Jesus meant for His kingdom to expand by the might of the sword, and that's what it amounts to. Now that Constantine has declared himself on the side of Christianity, the church is the strongest institution in the empire, excluding only the army."

Conrad nodded sagely. "It's the same here. The bishops in each of the synods are increasing their power over the laity. While I rejoice that so many are calling upon the name of the Lord, I fear that it is not good for the faith."

"Felice is displeased with me when I talk this way, and I acknowledge that Constantine has done much for the church in a physical way, but spiritually, I believe that Christians are drawing away from the teachings of Jesus."

Lucius leaned his back against an olive tree. As the sun dipped slowly behind a cloud and then disappeared from view, the radiant streaks of red and purple left in its wake reminded Lucius of the day Constantine had seen the vision on the eve of the battle at Milvian Bridge. "Constantine considers himself a man with a mission," he mused, "with two objectives—to restore the empire and to renew the world. He believes this can only be done by enrolling men in the service of Christ and allowing almighty God to lead them to make a better world. He says that he's the tool God has chosen to effect this change."

"And he may well be the one if he goes about it in the right way."

Lucius nodded agreement. "But it bothers me that he has never declared himself a Christian. He's become the champion of the church, but he has never formally become a member of the body of Christ. Am I wrong to be troubled about that?"

"Possibly, for he may be succoring the Christians while keeping one foot in the pagan camp."

"That's true—though he's been a big help to Christianity, he has never made war on the pagans. And there are times when he doesn't act like a Christian."

Conrad interrupted him by laughing. "That could be said of all of us, my boy!" Sobering, he said, "But what of the Donatist revolution? Our news is sketchy here in the West."

"Constantine's first attempt to restore unity in the church has failed, and he has become disgusted with the situation. After two councils and the emperor himself issuing a decree that the Donatists were in the wrong, he ordered their suppression by force and the confiscation of their property. But since this only increased their fanaticism and prolonged the strife in Africa, he's decided to leave the agitators to the judgment of God."

"The Scriptures plainly tell us to leave vengeance to God, so this may be Constantine's wisest move," Conrad said as he rose and led Lucius through the olive grove.

"Yet another schism has developed in the Egyptian church that threatens to disrupt the peace and unity of Licinius's realm," Lucius continued. "A controversy is raging between Arius, an ascetic of exemplary life and unquestioned moral character, and the bishop of Alexandria. At first, their disagreements were similar to those causing the Donatist schism, but now it has developed into a more serious conflict."

"Jesus expected His followers to live in peace and harmony, and to love one another, and the church has fallen into conflict such as this! It's discouraging, my son."

"In the apostle Paul's writings, we read that the church of his day had many problems, and this Arian heresy is similar to some of those that Paul had to deal with. Arius is advancing the theory that Christ was not of the same substance as God, meaning that He was not the Son of God and equal to the Father, but rather a created being. Arius has been excommunicated from the church, but he continues to expound his beliefs."

"That's too deep for me, Lucius. I opt for a simple faith based upon Jesus' teachings."

Smiling, Lucius said, "I've more than answered your question on the state of the church—outwardly the church is at its height, but the state of the empire is another situation. It's my opinion that in his objective to restore the empire to its former glory, Constantine intends to do so under a single head—himself. He's not said that in so many words, but he talks often of the great emperors of the past—Julius Caesar, Augustus, Hadrian. And he speaks disparagingly of the tetrarchy and the problem it has caused."

"His son Crispus seems to be holding the line here in the West. We have heard that in the past few months, in spite of cold weather, he has inflicted a tremendous defeat on the Alemanni and Franks. Many of the latter have sworn their loyalty to the empire."

"I hadn't heard that, but it comes as no surprise. The boy has shown amazing qualities of leadership. Felice and I are fond of Crispus."

"With subordinates like his son, do you think Constantine is capable of ruling such an empire?"

Lucius considered for several minutes. "Yes, I do. If I didn't recognize his superior leadership—both militarily and politically—I wouldn't have stayed with him this long. Without a doubt, Constantine is the answer for the future if he can control the many forces around him."

"But how near is he to becoming sole ruler? Licinius won't capitulate easily."

"No, but Constantine is like a cat waiting to pounce on a mouse. He's staying in Asia most of the time, and when he has the least excuse, he'll attack Licinius. There's been an uneasy truce since they ended their civil war four years ago and signed a peace agreement. And Constantine may soon have an excuse for war—if rumors are true, Licinius has violated the Edict of Milan and is allowing Christians to be persecuted in his domains."

"May God have mercy!" Conrad exclaimed. "Must every generation go through these trials to prove its mettle?"

Lucius shook his head. He had no answer for that question.

15

A s the small ship threaded its way slowly through the Sea of
Marmara, Lucius gazed around in awe. Less than two
weeks ago he had returned from Gaul, and now he was approaching Nicomedia, the city he'd wanted to visit for years. Shortly
after his return, he had been called into Constantine's living
quarters where the emperor sat with Fausta and her two sons.

"We are blessed to have you and your family back at the court
again," Constantine said. "No other scribe pleases me as well.
While you enjoyed your holiday, I trust you surveyed the political situation in Gaul."

"The area is peaceful, sire, and according to Felice's father,
Caesar Crispus is conducting himself wisely as a ruler and military leader."

"Your words please me, Lucius, for the boy reminds me of
his mother, who had more wisdom than I. It's time for him to
provide some heirs for me—I can't wait on these children," he
said, motioning to the boys playing at his feet. "I intend to arrange a marriage for him in the near future."

In spite of himself, Lucius's gaze shifted to Fausta, and the
rage mirrored in her eyes stunned him. *Why is she so angry—
because she doesn't want Crispus to be married, or because
she thinks her own sons will be passed over?* Lucius looked at

the youthful Constantine II, now four years old, who had been appointed a Caesar the same time Crispus had been. *Surely Constantine will deal fairly with all his children, so is there some validity to Felice's suspicion that Fausta is enamored with her stepson?*

Lucius snapped to attention when he realized that Constantine was addressing him again. "I hope that you're rested from your journey. There's a mission I want you to undertake for me."

Why me? Lucius thought, but his question was answered when Constantine said, "I want someone I can trust to go to Nicomedia and ascertain the conditions there. My closest advisors are well known to Augustus Licinius, who would look with suspicion upon their presence. You, however, could travel to Nicomedia to see your cousin Cassus, who is also a trusted friend of mine. He could give you an adequate picture of the situation. I will not order you to do this, but I would appreciate your cooperation.

"I will gladly go, sire. I haven't seen my cousin for many years."

Constantine had immediately dispatched a servant to book passage for Lucius across the Sea of Marmara. As he approached the port of Nicomedia, Lucius hoped that Cassus had been at home to receive the hastily sent letter about his arrival, for Constantine had not allowed time for an answer.

When the captain of the vessel told Lucius that it would be another hour before their arrival, he retreated to a sheltered place on the leeward side and patiently settled down to wait, but his leisure was interrupted by the words of a song that swept over his head.

> God is the only God
> So why should we argue
> About the substance of Christ?
> He's a created being
> But who can convince old Alexander?
> Who just for spite,

Has jailed the good Arius
and expelled him from the church,
An action he's fought with all of his might.

Startled, Lucius looked around and discovered that the singing came from a seaman who sat on the top deck mending a rope. He'd heard that Arius had written songs to promote his beliefs in the inferiority of Christ compared to the Father, but he'd hardly expected them to be so widespread that a common sailor would be spouting the words. *It's heresy!* He tried to close his ears to the words that the seaman sang over and over while the boat approached land and sidled up to the dock.

Lucius forgot his dismay over this incident while he enjoyed the reunion with Cassus, who looked enough like Octavian so that Lucius had no trouble recognizing him. The trip to Cassus's home and the evening passed quickly as he made the acquaintance of Lanitra, who proved to be an entertaining hostess. She obviously ruled the household *and* Cassus, but Lucius had never seen a man who more obviously enjoyed being subservient to a woman. After the meal was finished, Lanitra retired from their presence, shooing the children before her, leaving Cassus and Lucius alone.

Lucius unwrapped the bundle he had carried from his bedchamber. "I brought the Alabaster," he said.

Cassus quickly grasped the vase. "Thank you. Thank you. I had hoped to see it again. After the turmoil of the past decades, I didn't even know if you had been able to keep it intact."

"There have been some close calls, but God has allowed me to retain control of it. The truth represented by the Alabaster has been a source of comfort to me during some trying times."

Cassus continued to hold the Alabaster as if the contact gave him a sense of peace. Then he said, "The winds of change are threatening the church again here in the East. The controversy between Arius and the bishop of Alexandria over the nature of Christ is causing so much turmoil that Augustus Licinius is threatening to intervene."

"I heard a seaman singing about the controversy today."

"Oh, it's the talk of the empire. I had hoped that Licinius would just ignore the situation, but even though Arius has been excommunicated from the church, he will not give up. He's traveling around the empire to gain support, and he has some powerful supporters, including the bishops of Caesarea and Nicomedia, and the Empress Constantia."

"As I told you in my letter, Constantine sent me to gain some insight on conditions in the East. He's not sure that Licinius is upholding their past agreements, but I don't expect you to tell me anything that might bring you trouble."

"Licinius is suspicious of everything that causes a disruption because he senses an impending power struggle with Constantine. He believes that Christians are sympathetic to the western emperor, so he's preparing edicts to ban all church synods and to restrict worship services to outdoor meetings beyond the gates of cities. Women will be forbidden to attend services with men. Already he's dismissed Christians from his court, the army, and other governmental offices."

"But what has caused him to change? While Licinius has never shown any particular friendship toward the church, he hasn't been a fanatic pagan, either. And I'd hoped that the Empress Constantia would exert influence over him."

"He's afraid of Constantine, especially now that he's using Sardica as his chief base of operation. Actually, I don't believe that Licinius has any animosity toward Christians, for up to this point, he's chosen to ignore us. Now that Constantine has so wholeheartedly embraced Christianity, Licinius apparently believes that he must move in the opposite direction."

"Do you expect a full-scale persecution again?"

"I fear so. It's been many years since my parents were killed in the persecution under Diocletian. Will I face the same fate? Will I have the courage to stand firm in my convictions? It frightens me when I think that I might not have the courage they had."

Lucius laid a hand on his cousin's arm. "Don't worry about it. You've heard about my arrest and escape from death several years ago?"

"Yes, Marcus was here in Nicomedia soon after that and he told me about it."

"I'm ashamed to admit that I was terrified, but when it came to the moment when I walked out into the arena, God gave me a peace and calm that was unbelievable. I was unafraid when it came to the testing time, and you will be, too."

Lucius limited his visit to three days, and when Cassus accompanied him to the wharf, their leave-taking was strained. If it came to civil war between the two emperors, the cousins would be enemies—with Cassus in the employ of Licinius and Lucius in the employ of Constantine.

Their fears remained unspoken, but Lucius knew that Cassus's thoughts were the same as his when his cousin embraced him. "We are always brothers in the Lord, Lucius. Nothing can change that."

❈ ❈ ❈

Through the next year, Cassus watched helplessly as edicts were posted in public places forbidding Christian services and instruction. Churches were locked, others were destroyed, episcopal synods were prohibited, and bishops imprisoned. A few believers were martyred, but the persecution in Nicomedia didn't rise to the oppression under former emperors. Cassus was not arrested, so he never knew whether his faith would have stood testing, but he mourned for the faithful who paid for their faith by death and torture in the part of the empire controlled by Maximinus Daia.

As the year merged into 321, it became evident that war between Licinius and Constantine was inevitable. Contact between the two halves of the empire was punctuated by reproach, distrust, suspicion of plots, and bad faith. The situation caused

Cassus many sleepless nights. His cousins and sister were with Constantine, and while he owed no particular loyalty to Licinius, he had profited in his employ as an architect on the public improvements of Nicomedia. *If Constantine's army besieged the city, what could he do?* He wouldn't want to fight his relatives, yet he would have to protect Lanitra and their two children.

Licinius became more and more unpopular with his people when he increased taxation to finance the conflict he envisioned for control of the empire. And in spite of the influence of his Christian wife, Licinius gathered a group of diviners, wizards, seers, and pagan priests to serve as his advisors. Their sacrifices resulted in a promise of victory over his enemies, and the oracles blessed his enterprise. As conditions worsened between the two divisions of the empire, Licinius called his closest supporters to a sacred grove, studded with statues of the gods, where he delivered a speech contrasting the old and the new, the Christians and the pagans. He asserted that the former had betrayed the religion of their ancestors but that the current sacrifice would prove which group was mistaken in its judgments. "Let the decision of this present occasion determine between our gods and those whom our opponents profess to honor."

Of course the augur's interpretation of the sacrifice was complimentary to the pagan gods, and sporadic persecution of the church continued throughout the East. Cassus believed that Constantine would use this persecution as an excuse to attack Licinius, but with the coming of 322, he heard from Octavia that Constantine had problems in his own realm.

To assemble an army to attack Licinius, Constantine drew detachments from his western front, thus opening the door to invasion. The Sarmatians crossed the Danube into Pannonia in the spring of 322, and by midsummer, the Romans had defeated the barbarians, killed the Sarmatian king, and scattered numerous captives as slaves and tenants in the lower Danube Valley.

The following winter, Constantine took to the field again to drive the Goths out of Moesia and Thrace. Once again victorious, he laid down rules for a better defense of his borders, punished civilians who helped the barbarians, and chastised garrison officers who had granted furloughs when these Gothic raids impended. But this victorious campaign gave Licinius the excuse he had wanted, and claiming that Constantine's operations had violated his territory, he declared war on his fellow Augustus. After three years of expecting war to start any day, it was actually a relief to Cassus when the declaration was made. *But how should I pray? What would be better for the church? If Licinius wins, Christians will be persecuted, but doesn't the church always grow at such a time? But should Constantine win, the church in its security as a state institution will stray farther and farther from the teachings of Jesus.* All Cassus could pray was, "Father, your will be done."

❋   ❋   ❋

"I've lost count of the many capitals we've lived in with Constantine," Felice said, with the first hint of complaint Lucius had ever heard her utter about their lifestyle.

Lucius couldn't blame her, for it always fell to her lot to make their new quarters seem like home, and as soon as she had the dwelling to her satisfaction, they had to vacate for a new site. Constant years of relocating were bound to be grueling to a woman, for Lucius himself had grown weary of moving so often.

"We've been here at Sardica for two years, and I doubt that Constantine intends to move his headquarters now. Though he's commanded the troops to congregate at Thessalonica, I assume his court will stay here. If I'm called upon to travel with the emperor, you can remain here, for as long as Helena is in Sardica, you can be assured of protection."

When Felice spoke again, Lucius realized that it was more than a possible move that had disgruntled his wife. "Must he always wage war, Lucius? If Constantine has embraced Christianity as he seems to have done, why can't he exemplify our

Savior's teachings about peace? 'For those that take the sword shall perish by the sword.' It was bad enough to have so much fighting when he was protecting the empire from barbarians, but a civil war is so much worse. Lucius, I fear for our son," Felice added, voicing the real reason for her concern.

Lucius moved to comfort her when tears spilled over her cheeks. *There is more of Felice to embrace now than there used to be*, he thought as he pulled her close, but her plumpness hadn't dimmed his love for her. "Titus thinks of himself as a man, old enough to make his own decisions. I would have preferred that he follow the ways of peace, but I couldn't dissuade him. He's always held Crispus as an idol even when he was a child. He wants to fight under him."

"I know that, and I'm proud of his courage, but it's a mother's way to fret over her son."

"A father's, too," Lucius admitted, "though we do not show it as readily. But as for Constantine, this conflict with Licinius has taken on the nature of a crusade—a holy war. His counselors have advised him to be cautious, to try to work out the differences with Licinius peacefully, but he emphasizes his need to rescue his fellow Christians from oppression."

"Was the recent legislation forbidding anyone to force Christians to perform pagan sacrifices directed against Licinius?"

"Indirectly, yes."

"Is it possible that we might yet avoid civil war?"

"Only by a miracle—there's been too much preparation on both sides. Gothic prisoners of war have improved the harbor at Thessalonica to accommodate two hundred naval vessels, two thousand transports, and thousands of rowers and sailors."

"And one of those sailors will be my son."

"Most likely, for Crispus has been called from Gaul to take command of the navy. Besides this naval buildup, Constantine's army numbers 130,000."

"And I suppose Licinius has equal numbers."

"Even greater, or so the spies report. His army exceeds ours by at least 35,000 men, and he has a navy of 350 ships. Trying to prevent war now would be like attempting to stop the ocean waves. I believe it's a war to the finish, and the victor will rule the empire."

"I hope you're wrong," Felice said.

"So do I," he agreed.

❀   ❀   ❀

In February 324, Constantine left Sardica for Thessalonica, and Lucius and Marcus set out with him. Elissa and Tonio had spent the winter months in Constantine's camp, and in spite of the fact that Elissa still refused to marry Marcus, she and Felice had become like sisters, and they encouraged one another while the men marched with Constantine.

When Constantine's company arrived on the high bluff above the city and looked down upon the assembled navy and army, pride swelled in Lucius's heart in spite of his lack of enthusiasm for this fight. Love and respect for his emperor overshadowed the fear for his son. If Titus died in this conflict, he would die for a great cause. Even if Constantine's ulterior motive was for conquest and power, he still spread the Christian message, and Lucius was thankful for that, even though he believed that Constantine had a distorted understanding of Christianity.

Constantine and his advisors took up residence in the palace where he had spent several winters, but the emperor's private chapel, which housed the labarum, was moved close to the army encampment. For many years, Constantine had taken this chapel with him on every expedition. Before each battle, he went into the chapel to ask for victory and divine guidance.

The next day after their arrival, Lucius approached Constantine. "Sire, may I have leave to seek out my son? I have a message for him from his mother."

Constantine waved his agreement. "I will not need your assistance the rest of the day. I desire to see my son, too, so if you encounter him, command him to attend me. He doesn't want the other commanders to think I'm showing him favoritism, so he may not approach me until I send for him. Not only do I want to see him, but I would like some information about my granddaughter. And if the news I've heard is true, I may expect still another grandchild in the near future."

"Your granddaughter is about two years of age now, isn't she?" Lucius inquired politely, although he was eager to be on his way to Titus. He knew that Constantine doted on Crispus and his family at Treves. When the child was born, Constantine had shown his happiness by a general amnesty to most criminals in the area—with the exception of enchanters, murderers, and adulterers. These prejudiced exceptions convinced Lucius that Constantine still hadn't completely embraced all Christian principles.

"But I mustn't hold you with tales of my family. Seek out your own child and give him my greetings."

Carrying a basket of food for Titus, Lucius walked through the army encampment on his way to the waterfront, and he was impressed as always with the efficiency of a Roman camp. Constantine's army might not rival the one of the great Julius Caesar, but these were well-regimented troops. There was no idleness—some men polished their armor, while others were sweeping, digging, chopping wood, or loading supplies.

He waved to Marcus, who was overseeing the repair of a barracks to be used by his men while they were in Thessalonica. His brother was a fair taskmaster, but the vinewood stick that he held had a purpose other than to serve as a badge of his newly received centurion's rank, as the soldiers soon found out if they slacked at any task he assigned them.

Although eager to find Titus, Lucius paused to observe the troops in training. New recruits were being instructed in the building and use of siege machines—equipment built on the spot, such as battering rams to knock down barricades or towers to enable the soldiers to climb to the top of walls. The outside surfaces of the machines were covered with padding, metal plates, and wet hides to serve as protection against the enemy's stones and fire-arrows.

Several recruits were grouped around some practice wooden catapults, which threw either large or small stones, depending on whether the goal was to slay a man or break down city walls. Each legion had catapults of several sizes.

Lucius shook his head in wonder as he watched the soldiers quickly deploy a tortoise formation, the maneuver saved for a final assault. Fifteen soldiers raised shields above their heads to make an interlocking roof, while men at the edges formed walls with their shields. This moving tortoise formation protected the soldiers from enemy fire until they were close enough to again form fighting ranks. Lucius knew the strength of this formation, for he had once seen a chariot drive across the top of one without crushing it.

Lucius spent more than an hour searching for Titus, and when he found him, his heart trembled and his eyes moistened at the sight of his handsome offspring. Believing that his son would want to appear hardened before his comrades, Lucius almost omitted the customary embrace, but love for the boy overpowered his other emotions, and he held out his arms. He need not have feared Titus's reaction, for the boy enveloped Lucius in a clasp that left him short-winded. "Father! I didn't know you'd come with the emperor."

Gasping for breath, Lucius said, "Your father isn't too old to take the field with the army, but I'll admit, staying at home with your mother was tempting."

"Then she didn't come with you," Titus said, obviously disappointed.

"No, but she sent her love and greetings, and also a basket of food. She feared the army wasn't feeding you adequately, but from the looks of you, I think her fears are unfounded."

"Does she think I'm still a child?" Titus said severely, but he eagerly opened the basket. "Honey cakes! My favorite."

While Titus ate the pastries and shared them with his friends, Lucius squatted beside him. "How do you like the military life?"

"It's wonderful," Titus answered stoutly, but lowering his voice, he added, "but more grueling than I'd expected, and more than once I've considered coming back home. Do you think I'll ever be as tough as Uncle Marcus?"

"Perhaps in twenty years. Is the navy ready to sail now?"

"Yes, we've been waiting for orders from Constantine. Crispus is a good commander."

When Constantine received word from his military leaders that all preparations were finished, the emperor entered his tent chapel to meditate, for he never made any important decisions without this time of searching. While Constantine was in the chapel on the day of departure, Lucius knelt with the emperor's advisors and prayed for victory. Near the chapel, a select squad of soldiers surrounded the labarum, much more ostentatious than the simple one the soldiers had made before the battle at Milvian Bridge. The gold-overlaid lance with a crossbar was topped by a golden wreath framing the Christ monogram. From the crossbar hung a golden, jewel-studded cloth bearing three medallions, representing Constantine and his two oldest sons. To carry the labarum into battle was a hotly contested honor.

On this morning, Constantine must have received his message quickly, for in less than an hour he rushed from the tent, lifted his sword toward heaven, pointed toward the labarum, and shouted, "In this sign conquer! God will give the victory!"

A mighty shout lifted from the assembled army as Constantine mounted his horse and headed eastward. Lucius glanced toward the harbor as he followed the emperor out of the city, hoping to catch a glimpse of Titus, but in the flurry of activity he couldn't tell one sailor from another.

✸　✸　✸

By the latter part of June, Constantine's army arrived at Adrianople, a city on the east bank of the Hebrus. With a mock attack, Constantine diverted attention from his main force, which crossed the Hebrus on the third day of July to engage Licinius's army, firmly entrenched in the city. Constantine encircled the enemy with his cavalry, and by nighttime he had routed his foes. Many of Licinius's men fled to the mountains, but the emperor of the East rallied what troops remained and escaped to fortified Byzantium. Constantine laid siege to this city and notified Crispus to break into the straits between the Aegean Sea and the Sea of Marmara.

The ships took the fleet of Licinius by surprise, and Crispus's bold and skillful offensive caught the enemy ships out of formation, which threw the sailors into such confusion that with approaching darkness, they lost contact with their comrades. Neither side could claim a victory that first day, and under cover of darkness, both fleets escaped to their respective harbors in Europe and Asia.

By midmorning, the vessels were engaged again, but about noon a strong southwind caused shifting storms that cast many of Licinius's ships on the rocks. The wind further carried the vessels of Crispus into the enemy's midst, giving him an advantage that he quickly turned into a complete victory.

The Hellespont was opened without further resistance, allowing provisions to flow into Constantine's camp, where he was already moving siege equipment into place along the ramparts of Byzantium. From lofty towers erected on artificial mounds, large stones and darts from the military machines were tossed into the city. Battering rams attacked the walls. Before he was surrounded, Licinius gathered his treasures and escaped to Chalcedon in Asia. Constantine won a decisive victory on September 18. While his troops held the attention of Constantine's army, Licinius retreated once again, this time to Nicomedia, where citizens had already destroyed his statues and, with a hastily written edict, abolished the laws and judicial proceedings of Licinius's reign.

While Constantine debated an advance on Nicomedia to capture his brother-in-law, his sister Constantia approached the encampment and asked for an audience with her brother. As she entered the camp, Lucius compared the empress to how she had looked when she'd departed from Milan with Licinius many years ago. Still proud of bearing, the years with her pagan husband had nonetheless taken a toll. Gray streaked her dark hair and her face was wan and wrinkled. Though he watched her for signs of nervousness, Lucius saw none as she bowed slightly to her brother.

"Well, Constantine, you are to be congratulated. Your men have defeated the best army on the earth."

"Not without help," he answered as he pointed to the labarum exhibited behind him. "The God whom we both serve has given the victory."

"I have come to ask for my husband's life. Surely, since you have taken all else that he holds, you will be gracious enough to spare him."

"Your request is granted, but he will have to be exiled. I can not trust him otherwise. And you, will you depart with him? You will be welcome at the court of Constantine."

"He's my husband and the father of my son. I'll stay with him."

"I'll give you one week to leave Nicomedia before I occupy it. You will be conducted to Thessalonica, where you will have opportunity to live a normal life. However, please warn Licinius that this reprieve depends upon his good behavior."

That night when Lucius wrote an account of the campaign to Felice, he ended his letter, "After almost forty years, the empire is united under a single lord who claims Christianity as his religion, though he has not been baptized into the established church. As one of the priests who accompanies us said, 'At last we have one ruler, one world, one creed.'"

16

NICOMEDIA, NICAEA, 325

Another new home," Felice said as she wearily surveyed their living quarters in the palace at Nicomedia.

Smiling, Lucius said, "Maybe this is the last one. Now that Constantine is the sole ruler of the empire, perhaps he'll make this his permanent residence. I don't believe he'll live in Rome."

"Of course he won't. How many times has he been there in almost twenty years of his reign?"

"Not many, I'll admit. At least for now, perhaps, we're finished with change. I welcome this chance to be with Cassus and his family."

Lucius wasn't finished with change, for shortly after Constantine established himself in Nicomedia, Marcus stopped by their dwelling.

"Why, Marcus!" Felice said. "I hardly recognized you."

Marcus no longer wore his armor and the red cape of the Roman centurion, and he looked naked without his javelin, sword, and helmet. His muscular shoulders were draped in a brown woolen toga. Lucius's startled eyes caught and held his twin's gaze.

"I'm no longer a soldier," Marcus stated jauntily, but Lucius was quick to catch a hint of sadness in his eyes.

"I suppose your twenty-year stint has been completed."

"Actually, I've been in the service more than twenty years, but I didn't want to leave Constantine in the midst of the biggest battle of his career. But I can't trust my luck further—I've come through more battles than I can count without major wounds. It's time I give it up, although I'll admit it's difficult."

"Will you be staying here in Nicomedia?" Felice inquired.

"No, we're leaving for Rome in less than a week." He reached out a hand to Lucius. "Since the death of Father, our mother needs me at home, but I will miss you, brother. Is there any chance of persuading you to go with me? You've given Constantine the best years of your life—he'll surely release you."

"No, I won't leave him as long as he's still making policy for the church. I don't have much influence with the emperor, but just enough that I can sometimes sway him in decisions that would harm us greatly. We'll hang on a bit longer."

"And you'll be happy to know that Elissa is going with me as my wife. She says that her association with you made her want to become a Christian, and she believes she has to forgive me before her sins can be forgiven."

Lucius put his arms around his brother. "I'm happy for you," and a tearful Felice said, "She's loved you for a long time, but her pride kept her from admitting it."

"So we lose more of our family," Lucius said after Marcus left. "To lose Marcus and Elissa, coupled with the departure of Titus to the West, seems more than I can bear.

"I still don't see why Constantine sent Crispus back to Gaul so quickly. After the great victory he directed, he was the most popular person in the whole empire."

"Perhaps that's the reason! Constantine may be jealous of his son's popularity."

Felice shook her head. "I don't think so. According to Octavia, Fausta is the jealous one, and Helena is quite concerned about it. Fausta hasn't had a good word for Crispus since he married, and she believes that Constantine is favoring Crispus over her sons. She's trying to poison Constantine's mind about Crispus."

"She doesn't have that much influence over him," Lucius protested.

"She didn't in the past, but I'm not so sure now. Constantine is getting old enough that it swells his pride to have a young woman like Fausta fawning over him."

"If there is trouble between Constantine and Crispus," Lucius fretted, "I hope Titus isn't involved in it."

Now that the empire was established under his control, Constantine devoted more of his energies to spiritual matters. His residence soon took on the appearance of a church, which one entered under a vivid allegorical painting that showed Piety at war with Evil. The first day of each week, Felice and Lucius, along with other members of the staff, gathered in the great audience hall in answer to a summons from Constantine to hear personal sermons dealing with prayer, instruction, and devotion, on which the emperor often worked far into the night. He delivered each dissertation with earnestness. When emphasizing an important point, Constantine rose from his throne.

As he had done in other parts of the empire, Constantine set aside the first day of the week for worship, and he held services in the chapel that all of the court was urged to attend. Praying daily either in his private apartment or in the chapel tent that he transported with him, he tried to urge this practice on his people. He encouraged Christianity in the army by marking off the day for rest and worship, and he composed a prayer that all soldiers were expected to recite.

> We know Thou art God alone; we recognize in Thee our king. We call on Thee for aid. From Thee we receive victory; through Thee we are made greater than our enemies. We recognize Thy grace in present blessings and hope on Thee for the future. We all beseech Thee, we implore Thee to preserve our king, Constantine, and his pious sons safe and victorious to the end of our days.

When Lucius made his first copy of the prayer, he said to Felice, "There won't be any trouble over this, for even the pagan soldiers can recite these words. The Christian day of worship falls on the old pagan-appointed day of the sun god, and Constantine refers to it as Sun Day, not the Lord's Day."

"Yes, even Marcus wouldn't have objected to this prayer."

"Not now, anyway, for Marcus has mellowed a lot since he became a family man. He thinks of his loved ones before he acts." Lucius flexed his fingers. "I'll have to finish these when I return. The emperor is having a meeting with his religious advisors this afternoon, and he wants his scribe to attend."

"And, of course, his scribe wants to be there!" Felice smiled.

"Yes. Constantine never forgets that I'm guardian of the Alabaster, and I'm sure he has some superstitious belief about it. At least enough that he asks for my advice occasionally, especially when his chief advisors disagree."

"Why has he called this meeting?"

"Constantine is determined to restore religious unity in the empire just as he's united it politically. He's distressed because Christians are fighting among themselves. Of course, I'd prefer it wasn't so, but when the church deviates from scriptural precepts, it's time for argument. It isn't a matter of principle with Constantine; he simply wants to curb disharmony. He doesn't care what people believe as long as peace is maintained."

"You're not quick to speak your mind, but occasionally you do so with force. Watch your tongue, husband."

He waved at her reassuringly, walked along the corridor from his quarters to the main courtyard of the palace, and entered the emperor's private quarters. The bishop of Nicomedia was present, as well as Ossius, Constantine's Spanish Christian advisor from Cordova. A few other priests lined the benches below Constantine's throne. Lucius walked to the small table set aside for his personal use in taking notes on the emperor's councils or writing down sacred revelations that Constantine wanted preserved.

"Men," the emperor began after a few more priests entered, "it's time that something is done about this dispute between Arius and Bishop Alexander. When the church forsakes the law of God and engages in dissension, it jeopardizes the influence of the church, shakes the empire, and angers your emperor."

Bishop Ossius lifted his hand for permission to speak. "It isn't a simple matter to settle, sire, for too many people have become involved."

"In my opinion, it's a foolish argument that started when Bishop Alexander asked Arius, his presbyter, a question that should never have been asked in the first place."

As Lucius's stylus moved over the crackling parchment, he listened intently to the discussion with a feeling of despair. It was unfortunate that Constantine failed to understand the point of controversy between Arius and the bishop of Alexandria. Bishop Ossius apparently realized this, too, for he said, "Sire, may I review for you again the nature of the controversy?"

"Briefly. Briefly. You've gone over it before without convincing me of its importance."

"One of the basic tenets of our faith is that Jesus is the Son of God. Although He came to earth and lived here for thirty-three years as a human, He never lost His divinity. When He returned to heaven, He sent the Holy Spirit to be His representative in human hearts."

It was obvious to Lucius that the emperor had no comprehension of what Ossius was saying, but he nodded for the priest to continue.

"The Bible teaches that the Father, Christ, and the Spirit represent one indivisible godhead—the Trinity."

"A difficult principle to believe."

Ossius nodded agreement. "It's a belief that comes only by faith—it isn't something that can be determined by reason."

"But what's the main issue?" Constantine said impatiently.

"Perhaps it can be simply put: In what sense was Christ divine? Arius and his followers deny that Father and Son participate in a common divinity, teaching that God originally lived alone and had no Son. They say that at some unknown time, God created Christ out of nothing to be His building agent in the material world."

"That makes sense to me—one supreme God Who creates lesser gods to do His work. This is similar to our pagan beliefs and easy for us to understand."

"But it's contrary to the teachings of the Scriptures, which state that Christ existed from the beginning and is equal to almighty God," Ossius was quick to point out. "Before Arius began to dispute this belief, he was a favorite of his bishop, Alexander of Egypt, but when he refused to curb his writing and teaching on this subject, Arius was condemned as a heretic and excommunicated from the church."

Lucius looked up from his writing to glance at the Bishop of Nicomedia who was known to be an Arian. *Why isn't he defending his belief? Or does he prefer to influence Constantine privately?*

"Then the matter should have stopped there," Constantine argued, "but I understand this Arius has been traveling throughout the empire gathering adherents to his views. Now the church is divided into two camps—the believers in Arianism and those who hold to the orthodox view that Christ is divine. And what purpose has all this controversy accomplished? Nothing but division, and I want it stopped."

Constantine reached for a wax tablet lying on the table beside him and handed it to Lucius. "I have here a message addressed to both Alexander and Arius. I want you, Lucius, to make several copies of this letter. Then, Bishop Ossius, you will carry these missives to the two major disputants in this case. Will you read the general text of the letter, Lucius?"

Lucius stood to read the brief message.

I am displeased with the controversy which is not only affecting the church, but the empire as well. This question over the divinity of Christ is a matter that cannot be settled by human minds, besides being a dispute of minor details. You agree on the most important aspects of our faith—morality and worship. As learned as both of you are, you surely know that philosophical sects often disagree on details of their beliefs, but they remain together because of what they have in common and still respect the differences of the other on general matters. I urge you to do the same. I will expect an assurance upon Bishop Ossius's return that you have done this.

❋ ❋ ❋

The first of the year had passed when Ossius returned to Nicomedia, and his news did little to please the emperor, who had expected his representative to have a signed agreement to end the controversy. Instead, Ossius had joined forces with Alexander and Athanasius, another Egyptian presbyter, to oppose the struggle that Arius had started. Constantine was enraged that instead of bringing a peace settlement, the bishop of Cordova had become personally embroiled in the argument.

"I've had enough," Constantine declared when he received Ossius's report. "I'm going to mediate this situation. Lucius, draft letters to every important bishop and priest in the empire. I want it done speedily, so you will need to hire additional scribes to help you. Command these church leaders to come to Nicaea for a council beginning in June. The transportation of these men will be at government expense, so none will have the excuse of cost to stay away. While you're preparing the letters, I'll choose messengers to carry them from the western borders and eastward to the lands of the Tigris and Euphrates. Urge haste."

Lucius sketched a draft of the letter and handed it to Constantine for his approval. "That is exactly what I wanted written, Lucius. You're a valuable worker and friend. Prepare these drafts as quickly as possible. When you have fifty ready, send them to me, and I will dispatch them to the farthest regions of the empire."

When Lucius reached his apartment, Octavia and Helena were visiting with Felice. He didn't mention the intention of Constantine—let someone else share this surprising news.

"We have come to say good-bye," Helena said.

Startled, Lucius said, "What! All of our friends and family are leaving. I didn't think about losing you—I thought you would always stay with your son."

"It won't be forever, Lucius, but Octavia and I are leaving for Judaea next week. You know we've talked about it for years, and now that peace has come, it seems the appropriate time for our journey."

Lucius shook his head, and Felice said, "It seems such a long journey for you."

Helena smiled wryly. "I'm not getting any younger, and I'll admit that a journey of this magnitude may be difficult for a woman of seventy-three years, but I have so little time left. If I'm to serve my Master, it has to be now. Still, I would never try it without Octavia's company."

"Your son has heaped much worldly goods upon you," Lucius said, "no doubt making you the richest woman in the world. I would think that would be enough honor for anyone."

"Oh, it isn't honor I'm seeking." Helena paused and for a moment seemed lost in memory. "When I was a young Christian and Diocletian issued an order that everyone in his palace should sacrifice to the gods, I did as he commanded. I recanted belief in my Savior, and I've never forgiven myself. Years ago, I had a vision that I would be able to do some service for my Master to atone for that recanting. In Judaea, I will try to locate some of the holy relics identified with Christ. That will be my atonement."

"You don't have to atone for your own sins. Christ did that when He was crucified," Lucius said.

"It's easier for me to believe that I can work out my own salvation."

"Helena also has permission to stop at Antioch and depose the bishop there because he does not believe in the Arian philosophy, which Helena espouses," Octavia said with a piercing look at Lucius.

Lucius heard this comment with dismay. He knew that Helena, as well as Constantia were Arians, and both women exerted a great deal of influence over the emperor. Arianism, unchecked, could blight the true faith for centuries, and Lucius feared the outcome of the council at Nicaea.

"We wish you a joyful and rewarding journey," Lucius said as the two women rose for departure. "How long do you anticipate it will be before you return?"

"Probably a half year or more." Helena laid a wrinkled hand on Felice's arm. "We will miss your company while we are gone, but I'm looking forward to this pilgrimage.

❈ ❈ ❈

By the first of June, envoys began to arrive in Nicaea from places as far away as Arabia and Persia. As the council's opening day neared, the palace rooms were all occupied and the city's public housing had filled to overflowing with the nearly three hundred bishops and other church leaders who'd gathered at Nicaea. As Constantine's special scribe, Lucius had been commanded to attend all meetings and to keep records of the proceedings.

On opening day, the empire's spiritual leaders swarmed into the main hall of the palace. As Lucius recorded their credentials, he noticed an overwhelming majority from the eastern provinces, with especially large numbers from Egypt, where the controversy had started years ago. Only a few people came from the West, where Christians had little interest in the dispute.

Constantine's staff had arranged the bishops in two rows facing each other and seated in order of rank. When a trumpet heralded the entrance of the royal family, the bishops rose.

Constantia, the emperor's sister and a radical Arian, led the way. Lucius would have been just as happy if she hadn't come, but after Constantine had put Licinius to death for treason, Constantia had returned to her brother's court. Hearing of a military conspiracy in Thessalonica in favor of the deposed Licinius, Constantine ordered that the deposed emperor should be killed and his young son with him. Upon the death of her family, Constantia had little recourse except to turn to her brother. She had been a tremendous influence on Constantine in swaying him to the Arian point of view. Fausta and Constantine II preceded the emperor.

Out of respect for the Christian leaders, Constantine was not accompanied by his palace guards. Lucius had never seen the emperor more elegantly arrayed than he was today in a jewel-encrusted purple and gold brocade robe. Most of the bishops had never seen Constantine, and the mere majesty of his presence must have stunned them to silence, for even with the heat in the room generated by more than three hundred bodies, no one twitched in his seat, and not a cough nor a sigh attended the entrance of the sole ruler of the empire. As he hastily recorded his impressions of this scene, Lucius wondered if the gentle scratching of his stylus on the parchment was heard by everyone in the room.

Constantine stopped in front of the modest golden chair provided for him, for he had chosen not to sit on a throne. The emperor signaled for the bishops to be seated, but Ossius, who had been appointed to preside at this occasion, indicated that the emperor should sit first. Lucius smiled, thinking that this impasse might continue indefinitely, until they solved the issue by everyone sitting down simultaneously.

The bishop of Nicaea gave a welcoming address to the visiting bishops as well as Constantine. Then the emperor spoke briefly. "I have called you together for the purpose of settling a crucial question that is affecting the peace of the empire. Division in the church is worse than war. I thank God for granting us this special occasion, and I further pray that we will not allow the Devil to influence our deliberations. I urge you to approach this matter in the spirit of peace and harmony."

As he surveyed the assemblage, Lucius realized how difficult it would be to have agreement among these delegates, many of whom showed the marks of persecution. Some bore the scars of the imperial lash. One priest from Egypt had lost an eye, another's hands were disfigured from the application of red-hot irons. These men, who had stood firm in their faith during persecution, were not likely to compromise with those who had recanted and had been restored to places of leadership.

Eusebius, the bishop at Nicomedia, started the council with a statement supporting Arianism, but when he presented the document for the approval of the delegates, an irate bishop tore the parchment to shreds. In spite of the passion of some churchmen, Lucius was surprised that the majority of the delegates favored compromise.

Another creed was presented by Bishop Eusebius of Caesarea, a friend of Constantine and a nominal supporter of Arius. The emperor immediately threw his support to this creed, but he interfered little in the debate that raged over the next two months. Finally, a document emerged that all of the delegates except two bishops found acceptable. One of the dissenters was, understandably, Arius, who by an imperial decree was ordered into exile with his followers. His writings were condemned to be burned.

Constantine asked Lucius to quickly copy the adopted creed, and as he drafted the words, his hands trembled, wishing that he could glimpse down through the centuries. *Will this hard-fought victory supporting the deity of Jesus withstand the tides of time? Will succeeding generations even remember what has been done here at Nicaea?* But Lucius knew that it was not his responsibility to insure the perpetuation of the Nicaean creed—his job was to copy it and send it on its way among the churches.

We believe in one God, maker of all things visible and invisible, and in one Lord Jesus Christ, the Son of God, only-begotten of the Father, that is, of the substance of the Father, God from God, Light from Light, true God from true God, begotten not made, consubstantial with the Father, through whom all things have come to be, both things in the heavens and on earth; who on account of us men and our salvation came down and was made flesh, became man, suffered, and rose again on the third day, ascended to the heavens, and will come to judge the living and the dead; and in the Holy Spirit. But those who say there was a time when He did not exist, and He did not exist before He was begotten, and that He came into being from nothing, or who declare that the Son of God is of another hypostasis or substance, or is created or changeable, these the church anathematizes.

While Lucius struggled to organize this document to define the essence of the decision reached by the council, the delegates debated other matters. Some churches were celebrating Easter on the same day as the Jewish Passover, but Constantine's anti-Semitism wouldn't permit this, and a date was finally agreed upon that was satisfactory to all. The resurrection of Christ would be celebrated on the first Sunday following the first full moon after the vernal equinox that occurred on or near March 21.

The end of the council coincided with the date marking the twentieth year of Constantine's rule, and while towns and cities held festivals celebrating the prosperity and security of the empire, the emperor invited all the bishops to a state banquet before they departed for their homes.

Lucius was appointed to oversee the seating of the guests, who passed through files of imperial guards to the private dining rooms where Constantine personally welcomed them and ushered them to their dining couches. In appreciation for their work in solidifying the empire, Constantine presented gifts to every guest when the feasting ended.

❋   ❋   ❋

The rapid hoofbeats of his mount kept pace with Lucius's active thoughts as he urged the animal on to greater speed. It had been two months since he'd seen his family, and he was eager to be home. He especially wanted to discuss the disquiet in his heart with Felice, for his mind was not at peace as he considered the big change that had come to Christianity since Constantine had involved himself in the faith.

For over three hundred years, the church had grown through the witness of believers who had often been out of favor with the government and who had followed Christ with considerable danger. Now Constantine had introduced problems previously unknown, for instead of Christians being in disfavor with the authorities, a man was more likely to succeed in the imperial government if he was a member of the church. Decrees of church councils had become imperial laws, and the emperor was looked to for important decisions on church matters. Priests and bishops who had served their parishes at great risk a few years ago had now come under the protection of the Roman government. Lucius shook his head in dismay. He feared that such close connection between the church and the state would eventually spell disaster, although not many of his fellow Christians agreed with him.

The imperial palace at Nicomedia seemed strangely quiet after all the ceremonies at Nicaea, for since Constantine would not return for another week, no activities had yet started in preparation for his arrival.

Lucia and Panetta were playing in the courtyard, and they rushed toward him. He hugged both girls to him and hustled into the family's quarters. Felice embraced all of her family as much as she could with her short, plump arms. "I had not expected you to return today," she said with a smile.

"My work was finished for the present, and since Constantine and his family intended to spend some holiday time along the seacoast, he didn't need a scribe. He granted me leave to return home."

"And the proceedings must have pleased you," Felice said as she ushered him to his favorite chair and brought him a glass of wine.

"The council approved of what I consider the scriptural teachings of the deity of Jesus, so that did please me. Constantine is content, believing that he's put all religious wrangling behind him. Personally, I'm not that confident. I do not approve of the emperor exerting so much influence over religious matters. I fear the church may have to go through many years of testing before we are the followers that we should be. But, wife, I bring you other good news."

She looked toward him with questioning eyes, and he drew his children close. "How would you like to visit your grandmother Domitilla?"

The two girls beheld him mutely, for Panetta had never seen her grandmother, but Felice shook him by the shoulder. "What do you mean?"

"Constantine has decided to celebrate his vicennial in Rome together with the decennial of his sons. We will be traveling with him."

"I don't relish the long trip, but I would like to see the rest of the family." She paused suddenly. "The decennial of his sons," she repeated, "then that means Crispus will be there, and . . ."

"And Titus, I would assume. So we'll have all our family together."

Felice laughed and cried at the same time as she started planning for the trip, and their apartment was full of laughter.

"It's been quiet without you, Father," Panetta said. "We're happy you're home."

After they had supped and retired for the night, Felice said, "In all our rejoicing, I forgot to tell you about Octavia's letter. She writes that Helena has made some amazing discoveries in Judaea and that she has great plans for marking some of the sites connected with Jesus. She said nothing about their return. It's too bad that she will miss the celebration."

"Never fear. Constantine would not observe such an important event without his mother. He's dispatched a messenger to command her return from Judaea to Rome by water. She may well be in Rome before we arrive."

"And Octavia also writes that she has some very important news for you—it's something about the Alabaster."

Lucius sat upright in bed. "What could that be?"

"I don't know," Felice said sleepily, "but she sounded quite excited about it."

Felice soon slept soundly beside him, but any thought of slumber had fled for Lucius. *After more than three hundred years, how could anyone in Judaea know about the Alabaster?*

17

Rome, 326

The imperial entourage, slow and lumbering, wended its way from Nicomedia toward Rome. Gold coins had been struck to honor Constantine and his sons and to extol the eternal glory of the Senate and the people of Rome. These coins were issued in towns and villages along the way where elaborate festivals were planned to vie for the attention and the patronage of the emperor.

"I'm tired of all of this celebrating," Lucius complained to Felice more than once. "Whatever we do in Rome is going to be anticlimactic. And besides, I want to see my family."

"Especially Titus, I suppose," Felice teased.

Lucius didn't respond to her quip. "But in a way I dread going home, too. It's been so long. My father is gone now—the lions, too. Many of the familiar things of childhood will not be there."

"But we will see Marcus and Bernice and their families. This is part of growing old, my dear husband. We may as well as accept it."

He pulled her into a tight embrace, and his passion flamed for her as much as it had in his youth. "Some things never change," he said laughingly. "My love for you is as strong as ever. You've been a good wife, Felice."

❋ ❋ ❋

Considering the accolades he had received en route, Constantine's entrance into Rome was frigid by comparison. The emperor chose to overlook the coolness of the senators, who had not forgiven Constantine for his repudiation of the ancient gods on his first visit to the city. This time, the emperor seemed determined to be conciliatory. He wooed the Romans with dazzling displays and brilliant games, and he even gave audience to the astrologers and magicians, but he didn't offer any compromise on his Christian goals. He made it plain that there would be no reconciliation with the Senate on any terms other than submission to the Christianization of Rome. To prove his point, he appointed a Christian governor for Rome over the will of the mighty Senate.

Arguments raged in the Trento house over who would be the victor in this impasse between the Senate and Constantine, with Marcus and Cato united in their belief that the emperor would be defeated by the senators. "The Senate has a tradition of controlling the rulers, and they aren't about to change now," Cato said.

"And they will not submit to Constantine's Christianization of Rome," Marcus asserted.

Lucius remained passive most of the time, listening to his relatives discuss the changes the emperor was making in Rome, but occasionally he gave them a thrust. "Marcus, you were with Constantine for years. Do you actually believe that he will back down from any position he's chosen?"

"He may have to."

"You will see," Lucius said. "If the citizens of Rome do not follow his leading, he'll abandon the city. He's often considered the advantage of having his headquarters farther east. If he intends to establish the imperial capital elsewhere, Rome will suffer. But that's enough of argument. Octavia and Helena will be calling here this afternoon, so I pray you will not start on this chatter in their presence." Lucius stooped to kiss Domitilla, who spent most of her time reclining on a couch. Though she was still beautiful and alert, her health had deteriorated, but she remained comfortable under the ministrations of Elissa, who had resumed management of the domus.

"I've promised to take the girls for a walk before our guests arrive," Lucius said. He held Panetta's hand while Lucia walked beside him as they went toward the garden. He paused for a moment to look into the empty outbuilding where he had once kept all of his pets. He half-expected Dan and Beersheba to jump out at him. They walked along the creek that had separated the Trento property from the home of Plotina Flavius. *Does Marcus ever walk here and think of his secret meetings with his childhood love?* The forest where Lucius had hidden the night he left Rome was no longer there. Instead the trees had been cut and the land sold to provide a site for the church that Constantine planned for the city. The Church of the Martyrs was to be constructed on a scale unprecedented anywhere in the empire.

Lucius deplored this progress and wished at times that his life could stand still. But when he looked at Lucia, who was almost as tall as he was, he realized how much had transpired in his lifetime. He remembered Bernice's wedding, knowing it would not be long until he would see Lucia given to another man, and he shook his head over his shock when he had seen Titus.

Lucia voiced his thoughts by saying, "Father, it's hard to believe that Titus has grown into a man. He seems almost a stranger to me."

Crispus and his bodyguards, which included Titus, had not arrived in Rome until a week after Constantine's arrival. Titus had visited the Trento home twice, and although he had grown as tall as Marcus and almost as brawny, he maintained a boyish love for his parents and family. And as for Crispus, Titus still looked upon him as a hero, as he had all of his life.

Lucius put his arm around Lucia. "All of my children are

growing up too fast to suit me. I was just thinking that it won't be long until I'll have to give you away in marriage."

"Not yet, Father, please. I haven't found anyone that I love that much. I do like my cousin Tonio since he's so much like you, but I suppose he's too near a relation for marriage."

"Yes, especially since his father and I are twins. But I have wondered about Cassus's son, Octavian II."

Lucia flushed and dropped her head, but Lucius sensed that the idea did not displease her. He patted her shoulder. "Don't worry about it yet—when the time comes, we'll find someone that suits both of us."

When Helena and Octavia arrived a while later, Lucius exclaimed, "I should never have questioned whether you were able to take the trip to Judaea, Helena. You appear younger than ever." Her radiant appearance seemed to stem more from an internal quality than from a physical one.

When she spoke, her tones were hushed and reverent. "The journey exceeded all of my expectations. I found the cross on which Jesus was crucified, and even one of the nails that pierced His flesh. I was directed in my dreams to go to Jerusalem and search for the site of the tomb of Jesus. We discovered the place, but it was covered with earth and a temple for Venus had been erected upon it. Constantine had given me a great amount of power to be used at my discretion, so I ordered the pagan temple destroyed and workmen are beginning to erect a Christian basilica over the cave where He lay."

"You can't imagine the awe I experienced when we stood at the spot where the disciples had seen Christ's empty tomb," Octavia said. "I thought of the Alabaster, Lucius, and knew that it had been at that exact spot. It gave me a sense of eternity to know that in spite of the passage of time, there are still physical evidences to show that Jesus is alive."

"The bishop of Jerusalem is assembling artists and craftsmen," Helena continued, "and I've asked Constantine to release Cassus to be one of the architects for this church. We brought with us a list of needed materials, including marble for the pillars and gold for the roof."

"That's a great privilege for Cassus," Lucius said.

"We will return to Judaea to oversee the building of that basilica and others within the next few months if conditions here at home don't warrant my presence," Helena said as her face clouded and the radiance vanished.

"What other sites do you intend to mark?" Felice asked.

Helena nodded for Octavia to answer. "There will be a church built at Bethlehem on the site of Jesus' birth and another on the Mount of Olives where He ascended to heaven."

When they moved into the atrium to have wine and pastries with Domitilla, Octavia laid her hand on Lucius's arm. "Will you go with me to the chapel?"

Closing the door behind them, they walked to the front bench. The Alabaster had been returned to its pedestal for the time Lucius remained in Rome. "Do you remember the time the two of us sat here and you told me the story of the Alabaster?" Octavia asked.

"Yes. It was the day I learned I was to be its guardian. I also remember how frightened I was, though I never imagined then what the future would hold for me."

"I was amazed while we were in Judaea to learn more about the vase," Octavia said, and Lucius turned startled eyes toward her. "Do you know a man named Matthew, a collector of rare items, who once lived in Egypt?"

"I know whom you mean—both Cassus and Marcus have had contact with him, but not I."

"He lives in Jerusalem now, and Cassus asked me to call upon him. He operates an antique shop with the reputation of having the most complete set of ancient Christian writings in the world. Imagine my surprise when I entered his shop and saw some ornate vases that seemed duplicates of this Alabaster."

"What!" Lucius exclaimed. "I assumed that our Alabaster was one of a kind."

"No, there are at least nine more like it. Isn't there a numeral on the bottom of this vase?"

Lucius rose from the bench and brought the Alabaster to her. "Yes, it's numeral three."

"Then it's the one missing from the set Matthew has. According to him, these vases were fashioned by a Jew living in Caesarea prior to the birth of Christ. The illustrations are based on the story of the Jewish people from the time of Abraham through the reigns of David and Solomon. Matthew has searched all over the world for the missing Alabaster."

Lucius looked pointedly at Octavia, but she wouldn't meet his eyes for a moment, and when she lifted her head, chagrin was mirrored in her face. "Yes, he knows now that you have it. I was so amazed to see another vase like this one that I spoke before I thought. When Matthew quizzed me about it, I told him it was not for sale, but he doesn't seem to be the kind to give up easily. I fear you must guard the Alabaster, Lucius. Matthew isn't dishonest enough to steal it, but he'll try to buy it, I know. I'm so sorry I gave away the secret."

"I probably would have done the same thing in your place and under those circumstances, so don't let it concern you. The Alabaster will stay in the Trento family. Perhaps when you return to Jerusalem, you can tell the esteemed Matthew that you talked to me and that it's impossible for us to dispose of the vase."

"I'm not sure when we'll return," Octavia said. "Helena is quite concerned over Crispus. Have you seen him?"

"No. Titus has been here, but not Crispus."

Octavia couldn't have loved Crispus more if he'd been her own son, and she smiled. "He looks like a young god. He has Constantine's features, but he's much more handsome. His smile will melt the heart of a marble statue. His winsome disposition is sunny and warm."

"I don't know why Helena would be concerned about a grandson like that."

"Ah, that's the trouble! If he were less handsome, there might not be a problem. He made this journey without his family because he intends a quick return to Treves. Apparently seeing him again has rekindled Fausta's passion, and she's throwing herself at him. Crispus admits that he's only human and doesn't know what he will do if Fausta persists. However, to forestall her advances, he's removed himself from the emperor's palace and has come to live with his grandmother. We're glad to have him, and it gives us an opportunity to visit with him as well as Titus."

"I've never believed the gossip about Fausta and Crispus, but perhaps it's true."

"Whatever their relationship may have been in the past, Crispus is not interested in her now. So perhaps we have nothing to worry about."

Lucius wasn't so sure, for Fausta now had enough influence with Constantine to be dangerous, and if Crispus had finally repudiated her, there was no telling what she might do. Crispus had long been one of his favorites, so he acknowledged that he was prejudiced in the young Caesar's favor.

✸   ✸   ✸

Two days later, Lucius was summoned to Constantine's private chambers. "Lucius, I have some correspondence that I want you to handle for me. I assume that you've heard that my mother has located the sepulchre of Jesus."

"Yes, sire. That's an amazing discovery."

"Address a message to the bishop of Jerusalem. My mother gave instructions before she left Judaea to raze the temple to Venus that was erected there by the emperor Hadrian. This site of the burial of Christ has been miraculously brought to life again. I want the stone, the wood, and the earth that filled the grave carried away lest it has been contaminated by demons. Then the grave cavity must be richly adorned with gold and jewels. Once the holy place has been purified from idolatry, the most wonderful site in all the world must be marked with an edifice that will witness the glory of His resurrection."

Remembering the simplistic life of Jesus and His disciples, Lucius doubted that God would be pleased with the emperor's plans, for it was not the grave that was important, but the fact that Jesus was no longer there. Constantine hadn't asked for advice, so Lucius held his tongue.

"I have drawn a plan for the basilica. The portico will be sustained by marble pillars with corridors on the sides. The building will be entered through five aisles formed by plain square columns. The nave will be of great height, and its ceiling when covered with gold should shimmer like a great sea. At the end of the nave will be a semicircle of twelve pillars crowned by silver vessels, representing each of the apostles. The walls will be of colored marble."

Lucius was quickly recording Constantine's plans for the other churches to be erected in Judaea when Fausta burst into the room. Her richly embroidered silk robe was torn and gaped open to reveal a pearly white shoulder. Her hair, usually neatly coiffured, fell around her shoulders in disarray.

"Fausta," Constantine said, rising from his throne. "What has happened?"

"I was napping in my room when a man entered my chambers and assaulted me. He was in bed with me before I knew anyone was around."

"Why didn't you call out? Where were your attendants?"

"Perhaps I did shout—I don't know. It was all so startling."

As he watched Fausta's performance, Lucius's blood chilled at the import of this accusation, for he feared where it was leading. Lucius had to admit that she related a convincing tale. Constantine elicited all of the information from her that he could, but still he hadn't asked the name of her attacker. *Is he, too, fearful of what she might disclose?* Lucius wondered.

At last Constantine said, "And who was the man? Did you know him?"

"Oh, yes," Fausta cried wildly. "I know him. It's that son of yours that you've been pleased to raise above my own children. That one who has pursued me for years, and when he finally realized that I wasn't going to betray you, he attacked me."

"Not Crispus!" Constantine said, barely above a whisper.

Fausta drooped before him, an example of wronged womanhood, and as she sobbed, her shoulders shook. Lucius watched the changes in Constantine's face as he vacillated from unbelief to acceptance, then to anger and livid rage. He left the throne and stalked around the room, apparently too angry to speak. In that moment while Constantine was ignoring him, Lucius scribbled a note to Helena: *Get Crispus out of Rome immediately.*

A servant knocked on the door bearing the morning's refreshment, and Constantine said, "Send him away." Lucius went to the door, and while he relayed Constantine's orders, he laid a note on the tray. "Have this delivered to Helena at once," he whispered.

More than a half hour must have passed before Constantine returned to his throne. He looked at Fausta drooping on the floor. "You will remain secluded in your rooms until I order you conveyed to the palace at Sardica."

Fausta jumped to her feet, her misery forgotten. "Why am I to be punished? I've done nothing wrong. I won't go. My place is with you."

"You will go," Constantine thundered. "If I can't rule my own household, how can I hope to control the kingdom? You'll go if I have to send you in chains. Now that you've provided me with sons, I have no further need of you. I'm not convinced that you're an innocent party in this incident. You're banished from my presence." He rang for the palace police, and they conducted Fausta from the chamber. Lucius felt as conspicuous as if he had two heads, wishing he hadn't witnessed this tragic moment.

"I assume that you've warned Crispus to flee. I saw you writing the note," the emperor said unaccusingly.

Lucius flushed. "Yes, sire. I sent a note to your mother."

"Send another, then, and tell her that I want Crispus to go to Pola. I'm too angry to see him now, and I want to do some investigation before I act."

Before nightfall, Crispus and his bodyguards, including Titus, were on their way to Pola, a resort town on the Adriatic coast. If Crispus was exiled to a vacation spot, Constantine must not be too angry with him, Lucius concluded.

Helena came to beg Constantine to give Crispus an audience, but he refused to even see her. For a week he kept in solitary isolation, seeing no one except the servants who attended to his physical needs. When he finally sent for Lucius, his face was haggard, his eyes sunken into their sockets, and his hands trembled when he asked Lucius to record his plans for the remainder of time in the city. "There is to be a pagan festival in Rome in a few days, and the emperor and his court have been invited to attend. Send word to the Senate that we will do so."

Lucius darted a quick look in his direction. *Is the emperor demented? Is he ready to start cooperating with the pagans?* While he scratched out the message with his stylus, a servant entered.

"Augusta Helena is in the atrium. She desires to speak with you."

"Tell my mother to enter."

Helena glanced toward Lucius, and he raised his hand in greeting. For the first time, he noticed that she looked old. The regal bearing was gone, and she trudged on unsteady feet. Though her eyes were wary, determination marked her face. "Since you would not speak to Crispus, will you at least give me leave to plead his cause?"

After a momentary hesitation, Constantine nodded.

"Have you ever known me to lie to you, son?"

"Never. I revere you more than any other human on earth. You should know that, but I also know that you are very fond of my son."

"But I love you more, Constantine, so perhaps that will help you to believe what I say. Crispus was not here in the palace when Fausta says she was raped. He was at my residence that whole day, and I can produce dozens of witnesses to that fact if you will not believe me."

Constantine's body trembled, and he half-rose from his seat. Then his face blanched and he collapsed on the throne, covering his face with his hands. "Why would she lie?" he whispered, but Lucius could tell by his tone that he believed his mother's words.

"She has tried to seduce Crispus from the time they were children, and she renewed her efforts during the past month. That's the reason Crispus removed himself from this palace. He has avoided her, and I believe she has lied about him out of jealousy. Frankly, in the past few years, I don't believe that she was so much enamored with Crispus as she was obsessed with the idea of trying to discredit him in your eyes. She wants her sons to succeed you."

"But I have told her that her sons would share equally with Crispus!" Constantine exploded.

Helena shrugged shoulders that were bowed under the worries of her family. "Equal division is not enough for some people. They want it all. And, of course, I need not remind you that she didn't have all of you either, and she knew it."

Constantine nodded slowly. "Ah, Minervina, would God you had not died!"

After Helena left the chamber, Constantine sat with bowed head, and then he muttered, "It's too late. Why didn't I listen to her before it was too late?"

"Sire?" Lucius said, and his voice shook.

"It's too late, Lucius. By this time, Crispus is already dead. I simply removed him from Rome so that his grandmother would not know, but I sent my orders that he was to be killed at Pola. If the deed has not already occurred, I could never send a message in time."

Even though he was appalled at what the man had done, Lucius moved to the side of the grieving emperor and dared to place his hand on the man's shoulder. "Perhaps it would be worth a try, sire," he urged. "Weather might have delayed their crossing of the Adriatic. Your message might stay the hand of the executioner."

"No, I will not rescind the order. You see, I'm not yet convinced that Fausta and Crispus haven't betrayed me—not this time, for I believe my mother—but I've long been suspicious of their relationship and have suspected that they might be conspiring against me. That thought has entered my mind often since Crispus became so popular after fighting in battle." He sighed. "That's the curse of ruling, Lucius. One is always subject to treason from his friends and family. But Fausta must pay, too, since she has caused me to take the life of my son by telling me a lie."

Constantine stalked out of the room and headed toward the Augustus's quarters, though Lucius reached out a timorous hand to halt him. Soon his voice could be heard throughout the palace like a thunderbolt as he accused his wife of deceiving him. The door of his wife's chamber slammed after him, and Lucius heard no more, but he knew that Fausta's doom was sealed. Later that evening, the news circulated through the palace that Fausta had entered the caldarium of the palace baths, where she had suffocated when the room was heated far beyond its normal temperature.

Constantine secluded himself in the room he had set aside as his private chapel during his stay in Rome and didn't come out until the next day. By that time, Fausta's body had been removed from the palace, and Helena had gone into mourning because she blamed herself for the woman's death.

That morning in an unemotional voice, Constantine dictated an order to Lucius. "The names of Crispus and Fausta are to be removed from all statues and public edifices. Circulate the order throughout the empire."

With the treachery of his wife clouding his mind, Constantine was in no mood to compromise. On the day of the festival to the pagan gods, which the emperor had agreed to attend, he succumbed to fury when he saw the elaborate procession honoring the ancient gods and compared it to his own reception into the city. Lucius had never seen him so angry as he cursed the senators who had gathered in his presence.

"I will be no part in a procession that pays honor to gods made with hands. There is one God, and I've spread my banner under His protection. If Rome is not willing to go along with my convictions, then I will live elsewhere. I can get along better without Rome than it can get along without the emperor!" Constantine stormed.

The senators left in haste, and Constantine turned to his advisors. "We will depart this city within a week. Make preparations."

In spite of his anger, Constantine still wanted to leave his stamp on the city, so before he left Rome, the emperor gave orders for the building of several churches and conveyed a few pieces of public property to Helena. He also issued an empirewide edict that would ban killing of beasts in the arena and the execution of prisoners in gladiatorial combats. His concessions came too late to prevent Lucius's complete disillusionment with Constantine. The overtures he'd made to Christianity couldn't compensate for the deaths he'd ordered nor for the fact that he had made no move to eradicate slavery in the empire. Once again, Lucius considered leaving Constantine, but the habit of years was hard to break.

A note from Titus arrived the evening before they left Rome, delivered to Lucius at the Trento domus, where he and Felice were taking leave of the assembled family.

Dear Father,

A terrible tragedy has befallen the empire. Crispus has been murdered—suffocated in the bath buildings here at Pola. No one will admit to the deed, but we know that it was carried out through the emperor's orders. How can he justify such action with his beliefs in the Christian faith? With Crispus's death, my hope for the empire has faded. I intend to apply for my discharge from the army. When it comes, I'm leaving for Gaul to live with Grandfather Conrad. How I wish that you and the rest of the family would join me there.

Upon hearing of her grandson's death, Helena had fallen ill and was unable to have visitors, but before they left Rome, Lucius and Felice tried once again to see Helena, and she received them.

"We want you to know that we share your sorrow," Lucius said. Holding out her hands to them, Helena said, "And you loved him, too. How could my son have done such a thing? I went to him upon hearing of the death of Crispus, and he admitted that he had ordered the execution, but I take full responsibility for the deaths of both Crispus and Fausta."

"You shouldn't blame yourself," Felice protested. "Fausta brought on this tragedy when she accused Crispus unjustly."

"I know, but I must do my penance also. We're leaving soon for Judaea, and I will carry out Constantine's orders to build certain churches. Then I will return to Rome to live in this property my son has given me."

Felice and Lucius were subdued as they returned to their home. "Will we ever see them again?" Felice wondered aloud.

"Octavia, perhaps, but probably not Helena. Weighed down as she is with remorse and pain, she may not survive this coming journey."

"And what about us, husband? We become more disappointed with the emperor each day. How much longer can we stay with him?"

Lucius had no answer. He had been clinging tenaciously to his hope that Constantine was the answer to the spread of Christianity throughout the world, but his optimism had almost completely disintegrated.

18

Whatever remorse Constantine may have felt for the deaths of his son and his wife, Lucius never knew, for the emperor didn't mention them again. Upon his return from Rome, Constantine plunged into plans for his new capital, and Lucius spent many hours with the emperor and his advisors taking notes on their plans.

"Rome is too far removed from the center of the empire for me to dwell there," he said. "In the hours of the night upon my bed, and during long periods of meditation in the chapel, I've considered Sardica, Thessalonica, and even Chalcedon, but none of those seem suitable for my purpose."

When his advisors suggested that he should simply remain at Nicomedia and build upon the work of Diocletian, he shook his head. "No, I intend to build a city dedicated to the Christian God, and I will not defame His memory by building in a city where the blood of the martyrs has been shed repeatedly. The new imperial residence will express the improved conditions of this state, its religion, and life. I want a neutral location. Tomorrow, we shall ride toward the straits."

The next day as they traveled, Constantine had little to say to any of his companions. Lucius noted that the portable chapel that had always accompanied Constantine into battle was being pulled at the end of the procession. At dusk, Constantine entered the chapel and was not seen again.

Early the next morning, Constantine sallied forth looking like a man with a purpose. "Have my mount saddled," he ordered, "and all you who will see the foundation of the new city, follow me."

A sizable entourage accompanied the emperor until he stopped at the walled city of Byzantium. Lucius's surprise couldn't have been greater. He had supposed the emperor intended to choose a new site. *Why would he choose to build on this spot?* On second thought, Lucius recognized it was a strategic position, where the land route from Europe to Asia crossed the sea route from the Mediterranean to the Black Sea. It was one of the most impregnable spots throughout the empire. And since it was the site of the ancient city of Troy, from whence Aeneas had set forth to build Rome, perhaps the emperor thought that this site of Rome's origin would be a place where he could build a replica of Rome. But none of these considerations seemed to have swayed Constantine, for when he finally stopped his horse, he looked around and said, "God has led me to this spot." He dismounted and took his spear in hand. "I will walk the path where the foundation of the new city will be laid. Mark it."

Constantine looked straight ahead, not deviating to the right nor the left, and his attendants found it difficult to keep up with his rapid stride. As the day wore on and the circle became larger, Lucius said, "How much farther, sire?"

Bearing the same look on his face that he had displayed when he'd seen the vision before the battle at Milvian Bridge, Constantine said, "Until He who walks before me stops walking."

If the emperor believed that the building of the city was directed by God, nothing would stop Constantine's plans, and Lucius decided that he would stay with the emperor for a little longer, even though his hopes for the future were not bright. The building of a great city on the Bosporus would divide the empire. *How can Constantine reconcile this decision with the many battles he's fought and the lives that have been lost to unite the empire?* If he continued to travel from city to city as he'd done before, he would have been the emperor of all the people. But this city would definitely be an eastern capital, leaving the West to fend for itself. And without Crispus to rule Gaul and Spain, Lucius could forsee the disintegration of the empire.

Once the site was chosen, Constantine went full speed ahead with his plans. He gathered materials by raiding precious treasures from cities throughout the East, and he drew heavily upon the financial resources of Rome and other cities of the empire. He enticed an adequate labor force for the necessary building. Skilled workmen were imported from as far away as Naples, and the new city was soon populated with architects, plasterers, mosaicists, cabinetmakers, masons, gilders, marble workers, and glaziers. Much to Cassus's delight, Constantine recalled him from Judaea to aid in the construction.

"I enjoyed seeing the sites connected with Christ's earthly ministry, but I missed my family," Cassus confided to Lucius and Felice on their first meeting. "Octavia and Helena send their love."

"And how is Helena surviving the trip?" Felice asked anxiously.

"She's failing physically, but everywhere she goes she distributes generous gifts to the soldiers, pardons prisoners, and gives bread and clothing to the poor. Constantine has granted her unlimited powers, and the people in that region look upon her as their savior. She thrives on their adoration."

"Is she reconciled to the deaths of Fausta and Crispus?"

"Not reconciled, but at peace with it. She's forgiven herself for what she considers her negligence in not bringing the matter to Constantine's attention before. She believes that God has forgiven her, especially now that she's had opportunity to present thank offerings in Jerusalem to honor her son and grandson."

"We had a communication from Octavia saying that Helena considers atonement for her past sins has been made by undertaking this pilgrimage to the Holy Land and honoring the footprints of the Redeemer," Felice said.

"Now that she's seen the work underway on the various basilicas that Constantine has ordered, I expect them to return to Rome," Cassus said. With an apologetic glance toward Lucius, he continued, "As you know, Octavia has a guilty conscience because she revealed to Matthew where the tenth Alabaster is located, and she's concerned about it."

"I've had several communications from him wanting to buy the vase, and he is quite persistent," Lucius said with a smile.

"We know that, and Octavia sends you word to guard the Alabaster. She believes that Matthew isn't above procuring it by unorthodox means if he can't persuade you to sell it."

"What do you think?"

Cassus shook his head. "I'm not so sure. A few years ago I would have said that Matthew was incapable of unethical behavior, but he's changed. He's quite ancient, and I'm not sure he's altogether rational, so it might be well for you to hide the Alabaster."

When Cassus rose to leave, Felice nudged Lucius, and he said, "Cousin, we have serious matters to discuss concerning our own family. My Lucia and your Octavian say that they want to marry, and they're asking for our blessing. We've put them off, waiting for your return, but now I believe that we must deal with their request."

Cassus laughed. "Lanitra has communicated with me about it, and I have no reservations."

"Lucius has reservations, not because he doesn't like Octavian, but he doesn't want to lose his daughter," Felice said with a tender look toward her husband.

"I do not like to see my children leave home, but perhaps we can at least keep Panetta for a few more years," Lucius said with a smile.

❀   ❀   ❀

Remembering how easily the Alabaster had been stolen that time in Gaul, Lucius took Cassus's advice and built a small shelf in his quarters to hold the box containing the Alabaster. Then he plastered around the shelf to make it part of the wall. Only Felice knew where he had hidden the Alabaster, but he often reached out to touch the spot where the family relic was hidden away.

Apparently their fears were unfounded, for after two years had passed, both Cassus and Lucius decided that no one from Judaea had been dispatched to steal the Alabaster. Concerned that being sealed in the wall might not be good for the vase, Lucius brought it to light.

Those years had been busy ones for Lucius and Cassus as they worked together to do Constantine's bidding on the new city. A wall from the Golden Horn to the Sea of Marmara, four times larger than the original wall of Byzantium, protected Constantinople against attack. In many ways the new city imitated Rome, for it was built on seven hills and divided into fourteen districts, complete with a forum, a senate chamber, and an imperial palace.

The most outstanding feature of the palace was the great throne room, where a cross in gold mosaic inlaid with costly stones occupied the middle of the ceiling. The palace gardens and the smaller buildings reached to the shore of the Sea of Marmara. On the lintel of a door leading to the sea was an inscription addressed to Christ.

In his effort to make the city Christian, Constantine planned churches of rich marbles, gilding, and carvings. There was no place in the new capital for the old gods, although a few shrines still survived.

Lucius was with Constantine examining the newly laid foundation of the Church of Holy Peace when Panetta ran into their midst. Brushing past the emperor as if he weren't there, she grabbed her father's arm. "The Alabaster is gone! Mother was knocked unconscious by an intruder, and when she revived, the Alabaster had been taken."

Cassus, who was standing nearby, threw down the tablet he held. "Let's go, Lucius," he said, but Constantine grabbed Lucius's arm.

"Just a minute, you Trentos. This is the second time the Trentos have forgotten their duty to the emperor to chase that Alabaster."

"It was Marcus the other time, sire," Lucius said, desperate to go see about Felice, but hardly daring to shake off Constantine's restraint.

"It makes no matter. I don't like for my subjects to disregard my presence. Where does your loyalty lie, man?"

Knowing he was putting his life in danger, Lucius said, "My first loyalty is to God, sire. That vase is a symbol of His Son, and it's been placed in my care. I have to find it."

Constantine laughed. "You're right, of course. The Scriptures say that we should place our loyalty to God above all else. Do you have any idea who would steal the vase?"

"Yes, sire. A merchant in Judaea has tried to buy it, and we feared he might try to take the Alabaster, but as the years have passed without trouble, we considered the threat to be groundless."

"Judaea? That means the thief will probably travel by water. I will dispatch troops to help you. They're under your command. How long ago did this happen?" he asked Panetta.

"Within the hour, Mother said."

"Then the thief can't have gone far. We will cover all routes from this city by water and by land. God go with you," he added, dismissing them with a wave of his hand.

Lucius and Cassus couldn't keep up with Panetta's running feet as they hurried to the nearby house where they had moved during the construction of the city. When he was assured that Felice was all right except for a lump on her head, Lucius said, "Tell us everything you remember."

"I don't know for sure who struck me, but several times in the past few days I've seen an old man, a stranger, walking on this street. I hadn't thought of it then, but could it have been your aged friend Matthew, Cassus?"

"Quite probably," Cassus answered. "He's a determined man, and he wants the Alabaster. If it is Matthew, he'll travel by water, so let's cover the seaports, Lucius, and leave the land routes to the soldiers. Knowing Matthew's habits, I'll wager he's gone to Alexandria Troas to await passage. That's what he did years ago. Let's hurry there, for my wife's relatives will know if he's in that town."

In an hour's time, Lucius and Marcus, with a dozen soldiers flanking them, took their horses out of the city. Cassus's hunch had been correct, and a week later they apprehended the aged scholar as he was boarding a ship in the harbor of Alexandria Troas. He showed no fear when they confronted him.

"Matthew, we want no trouble, but you cannot leave here with the Alabaster," Cassus said. "I've explained to you more than once why it's important to us."

"It's important to me, too, to finish out my set." With a vicious look in Lucius's direction, he said, "I've offered him a king's ransom for it, but he will not sell."

"And I still won't," Lucius said firmly. "Would you sell your birthright, sir? That's what the Alabaster means to me. Now hand it over."

Matthew halted indecisively, noting the dozen soldiers with them, and looking from one to the other of the cousins, he could tell by the determined set of their jaws that they would not leave the ship without the Alabaster. He pulled the old box from his pack. Lucius grabbed the box and quickly checked the vase—it was definitely the one bequeathed to him by Ignatius.

When orders for sailing were shouted by the crew, a crafty look entered Matthew's eye. "Then if you will not sell me that one, could I interest you in buying the other nine?"

"I'm afraid not, sir. I'm a simple scribe, and even if I wanted the others, I couldn't afford them. Besides, this is the only Alabaster I want."

When they returned to the burgeoning capital city, Constantine sent for Lucius, with the message, *Bring the Alabaster*, as he'd once before commanded.

"What does that mean?" Felice asked with troubled eyes.

"I'll soon find out, I suppose," Lucius said, and his heart beat strangely. *What does Constantine have in mind?* The thought tormented Lucius as he approached the royal headquarters. The emperor didn't keep him long in suspense.

As soon as Lucius entered his quarters, Constantine said, "I'm glad to hear from Cassus that you recovered the vase, but I've decided that the relic is too valuable to be kept by one family. I'm going to take it and place it in one of the new churches we're constructing in the city." He reached out and plucked it from Lucius's hands. "Now, no arguments. I know you're fond of this vase, but after all, it is a holy relic."

Lucius was speechless with rage as he wended his way toward his home. *How dare he commandeer the Alabaster when he knows how important it is to our family!*

When he staggered into their house, Felice cried, "Lucius, are you sick? I've never seen you look so terrible."

"The emperor has taken the Alabaster to put in one of his churches. How am I going to get it back? You know how obsessed he is with bringing anything of worth to his capital."

"I can't believe he'd do that after all the years you've served him," Felice said in amazement.

"But you know that he's taken many another item that he considers a holy relic. I'll have to steal it from the church. I am *not* going to allow the Alabaster to go out of our family."

"You can't fight the Roman government," Felice said, resignation dulling her voice.

"I believe God will fight for me. Constantine is becoming too powerful, and his lack of spiritual insight disturbs me. I don't believe he has the first idea of the change Christianity should make in a man's behavior."

"Perhaps that's why he's never been baptized, never actually aligned himself with the Church," Felice said.

"The man baffles me. In all my years with him, I've never been able to determine whether he really believes that Christ is the Savior of the world or whether he's an astute politician who hitched his star to Christianity because he thought that was the best way for him to rule the empire."

Neither Felice nor Lucius slept throughout the night as he wrestled with the problem facing him. *How can I retrieve the Alabaster from the clutches of the emperor?*

Morning found Lucius tired and listless, and Felice said, "Why not stay here today? Send word you're not able to work."

He shook his head. "No, I must continue in Constantine's presence for the time being, but I promise you, wife, that as soon as the Alabaster is back in my possession, I intend to leave the imperial court. In this stilted atmosphere, sometimes my own thinking becomes warped and I forget the teachings of Jesus."

Smiling fondly at him, Felice said, "I believe I've heard all of this before."

"Yes, for twenty years or more I've threatened it, but this time I'm serious. Within the year, we'll be living in Gaul with your parents and Titus."

Felice put her arms around him. "I would like that, though if we leave here, Lucia will be lost to us in the household of Cassus. But wherever you are, that's where I want to be. I love you, Lucius," she said as she put her arms around her husband.

They broke their embrace when a hasty knock sounded at the door, and Cassus rushed into the room, his face beaming. He unrolled a leather bag that he carried and handed a box to Lucius.

"The Alabaster! Have you stolen it?" Lucius asked with surprise.

Laughing, Cassus said, "No, the emperor sends it with his blessing."

"But, what . . . ?"

"Constantine placed the Alabaster in the new basilica he's having constructed across the street from the imperial palace. Last night the east wall of that building collapsed, almost crushing the two soldiers who were guarding the Alabaster. Constantine takes that as a sign that it should remain with the

Trentos. He's sent the vase back and says he never wants to see it or hear about it again."

Lucius breathed deeply as he clutched the Alabaster. "The emperor has always been superstitious about the power of this vase. But what did cause the wall to collapse?"

"Nothing miraculous, simply poor workmanship. We architects have tried to impress on Constantine that he's building too much and doing it too rapidly. He's using poor construction methods that will necessitate rebuilding many of the city's edifices in a few years. But he's set the dedication of Constantinople for May of next year, and he's rushing us to have it finished by then."

"A beautiful city on the outside, but crumbling underneath, eh?"

With a look of concern, Cassus said, "Just like the empire and the church."

"You feel that, too?"

"Very much. You and I may not live to see it, but our grandchildren will witness a decadent empire, and the day is coming when one won't be able to separate the church from the government—when it will be against the law of the state not to be a Christian. That is not the way Christ intended it to be."

"And I desire to live out my remaining years where I do not feel that pressure. I'm asking Constantine to release me," Lucius announced.

❀　❀　❀

The next week when Lucius was alone with Constantine and noted that the emperor was in a benevolent mood, he said, "Sire, I have been in your service for more than twenty years, and with your permission, I should like to retire and return to Gaul where my son is. We have not seen Titus for three years, and Felice is eager to see him, for the boy has married and has given us a grandson."

Constantine looked long at Lucius, and a wave of sadness filled his eyes. The emperor's stalwart physique was softening, and his shoulders sagged. Wrinkles lined his face and dark circles rimmed his eyes, making them seem more deep-set than ever. Despite his eagerness to leave the court, Lucius couldn't help but mourn for the days that had been.

"I do not blame you for wanting to leave," Constantine said. "There are times when I long for the early days at Treves when we had little to concern us except an occasional battle against the Alemanni, and there were many occasions to go on hunts and celebrate the festivals with my friends. Most of my old friends are gone, and now I must lose you. Against my wishes I'll release you from my service, but with one stipulation. Will you stay through the dedication of the city? I would like for you and Felice to be by my side on that day."

"Gladly, sire. We will plan our departure for the latter part of June, if that pleases you."

❁   ❁   ❁

The next few months sped by quickly as Cassus and Lucius spent hours doing the emperor's bidding to complete his city. Helena and Octavia came home from Judaea to be present for the celebration. When Felice went to visit Helena, she returned with a gloomy expression.

"She will never travel anywhere else," she reported to Lucius. "Octavia says that only the most constant care has enabled her to reach here alive."

"So Constantine will not only be losing us, but also his mother. I suppose she is nearly eighty years old."

"He has Constantine II, who is fourteen now," Felice pointed out.

"But he intends to send him to Gaul as a Caesar, so he's going to be lonely."

"I'm afraid that's his own doing," Felice said, not unkindly.

"He should have thought of the future before he murdered Fausta and Crispus."

"So you haven't forgiven him for that?" Lucius said.

"Have you? I've tried, but it will take more time and prayer."

Lucius bowed his head and didn't answer. Those impulsive acts of the emperor had been a blow to Lucius, causing him to lose respect for the man he'd served for so many years. He hated to leave the emperor's service with such disillusionment, but he knew of nothing that Constantine could do now that would change his point of view.

The festivities to mark the birthday of Constantinople started on May 11, and they lasted forty days. Crowds gathered into the new, marble-paved, oval forum, which was surrounded by a tall marble portico. The middle of the portico was marked by a porphyry column displaying a gilded image of Constantine. To the east of the forum, the main street was lined with numerous statues. Beyond these statues stood the meeting place for the Senate, and nearby was the imperial palace, where Constantine could observe most of the activities from a special box that overlooked the Hippodrome.

To please the pagans, the birth of the city was celebrated by an astrologer who read the signs of the heavenly bodies, which indicated peace and prosperity for Constantinople and its emperor. Other than these small concessions to his pagan subjects, Constantine had decreed that all other rites would be Christian. Singing worshipers moved through the forum, and bishops conducted rituals of worship. A new silver coin was minted bearing a cross that was joined to the circle of the earth and superimposed on the imperial scepter, thus expressing the importance of Christianity to the empire.

Chariot races, games, excessive doles of grain and bread, and religious observances marked the celebration until the final day, when smartly uniformed soldiers paraded through the streets. They carried white candles in advance of a golden statue of the figure of Constantine, which was borne on a wagon pulled by white oxen. The procession circled the Hippodrome and stopped before the imperial box. Constantine rose and saluted the statue, and Lucius exchanged a disbelieving glance with Cassus that he would thus pay homage to himself.

"This magnificent symbol of Constantinople will be placed in a new chapel, and the statue of Tyche from Rome will join it. I decree that every year on this same day, a celebration will take place to honor the founding of this city. I declare that the dedication is complete," Constantine announced.

Lucius's heart seemed to drop with a thud to the pit of his stomach. This was the end, and it seemed so final. His association with Constantine had ended. After he helped Cassus escort the wilting Helena from the imperial box to her home, Cassus gave his cousin a look of understanding.

"So you will go, and I will stay on," he said. "There is still a lot of building to be done before this city is complete. Architects are desperately needed. After all, it is my home, but I will miss you, Lucius. I suppose a reminder of you in Lucia will always be a part of my household."

Lucius and Felice had intended to quit the city the next day, but they delayed their departure once again because of the ill health of Helena, who had kept up her strength only until she had witnessed her son's greatest triumph. She sank immediately into a decline and died within a few days. Constantine stayed at his mother's bedside and was there when she died, as were the Trentos, who had been her friends for years. Octavia wept as she had not wept for her own mother, since she had only been a child when Atilia was martyred.

When Felice and Lucius went to their home after Helena had died, Felice said, "These changes are more than I can bear. Will life ever stand still for us, Lucius?"

Lucius shook his head gloomily, "No, not here, nor in Gaul where we're going. We'll go to Rome with the cortege of Helena, where we will see our family. Then we will go back to our home on the hill overlooking the Rhone. Think of that, my dear, not the sadness you feel. We will enjoy a great future. For the past few weeks, I've been dwelling on my future, and one thing I intend to do is to start writing a history of the Alabaster to leave to our descendants. That will occupy much of my time."

❀　❀　❀

Ten days later Felice and Lucius, accompanied by Panetta, bade a final good-bye to Constantinople and the imperial court as their carriage moved out of the city. A cart behind them held all of their possessions. They followed in the wake of a magnificent sarcophagus of porphyry that Constantine had ordered constructed for his mother's body, which was being escorted to Rome by a large military guard. She was to be laid in a mausoleum that Constantine had built for his mother several years before.

Lucius held loosely to the reins and gave no guidance to the horses, who followed the procession without his help. Through tear-blinded eyes, he looked toward Felice whose still-beautiful face was shiny with tears. She tried to smile at him, made a poor job of it, and lowered her head to his shoulder.

Tying the reins around the post of the carriage, Lucius pulled her into an affectionate embrace. With the other hand he touched the Alabaster, safe on the seat between them. "The sadness of this moment will give way to something better. Remember, there is life after Constantine. In Gaul, I can concentrate on my true destiny, the one given me by Grandfather Ignatius thirty years ago—to teach the story of the Alabaster to my descendants so that they'll carry on the eternal message of Christianity. Earthly rulers will come and go, but the message of Christ remains— 'No man can be acceptable to God unless he comes through My death and resurrection.'"

EPILOGUE

In 337, Constantine became ill. Suspecting that death was near, he at last asked Bishop Eusebius of Nicomedia to baptize him into the church. He was still dressed in the white robes of a Christian neophyte when death claimed him.

After his death, his three sons and two of his nephews fought for control of the empire. When one of the nephews, Julian, became emperor in 361, he tried to halt the spread of Christianity and restore worship of Rome's traditional gods but without success. From Constantine's time on, Christianity became the official religion of the Roman Empire. Bishops gained increasing dominance, superseding in some cases the power of emperors.

Only eighty years after the last great persecution of Christians under Diocletian and Galerius, the church began to put heretics to death.

The western empire grew steadily weaker as barbarians invaded Gaul, Spain, and northern Africa. Most historians date the fall of the West Roman Empire at 476, although the eastern empire survived until 1453 when the Turks captured Constantinople.

PONTIUS PILATE
A Novel
Now in trade paperback!

PAUL L. MAIER

Follow Pontius Pilate, Roman governor of Judea, as he rises from the political intrigues of imperial Rome and survives the treacherous plots of Herod Antipas. Behind him stands Procula, a wife who fires his ambition for political advancement; before him stands the bewildering clash of Jewish leaders, national extremists, and religious zealots.

"A tremendous story. . . . In drama, romance, color, scope, and depth, this novel is comparable to *Ben Hur*, *The Silver Chalice*, and *The Robe*." —*The Christian Herald*

"Unique in biblical novels . . . raises the genre of the historical novel to a plateau it has rarely reached." —*The Chicago Daily News*

"We commend this book as an exciting supplement to the New Testament itself." —*Moody Magazine*

PAUL L. MAIER is professor of Ancient History at Western Michigan University and an award-winning author whose expertise in first-century studies and extensive travels in the Middle East and Asia Minor provide historical authenticity and compelling drama to his writing. His other writings include the ECPA Gold Medallion Award-winning volume *Josephus: The Essential Writings; The Flames of Rome* (a companion to *Pontius Pilate);* and the 1994 best-selling novel, *A Skeleton in God's Closet*.

0-8254-3296-0   paperback   384 pp.

THE FLAMES OF ROME
A Novel
Now in trade paperback!

PAUL L. MAIER

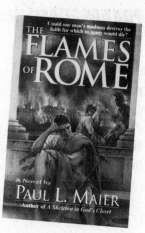

In the years preceding and following the Great Fire of Rome in A.D. 64, the splendor, sensuality, and pagan excesses of Roman society are illuminated against the explosive struggle between the established power of Rome and the life-changing faith of Christianity.

Based upon the experiences of the family of Flavius Sabinus, the actual mayor of Rome under Nero, this work recounts their own history as crucial converts to Christianity.

"A soul-shaking novel of the time when society was at its worst and Christians were at their best!" —*The Christian Herald*

"Impressive . . . illuminates a crucial time and place in world history." —*Publisher's Weekly*

"Flames sizzles [and] doesn't fiddle with the truth." —*The Detroit News*

PAUL L. MAIER is professor of Ancient History at Western Michigan University and an award-winning author whose expertise in first-century studies and extensive travels in the Middle East and Asia Minor provide historical authenticity and compelling drama to his writing. His other writings include the ECPA Gold Medallion Award-winning volume *Josephus: The Essential Writings; The Flames of Rome* (a companion to *Pontius Pilate);* and the 1994 best-selling novel, *A Skeleton in God's Closet.*

0-8254-3297-9 paperback 458 pp.

THE HEART OF A STRANGER
A Novel

KATHY HAWKINS

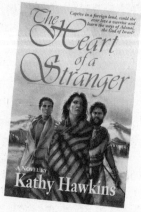

King David's reign and the greatest battle
of the Old Testament provide the setting for
this captivating story of political intrigue
and romantic love.

Jonathan, one of David's thirty "mighty
men of valor," returns from war with Ailea,
the beautiful, spirited daughter of the
defeated Aramean commander. Her own inner battle between love
and mistrust is equally matched by her struggles with the cultural and
religious life of the Jewish people. The battle for her heart is waged
not only by Jonathan, the perspective bridegroom, but by Adonai, the
God of Israel, as well.

KATHY HAWKINS is a graduate of Southeastern Bible College and holds
an M.A. in Biblical Studies from Dallas Theological Seminary. She
and her husband—Christian broadcaster and author Don Hawkins—
frequently speak at Bible conferences and seminars across the U.S.

0-8254-2867-x   paperback   304 pp.